2595

GENIUS JACK

By the same Author

GENIUS JACK

A Novel By

Thomas Wiseman

Marion Boyars
London • New York

F

Published in Great Britain and the United States
in 1999 by Marion Boyars Publishers
24 Lacy Road, London SW15 1NL
237 East 39th Street, New York NY 10016

Distributed in Australia and New Zealand by
Peribo Pty Ltd, 58 Beaumont Road, Mount Kuring-gai, NSW

© Thomas Wiseman 1999

British Library Cataloguing in Publication Data
Wiseman, Thomas
    Genius Jack: a novel
    1. Motion picture producers and directors — Psychology —
    Fiction   2. Motion picture industry — Fiction
    I. Title
    823.9'14 [F]

Library of Congress Cataloging-in-Publication-Data
Wiseman, Thomas.
    Genius Jack: a novel/by Thomas Wiseman.
        p. cm.
    I. Title.
    PR6073.I77G4   1999
    823'.914—dc21   98-36190
        ISBN 0–7145–3041–7 Hardcover

Typeset in 11/13 pt Times by
Ann Buchan (Typesetters), Shepperton
Printed and bound in Great Britain by
Redwood Books, Trowbridge, Wiltshire.

Once again for Malou and for Boris

‘Genius is a terrible malady.’
— Balzac

YOUNG GENIUS STAKES

Jack Strawley's *Killers Kill* is a thriller of New York's lower depths, and our own. With dazzling brio, Strawley uses the traditions and trappings of film noir to explore the character of a mobster hitman who claims he only rubs out those who've got it coming and hence can regard himself, in his own sort of way, as a moral force. He also considers himself an artist, since he likes to paint nudes, admires Constable and carries out his hits with 'artistry'.

In outline the story is pure pulp, in the style of the Forties city thrillers of Siodmak and Lang and Curtiz, but there is more to it than just mayhem and melodrama. The focus is on the odd 'friendship' between a young, unformed photographer, working for a small neighbourhood newspaper, and the hired killer. The story is seen through the photographer's eye, and the camera is unjudgemental, it merely records, and in doing so discovers an unsentimental sleazy sort of beauty in the West Broadway bars and dives frequented by the hitman and his clients and targets. At one point the photographer says that 'very bad things can *look* very good in a photograph', a point that Strawley proves with a rich flow of chiaroscuro images. He shows us the way the dark can glitter.

But the film is not all low-key lighting and darkness. Characters step out of the shadows and move with blinking eyes into a clean sunlit world of suburban rectitude, and it is here, in the glaring light of day, that the hitman strikes down his 'subjects' — out of the blue, without build-up or Miklos Rozsa music, an artist of death. When you are expecting something terrible to happen, the threat turns out to be false, shadows turn into benign everyday faces.

'You never know who your friends are, or your enemies,' the hitman says at one stage, and this is borne out when Pete, the photographer, unintentionally breaks one of the rules of the underworld, his pictures 'inform' the police, and he there-

fore 'has got it coming', and has to be hunted down by his
erstwhile friend. Each in his way has to do what he does and
to become what he is: the photographer has to take pictures,
and the killer has to kill. As Pete is hunted from place to
place, his only means of defending himself is by taking
photographs of the men intending to kill him and putting
these snatched pictures in envelopes addressed to the police.
If he is rubbed out, these photographs will identify his killers.
One extraordinary shot in the film shows Pete walking along
the aisles of a dim church, with the killers behind him, unseen
in the dark. The camera shows the first glimmer of the setting
sun on the edge of a stained glass window, and as the killers
are about to close in, a burst of sunlight illuminates them, as
in a police identification parade, rendering their faces recognizable by potential witnesses. And so, as if by a miracle of
light, they are forced to stay their hand, this time. (The scene,
we are told, was filmed at night with powerful sunlight arcs,
and the intensity of the sunlight was obtained by spraying a
highly reflective dust, composed principally of ground-down
mica, into the light beam.)

Another stylistic touch is the way Strawley creates a sense
of claustrophobia by showing the fleeing man shut in by rain
backlit to be as clearly defined as the bars of a cage. He also
has a highly original way of entering scenes already in progress,
so that you don't know where you are, or who anyone is. This
creates in the audience a visceral sense of disorientation,
mimicking the confusions of panic or derangement. His 'broad
daylight scenes' have an unruffled stillness, a lulling tranquility,
that is shattered without recourse to the usual build-up shots.
Violence explodes with shattering suddenness, as if a newsreel camera had swung abruptly to catch the tail-end of
something that began outside its field of vision. The result is
that Strawley re-trains our sense of apprehension so that the
greater the surface calm of a scene, the more intense the
suspense becomes. The overall effect is to depict the criminal
underworld, with its strict rules, shibboleths and conventions,
as a kind of darkly mocking mirror-image of the normal
daylight world.

The feeling of danger that comes from the screen is com-
pounded by Nik Ransom's brooding, groping-in-the-dark 'death
artist', spelling out the big questions in words of one syllable

and terrible silences. His is a new and powerful screen presence. Lila Karr depicts the floozie Slither Slither as a foolproof man-trap, and since she has the physical endowments to make a poker game for her favours thrillingly suspenseful, she should have a glittering future on the screen.

Now that Orson Welles has reached his fortieth year, the cinema's young genius stakes are wide open, and with this film twenty-four year old Jack Strawley enters the lists.

Stephen Dall, *Sight and Sound/* Autumn 1954

PART I

THE EYE OF THE SAVAGE

1

The enthusiasms of one's youth can be dangerous. In later years I was to wonder if I had done Jack Strawley actual harm by my rash, if somewhat tongue-in-cheek, coupling of the epithet 'genius' with his name. For I started a snowball rolling that was to grow to unjustifiable proportions, as almost everything does in the movie business, and in the long run the tag — and the role — 'Genius Jack' (which not I but the popular press bestowed upon him) did not allow him a tranquil life. But then Jack Strawley wasn't cut out for tranquility. I remember him saying with eerie prescience, when he was getting all that acclamation for his first film: 'Once you've been called a genius, what else can they call you, except a fake genius?'

It has been said that as a journalist, biographer and memoirist I have been overly attracted to birds of the brightest plumage. It is a charge to which I plead guilty. To trace giant footsteps, where they have come from, where they are going, has been for me a passionate pursuit, as well as a livelihood. Which may explain why I was trudging through the snow-bound streets of New York, in the winter of '88 — no cabs to be found, wind howling about my ears — in response to a phone call out of the blue (yes, that was the way things happened with Jack in life as well) from a girl called Alice, saying that Jack wanted to see me urgently.

The address that I had been given turned out to be an industrial building in Lower Manhattan, with a handsome façade from which quite a lot of the decorative fake French and Italian Rennaissance motifs had fallen off in the course of time. The immediate vicinity was uncertainly poised between seediness and chic. There was an art gallery in the former loading bay of the building next door. On the corner there was a car park. Some of the buildings were still in use as warehouses, and there were big trucks drawn up along the kerb. It was a far remove from his former house in London's Carlyle Square. On a vertical panel of door bells I saw one marked 'film shoot' and pressed it, and when nothing happened I pushed at the graffiti-embellished door, found that it opened and went in. There was no elevator and it was a long climb up, passing the doors of small businesses: Fabulous Fabric Stylesetters, Inc.; J.G. Landau, literary, theatrical and film agency; Eisenstoffer and Bucci, attorneys-at-law. When I got to the top floor, the door was ajar: in the triangular wedge I saw an upright manual typewriter on a table, and on the floor a pile of scripts; an Arriflex with its body harness; cans of film covered in stickers. A large bed standing well away from the wall. There was someone in the bed and a girl in a grimy smock was bent over him, working on his face with a bushy make-up brush. She looked up and said: 'Jack, I think it's Stephen. Stephen Dall?'

The man on the bed struggled upright, frowning.

'Stephen? Well so it is. So it is. The Critic in person, the Lord protect us.' Gathering his breath, which seemed to call for some considerable effort, he added, 'Glad you came, Critic. Alice explain to you?'

'Only that you'd like to see me and . . .' He cut me off, was not going to waste time on social niceties, perhaps due to being in the middle of shooting, or his shortness of breath.

'See, we're doing this film, which is about a once-famous film director who's suffered a fall.' He gave a sour chuckle, wincing as he did so, which may have been due to the battering that his face had recently received. The puffiness beneath the eyes, the blue bruise patches, the scar tissue on the forehead were not make-up, as I had momentarily thought. 'I got mugged,' he explained, 'so we wrote it in. This film is part fiction, part fact. As to which is which, I wouldn't know, I've never known. It's about this . . . this famous movie director who's fallen on hard times, and he has a scene with a critic who once called him "a genius". Long while back. We make up our own dialogue. Because it's supposed to be true, you see.'

A couple of movie lights threw their luminosity onto silvery reflector panels held in stands. The light falling on Jack Strawley gave his pallor a phosphorescent glow. He laughed and it was as if iron filings were rattling around in his throat. His breathing was becoming more strained; he reached to his side, picked up a mask, and took a deep drag of oxygen from the cylinder by the bed. I knew that he had, for many years, suffered from emphysema, and it seemed to have now reached this advanced stage. He minimized it. 'Picked up a chest cold. It's this glacial weather. Getting mugged didn't help. Be okay soon's I get my breath back.'

His pallid-grey face, beyond the recent injuries at the hands of muggers, showed the signs of the sort of life he had led for a long time. Craggy fault-lines could be made out through three or four days' growth of white beard. His hair was an ash-coloured mane. His eyes were pale violet, other-worldly.

'This film, it's a story of what it meant to be a film-maker in the fifties, sixties and seventies . . . the times you and I knew well, Stephen. From our different ends.' His breath was rattling in his throat, the harsh raw sound of the body's struggle to obtain air. He stopped speaking. 'Oh, damn and hell, I . . . got . . . to . . . rest minute.' He lay there, chest heaving as if he'd just done a 100-metre sprint. The camera had started rolling on some signal that he must have given: evidently he wished to be filmed in this state. The new realism. It seemed pretty sick to me.

'Listen,' he said, speaking with difficulty on camera, 'remember those tapes we made years ago, when you were going to do that book with me? When you were going to help me write my autobiography. Be my ghost! You still got those tapes?'

'I think I have, yes.'

'Well bring them. I could use some of that stuff as voice over. I seem to remember we got onto some clue there somewhere.'

'A clue?'

'Yeah, probably a lot too many clues. Difference between detective stories and life, in detective stories there always too few clues, in life too many. Anyway, bring the tapes, will you?'

I nodded and said I would.

This was all being filmed and recorded, and I realized that I had been unceremoniously drawn into the film, like it or not.

'Want you to play yourself, Stephen,' he said, 'because . . .who else can play you . . . as well as you play yourself . . . hah? Want to have people who had some role in my life, even if they weren't aware of it.'

The loft was serving as a film set and at the same time being lived in by Jack and the girl called Alice. It looked as though everything was being mixed up quite deliberately, life and cinema, fact and fiction.

He was having a lot of trouble breathing now, was gasping, and it was distressing to watch, although he was making gestures for the cameras to continue rolling, since he didn't want to lose any dramatic material. When he was eventually able to spill out a few words, he said:

'Not so good today. We'll do our scene next time, Stephen. Bring the tapes, huh? Bring the tapes.'

At my apartment, looking for the tapes, I remembered our long recording sessions in his suite at the Hotel Alphonse XIII in Seville, back in 1974 when he was making *Heart of Darkness*. If he couldn't sleep, which was often the case, we'd sometimes work all night — memories pouring out of him in a rush of chaotic images spiced with his ribald black commentaries. I was supposed to keep him to some sort of storyline, but it was an impossible task. Invariably one story led to another, with no respect for chronological order, or any of the unities of time and place, and indeed there were chunks of time that he had totally obliterated from his recollections and I was supposed to track down what had happened to him in those periods. There were other areas of his past of which he could forget nothing: was plagued by an eidetic memory that reproduced images of great accuracy and amazing detail. With his inability to forget certain things — and to forgive, which I suppose was part of it — he was in thrall to his images, and his ghosts.

I thought at the time that it was all rich material coming up, but so uncontrolled, so hopelessly indiscreet, unrespectful of anyone's privacy — his or of those who'd been involved with him — that I couldn't imagine much of this stuff getting beyond a first rough draft. As it happened, the autobiography was never written, it was one of many projects of his that were to fall through at this time, and so there had been no occasion to edit his calumnies and indiscretions.

After some searching, I found the cassettes in a shoe-box on a high shelf of the hall closet, where I kept other material for which I had not foreseen any immediate use. There was not much interest in Jack Strawley at this time. During the past ten years or so he had disappeared from view and been largely forgotten, but now that I'd seen him again I had a sudden shivery feeling that it was wrong to have written him off, and that even if he was a name out of the past, that past was a part of movie history, as he had been.

What clue had he been talking about? Clue to what?

I got down the shoe box and started reading my index notes: they indicated the free-wheeling leaps and bounds of his mind, as we worked at recollecting his life. Now I was remembering some of the material that had come up, and how he'd contain himself, sitting completely silent, until the tape recorder was switched on and he could see the spools turning. There'd be a bottle of brandy on the table, and he'd be hunched up on the sofa, hardly looking at me, addressing the table microphone as if it were the interlocutor to whom he had to answer. I had the odd feeling that for him I was simply an instrument, like the tape recorder, through which he was seeking to come to terms with the events of his life.

I put the tape marked 'Seville 1' in my machine, and without bothering to rewind to the beginning, since there was no consistent chronological order to his recollections, pressed 'Play', and I had come in at a point where he was talking about his mother.

'My mother, she got swept out the way. Part of the ground clearing. It was — awful to say — something that couldn't be helped. She suffered with her nerves. If you want to know, she was a hysteric. Finally had to go into a "rest home". History of that in her family. She thought I didn't love her. It's true, I couldn't love her on the scale that she demanded love. I don't let myself be swallowed up. So she had to be cleared. And there was Carl . . . he had to be.'

There was a gap here on the tape, a longish silence, and I

remembered how he'd got up and started pacing, his face deeply lined, and that there was a painted-on smile in his eyes that didn't budge. Frothing saliva had dried on his lips, giving him a white clown's mouth in a rigid face. There was the long gap, and then he continued in a kind of snarl:

'That's another story that we'll have to get to eventually . . . Carl's another story, I loved Carl, and when Gloria said, that time, what I was doing to him was going to destroy him, I said: "I'm afraid I don't care." It's what I said. I can't believe it but others have confirmed it, so I must have said it. In addition to "Genius Jack" I was also known, to some, as "Jack-the-Talented-Shit". Leave Carl out of it for now. He's a chapter to himself.'

I remembered the wolfish flash of the eye. You could see him speeding up, wildly speeding up, his eyes shiny with the flashing pictures racing through his overfull mind, which he was trying to empty, trying to empty into the tape recorder, into me. The horror when the visions all stay there, impressed in minute detail, unwipeable matter.

There'd be periodic interruptions to the restless flow of words: sometimes he paced, sometimes he got up and went to the window, and sometimes he called room service for smoked salmon sandwiches, or another bottle of brandy, or coffee . . . and some nights, with the tape recorder recording some steamy love affair or other, his mouth suddenly opened wide, his eyes closed, and he'd drop off. Not altogether surprising since he was getting so little sleep during the shooting. He'd re-awaken with a start and continue from where he thought he'd left off, but now he'd picked up some other thread: about how he'd gone off to New York, as a kid, and lived the life of the streets, always mad about films, looking at everything with that intense eye of his which he thought of as the 'the eye of a savage'.

2

The hard daylight burned his eyes coming out of the Sheridan into the overbright street. He'd had to see *The Lady from Shanghai* a second time, it was such an amazing experience, and that had meant sitting through *The Mating of Millie*, and the cartoon and the trailers and the newsreel and the short. The street had a white sheen over it, and a ghostly crowd thronged the sidewalks. His head was spinning, his eyes having trouble adjusting to the brightness. He was under the spell of the hypnotic images. In Acapulco and San Francisco and inside the baroque genius mind of Orson Welles. A masterwork! The great opening. *Off the hump of Brazil I saw the ocean so black . . . the sea was made of sharks and more sharks still . . . the beasts took to eating each other. In their frenzy ended up devouring themselves.* What a lead-in! He was still in the grip of the magical imagery, he remembered every shot, every camera angle. Every cut. The cinema had been half empty, though. And some members of the stupid audience had clearly preferred the awful Glenn Ford-Evelyn Keyes to the Welles. Welles was too dark for them. Too monstrous. And too dazzling.

The sudden daylight was too much after all that murkiness of soul. Those bizarre characters — Everett Sloane's crippled brilliant defence attorney getting onto the witness stand to cross-examine himself! What a performance! What an idea! His head was bursting with images. Reducing valve had bust and everything was flooding in at once. Screaming kids kicking a soggy half-inflated football around. Their wild faces. Any moment a goal was going to be scored on a shopkeeper's glass door — he was emerging, fists waving. Jack had his camera out. The colour was coming back to his eyes. There was a high hum in his head. He could make out the tiny pleats and wrinkles in the goalscorer's pants. *When I set out to make a fool of myself, there's not many people can stop me.* Orson's rich Irish brogue. He could see what Rita Hayworth meant about not being able to take his genius anymore. In the film, husband and wife killed each other in the hall of mirrors. He felt the sugar shortage in his brain. In the cluttered window of a Chinese laundry, steam was rising from the the big pressing machine: a jumble of garments hanging from a line in their skirts of fine tissue paper. Dangling from the pressing board were a pair of grey flannel trousers. The intricate folds of the hanging pants, the rich heavy texture of flannel. The way the flannel fell and lay and folded up on the floor. He was speeding up now. Sometimes something happened to make a picture. You had to put yourself in the position where it might happen. You had to put yourself in harm's way. Otherwise nothing happened. You had to have the eye to see it. The eye of the savage. You had to be able to isolate one moment from all the rest. A massive tree trunk. He saw the movement in the sharply etched lines of the bark. That was the picture. His reducing valve busted, he could keep nothing out. There was the pounding of jackhammers, the fast dense traffic, the teeming human flow. A girl in a light cotton dress strutted past and he couldn't keep her out either, she infiltrated his mind with the crazy motion of her limbs: he could see the slowed-down sway of her thighs rubbing together as she strutted along the street, and saw her sex come moistly into bloom. From the Cuban bakery came a fresh white doughy smell. Then, from the next store, a subtle aroma of dark brown coffee beans in burlap sacks. A barber's shop redolent of men's pomades and lotions. The strutting girl had disappeared into the crowd: this hurried girl with the lithe limbs. After Broadway, the streets weren't so salubrious. An intensely bright circular spot in the sun's halo, a mock sun, threw a thin arc onto the black mouldering brickwork of basement entrances where second-hand clothes merchants held aloft their wares on wire clothes-hangers, beckoning to passers-by to enter their dim underground emporiums. Drifting smells emanating from the Gashouse district. Lower Broadway's overflow was descending in a thick gluey mass towards the dimness and the metal clatter of the Third Avenue El. That amazing court room scene with all the dialogue overlapping. The way he tracks in and then, without completing the track, in the next instant, the actor's face fills the screen. On the teeming sidewalk he'd caught up again with the strutting girl, jostling flesh cohering damply beneath transparent cotton. Oh gosh, oh boy! You couldn't hide anything from his all-seeing eye. He can picture this rippling beauty in every whichway. He wished powerfully that this strutting girl would stop by a shop window so he could get her reflection as well. But no luck. However much you willed them there were certain things that didn't happen when you wanted. He was speeding nicely without strain. The sun had left the highest of the buildings, its diffused rays sneaking out between West Side setbacks. There was a frosty edge in the air. In the gridwork of shadows under the El, pushcarts selling fruit, goats' cheeses, ripe and green olives, finocchio, ready-to-eat pizza, satin neckties, cheap watches, scarves. The haphazard early evening drift from the Bowery had deposited a group of derelicts, clutching bottles wrapped in brown paper bags, in the doorway of a closed and padlocked pawn shop. Seated nearby, on a folding stool, at her usual pitch, was Melina Karamouzis with her deeply lined face. He had never seen so many lines in one face. At the corners of her mouth the lines were like tangled-up cotton thread, life scars which she wore boldly, without attempt at concealment. She was fitted out for the street in long heavy skirt and quilted waterproof, a black woollen scarf tied tightly under her chin, half-mittens on her swollen fingers, two pairs of socks on her feet. Her wild white hair straggling out through the headscarf jutting out in all directions. Her eyes darkly pouched. With her stiff arthritic fingers her fingering on the violin was clumsy but her bow work was still good. Her violin case was open on the ground with nickels and dimes gleaming dully on the blue velour. Stuck inside the lid of the case was a photograph of herself as a good-looking middle-aged woman, wearing a long sequinned white evening gown, playing her violin on a concert platform. He'd heard she used to often play at Carnegie Hall in the twenties and thirties. It was rise and fall, just like the Roman Empire. All part of life's rich pattern, yeah! He got a couple of quick shots of her with his savage eye, and the old violin-witch told him to get lost. People didn't like it when you saw them as they really were.

The whole 'city phase' of his life had begun when his Ma took up with the fat Yugoslav. It happened because Dad was an insurance adjustor and was never home, and mom was a hysteric, always exaggerating everything. As a result, Jack had come to live with his Auntie Dawn. She was about thirty-six, thirty-eight, but dressed like a young girl with those off-the shoulder nylon blouses and tightly pinched and puckered skirts, which seemed not right for an aunt. The good thing about Dawnie was that, as an usherette at the Paramount, she could get hold of comps and occasionally even passes for press-shows. And she wasn't too restrictive of his freedom. Didn't fence him in. They had cut a sort of tacit deal about that. In her smart mauve army-style usherette's uniform she could look pretty good in the dark of the cinema, and men who came to the Paramount by themselves and had been lit up by Dorothy Lamour or Deanna Durbin on the screen, sometimes asked Aunt Dawn to go out with them, and if she liked the look of someone, even from just a brief glimpse, she did, and sometimes she didn't come home all night. Other times she came home when it was practically morning, after having been taken to a nightclub, and young Jack Strawley creeping to the bathroom could hear her carry on, the rapid breathing and all that: sounded like she was having a seizure. There was no holding back Auntie Dawn when she got going. Their deal was to respect each other's privacy.

On nights when she knew she had a heavy date, Auntie Dawn brought liquor to the apartment, to get in the mood, and she'd offer him a drink. After two big scotches and a smoke he entered a sepia-coloured world in which all the messy and jagged little wrinkles in his brain were smoothed out, and there was a beautiful sense of ease, of everything having become suddenly easy, and he told Aunt Dawn of his projects, then, told her he was going to make films, was going to raise the money, write the scenario, and direct. Like Orson Welles. One of these days, Jack was going to make his film, and it was going to be a big hit, he knew that. When she asked him teasingly, How d'you know? he replied grinning broadly, nicely smashed by then: 'I'm a genius, that's how.' To which she replied with a coarse, intimate little Dawnie laugh: 'Yeah, sure. Just have to rub your little magic lamp, right, and straight away the genie-genius comes popping out?'

Though she teased him, he could see she took what he said seriously. He knew what he was talking about, knew his cinema: not just the stars but names of directors and even of cameramen and art directors and music composers and could tell the work of one from the work of another. There was no mistaking music by Miklos Rosza or Bernard Herrmann or Max Steiner, or the camerawork of Karl Struss or Stanley Cortez or James Wong Howe or Lee Garmes. No mistaking a Robert Siodmak film . . . or a Howard Hawks . . . he knew all their styles and mannerisms and tricks because he'd seen their films many times over and remembered everything.

Beyond Third Avenue it got to be seedy. Some of the houses along here had once been fine town residences but now they were all in multiple occupation and pretty run down mostly, though here and there little enclaves had held out against the general rot. It was a mixed, lively area. He liked it because of the liveliness and the variety. In the space of a couple of blocks you could come upon Greek Orthodox priests with long black beards, and flashy-eyed exuberant Hassidic Jews with broad black hats and long sideburns, and sleekly shod Italian Lotharios with shiny hair and expensive watches, and sombre-faced thick voiced Russians, violently pro- or anti-Soviet, and Ukrainians and Poles and Romanians and Hungarians and Greeks. Lately, a whole new influx of Americans from the sticks had been added. In scruffy torn denims and sweat shirts and cowboy boots, they were drawn to the bulge of Lower Manhattan by the stories of low rents and cheap places to eat and tales of wine and wild women and of publishers hungry for new talent and reports of new theatre collectives starting up. Where he lived at Aunt Dawn's, you were just a face in a madly rushing crowd, whereas down here, in the Tompkins Square area, though it might be rougher and dirtier, people weren't in so much of a hurry, had time to talk to you.
Which was how he'd got to know Carl. Carl Schmidlin. A writer. He was often at the Black Swan Café on Avenue A, drinking one coffee all morning and writing with puckered brow, mouthing dialogue to himself, sometimes speaking it out loud. Engaging in his daily struggle with the Word, high domed fore-

head crunched up in pained concentration, eyes firmly fixed inward, a battered fraying-at-the-elbows-and-cuffs old English Daks sports jacket draped around his shoulders.

Carl was Austrian, from Vienna. Living in England during the war, a Jewish refugee from the Nazis, he'd wanted desperately to get to America, because America was where everything could happen, unlike dull old England. America wasn't stuck in the past like England was. Finally, in '47, his visa came through and he could set off for dreamland. When he reached it he was disappointed. Bitterly disappointed. America wasn't the dream it was made out to be. He wasn't sure he wanted to stay. Seen from England, it had looked like the legendary place of opportunity for a young budding writer: but the price you had to pay was becoming part of the System, becoming part of the rat race, and subscribing to American values. America was maniacally competitive: you had to sell yourself all the time. Everything was money-oriented. Success-oriented. You couldn't get anywhere without contacts. It had taken him two years to acquire a precious few of these, but even if you managed to get a foot in some door, you had to keep hustling, because editors and publishers and producers soon lost interest in you and turned to someone else. New York was lousy with budding playwrights, budding radio script writers, budding movie scriptwriters, writers budding all over the place and trampling over others. When you'd achieved an actual production, your troubles were only just beginning, because directors in America had no respect for authors, Carl said. They took terrible liberties with your texts. Actors wanted to be free to improvise around your dialogue. He'd had one play produced by a semi-professional fringe group. And had sold a couple of playlets to a TV station. $60 was what he'd been paid by the TV station. Nothing by the fringe company. The way he was making ends meet was by giving classes in drama appreciation. He'd formed regular play-reading groups which read plays by Ibsen and Chekhov and Strindberg and other European masters. Each group consisted of about ten people, mostly women, and each member paid him $1 per meeting, so with three or four groups a week he could make $30-$40. Recently he'd branched out into cinema appreciation courses, linked to the Tompkins Square film society which he'd started. After a showing of one of the great masterpieces of cinema — a Chaplin, a René Clair, a Jean Renoir, a Donskoi — he'd dissect and analyze the film for the benefit of the class and then lead a discussion about it. By these means he was earning just enough to keep going while he waited for something to happen with one of his plays. Carl had read some of these to small groups of friends and fellow artists, and Jack had attended one or two such readings. Carl sounded just like Paul Henreid in *Now, Voyager.* He had an impressive success rate with women. He'd go up to them in the street and smell their perfume — even if they weren't wearing any! — and try to guess what it was. It was a great system. The way he did it none of these babes — at any rate, none in Jack's presence — had ever gotten mad at him. 'Let me guess. Christian Dior? No — Chanel? No—? No, wait a minute.' More sniffing, ever closer to the desired flesh. 'Balmain. It's Balmain's . . . no, I've got it wrong, it's Schiaparelli, I recognize the saffron in it. Saffron, the sweet-smelling herb in "The Song of Solomon". Also used in bouillabaisse.' Laughing, they let him guess and sniff away until he'd got it right. Or until they decided to say he'd got it right. 'Since I guessed it right, you must let me buy you coffee,' he'd say, and they usually did let him. He never offered them more than a coffee, explaining that he was a struggling artist who couldn't afford expensive restaurant meals. These girls usually ended up taking him out to dinner. They liked his worried frown, his troubled dark eyes. His Paul Henreid accent.His gentle irony. Made a change from the New York hotshots with slippery eyes. They were career women, the ones who bought him dinner. They worked for Merrill Lynch or Sullivan and Cromwell or Time-Life or NBC, and Jack had heard Carl say to them, with his great gloomy smile, which took the edge off his most incisive remarks, that they were the gilt on the mouldering gingerbread. Whether it was a question of flour being burnt while the world starved, so as to keep up stock market prices, or two ignorant human beasts battering each other insensible in the ring to make money for the fight promoters, in back of it all lay the capitalist system, of which these girls were at the same time the myrmidons and the camouflage. Pretty myrmidons, pretty camouflage, he said, smiling sharply. What were myrmidons, they asked. And he told them that they were killers.

He'd liked Carl immediatly. You could have serious discussions with him. Like the talk they'd had about *The Naked City*. Jack said that he'd really liked the way Dassin brought in chance factors like Garza's bumping into a blind man and being set on by the man's guide-dog, and the voice off saying 'It's only an accident, Garza. Pass it off! Don't lose your head! Don't lose your head!' They'd talked about it for hours, analyzing practically every shot in detail. Breaking it all down to see how it worked.

Jack was eager now to discuss *The Lady from Shanghai* with Carl and was looking around for him in the Black Swan. He spotted him at a table, drinking lemon tea, and pulled up a chair.

'Did you hear Winchell on Sunday?' Carl asked him straight away with a look that was at the same time worried and contemptuous. 'His usual sneer at the "poor Britishers", then off on his favourite hobby horse. Rat-a-tat-tat. Atomic war with the Ruskies! Drop an A-bomb on Moscow! Oh, don't make any mistake, Jack. America's ready to go to war with the Soviet Union. All that is required is one mistake. If by accident the Russians shot down an American or British plane over Berlin.'

'You can't pussyfoot around with the Russians,' the fat chess-player at the next table interposed, his mouth full of club sandwich. 'The Ruskies understand toughness . . . and that's all they understand. We got to show 'em we mean business.'

'Business being the operative word,' Carl muttered, sharply smiling. He got up, his long forehead finely creased.

'Are you in a *huge* hurry today, Jack?' It was said with that slight downturn of the mouth which implied a light reproof.

'Got a few things to do.'

'What I was going to suggest — if you weren't in too much of a hurry — would only take half an hour — I'd like your opinion of something I've written. It's short. Oh, I promise this time.'

Carl's readings, great though they were, sometimes could go on interminably through innumerable versions of the same text, in order that the listener could indicate his preference for version A or B or X. Jack wasn't sure if he could face one of these marathons today.

'What's the great hurry, Jack? A pressing appointment with the Warner Brothers?'

'Oh, I dunno.'

'I know, Jack, that you have faith in the beautiful American dream of Success and I'll allow you it's a great dream. I had it myself at one time.' He gestured vaguely in the direction of the downtown shrines of Wall Street, and frowned in the way that the women whose perfume he smelled considered so attractive. 'Where in the history of mankind has there ever existed such material splendour before? But . . . but . . . ,' he wagged his finger severely, 'tell me this, amid all the riches and the glories of America, where's the skull in the corner of the canvas to remind Sam Slick of the vanity? Who's there to tell him of the charlock's shade?'

'The what?'

'It's one of the Enemies,' — Carl's lip had that little secret ironic twist to it — 'a great corruptor of the artist's will to work. Sex! It's all in *The Enemies of Promise,* a book you absolutely must read, since "Success" interests you so much. Find out about all the traps awaiting you . . . some are very clever. Oh, very clever indeed. There's the slimy mallow. And the nodding poppies. And money-on-the-nail. Now there's a trap I'd gladly embrace right now . . . not to mention praise-on-the nail.'

Carl had a taste for books of dark prognostication. Jack couldn't argue with him about books, since he'd read so little, but he could hold his own talking about cinema. That day they argued about Frank Borzage. And about Joseph L. Mankiewicz. 'I'll agree with you that Borzage gets that dark broody heavy feeling,' Jack conceded. 'Only then it gets slow . . . it really gets slow, and the ending is sentimental . . . by then I was bored.'

'Could it be,' Carl asked, 'that boredom lies in the eye of the beholder, in your case, since I notice that everything's got to grip you by the throat or else you're bored.' This was true but he couldn't help it. There were times when his eyelids just drooped, his eyes began to water profusely, his mouth and jaw were wracked by convulsive yawns and his brain filled up with an impenetrable fog.

They had reached the entrance of Carl's lodgings.

'So will the Warners wait? While you come in and have coffee and I read you my new one-acter? I need an opinion because I'm thinking of sending it to a theatre group I'm in contact with . . .'

By the time Jack got back home, three hours later, his mind felt like a squeezed-out sponge, he was panting from mental exhaustion, from trying to keep up with Carl's swiftly darting, many-tracked, endlessly annotated flow of ideas. No question that Carl was pretty clever — all those books he'd read. Problem was he could never stick to any one subject, once he got going. Had to go down every sidetrack, till you were good and lost.

3

He walked all the way over to the Hudson and then down until he came to a spot where there was access to the bank and he could lie there and dangle his hand in the water. Higher up a big French ocean liner was departing for Europe, eased out by tugs, and he could see, faintly through the evening haze, the Statue of Liberty in the harbour mouth, covered in a shimmer of bluegreen rust. His hand was being washed by the wide river with all its floating trash. He felt he was dipping his hand in the deep life of the land, filthy and smelly though it was — there was the drifting smell of spoilt fruit coming from the United Fruit Company's pier and the raw stench of meat from the boats of the Chicago meat companies. Didn't matter how big and fat and dirty the river was, it was great because it flowed through time and time washed out the worst things you could think of, made it all into history.

Under the Third Avenue El he bought a ham and leberwurst

sandwich and walked back eating it in the grid-patterned late sunlight, amid the swarming dust motes. People sleeping in doorways, head down on formica-top tables in all-night restaurants, dossed out on loading platforms. He had to jump clear of the revolving jets of the water wagons. Through the red hue at the island's tip he saw the ziggurat towers rise up, and his mood abruptly changed, which sometimes happened: he was feeling high again, with the knowledge that everything was going to happen. Only it was taking a long time. Assisting Mr Bridewell wasn't regular work, the photographer just called him up when he needed extra help . . . which was maybe once or twice a week, and sometimes less. Doing nothing could get pretty dull. And tiring, as well. In films when somebody went somewhere *something happened to him*, something *always* happened, that was the rule of the Story, but in the life of Jumping Jack the Strawman there wasn't anything happening — in his restless flashing mind he had a picture of 'the Centre', where things happened all the time, an endless flux of *movement,* but it was a milieu from which he was excluded by virtue of his youth, inexperience and lack of Success. The trouble was that he was on the Outskirts when where you *had* to be was in the Centre.

He'd decided to go out and have a drink someplace and a bite to eat, since there was nothing in the fridge except a piece of pie left over from three days ago and a stale-looking yellow corn muffin, and some Jell-O butterscotch pudding. Aunt Dawnie wasn't what you'd call a housekeeper. More of a nymphomaniac, really. He found there was some J & B left in the bottle and he drank that before going out.

His first stop was Johnny Romero's in the Village which had a reputation as a pick-up joint. They said white women went there to get picked up by black guys. But no sign of women on the loose tonight, and he went to the next place on his list, and then the next, and by midnight his soggy brain was telling him that the stories of wild women were a big swindle. There weren't any wild women, and he'd best go home and eat some of the pie, write it off as another wasted night on the Outskirts. Where things didn't happen, because it wasn't the Centre.

He was drifting down through desolate streets of dark warehouses with grime-encrusted windows and iron steps leading up
to loading platforms. Ahead he could see one or two Chinese
signs, indicating where Little Italy and Chinatown began to
overlap, and he decided this was far enough downtown, he didn't
want to walk any further tonight, and he turned around and
started back up. He'd taken a street he didn't know that ran
parallel to the one he had come down: names of shipping and
storage companies on the dark buildings, trash being blown
along the gutter and spiralling out into the roadway, double
padlocked heavy doors, iron shutters covered in graffiti, overflowing metal garbage cans. A sudden mewing of tomcats racing
across a patch of rubble-strewn ground between two buildings
where automobiles were parked. Up the road a few doorways he
saw a faint light coming from below ground level, and as he got
nearer felt the sidewalk vibrate with muffled sound. Standing on
top of the vibes and looking down, he saw faint lines of light
coming from between the slats of a closed venetian. He went
down three iron steps and put his eye to the smudged porthole
window. He made out a narrow barroom, like a long corridor, a
few people sitting up at the bar, a jukebox, sawdust on the floor.
No reason to suppose that this dive was going to be any more
productive than the others he had investigated, but he thought try
it. Last one tonight. Then home.

The place had an appealing sort of tackiness, with electrically
illumined plastic daffodils up on the wooden bartop, and there
was a tacky jukebox bellowing out raucous music to the accompaniment of coruscating pink and mauve and yellow lights. Two
girls sat at the bar. They looked as plasticky as the electric
daffodils, though the blonde one, he thought, didn't look too
bad, considering. She had bright eyes and an air of innocence
surprised, even if it had been surprised a long time ago. He took
a seat at the bar and ordered a scotch, then turned and peered the
other way, along the narrow corridor to a second bar, this one
without electric daffodils, or much of any other lighting, a sort of
back room bar that petered out at the end into an even darker
back area about which there was something definitely sordid.
Glass in hand, he ambled over. In the dark at the back he made

out a big guy talking on the phone in the corner, one long leg propped up against a door-jamb, his large form gradually sliding down the wall, as if slowly falling asleep on his feet. His heavy eyebrows twitched together densely above eyes whose focus appeared fixed. Periodically he stirred himself out of his somnolence to mutter chopped-up sentences into the mouthpiece on the wall: '. . . in Patsy Sorago's, yeah . . . in the meat market . . . yeah, front of all his pals . . .' A sleepy chuckle cut off by a yawn. '. . . Billy wanted him taught a lesson . . . I taught him good . . . Motherfucker needed thirty stitches.'

He let the earpiece drop and dangle by its cord from the wall instrument, then dropped the propped-up leg too and asked the sailor, all in white, who'd come up to him: 'Wanna see me?'

'Told you could . . . fix me up.'

'What is your fancy, friend?'

The sailor leaned forward close, jerked his head back to the first bar where the electric daffodils cast their watery light on the two girls at the bar.

'The blonde,' he said stiffly.

'Yeah, she's great,' the guy with the eyebrows said, 'Pure cream'n black satin.' He was more awake now. He went back to the dangling wall instrument and said into the mouthpiece: 'Call you back.' and dropped the earpiece into its cradle. 'Come on in here,' he said to the sailor. A swift low-voiced discussion ensued, and while it was going on Eyebrows was signalling to the blonde who promptly slid off the high bar stool and with hissing nylon thighs, eyes flashing, made her way to the back of the bar, her slithery walk stretching the material of her skirt around her like an elastic band. Eyebrows was wearing a lavender silk shirt with an exactly matching lavender silk tie tied in a large windsor knot and a lavender silk handkerchief in the pocket of his loosely draped jacket. His hair gleamed. His dice cufflinks clinked softly. The sailor was moving his cap around in his hands nervously. Eyebrows signalled with his fingers a certain sum of money, and the sailor counted off the notes. By the time the slithery blonde had come up to them the money had changed hands. 'Here's our little happiness factory,' Eyebrows said by way of introducing her. She slipped into the dark area at the back and the white-clad sailor followed, squeezing his cap into a roll. Eyebrows resumed his position between the door-jambs, raising a long leg as a sort of temporary barrier across the space. Then, twisting sideways, he unhooked the earpiece, dialled rapidly, and resumed the phone call he had been making. After about ten minutes slithery blondie came out of the dark space picking hairs from her tongue and tugging at the stretch material of her skirt and smoothing it down over her hips. The sailor, a big sheepish grin on his face, emerged a little after her, tidying himself up and breathing hard. 'Was that to your liking, friend?' Eyebrows inquired solicitously.

'Great.'

'Come and see us again,' Eyebrows said after him.

'Yeah. Sure,' the sailor said, walking away fast.

Seeing Jack observe the scene, Eyebrows gave him a wink and asked:

'In'rested in a li'll action, friend?'

'Not right now, thanks.'

'Make you a price. I promise you, blondie here is *g-e-r-e-a-t.*'

'Bet she is too.'

'Give yourself a present, young fella.'

'Not my birthday.'

'Who's gonna know?'

Letting himself quietly into the apartment he heard Aunt Dawnie's agitated breathing. Nympho! He went into the kitchen and ate the stale piece of pie, followed by the butterscotch pudding, after which he got undressed and went to bed. He didn't bother to put on pyjamas and he left the door of his room slightly ajar. The sounds from Aunt Dawnie's room was still going on, underscored with the jangle of bedsprings in varying rhythms from slow slow soft to frenzied fast and back to slow slow soft. Speeding up, slowing down. Sharp harsh strong cries, gasps, the roll of bedsprings. Then mysterious periods when the sea was calm. Then another sudden dramatic squall. He synchronized his own movements to the course of the storm in the other room, slowing down when it slowed down, and speeding up as the tempo accelerated there. Somewhere in the course of these stop/

go frenzies he fell asleep and dreamt about going up to Orson
Welles in a low bar and saying to him, 'I want you to kill me!'
and then, later, twisting round with a sense of someone having
come into the room, he saw the prince of darkness standing by
the window in his lavender shirt and all his evil glory, dice
cufflinks tinkling enticingly.

4

Chuck's 'hole-in-the-ground' was far from being the Centre,
but things were going on there, even if only visits to the doorless
back-room by happiness machine Slither Slither and sailor boys
or denim wholesalers from Walker Street. He had got in the habit
of dropping in at Chuck's whenever he was in funds, and Eddie
Max, whom he'd first thought of as Eyebrows, was usually there.

Eddie Max liked to think of himself as an artist — at any rate
he painted, painted naked girls one step more naked than in the
girlie magazines, a jungly array of pudenda — and since he
considered Jack an artist too, on the basis of his photographs, he
felt that a basis for friendship existed.

The first time he'd gone to Eddie Max's apartment in Sullivan
Street, Eddie Max was wearing a long Japanese silk kimono and
was bare-legged and barefoot and bare-assed underneath. He
jingled his heavy bunch of keys (his front door had four separate
locks, he said there was a lot of crime going on in the area) as if
it was some kind of musical instrument. Inside the apartment the
windows were thickly curtained. Black silken canopies covered
the ceiling and striped black velvet velour the walls, and the
huge bed that could be glimpsed in a deep recess had black satin
sheets, upon which floated what looked like blond water lilies.
There seemed to be only this one room, the front part serving as

living quarters, the rear as bedroom. A piece of furniture that looked like a treasure chest on a stand stood with its lid up revealing that the top section contained a selection of variously coloured liquors and liqueurs and an array of Venetian glass goblets. The walls were covered with paintings, all in the same bold garish style, and evidently by the same hand, and all of nude and semi-nude young women in provocative girlie magazine poses, but without any coy concealment of pubic hair and genitalia, and a kind of living picture of the same sort, Slither Slither the happiness factory, lay sprawled on the bed, partially covered by the black sheets, her long blond tresses outspread in riotous disarray. She seemed to be deeply asleep and did not stir.

He'd been invited to look at the pictures and to give his honest opinion of them from the point of view of a fellow artist who 'had an eye', as anyone could see from his photographs.

'Tell me whatya think . . . they're pretty good, uh? So why don't the Jew-boys buy 'em, you wanna tell me that?'

'Maybe because they're all the same,' Jack Strawley said.

'I paint what in'erests me.'

'I can see that, ' Jack said, smiling tensely. He went to examine some of the paintings from up close. Bold splashy colours laid on with verve. A kind of innocent relish, a childish glorying in the fantasy of flesh. Executed with elementary art-school skill.

'They've got something,' he said, 'only you don't paint what you see, you paint what you'd like to see. That's why they're all the same.'

Eddie Max didn't look too put out by this criticism.'What's wrong with that? I like the same. Don't you?'

He jerked his head meaningfully towards the floating mass of candyfloss hair on the bed. 'I can see from the way your eye keeps sorta loitering over there. *That's* more o' the same . . . oh, that *is*. Much more of the same.' He paused and asked in a sudden impulse of uncontrollable generosity. 'You wan'er? Said you like the way she walks. Slither slither, huh?' He gave a shrug. 'It's a present. On the house. I like you, and you take good pictures, and when I like someone that's what I do, I give them a nice present. I like to do it.'

Their conversation had finally penetrated down to the subject herself in the deep dream world in which she was suspended, and Slither Slither began to stir restlessly, dislodging enough of the partial covering of black sheets to expose the opulent rotundity of one buttock. The murmurings and sighings and faint moans of the half-world between sleep and awakening. And then there came the vague slithery movements from the bed, and presently a certain regularity entered into these movements, and they were becoming stronger and more definite, and her breathing too.

'See what she's doing, hot little bitch, always hot when she wakes up out of her dreams, ' Eddie Max said. 'She don't mind you looking. Don't be afraid. She likes being watched.'

Jack Strawley mentioned that he had to be going.

'Don't wanna stay for the show, kid?'

'Another time maybe.'

'Listen,' Eddie Max said, 'even you don't want accept my present, about which I'm very insulted I gotta tell you, even you don't, here's a strictly business proposition for you. I need some photos of our friend. You know the kind I mean? People writing in reply to box number ads I put in some magazines. I have a little mail order business going. You wanna do that for me? Pay you twenty-five. And there are other compensations if you want other compensations.'

Eddie Max peeled off five five dollar bills and handed them to Jack. 'Come back with your camera.'

These photo sessions took place while Eddie Max strode about barefoot and bare-assed in his kimono dressing-gown, supervising the photography and holding forth about himself.

'I keep fit, see, I go to the gym every day, got to, got to be fit for this work, I don't drink, I don't smoke . . . bend the other leg outward, honey, yeah, like that . . . let's see some pink. See, I got to be in training like a fighter, it's the same . . . the bread 'n butter is escort jobs. Try it with one leg over the armrest, honey, that's good, that's good. You got to understand that when Billy the king goes anywhere he gotta have an escort. It's protection and it's prestige and it's rank. He don't go anywhere alone. He don't go to shit alone. I like good things,' he avowed with convincing sincerity. 'Good quality leather. Good quality clothes.

Vicuna, camel hair, silk . . . satin. I love the feel of camel hair, I love to have silk against my skin, all my underwear's silk. I always had the best. Whatever it was. Shoes, I like the leather to be soft like glove leather . . . antelope skin, lovely. Glass, I like to drink out of crystal, out of the best Venetian. So how about that Studebaker convertible . . . all white with white upholstery leather? Is that the most beautiful automoble in the world. Or isn't it?'

One day there was this girl there with the Linda Darnell hair-do, with the double rolls of hair at back, wearing — at first — a long velvety jet black outfit with gleaming buttons all the way from neck to hem and down each sleeve.

'Don't get me wrong. I intend to make it as a serious actress,' she said, 'but you've first got to get their attention, haven't you? You think I'll be able to use any of these photos for sending to agents?'

'Lie on your belly,' Eddie Max told her. 'Let one leg dangle down to the floor. Look like you're having fun.'

'Oh, I am. I am.'

'Show it. Put that cushion between your legs.'

'I won't be able to use these pictures for agents, will I?'

'I'll crop some for you. The expression on your face is very nice,' Jack said.

'I think you should always have a nice expression on your face, whatever you're doing,' the girl said.

After the photography was over, the girl with the Linda Darnell who was going to be a serious actress had gone into the black-tiled bathroom, and Eddie Max was arranging the lighting. Coming out of the bathroom wearing only the black fishnet stockings and garter belt which she had got down to in the picture session, her eyes had a belladonna-bright sparkle in them. Eddie Max was regulating the recessed lighting to give the walls the right soft pink flesh-like flush. Then he took off his camel's hair jacket, though not his dark glasses, hung it over the back of the high-back Spanish chair, and gave a little tidying touch to his hair glistening with Luster Life. He went to the deep treasure chest which contained the range of alcoholic drinks, fixed a screwdriver for the girl, after which he poured orange juice into a

pewter beer mug for himself. He was humming an accompaniment to 'Zip-a-dee-doo-dah' on the gramophone. Then he sat
back, seignorial fashion, in the Spanish-type chair and broke a
capsule under his nose, shaking his head from side to side and
snorting deeply. The girl was still standing, holding the drink in
her hand, as if she was at a cocktail party, a nice expression on
her face.

'Come on here,' Eddie Max told her with a rough, authoritative hand movement. And when she was seated within the wide
angle of his thighs he started to unbutton himself with one hand
while pulling her head towards him with the other.

'You can have her after me,' Eddie Max offered. The girl
nodded vigorous consent while keeping the nice expression on
her face. 'I'll be careful not to use her up too much. Heck, we get
sick of her, we always got each other. Ha ha ha.'

One day Eddie Max came up with a strictly business proposition
that did not consist of photographing naked girls. They were
walking along the waterfront, dark river water lapping over
rotting wooden piers. 'Only schmucks don't walk while they
talk, when you could go to jail rest of your life for what you're
saying. Remember to walk, Jacko, always walk when you talk.'
Grass invaded by stiff high weeds prickled their ankles as they
passed the wrecked wooden benches and the rusty railings that
sagged out over the fast moving river. The other side of the road,
the big windowless entrance of a newly fashionable nightspot
was wide open, and the high trill of a saxophone drifted in sharp,
quick spasms through the humid air. On the river, the beam of a
police boat spotlight was slicing through the water-borne trash
carried by the strong current and stopped in its random trajectory
on a dark inflated form.

'Yeah, this is where they find 'em floating,' Eddie Max pointed
out, indicating what might be a corpse.

Between pier 88 and 89 it was desolation. There was a big
black shiny Packard standing in the midst of the concrete waste
ground. *The Queen of Sardinia* unloading. Rainbow colours in
the gasoline spills. Fifty yards in front of them, the short bulky
man getting out of the black Packard was moving a cigar around

his mouth without touching it with his hands: his hands stayed deep in the pockets of his long overcoat. They watched the metal-bound wooden crate being hoisted down slowly on pulleys.

The man moving the cigar around his mouth was coming forward slowly.

'That's Billy's right hand,' Eddie Max said with low-voiced respect. 'Big noise. Wants some pix took to show Billy that I done a good job. Wanna come along and be my personal cameraman? Pay you fifty.'

'What sort of a job?'

'Gonna be some blood. Got a strong stomach?'

'How much blood?'

'Not too much. Some. Depends, of course. Wanna do it?'

'You're not going to kill him, are you?'

'Nahhh. Just teach him a lesson.'

They stood a little way back outside the barber's where Colleano went for a shave before going to see his girlfriend Janey on Mott Street. Waiting for Colleano to re-emerge, Eddie Max took the opportunity to acquaint Jack with the tattooing art of Rocks Grillo. Photographs in the window showed a big wrestler covered all over in a dense pattern of intertwining roses. Next to him, a circus strongman exposed jungly buttocks swarming with snakes and birds and butterflies, while his belly bore the image of Jesus Christ on the Cross.

'Rocks is the best. Beautiful work,' Eddie Max said. 'You may have noticed, had some done myself. The guy's a great artist. Maybe not as great as Constable' — he laughed — 'but pretty fuckin' great. You know who I'm talking about, kid? Constable . . . the British painter Constable? Did fields, and trees, and streams and rocks? And haystacks. Great! So great! What an artist! Beautiful countryside. I could paint like him, would I be doing this line of work? Wouldn't need to, would I? This stuff's to make a living, Jack. But what I am at heart truly . . . is an artist.'

Colleano had come out of the barber shop smoothly shaved and smelling of face lotions. He was a burly man with a raw reddish complexion and red hair, huge fists and small stone-like eyes. He went lurching down the street unaware of the two figures who'd stepped swiftly back into the dingy stairwell of the Progress Hotel. Eddie Max went after him, keeping about fifteen yards behind. Going north Colleano turned left into Pell Street and stood for a minute looking in the window of Chinaman Chung's 'love emporium' before going in: Eddie Max and Jack stayed outside. The love potions were displayed in decorated porcelain jars and bowls and on lacquered trays: ginseng root, preserved bear's testicles, sliced deer's horn, dried sea horses, blanched snakes. After a few minutes, Colleano came out carrying a small packet, and there was an additional bounce in his step as he headed back towards Mott Street and Janey-girl. Right here, outside the 'love emporium', was the place to teach Colleano his lesson, Eddie Max decided. It was quiet there. Nobody about. Yeah, do it while boastful Colleano, would-be pal of the great, was swelled up with amorous anticipation. He called out: 'Hey, Colleano.' The lumbering ex-boxer, hearing his name, swung round.

'What you want, Max?'

'Got a message for you from Billy,' Eddie Max said, approaching with Jack at his side.

'So what's the message?' Colleano asked.

'Billy don't like people boasting. About knowing him, see. He don't like people claiming to be close family when they're just distant cousins. Related only by marriage of convenience. That's all. So I hope you got the money, Colleano. Because Billy rarely extends a loan beyond the due date, only does it sometimes if somebody is close family, real close family, and has had a mishap, but you're not even related.'

'I'll have it by tomorrow latest,' Colleano said.

'Tomorrow's too late,' Eddie Max said coming up close to the big man.

'Okay, I'll remember next time,' Colleano said.

'I know you will, but just to make sure . . . Billy wants to make sure you remember.'

Colleano in a rush of bravado said tightly: 'Don't make me tread you in the ground, faggot.'

'All I got to do is give you a black eye, Colleano. Billy just wants you to have a little remembrance of him. You know? To jog your memory when it needs jogging. You won't get too bad hurt if you do this right, — he slapped his hands together pit-pat. 'On the other hand, you wanna do this the hard way . . . that's okay by me too.'

Colleano was squaring up for a fight, and Eddie Max shrugged. 'That's the way you want it.'

He shot a sideways look at Jack and nodded, giving the signal to start taking pictures. Moving forward, ducking daintily under Colleano's suddenly flailing arms, getting up close to the large, freshly shaved and lotioned face, he placed the big head as if setting up a coconut shy. The short sharp punch to the left eye produced a howl of pain from the man. Colleano was throwing wild punches, which Eddie Max was sidestepping without any trouble. He was under them or to the side of them. And then he had got hold of Colleano by the neck, his fingers applying pressure to the jugular until the veins in Colleano's forehead looked about to burst. Propping up the head with one hand, Eddie Max lashed out at the eye that was still open and not streaming blood, once, twice, three times, in rapid succession, and he followed up with a tight-knuckled blow to the broken-toothed mouth, and a rammed knee in Colleano's genitals. The big man went down screaming, clutching the Chinese love potions to his groin, whereupon Eddie Max kicked him in the face and the ribs. The writhing man on the ground, in a blind reflex, sought to kick back. So what d'you do when a man who's down tries to kick you? Teach him a lesson, kick him back. Having got into the swing of it, Big Eddie Max seemed loath to stop. Every slight attempt at retaliation — or even self-defence — from the man on the ground spurred Eddie Max to a renewed cold fury. Jack could see that if this didn't stop, Colleano was going to be dead pretty soon.

He stopped taking pictures and said hoarsely: 'You're going to kill him, Big Ed. You're going to kill him if you don't stop . . .'

Eddie Max stopped in mid-punch, cutting off as if a switch had been thrown inside his brain. He breathed deeply once or twice. 'Got some good pix, kid? The face? Get me some good shots of the face.' The face was a bloody pulp. Eddie Max, breathing hard but otherwise unruffled, examined with distaste the blood stains on his jacket. He shook his head. 'Bring the pix over soon as they're developed,' he said, then added, 'You was right to stop me, kid. No reason to kill him. Wasn't due.'

5

A quarter of a century later, in Seville, talking about this period of his life for the memoirs that in the end were never written, Jack Strawley said he knew — even if he didn't really know what he was going to do with his life — that, whatever he did, it had better make a good story.

And then one day something happened that gave him a sense of conviction about what his life was going to be. It was as if everything had been blurred up till then, only vaguely grasped, and now he was seeing things in sharp focus for the first time. It happened one night when he went along to the Tompkins Square film society, run by Carl. It was an occasion when they were showing Eisenstein's *Battleship Potemkin,* and there was going to be a talk afterwards by W.V. Kyser, who had known Eisenstein and worked with him at Paramount while the great Russian director was there to make *An American Tragedy.* At first Jack had been sure that he was going to be bored. He had been brought up on Hollywood movies, had hardly seen any European classics. Then the lights went down and the film began, and soon he was totally caught up in it. The great battleship at sea, the superior arrogant officers, the submissive crew, putting up with their conditions, with the disgusting food, and then the revolt, and the revolutionaries taking over the ship. He noted how little the camera moved, how Eisenstein told his story almost entirely

by cutting. And then the ship, with the revolutionaries commanding it, sails into Odessa, and there followed the sequence on the
steps, a pyrotechnic display of pure editing. He was unconscious
now of the body-smells and the pipe smoke and the wet rain-
coats: he was with the anti-czarist rioters as the soldiers of the
White Guard started moving in strict formation down the wide
steps, firing into the crowd. The rhythm of their advance, the
details that Eisenstein selected for the audience's attention — the
bayonets bearing down, the high boots descending, the soldiers'
shadows on the steps, the screaming woman in close-up, the
panicking crowd in long shot, and then the amazing sequence of
the woman with the pram who is shot and whose fall sets the
pram careering down the steps. At the end he had wanted to
applaud, but once the lights were back on, the stuffy classroom
atmosphere re-asserted itself, and such manifestations of enthusiasm seemed out of place.

After the film came the talk. Kyser said that though Eisenstein
had made only five films in twenty-three years, each one was a
masterpiece. And his theoretical writings would remain the basic
textbook of cinema for a long time to come. It was his application of Dialectical Materialism to aesthetics that was perhaps his
greatest contribution to film theory. At its simplest what he
demonstrated was that in the cinema the interaction of a and b
did not make $a + b$ nor even $a\,b$, but c. This principle, W.V. Kyser
said, was best illustrated by the famous experiment of inter-
cutting a man's face with an image first of food, then of a fierce
dog. Though the face remained unchanged, in the first case the
man appeared to be hungry and in the second afraid. This was the
essence of creative editing, of creating meaning by means of
counterpoint and opposition.

At the end of the talk, something had jelled for Jack. Speaking
of this in the Seville tapes he says: 'You have to call it an
epiphany . . . suddenly I knew what I had to do with my life. I
remember blurting this out to Carl, so excited had I been by that
film, and I was expecting him to be drily ironical, as he usually
was about everything. *Well, you better let Warner Brothers know
fast of your decision.* But, to my surprise, he didn't mock.
Treated my outburst with perfect seriousness, rolling up his

brow, puffing at that damned pipe of his and then he said one had to be mad enough, or desperate enough, to be ready to stake one's life on such an ambition, and yes, maybe I was desperate enough, or mad enough, to do that, and good luck to me, something like that, and the thing was that I realized as he said it that, mad or desperate, I *was* ready to stake my life on it. And the fact that Carl didn't ridicule the whole idea was, at that point, the crucial endorsement I needed. After that it was settled for me. That was what I was going to do.'

6

In the downstairs lobby, next to the dusty potted ferns, old Mrs Gutenberg, with her famished white arms and her famished white lapdog, wearing a cotton dress imprinted with giant yellow sun spots, and a straw bonnet, sat whitely under the bowls of imitation alabaster and yellow lanterns. 'Come and talk to me, young Jack,' she called to him. 'I've had such a trying day today. I need to keep my spirits up.'

He went right by her as if she was a ghost, which she may have been, because he was no longer sure what anything was, didn't know what was inside his head and what was outside. There was the curious situation that he himself was outside his head, watching in a deep daze the imposter who had taken over his mind and body rush like a madman past Mrs Gutenberg, taking no notice of her, and practically knocking her over. The wild stranger who was inside him heard Mrs Gutenberg say that young people nowadays had no manners, no consideration for others, while the outside man watched through the grille the elevator's endless descent, its oily noose of black cables sliding towards him like coiled snakes. He shook the lift cage in a mad fury at the elevator's slowness, seeking to squeeze his head through gaps in the ironwork. At the same time he was watching from afar while these strange things were happening to him. Where is everybody? Everybody left to go fishing? Nobody home? When was the cunthole ever in? Nymphomaniac. Better call a doctor because something is wrong here. Somebody's got into my skin, and I don't feel myself. The problem was he didn't know any doctors and nymphomaniac Dawnie was probably getting it stuck up her right this minute and would go on getting it stuck up her all night long, since she never had enough, so who could he ring?

There was nobody to ring. Except Carl. Carl was the only friend he had when it came down to it. The only one you could ring when you had a problem like being out of your fucking head.

He rang Carl and told him he was sick: his heart was going at about a hundred miles an hour, he said, and did Carl know a doctor? Could he send a doctor over to him? Carl got there first. Concern on his face. 'What's the matter?' 'I don't know,' Jack said. 'I feel sort of weird. Not myself, you know? I think I may be dying.' 'No,' Carl said, smiling tightly, lighting his pipe, he was not going to let that happen, was not going to let him die, which seemed like a funny thing to say, because what could Carl *do* about it, since he wasn't even a doctor? Then Carl's doctor arrived, a thin austere man with sharp eyes, a sombre expression, Viennese. A brow like the dome of a church. He took Jack's pulse for about five seconds, then abandoned it and produced a writing pad and a fountain pen and started asking questions. Felt his mind was going 'too fast', did he? That it wouldn't slow down and would crash. Into what? All these flashing images. Ah yes. Ah yes. Felt he was going crazy? Ah! ah! said Dr Krakower that was a sure sign that he wasn't: crazy people didn't feel crazy. It took a sane man to feel crazy. When had this feeling come over him first? He said it was after seeing *The Snake Pit,* that was when he'd had a foretaste of it. A warning flash. Ah yes, ah yes, said Dr Krakower. Some people were very quick to *identify.* Were born with one skin layer missing, so to speak. They put themselves inside others' shoes . . . and bodies and souls. He nodded his head with sombre knowingness. 'You feel trapped *inside?* You feel you have to get out? Whatever the cost.'

'Sometimes my mind's going so fast I can see things before they happen, I can see things all laid out in front of me.'

'What sort of things?'

'Part of me is sure, really sure, I'm some kind of a genius who's going to do all these amazing things which will dazzle the world, I really believe it, and the other part just keeps saying, "You're going to die, you're going to die, you're going to die, you're going to die . . ."'

'Well, I don't think you're going to die just yet,' Dr Krakower said. He asked Jack how much he smoked and drank, and whether he took any kinds of stimulants. Dr Krakower listened to Jack's heartbeat, without a stethoscope, with just the naked ear pressed to his chest. That way you heard the truth and sometimes could decipher the signal sent out by the frantic beats.

'Functional paroxysmal tachycardia,' he said, rising solemnly. 'Nothing to worry about.' The speeding of the heart was not due to any ailment but was purely functional. Since the soul could not speak, said Dr Krakower, it had to make its needs known by functional means through the body. He diagnosed nervous over-excitation due to the excessive use of alcohol, coffee, nicotine and pep-pills of the benzedrine type. Perhaps due to excesses of other kinds as well. He had been abusing his nervous system, which needed a complete rest. He must look at the beauty of nature, and seek to calm his spirit, which Dr Krakower could see tended towards excessive forms of excitation. 'The nerves become over-stimulated and quickly exhausted in natures such as yours.' He must try to find some stability. He must go away for a rest, find 'the green and pleasant land'. It could be found by those who looked for it. Meanwhile he prescribed Seconal so that Jack might get some sleep.

7

The Tramline Theatre Collective had been created in a former trolley-car depot in Greenwich Street. A couple of the old 42nd Street trams had been kept, one to serve as box-office kiosk and office, the other, sub-divided into curtained boxes, as a communal dressing room for the actors. In the remaining space they had succeeded in creating a good-sized open stage, with curtained off backstage area, and an auditorium that could seat 150 people: fifteen tiered rows of ten seats across. Since the seats were plywood stacking chairs, the stage could be enlarged or reduced by removing or adding rows of seats.

No full-scale production was running at the time that Jack turned up, so the only chance to see the theatre in action, Carl had said, was to come along to a 'public reading'. He was doing one himself in a few days' time and suggested Jack should come to that.

Arriving a few minutes before the posted starting time, he found no more than about fifteen people in the audience. The evening opened with 'incantatory new poetry for theatre performance' by a young Negro poet. This was followed by readings from a play-in-progress about Tolstoy and his wife, drawn from their respective diaries. Next came Carl, wearing black corduroy trousers, a black polo neck pullover, and smoking Gitanes. Through the cigarette smoke he announced in his soft ironic Viennese voice the title of the work: *Suicide Note, An Inconsequential Comedy in One Act.*

It was about a man sitting on a bench in Central Park in a snowstorm writing a suicide note. The man says he has taken 20 Nembutal tablets and is beginning to feel drowsy. He tells the audience that he is perfectly sane, even if the coroner should decide otherwise. What do coroners know? They only knew about the contents of the stomach and lungs, not of the soul. He is trying to write the suicide note but his fingers are frozen stiff and so he gives up and speaks directly to the audience. The pills are beginning to take effect and he is getting confused, but he is sure it was a totally sane decision to end his life. There was nothing else to be done. He notes that it is getting dark and that he is in a dangerous part of the park. It was a relief to realize that this didn't matter now. That nothing mattered now. Or ever did, if you came to think of it. The snow is piling up around his ankles. Soon it will be up to his waist, then his neck. Looks like it's going to blow up a storm, and he's only wearing a light coat. The temperature must already be around zero and during the night it could fall to ten below, and with an Arctic wind blowing that would be the equivalent of minus 40. He could freeze to death. Which of course didn't matter if you were committing suicide anyway. In America everybody worshipped the Bitch-Goddess Success. But all the same there was a certain beauty in being someone who has missed the boat. Lying in the gutter, you were closer to the real truth. How low the ground was when you were crawling over it, and how hard, but it was solid ground unlike the vaporous endless blue of the American Dream. This was some snowstorm! How many inches so far? A drowning man saw his life flash before his eyes . . . with Nembutal it was slower. Wasn't speed what life was all about in America? In his life he has taken everything too seriously. It is only now with the snow rising up around his shoulders, almost at his chin — soon it will cover his mouth and he won't be able to make himself heard, so much the better! They won't have to listen to his ravings — only in his present circumstances has he realized that he should have taken life more lightly. But you always discovered these things too late. The stage directions say that snow covers his mouth, and all that the audience can hear are choked mumblings and gurglings. Soon he will be completely buried in snow. Once he is dead, he finds his voice again and tells the audience, in the form of a brief obituary, that when found next morning he was sitting upright on the park bench, having metamorphosed into a snowman.

At the end the applause was mild, only Jack clapped with fervour. He continued to do so after the others had stopped. Feeling someone watching him, he turned sideways and saw a woman standing in the aisle scrutinizing the audience with sharp alert eyes. This must be Gloria Vanderveld. She fitted the bill —

'a clever, beautiful woman, dedicated to the theatre,' Carl had said about her. She was, he saw, very concentrated on what she was doing, which right now consisted of watching the audience leave. Her hair was uncomplicated, straight and long with a centre parting, and she dressed uncomplicatedly too — a white blouse-shirt with big practical button-down flap pockets from which pencils and pens protruded, and a long pleated practical skirt that didn't impede movement. She had a bunch of papers under her arm and was smoking with the quick hard drags of a serious smoker. She had a quiet, nervy sort of 'older woman' beauty — she must be twenty-seven or twenty-eight, he thought. Their eyes met and he said: 'You're Gloria.' She nodded curtly and made a sign that she was busy for the moment, but would be with him later. At the same time was giving nods and signals to staff: unobtrusively running the place. She was fully occupied in this way for some minutes. When the audience had left, she turned briskly to Jack:

'Sorry. Yes? You wanted to see me?'

'I'm Jack.'

'Jack? Of course you are.' She looked at him closely. 'Carl's told me about you. You fit the bill.'

'So do you,' he told her.

'Do I? How'd Carl describe me?'

'Glowingly.'

'Ah, did he? Did he?' She laughed a little shyly, which didn't fit with her general authoritative air. 'He's a terrific person, Carl. A very wonderful person. I love him very much.'

'He's my best friend.'

'That's what he said. I was glad to see, from the way you were applauding, that you liked the piece.'

'Carl's a good writer.'

'I think so too. But then we're on his side from the start, whereas audiences have to be won round. They have to be told something is good. Then they see it. Sometimes.'

'Well, I liked it a whole lot.'

He found himself being assessed in her clear bright eyes, which were obviously used to assessing people and good at it. He had a sense of being summed up. Realizing what she was doing, she looked down and said:

'Sorry if I seemed to be looking you over. It's because Carl's talked a lot about you. Cross-checking, that's all.'

'So am I what you expected?'

'I make up my own mind about people.'

'I can see that.'

'Anyway.' She smiled, looked at her watch. 'He won't be long. Not being an actor, I expect he can't "come down" as fast as some, has to do it gradually.' To fill in while they were waiting for Carl to 'come down' and emerge, she said conversationally: 'Carl told me you've been on a marathon reading jag this summer. The Thirty Greatest Books in twelve weeks? Amazing.'

'Twenty,' he said, 'it was twenty . . . Carl picked them out for me.'

'Still pretty impressive. I gather you went for Thomas Wolfe in a big way.'

'Yes . . . he's tremendous.'

'How about Faulkner?'

'Couldn't get on with him.'

'Why not?'

'Couldn't get into his world. I've got to be able to enter somebody's world, or I fall asleep.'

'Carl told me about that.' She laughed. 'Oh we're all spoilt by the movies. Expect to be thrilled all the time. Some books — and people — have a slower rhythm. Oh God, I hope that doesn't sound too lecturing .'

'It's okay. I can do with some lecturing. I skipped most of my schooling.'

'Because you fell asleep?'

'Yeah, I fell asleep a lot. But I got on great with Shakespeare. *Macbeth.* Terrific play. Had some ideas about how to do the witches. As gangsters' molls!' The interest in her eyes induced him to continue. 'When I get involved in something I can keep going non-stop, don't need to sleep at all.'

'Carl says you want to work in theatre and that you take good photographs. Are interested in stage lighting.'

'What else he tell you about me?'

She hesitated, and then said: 'That you'd been sick.'

'I had sort of a nervous breakdown,' he said lightly. 'I was overdoing things, using . . . bennies to give me a lift. For a while they can make you fly, but then you have a job coming down. You can crash.' He added quickly: 'I got cured of it.' And he added in reply to her initial question: 'Yeah, I'm interested in theatre. I'm interested in directing.'

'How about sweeping floors?' she asked, laughing gently at him.

'Stage floors? Sure,' he laughed back easily.

'We have lots of floors to be swept. And heavy stuff to be moved . . . you look strong . . . you get to be a director a teeny weeny bit later.'

'That's okay,' he said, 'I've got a *bit* of time.'

Carl was coming to join them: he put a firm, welcoming grip on Jack's shoulder, and then his high forehead crumpled into intricate folds as he fumbled for his pipe and started on the business of filling it and lighting it, in the course of which he demanded, without looking up: 'Well how did it play?' Having got the pipe lit and drawing, he fixed Gloria with his large soft brown eyes.

'Made a big impression on Jack. Yes?' she said, deflecting the question to him.

'Yes, it did,' he confirmed.

'And the audience?'

'They seem to have found it . . . interesting. But also bewildering. Buried up to his neck in snow in Central Park! They couldn't decide if it was meant to be "real" or allegorical.'

'Well, it's a dead man talking,' he said.

'Audiences are audiences: not very bright.'

'And you, darling? Did it work for you?'

She took a deep breath, looking momentarily unsure, then plunged on with an air of recklessness. 'It's something to be read, it's a fine short story. But I don't think it *performs*. I don't think reading it to an audience adds any value. That's being very honest, Carl. Which I think you want from me. I found myself asking: what is the action? Action defined as a change of relationships or of heart. It's not dramatic, the outcome being decided from the start. Where are our dramatic values?'

Carl asked her quietly: 'Are you saying I should forget it?'

'We have a workshop function. We're supposed to find out with the audience whether something works or not.'

'And you've found out that this doesn't.'

'It's . . . literary rather than dramatic, which is not a fault necessarily.' she began. She turned to Jack for help, less for his opinion than simply to shift the basis of the discussion, which was becoming tricky to handle.

'It's great,' Jack said flatly.

Carl laughed. 'I don't think Gloria shares your opinion, Jack.'

'Gloria's wrong,' Jack said in a quietly matter-of-fact way. 'So's the audience, if they didn't like it.'

'It's not that I didn't *like* it,' Gloria began defensively.

'I think why the audience didn't get it, ' Jack said, 'is because Carl isn't an actor. He read it, and it needs to be acted. A good actor'd find the dramatic values Gloria's talking about. They're there, but they have to be brought out. It wasn't directed.'

Gloria was watching Jack closely while he was talking.

'Have you ever worked in the theatre?' she asked him now.

'No.'

'But I expect you go to the theatre often?'

'No, practically never. Can't afford it.'

'Then, forgive me, on what basis do you make your judgement about . . . what makes a play work or not?'

'I just have a feeling about it,' he explained. 'I know what makes films work, I go to see lots of films.'

'I think theatre is a little different, you know. Plays don't work on quite the same principles as gangster movies.'

'You're pretty snobbish about movies, aren't you?' Jack said. He laughed. 'I think films can be great. As great as theatre. I know I'm right. This is something I really know.'

'You're very . . . sure of yourself,' she said smiling.

He shrugged. 'You mean for someone my age. Who hasn't done anything yet. I know what you mean. But I wouldn't say *very.*'

'What would you say?'

'Just sure enough.'

Gloria turned to Carl. 'Well,' she said, 'your friend certainly is full of opinions . . . and of himself. I expect we could use him here for something.' Smiling broadly she went and got him a broom. 'Good sweeping!' she told him.

'Yeah, you just watch me!' he said at once, taking the broom and determinedly raising a cloud of dust.

8

He was watching all the time while sweeping floors and moving scenery and setting up lights, watching how actors worked at their roles, and how directors worked with actors, and how set designers worked with limited means in a limited space. Some established stage directors had come to give seminars and in doing so revealed their work methods, and sometimes star movie actors came to work out in private, shielded from prying eyes in theatre-lab improvisations.

He had a secret timetable which was like a biological clock ticking inside him. He was learning about handling actors by watching others do it. There were different methods practiced by different directors: some gave the actors line readings, down to the tiniest movements and intonations. Others hardly seemed to direct at all, they worked by creating a situation or atmosphere that would play upon the actors' emotions and skills and get them to find the performance in themselves. He obtained practical experience of directing actors during photo sessions for front-of-house displays. It was acknowledged that he took good photographs, and since the actors knew that his stills could help them with their careers they gave up as much time as he demanded of them for these picture sessions. He took endless trouble to get the photographs right, made the actors run through their scenes again and again, and even re-directed them to some degree — 'do it like this for the camera, *looks* better'. There were people who said that these stills-sessions were sometimes better directed than the plays.

Most of all he learnt from Carl, the fount of wisdom. From Carl and Gloria. They really were a unit, an inseparable unit, a meeting of true minds and bodies. Gloria had come to accept Jack's hanging around them all the time, like a lost dog. He couldn't seem to let go of them. Well he didn't have anyone else, Carl said. Was all alone in the big city. Used to wander the streets by himself, now he hung around them instead. Carl had sort of come to feel responsible for the education of the savage. 'You have to watch out with this Eddie Max fellow,' Carl had warned. 'I know how the criminal mind fascinates you, but this man is no Hollywood gangster, he's the real thing.

'I can believe that he has his amiable side — paints, wants to be an artist, maybe *is* an artist of sorts. So was Hitler. I wouldn't give Eddie Max your address. I don't think that'd be prudent. Or tell him where you work. These people, one minute they're your greatest buddy, will do anything for you, give you their women, rough somebody up, bump somebody off, and then the next they've turned on *you*. Killers kill, you know. Watch yourself, Jack . . . oh, I can understand your interest in him, I can see that he's "material" for you, but be careful.'

At the end of fifteen months Jack knew that he was ready. He'd taken it all in through the corner of the eye, and through the ear, as he had gulped down the Twenty Greatest Works of Literature in one summer, while recovering from his nervous breakdown, as he had absorbed the photography of Cartier-Bresson and Ansel Adams and Steichen, and the film techniques of Eisenstein and Pudovkin and Hitchcock and Siodmak and Rossellini and De Sica. He had been thrilled by Meyerhold's assertion: 'Words are decoration on the hem of the skirt of action. The actor no longer occupies the leading place upon the stage. The director will determine all life there.' He had absorbed Strasberg's edict that 'the subtext is the play, and the subtext is sometimes contrary to the spoken text.' He had learned from those wonderful cumbersome great sentences of Thomas Wolfe's, and from Lee J.

Cobb's enormous performance in *Death of A Salesman*, and from Kazan's luminous direction, and Jo Milzener's set, and from the great lighting wizards of the movies like Stanley Cortez and James Wong Howe and Arthur Miller and Karl Kruss, and from the great chase in *Naked City*, and the overlapping dialogue in *Lady from Shanghai,* and the ballroom scene in *Ambersons,* and the ice-rink scene filmed inside a refrigeration depot to get the breath clouds, and the cuts within sentences that Welles used, and the way he 'pulled frames' to go into jump close-ups that took you right into the mind and soul of the character. And from Hemingway he had learned that provided you really know something you don't have to say it.

Since his internal timetable told him that he was now ready, he proposed to Gloria Vanderveld, with all the presumptuousness of one who has paid his dues sweeping floors for fifteen months, that she should let him direct *Suicide Note,* as a curtain-raiser to her own appearance with Nik Ransom in Strindberg's *Miss Julie.* She seemed taken aback by his audacity in demanding to be given this chance so soon. He had not been working in theatre for even eighteen months, he was twenty years old; there were actors in the group with years of theatrical experience behind them, who had directed plays at important theatres around the country, had worked on television, in films, and by rights they should get a chance to direct long before him.

'They were obviously no good,' he said, 'or they'd have gotten other chances by now,' then added: 'I know how to direct *Suicide Note.* It'll be a success for Carl . . . and I want to give him that. Don't you want to give him that?'

'You'd have to persuade one of the actors to play it,' Gloria said. 'Nobody wants to do it. They don't think it can work.'

'I can make it work,' he said, 'and I want Nik for it.' She laughed at the this. Nik was generally held to be the most talented male actor in the group, but also the most difficult, the most temperamental, the most undirectable and the most selfish.

'Alan, who has directed hits on Broadway, is having a hell of a time with him on the Strindberg, and you think you can persuade Nik?'

'Let me try.'

She laughed. 'He won't do it, Jack. Not with someone who's never directed a play before and an author who's not famous. Nik is very career-minded under all that contempt for the commercial. He knows exactly where he's going.'

'I know. That's why I think he'll do it. It'll be good for his career.'

'He won't do it with you, Jack. I'm sorry I have got to be so blunt, but that's the reality.'

'Okay. But if he said yes, would you let me do it?'

'He won't.'

'But if he did?'

'Look, let's stop talking about this, it's pointless. There's no chance he'd agree.'

'If there's no chance, it doesn't hurt you to say that in the unlikely event that he did agree, you'd let me do it.' She said nothing, was sullen. 'Give me a shot at it — to win the lottery. What's the risk, if it's such a way out chance?'

'Okay. You've got yourself a lottery ticket, satisfied?'

'So when can I have him to work?'

'When he's agreed.'

'He has agreed. He said you won't agree, but if you did — in that unlikely event — he'd do it.'

'Well, I let myself get trapped into that, didn't I? I have to hand it to you, Jack. You're a smart operator.'

'Not yet. But I'll get smarter. I'm learning.'

'Am I going to regret what I've let myself in for?'

'You won't. It's the best decision you ever made. You'll see.'

Persuading Nik Ransom to play the part in *Suicide Note* was one thing, directing him in any meaningful sense of the word was quite another. Nik did what he did, and directors, knowing what a difficult person he could be, settled for that, since what he did was always good, even if it was not always right. He had a raw sexual presence on stage that it was difficult to fit into parts requiring more variable qualities. Having been mentioned as *the* new actor to watch by some respected critics, and commercial theatre directors like Kazan and Logan, he was very conscious of being the coming man, and of having to plan his moves, and was doing so, while giving the impression of being a wild man who took heed of nothing except impulse. He had accepted Jack as director confidently expecting to eat him for breakfast, and then he'd direct himself in *Suicide Note*. A twenty-minute death scene preceding his role as the valet in *Miss Julie* would give him a chance to display histrionic range, even if the play was crap. Strindberg would supply the quality, Carl's play a chance to show his virtuosity.

Jack started the rehearsal period by getting Nik to read the piece through cold. Gave him no guidance, no orientation. Not a clue. Then he told him to go through it again and 'just play it this time the way you see it.' Just let him do it anyway he fucking wanted. Let the big shit get lost. People who were lost were usually grateful for some directions. Let him find out for himself, let him feel adrift. At the end of the first stumbling, incoherent reading (which Nik knew to be as bad as it was), Jack made no comment, simply said: 'Let's do it section by section.' When Jack made a suggestion about a certain nuance to be given to a certain line, Nik replied: 'I don't see that.'

'Try it, Nik. If we don't like it, we'll change it.'

When Nik started nodding his head up and down and doing nothing, his favourite way of outstaring directors, Jack just sat there and waited and waited and did not try to coax him out of it. He was ready to wait all morning, ready to wait all day. All week. Finally Nik came out of it, and said: 'Okay, want to do it?' and Jack said, 'Whenever you're ready.'

This process was repeated every few minutes, with long intervals when Nik was nodding his head up and down and that was all he was doing. At this rate it would take them all day just to read through the twenty-minute play. But Jack had decided that this was the bloody battle that had to be won, so he stuck it out.

When they came to the section where he was talking about the women he had loved, Jack instructed:

'Make it angry, Nik. It's sentimental on the surface but underneath he's angry as hell. Never mind the words, go against text, imagine yourself pissing on their graves . . . those cunts all failed you, they didn't give you what you really craved, you never admitted to yourself how much you *hated* them. Desired them and hated them. We've got to see the other side, you don't admit this even to yourself . . . just to the audience.'

Nik said he didn't see that interpretation and began nodding his head up and down while he worked out how the lines should be spoken, frowned a lot, and started to say things which never got out of his mouth, and after about ten minutes of this came to a dead stop. Jack gave him no more help, went off to get coffee, took his time coming back, and then seemed fairly uninterested in Nik's private wrestling with the lines. When Nik finally got around to saying them, he was seething inside and the lines came out angry as hell, and even as he was saying them he was conscious of how good his reading was.

Jack told him: 'I think you found it, your idea of doing it angry works a dream,' and Nik didn't contradict him.

Jack told him not to move from the park bench, not to get up, not to make any gestures, to play it all as if paralyzed from the neck down: the movement, the action was all in his head, he had to act it all with his head, using only eyes and voice. 'Where do I look ?' Nik wanted to know. 'I can't just look nowhere.'

'Look inside yourself,' Jack told him.

Nik hadn't the slightest idea of what the piece was about or what the direction he was being given was meant to bring out, but in some inexplicable way what Jack told him to do *worked,* and he sensed he was giving a performance which would attract attention.

Even though it was a one-man show Jack was lighting it with every single light that the theatre possessed, all dimmed down, at the start, to a tenth of their power. This was to create the effect of luminous twilight, and then he dimmed the lights fractionally, second by second, throughout the twenty minutes that the piece ran, thereby producing the effect of a slow fading of the light, right down to total darkness. At the very end he reversed the process, speeded up this time, from black night to a cold red dawn. When the stage was visible again to the eye, it was seen that the bench had become submerged in snow, and that there was a frozen form on it that looked like a crumbling snowman.

The tautly handsome woman in her fifties with the sharp eyes and sharp smile on her sharp face was Gloria's mother, Louise

Vanderveld. She was being conducted to her seat by a plumply middle-aged man with curly grey hair wearing a tuxedo and a dress shirt with diamond buttons: this was Louise's fourth husband, the theatre agent, George Jakes. The other clan members were the offspring of Louise's earlier marriages.

Carl's piece was listened to in a mood of puzzled politeness, and similarly applauded at the end.

The *Miss Julie* was enthusiastically received, with Gloria getting vociferous acclamation from the 'Gloria clan'. Taking her bow, she pointedly ignored them and afterwards asked the other actors to excuse her family's partisanship and rudeness. 'They think they're being supportive, and that family is family. Even though not one of us has got the same mother *and* father.'

The extended family was on its way backstage, congratulating everyone in sight with glazed eyes, strong handshakes, slaps on the back and, where called for, hefty kisses. The man with the diamond buttons spearheaded the backstage progress. Gloria introduced him as: 'George Jakes who's married to Mother.' Mother herself was introduced simply by her name, Louise Vanderveld, as if the actress and the mother were two different people.

With an air of deciding this on the spur of the moment, George asked them all, *all* — gesturing vaguely around — to come back to the apartment for a glass of champagne and a bite of something to eat, adding that it was just going to be simple, since there hadn't been time to organize anything.

9

'Going to let you introduce yourselves,' George Jakes told people as they arrived. 'Half those here I don't know myself.'

This was an affectation, since he was known for knowing everybody.

He was only just back from the coast, had had no time to organize anything fancy and had simply made a few phone calls. Have to wait and see who showed up. He'd heard that Orson was in town — as usual nobody knew where, but the office had finally tracked him down, an operation on a dragnet scale . . . and Orson had said he'd try and come, though you never could be sure with Orson, he was liable to have changed his mind and flown to North Africa. There were other lovely people who might or might not show up. What you could be sure of was that there'd be some knock-out girls at the party, new young actresses, movie starlets, dancers and models, all eager to meet the lovely, important people who might or might not show up.

George's girls, as they were collectively referred to, had been among the first to arrive, and they flitted around glowing on and off like fireflies on a hot summer's night, challenging the important men to excite them, amuse them, make them laugh, make them cry, make them horny, make them an offer.

Away from the girls, the talk was largely about money. But there also was talk of Nik Ransom's double-performance, and words like 'star-quality' were being used. Nik was weaving in and out of the tight circles, which all opened up eagerly to receive him and then closed around him embracingly, and he was lapping up the flattery while pretending not to. 'Yeah, fuck you too,' he was heard to say to one fulsome lady while grinning not entirely disarmingly. Gloria was talking animatedly with her mother, and there seemed to be tension on both sides, with Carl standing a little way apart from them saying nothing.

The apartment was the sort of place Jack had previously seen only in MGM films: there was a long curved black marble-top bar — of the kind you would expect Fred Astaire to dance on if he were there — and long white leather sofas and white deep pile carpets and curved chrome and black leather divan-chairs.

'We had to gut the entire space and re-configure it,' George was explaining to a guest in one of the tight little circles. What was so great about the apartment, he said, was its size and location and the outside aspects: the deep terraces here on the eighteenth floor, where the building narrowed down to a two-apartment setback, had made it possible to lay out a real lawn with real grass, not the plastic stuff. They'd taken advantage of this to create a mini-golf course. Which was something, wasn't it? Inside, there were round-backed chairs of a light-coloured wood, and ebony cabinets with inlaid zigzags of goldwork. On the walls there were high-relief panels of Nordic girls with backward streaming copper hair. The Jakes's nostalgia for the Twenties was understandable: it had been George Jakes's heyday as a man-about-town theatre agent, and Louise's as an adored young actress.

The knock-out girls who had shown up were flitting around in the vicinity of men who might turn out to be important, and a lot of diffuse erotic promise was being generated, though none of it aimed in Jack's direction. Whisky in hand, he slid back glass doors and stepped out onto the miniature golf course to take a look at the non-plastic grass. Far below, people were moving about like frenetic ants, while up here in the hanging gardens of Babylon he could see, through the glass doors, the king's golden carps swimming about feverishly, and he didn't know if he was destined to be an ant or a golden carp. It was too humid and hot in the Babylonian night and so he went back inside, to cool off in the air-conditioning, and edged up to some cigar-smokers avidly talking money. George Jakes was saying you couldn't disregard TV. It was getting to be big numbers.

There were paintings on the walls that, from the way they were framed and lit, could be valuable originals, only you couldn't be sure what was real and what was studio set stuff in this place. Were George's girls real, or had they been put there by the interior decorator, programmed to glow when anyone important looked at them. To find out if there was anything behind the many, glittering white doors, Jack tried one or two to see where they led. Louise Vanderveld, passing, said: 'If you're looking for the bathroom, it's over there. I know your face. You're with the Tramliners, aren't you?'

'Jack Strawley . . .'

'I know, I know . . . I never forget a face: not one as handsome as yours, anyway.' She was looking around distractedly and seeing George go by at great speed, stopped him to ask: 'Darling, has Orson arrived? I haven't seen him. He promised me faithfully he was coming. George, you know Jack? Don't you? He's with the Tramliners. Gloria has talked about him . . . Jack Dowley?'

'Be with you in a minute, darling,' George promised. 'There's a call I have to take . . . it's the coast. *Dore*. They want Nik — badly.'

'Oh, I'm not surprised, he's very good. And he has a very photogenic face. Ask a lot of money for him, George. And give Dore a big kiss for me.'

He went off striding purposefully to take the call from the coast, kissing one or two people on the way.

'Isn't it exciting,' Mrs Vanderveld said, 'when you're wanted like that? Suddenly the coast is ringing up, and they always want you *badly* when they want you. Everything they want they want badly. It *is* lovely to be so wanted. I remember its happening to me. Oh, that was quite a few years ago now. Then, later on, they just as badly don't want you.That's how it goes. What is it you do exactly, with the Tramliners?'

'Let me bring you a drink, Mrs Vanderveld,' he offered.

'Thank you, dear, but I never ever drink at my own parties, it's a golden rule of mine. Now who don't you know here? Who would you like to meet. There are lots of lovely girls. Oh, George never introduces anyone.' She lowered her voice. 'He can't remember people's names. Getting senile.'

Somebody came up claiming to have seen Orson Welles, and Mrs Vanderveld went off to investigate, saying to Jack: 'The bathroom — along the corridor, left, second door.'

He tried the first door to see what was behind it and found himself in a small room with blue wallpaper where there was a stunningly coloured gouache of a pubescent girl with one hand between her legs and a rapt expression on her face. He was examining this painting closely when one of the glow-glow girls came in and was about to glow-glow out again, since it was evident that there was nobody here of any consequence, when she saw the picture he was looking at with such interest and couldn't resist saying with a sumptuous smile, 'Enjoying yourself?'

'Yeah, what about you?'

'Sure am,' she said determinedly and added, 'I was just looking for somebody,' and started to go out again.

'I'm somebody,' he said smiling hard. She had long blond hair with a rolled fringe, and she wore a long white chiffon evening dress that was like some kind of de luxe nightgown, almost diaphanous — you had the illusion of seeing her luminous naked form through it, and when she moved, the dress went swish-swish around her silvery feet.

'It's a Schiele,' he said, having got the artist's name from the little brass plate.

'Actually it's Bonny Cashin,' she corrected him.

'I was talking about the picture,' he explained.

'And I was talking about the dress.' She laughed deliciously. 'Who did you say?' She looked at the picture more closely.

'Egon Schiele,' he read out.

'Looks as if he painted that with one hand, whoever he is,' she said with a marvellous little giggle.

'He's an important artist,' Jack said, concluding this from the fact that he'd got a brass plate with his name on it.

'Oh yes?' The word 'important' got through to her, and she became interested. Stepping up close, she studied the picture and asked: 'D'you know him personally?'

'No. Not personally. He's probably dead,' he guessed from the fact that important artists given brass name tags usually were.

'You can see that he's an important artist,' she now agreed with him. 'When you look close. From a distance you'd think it's a dirty picture, but from close you can *see* that it's by an important artist, can't you?'

That settled, she turned again towards where the action was. 'Anyway. Was nice talking to you.'

'You haven't really talked to me.'

Reprimanded, she regarded her fingernails sulkily. 'So are you someone I should know?' she asked finally.

'I don't know about *should*,' he said, trying to fathom the secret to these flitting girls' hearts. 'But I'd like to know you.'

'What for?' she asked practically.

'Oh — because you know an important artist when you see

one. What's your name?'
'Maureen.'
'Maureen what?'
'My screen name's Wynner. With a y.'
'And your real name?'
'Oh, we don't talk about that. Wynner's my real name now.'
'What was wrong with your previous name?'
'Mr Jakes thought it didn't have a very starry ring as a name.'
'And that's what you want to be: a stah, a stah?'
'Sure.' She embarked on an account of her career to date. 'I
started out as a photographic model, glamour pictures, and I was
very in demand as a model, only I wanted to get into something
more creative, more fulfilling than just *posing*, so then I started
to branch out. I've had *a few* parts in films, I can't pretend they
were big parts but they were satisfying to me, because I felt I was
doing something creative, and getting known. Then I got to know
Mr Jakes who's been very kind and says I have star-quality. He
says I have warmth and sincerity, and I do have those qualities, I
know. And so what do you do?'
'I sweep floors and move furniture.'
She laughed. 'Really what d'you do?'
'That's what I do. And I direct too.'
'You direct — plays?' He nodded faintly and saw the glow-
glow deep in her eyes quicken. 'What have you directed?'
'I just directed Nik Ransom in a one-character piece called
Suicide Note.'
'Oh, I do admire him. I'd love to meet him. Nik Ransom. I
think he's such a fantastic actor.'
'He can be. If well directed.'
'You really a director?' she asked frowning suspiciously. 'I
think you're kidding me. Are you? I think you're too young to be
a director . . .' She laughed, starting to leave. 'There are supposed
to be lots of important people coming, like Orson Welles, but I
haven't seen any,' she complained.
'Why d'you want to meet important people?'
'You have to. If you want to get somewhere. See, I'm very
ambitious.'
'If you like, I'll introduce you to Orson Welles.'

'You know Orson Welles?' She seemed impressed.

'Oh, sure.'

'Liar!' she said with flirty eyes. 'You're just trying to impress me, aren't you? I don't think you know Orson Welles at all. And I don't think you're a director. You're a big kidder, that's what you are.' She had been out of the action far too long and was turning from him with a little circular hand wave. 'See you.'

'Yeah, sure.'

He followed her back into the living room, and saw her eyes searching around for important people. There being no sign of Orson Welles, she zoomed in on Nik Ransom who was accepting congratulations from a matronly lady with ill-disguised ill grace.

Louise Vanderveld had reappeared. 'It was a false alarm,' she told Jack. 'It wasn't Orson at all.' She watched Maureen Wynner moving in on Nik Ransom. 'How they can smell out success with their little retroussé nose jobs. Look at that one. Maureen something. I can never remember these little girls' names, oh, they're utterly without shame . . . I know your face, young man — remind me who you are. Oh, that's right, you were the one who was looking for the bathroom.'

'I'm with the Tramliners.'

'Yes of course you are. What d'you do there?'

'I direct.'

'Of course you do. Gloria told me about you.'

She extracted a cigarette from a yellow enamel cigarette case and raised it demandingly before her. 'Gloria is not George's daughter, you realized that of course? She's the daughter of my first husband,' she explained, her exigent eyes demanding fire. Jack looked around for a lighter or a match. 'A sadly afflicted man, a real tragic O'Neill figure. I'm talking about my first husband, Gloria's father. A gambler and a drinker and an obsessive womanizer. It's fortunate that Gloria has inherited my character, and not his.' Jack lit Louise Vanderveld's cigarette with the heavy onyx lighter that was on the bar, and Mrs Vanderveld expelled smoke harshly from her lungs. 'George!' she called out to her present husband, who was passing, 'what happened with Dore? Has he made you a good offer?'

'Yes, but Nik's turned it down. Nik says that Hollywood is the graveyard. You know Orson is here, don't you? He's over there.'

'Orson is here? Where?'

She saw him now. The hulking figure had been cornered by tiny entrepreneurial Maureen. He was shovelling handfuls of peanuts into his mouth, drinking white wine from a beer mug and talking with his great jowl working like a concrete mixer, his eyes protruding. Maureen had gone into rapid glow-glow as a low rumble of deep-down laughter shook the mighty frame.

'These little girls are such a menace,' Mrs Vanderveld told Jack in his ear. 'Even with his prodigious appetite, Orson simply can't do it with all of them. I'm going to have to rescue him.' Diving into the rapidly forming circle, she took hold of Orson by the hand and tugged him free of Maureen, who sought to follow, but Mrs Vanderveld was too fast for her.

'Give you a number where you can reach me,' Maureen called after him, starting to write with an eyebrow pencil on a paper napkin while pushing to keep up. 'Can I reach you somewhere?'

'Ah, if only I knew where I can be reached,' he called sighingly over his shoulder, over the heads of people who had come between them, as he was tugged along through the crush. He was too far ahead by now for her to give him the paper napkin with her phone number, and she fell back disconsolate, until, spotting Nik Ransom, the glow-glow spirit welled up in her anew and she made a beeline to head him off, since she was determined to give her phone number to somebody important, or potentially so.

Five minutes later Mrs Vanderveld had lost Orson again, for there were other Maureens at large. She was opening one door after the other looking for him. 'Not in there. Not there . . . Well, he's certainly not in here,' she declared. And then saw Jack, who undoubtedly was in there.

'Tell me again who you are, young man. I keep seeing you.'

'Jack Strawley. I direct.'

'Of course you do,' she cut him short. 'You know, I think what I'm going to do is . . . have a little drinkee. To hell with the rules! Since this is *my* room.'

Back in the living room he looked around for Maureen again. He spotted her talking to Nik Ransom: she was writing something on a paper serviette and giving it to him. It appeared that she had finally found somebody to give her phone number to. Nik was called away by George, who was saying that Dore was on the phone again from the coast, upping his offer.

Jack went up to Maureen:

'Can I phone you some time?'

'I don't know where I'm going to be,' she said vaguely.

'You know where you're going to be tomorrow.'

'Not really,' she said.

'I can try. If you're not there, that's my bad luck. Let me give you a ring.'

'I don't want you to ring me,' she said.

'Why?'

'Because I'm going to be busy.'

'All the time?'

'Pretty much.'

Her eyes softened a little. 'It's not that I don't like you, Jack. I think you're very attractive. But I don't have time.'

'I think you're very beautiful, Maureen.'

'Thank you. But, you see, I'm not always going to be *that* beautiful. Am I? I'm at my peak now. And that doesn't last. Which is why I can't afford to . . . waste time, Jack. Listen, I'm sure I'll see you again sometime, somewhere, like the song says, but now I got to circulate . . . *really.*'

She was going to go away and he gripped her wrist to hold her there.

'Maureen . . .'

Her eyes were evasive. Her lips tightened determinedly.

'Jack, I do like you, really . . . but . . . I know what I want.'

'What?'

'You're hurting me, Jack.'

'What d'you want?'

'I want to be a star.'

'Okay. Doesn't have to stop you having a life meanwhile.'

'That's going to be my life.'

'So?'

'Anyway, it'd be awkward if I went out with you, because Nik's asked me to go out with him, and I said I would. But I'm sure we'll run into each other, Jack. Probably when we're both famous names. I really do like you . . . it's a shame really . . . just bad timing for me.'

10

Stella's, down the road, was practically an extension of the theatre. It was where everybody went for a drink or a quick meal or just to break the tension. It was another place to be, without really going anywhere else. There was a big upstairs room that they hired regularly for the early stages of rehearsals, and consequently Stella's-down-the-road had become almost an extension of Tramline premises. Considering it their place, they were always a bit put out discovering that they didn't have it to themselves, that outsiders came there as well.

'One pastrami, one crab mayonnaise, a Budweiser and a Hudepohl,' Gloria told Paddy who assisted Stella behind the bar.

They took their sandwiches and beers and looked for a place to sit. There was one of these outsiders clutching the earpiece of the wall phone and speaking insistently to the wall while she smoked, played nervously with small coins and turned the pages of her tattered phone book, held together with brown tape.

'So what would you suggest, Frank. . .? Tonight . . . what I do tonight, Frank? I don't have money to go to a fucking hotel.' The phone had gone dead in her hand, and she regarded it with murderous hatred, then realizing that she was being observed moderated her expression, found another number in her book and composed it with enforced calm.

'New York's no place to live,' Gloria said sitting down with her beer and sandwiches. 'It's a daily hassle. Every day is sink or swim. Something wrong with a rich country which does that to people.'

'Yeah, you have to be a swimmer in New York,' Jack lightly agreed with her. 'That's the American system. If you don't swim you drown.'

'You don't mind the system, because you think you can beat it.'

A carefree little girl laugh was being emitted by the girl at the phone, as if life in America was no hassle at all. 'That's right,' she was saying husky-voiced, 'at Ludmilla's. About a month ago? Oh, maybe it was six weeks. Lila? I'm the girl . . . well, how can I . . . lemme . . . okay . . . I was wearing this silk jersey sweater, kindof grey?' She gave a deep-throated machine-gun laugh in response to something said to her.

As he bit into the crab mayonnaise, Jack was angling himself slightly so that, while still facing Gloria, he could, out of the corner of his eye, keep a check on the girl with the rip-roaring laugh, which was both coarse and beguiling. She wore a white linen suit, cut tight to the body, stylishly waisted, with big mother-of-pearl buttons and wide revers, very creased down the back, and there were sweat patches under her arms. Her face was shiny with perspiration, and damp strands of disorderly hair had fallen down over one side of her forehead and face. You would have to admit she was a bit bedraggled, and also that she was almost jumping out of her skin the way she was twisting her foot, and agitating her knee against the wall, the way she gripped and ungripped the earpiece of the phone, moving it from one hand to the other, from one ear to the other — it was glistening from her sweaty palms. But bedraggled and agitated though she was, she was attractive, in a basic sort of way, and she was doing terrific things with her voice, laughing with it provocatively, sending caressing intonations down the line, and putting an upbeat little lilt to the ends of every sentence. A conspiratorial giggle. 'You remember me now? What? You remember *my laugh!* That's *all* you remember? Oh, you're *nasty.* Well, you did give me your phone number, otherwise how could I phone you? Well I know it was a few weeks ago . . . no, couldn't be *months.* Uhuh, I see. I see. Okay . . . okay. Well, good luck to you both. Sorry I bothered you.'

'Amazing performance that girl is giving on the phone,' Jack said to Gloria. 'Isn't it?' She responded with a vaguely sour expression, less impressed by the girl's amazing performance than he was. He bit into his sandwich and took a gulp of beer. The Hudepohl had a malty sweet flavour and a good head. 'He's really such a lovely guy, Carl, I really love him,' Jack said thoughtfully. 'Wish he wasn't having such a tough time. Keeps saying to me that he's failed in America and wants to go back to England. Expect he's told you that too.'

'He doesn't say that to me, because . . . well, for obvious reasons. But I can see with my eyes. You think he stays here because of me?'

'Listen, I don't want him to go either, he's the person I'm closest to.'

'Carl,' Gloria said, 'has no capacity for bending with the wind.'

'All he needs is the right break. It should happen. It should, because he's good, he's really good. He's an important writer.' He couldn't help sneaking a look again towards the girl on the phone, although he could feel Gloria getting irritated. While twisting the telephone wire around her fist, the girl was seeking to smooth talk somebody called Jason from her tattered little black book. Jack gave her a friendly smile of encouragement.

'Now don't go feeling *too* sorry for her,' Gloria advised, following Jack's gaze. 'She certainly is giving some performance. And it isn't for Jason, nitwit! She knows even with her back turned you're interested. Okay now: if you can switch your attention from her for a minute, there's something I want to discuss with you.'

'Go ahead,' he said. The girl on the phone had eased open the middle button of the linen jacket which showed the tight fit of the very creased linen skirt over her behind and belly and hips.

'I'm going to finish my beer,' Gloria said, 'and I'm going to go, Jack, and leave the problem of housing the homeless to you to resolve all by yourself.'

'You wanted to talk to me.'

'I did. But your mind's on other things, and I can't compete with that.'

'I can manage to think of two things at the same time. Maybe even three if you push me hard.'

She hesitated, and then spoke quickly. 'Carl's written a new play. It has things wrong with it, but basically it's good, very good, and I'd like for us to do it. It's a big production. There's a part I want to play myself, there's a good part for Nik. I think it's the play that could establish Carl, and I think it has both artistic and commercial potential. And it might transfer and make us some money, which we need . . . badly need to be able to continue. We can't do *any* more productions that lose money like the last three have done.' As an actress she could be in touch with some wild and weird character strains, but the administrator in her was businesslike, orderly . . . logical. 'It's going to be an expensive production,' Gloria continued. 'I think I can find the money, that's not the problem, the problem is that Carl insists on directing the play himself. He thinks anyone else will ruin it.'

'All sounds good. Don't see your problem, Gloria.'

'Carl thinks this is his last chance — in America . . . maybe anywhere. And you know how Carl can be . . . unbudging . . . I'm afraid he and Nik are liable to. . .'

'So what d'you plan to do?' Jack asked biting into his sandwich, drinking beer and shooting a quick sideways glance at the girl on the phone.

'I really don't think this is the moment . . . let's talk about it some other time.'

'I'm with you, Gloria.'

She gave a slow sigh. 'What I wanted to know is if you'd be willing to act as Carl's assistant on the production. You've shown you can handle Nik. And that's going to be crucial. Besides which, I think you're the only person from whom Carl would accept some discreet steering.'

'Not from you?'

'It's going to be difficult for me. I'm going to be in the play, I'm not going to be sufficiently outside it to have an overall view. But you would be, and he trusts you. And respects your judgement. He doesn't feel threatened by you. I know you've been hoping to get a play to direct yourself.'

'I'll do whatever you say, Gloria.'

The girl on the phone was now embarked on another call and making nervous fidgeting movements, agitating her knees from side to side inside the crumpled skirt. The way he was so fixed on this girl had become too much for Gloria and she suddenly stood up, tautly composed, angry underneath.

'We'll have to talk about this some other time, Jack. I can't talk to half of you, I need to have more of you than that.'

'Before our first read-through this afternoon, I'm going to give you some notes on the characters,' Carl told the assembled cast. 'Since they're my characters you will have to trust me if I say' — he smiled drily, professorially, the way he talked to his play-reading groups — 'that I know them a little better than you do *at this stage,* although I hope that will change and that eventually you will reveal to me things about them that will surprise me.'

The actors said nothing, they were listening attentively except for Nik Ransom who was looking all around the room. Gloria was very still and attentive and concealed. Eyes hooded. Carl was not getting much response from anyone but continued determinedly: 'I just want to say this. A work of art is not born out of some casual desire or even for some goal like money and fame, but out of necessity. That is what I am entrusting to your hands, my necessity.' He proceeded to outline the theme that he found he *had to* develop in his play.

The notes went on and on, and the actors were letting their attention wander. Finally, Gloria intervened to suggest lunch. 'Darling, it's almost one, I think everybody is getting hungry. Can you give us the rest of your notes after lunch?'

'I hadn't realized it was quite so late,' Carl said apologetically and folded away his notes.

After the lunch break, as the actors were filing back in and Carl was unfolding his notes, Nik remarked softly: 'Think we can pass on the notes for now, let's go straight to text, yeah?'

'Okay, let's do as Nik suggests,' Carl said with a touch of resentment in his voice that Nik had taken the initiative from him. 'I'll give the rest of my notes afterwards.'

The opening scene, set in the café of the Hotel Metropole, Vienna, involved Gloria as the journalist Camilla Bauer, Gene

Hobble playing Baron Rothschild, and Nik as a lieutenant in the Austrian Hussars prowling the café looking for women to pick up. The actors remained seated around an oval table, scripts in hand, and read their dialogue, leaving gaps for Carl to read out stage directions. It was a straight read-through with nobody attempting to give a performance. Nik was here and there giving tentative touches of characterization in his reading of lines, whereas Gloria's reading of Camilla was flat and without nuances. When it came to the seduction scene at the Opera, she read her lines in a determinedly clipped and mechanical fashion, whereas Nik was falling quite effortlessly into the part of the arrogantly determined seducer. Seeing that he was making an effort and she was not, Gloria said: 'I . . . I'm sorry, Nik. I'm not quite as far as you are in my reading of the part . . . you'll have to give me a little more time to get into it.'

The actors were arriving one or two at a time for the second read-through and taking their places in a semi-circle of chairs. They showed signs of restiveness while Carl was giving them five minutes of the dreaded notes, which Nik interrupted before the end, saying:
  'Carl, we've got the hang.'
  Nik's second read-through was very adjusted. A character was emerging. Rothschild also was good, on a more superficial level. Oskar, the dealer in lives, was doing lots of things that were wrong, but one or two things that were right, and it looked as though he could be steered. The Eichmann player was too sinister and hadn't seen the black comedy that existed in the part. But Gloria was the worst: she was floundering and especially lost in the sexual scenes which she read in an artificial actressy voice. Realizing how bad her reading was, she stopped herself and read the lines again, and then again, but could not succeed in getting them to ring true. It was almost as if she had a need to deride the sexual content of these scenes. Tensely lighting a cigarette, she threw out: 'Carl, maybe there's something wrong with these lines, I don't feel them, I don't feel she would say those things, in that way . . . Anyway *I* can't say them, it seems.'

'Darling,' Carl told her, smiling, 'please allow me to be the author, and you concentrate on the performance . . .'

In the next few days the rehearsals intensified with more and more emotion being put into lines, except for those lines which the actors had problems saying. Whenever an actor wanted to change a line or leave it out, Carl said: 'Each line has a purpose even if you don't see what it is . . . if you leave out lines you pull apart the play . . . the whole internal structure collapses.'

The more the actors complained and asked for changes, the more Carl dug in his heels, and by the middle of the second week of rehearsals the atmosphere between director and cast had become acutely strained. He was trying to explain to them: ' I want only to create a structure within which the truth of the characters can emerge, and the play can come to life.'

'Carl,' Nik said standing up, 'the truth of this character is he needs a coffee-break and not to drink coffee. Fifteen minutes?'

When the actors came back, not fifteen minutes but half an hour later, their faces were sombre, and they were avoiding looking Carl in the eye. Not even Gloria looked at him. Nik was starting to speak for all of them when Carl, very grey in the face and tense, interrupted him:

'I've been thinking about our various problems,' he said, 'and I've come to the conclusion that maybe you need a rest from me, and I need a rest from you, so what I'm going to do is go away for three days and let you get on with it, and then when I come back I hope both sides will have been refreshed by the break. While I'm away Jack will take the rehearsals . . .'

There was an exchange of looks between the actors; a decisive nod from Gloria swung the others behind her.

'Good idea,' said Nik.

Next morning, Jack was in the rehearsal room ahead of everyone else. He was drinking coffee from a large mug and marking the script on his lap with differently coloured pencils. In the margins and on the blank backs of the pages he had made sketches. When the actors had all arrived, Nik started to speak:

'First thing what we got to do,' he began, 'is we got to get to grips with what this fucking play is about, and in my view . . .'

Jack stopped him. 'We'll find out what the play's about by doing it, okay? Okay, everybody. From the top. "OSKAR: Allow me to introduce myself . . ." We're going to try a couple of changes in the opening scene. Oskar, instead of addressing the audience throughout the whole of your long opening monologue, let's see how it plays if you say the first few lines to the audience, and then start your walk through the café, stopping at different tables, and let's try breaking up the rest of the monologue.' He gave the other actors instructions for what they were to do. 'Old Pianist plays *Tales of the Vienna Woods*. With lots of smiles and bows and greetings all around. Eichmann is prowling about, clumsy, bumping into things, bumping into Oskar, muttering under his breath. Everybody is talking at once. High café buzz. Conversations overlapping . . . even if we lose bits of dialogue. We'll reduce the buzz for what's got to be heard.'

Some of the actors immediately started asking questions, wanting to work out who said what to whom and when, and Jack stopped them in their tracks by jabbing a finger at Old Pianist, and commanding: 'Play!', and Dolbitzsch silenced all discussion with the opening bars of *Tales of the Vienna Woods*. After a few beats, Jack indicated for the music to diminish and made a conductor's pointing gesture to Oskar to start his speech to the audience. While he was speaking, Jack pointed his finger successively at others in the café, giving each of them their cue for when they were to speak or do some stage business, and then he grabbed Oskar by the arm and took him table-hopping, feeding him the prompt lines in his ear. In this way he cut up the long opening monologue and varied its tone. Oskar automatically adapted his manner, all the way from flattering to offhand, according to the person he was addressing. While moving Oskar around the stage, Jack cued Rothschild to start making his move towards Camilla, and to begin his flirtatious conversation with her.

The effect of these changes was chaos. Actors got in each other's way. Crucial dialogue was drowned out, Carl's witty and sonorous monologue was broken up into scrappy bits of disconnected, overlapping dialogue. It was like being in a noisy café and not being able to hear yourself speak.

Gloria asked: 'Jack, have you got Carl's approval for these changes?'

'We talked for five hours last night,' Jack said. 'And a lot of new ideas came up.'

Jack spent the rest of the morning eliminating the worst of the snarl-ups and diminishing the sound level when lines were being spoken that had to be clearly heard. By four in the afternoon, the opening scene was in good enough shape for him to say: 'We can leave it there for now. I'd like to spend the rest of today working with Wirthof and Camilla. I just need Nik and Gloria. The rest can go home and work on their lines.'

Gloria was smoking more than ever, on her third pack of the day, puffing deeply at the little black holder as if it was some kind of essential source of sustenance, and then blowing out with eyes narrowed against the stinging smoke, upper lip curled in something like disgust. The prospect of having to finally get down to 'the sex scene', which so far she had been shirking, reading the stage directions instead of performing the actions, seemed to arouse intense anxiety in her. It showed in her pallor and her stillness and her unabated chain-smoking. She was brought black coffee which she sipped between puffs.

To relax her, Jack said easily: 'We can play around with it, whatever you like . . . nobody here except us . . . so let's do it and see how it plays.'

Gloria put another cigarette in her crystal holder and stayed poised and silent and wary, not really responding to the invitation to relax. Nik was walking about, mumbling to himself, eyes closed, head raised up, getting into the scene, getting sexed up. Gloria was sitting staring blankly ahead like someone on a railway platform waiting for a train to arrive. Unlike Nik, she gave no visible signs of preparing herself for the scene. Jack gave them both another couple of minutes and then said briskly:

'Okay, from page 32. Wirthof comes into the box looking for Oskar."I thought Oskar would be here . . ." '

Nik's normal, rather slouching, carriage had instantly changed to the upright, imperious, hand-on-hip posture of an officer of the Hussars. He stood poised over Camilla, hand to chest as if holding his brocaded pelisse in place over one shoulder, one leg insolently bent at the knee, the whole arrogant force of his body concentrated in his taut lower parts. He spoke the line, 'I thought Oskar would be here,' as a transparent excuse that he had no need to make. His demeanour and posture expressed a man who is completely sure of himself with women and sure of himself in the world. They went through the scene to the point where the stage directions said: 'Camilla is wearing sixteen-button white gloves, which she now starts nervously to unbutton. She shivers.' Since Gloria was not wearing gloves, she simply made a token gesture of unbuttoning them. Jack told her:

'Do more with the gloves, Gloria. When you take off the glove, it's as if you're undressing in front of him. That's what the shiver is about.'

Gloria started the unbuttoning again, but it wasn't any better.

'It's not dark enough. You're not playing it dark enough. This scene is the malignant worm in the bud. It's the rape of Austria that you're leading up to.'

'I don't think I'm right for this part,' she said flatly.

'Forget the gloves for now, take it through to the end.'

He could see from her increased pallor and stillness that a paralyzing sort of stage fright was aroused in her at the prospect of having to play this scene. She was on the verge of finding some pretext for refusing to do it.

'*Where* do we do it?' she asked bleakly.

'For the production there'll be a chaise longue. But for now it'll have to be the floor, Gloria.' She got up off the chair and sat on the floor, straight backed, with her knees tightly together, and Nik sprawled down alongside her.

Gloria was shaking her head. 'How am I supposed to play this?' she asked, solemnly tense.

'Like this,' Nik said, falling back, kicking his legs in the air and threshing about while he let out girlish gasps and moans.

'The solution,' she said trying to get herself in a lighter mood, 'is that Nik plays Camilla.'

Jack had seen the flash of panic in her eyes. But there was nothing to be done about that. What the hell: she's an actress, she can read, she chose to play this part, written by the man she loves — she was in a position to get him to change the scene had she insisted he do that, either by persuading him on a personal basis or by saying the play wouldn't be put on unless the changes were made. It's her production, she cast herself in it and Nik to play opposite her, she can't start back tracking now and expect support. He gave them a signal to start. She was scowling and scared.

Nik played the scene without making any concessions to Gloria's nervousness. He played the scene rough, as it was written. Perhaps a little too rough, perhaps a little over the top. But that could be toned down later. Basically it was right. A brutish seduction in a lush setting. The script called for Camilla to struggle half-heartedly against the invader: it was meant to be a metaphor for Austria's submission to Hitler. But Gloria was unable to play it in this way: she fought Nik off like a virgin fighting for her honour, not like a sophisticated worldly sexual woman offering token resistance to a man she despises but is attracted by. She seemed to be incapable of reconciling contempt and attraction.

'You're playing her too innocent,' Jack told her, 'and that's wrong. She's drawn to him sexually, against her will and her good sense and her moral standards.'

'Yes, I know that,' she said humbly. She wasn't disputing what the scene was supposed to be about, but in her playing of it what she conveyed was disdain and distance.

They tried it half a dozen times, but at the point when she was supposed to be overcome by passion she invariably froze-up, retreating into a kind of primness. As Jack was making her do the scene again and again, and being less and less circumspect in his direction, she was becoming almost hysterical. He was pushing her hard and she looked close to tears and was constantly fussing with her hair in a nervous, finicky way.

'Yeah, sorry about mussing your hair, Gloria,' Nik said. He seemed to be seething inside.

'Something bothering you, Nik?' Gloria asked him.

'Yeah.'

'What is it, Nik?' Jack asked. 'Spill it.'

He was keeping silent. 'Yes. Say what you have to say, Nik,' Gloria urged him.

Nik walked up and down with nodding head, hitching up his pants, clenching and unclenching his hands, venting energy levels that were getting too high in him.

'You know what I think, Gloria . . . you clearly have some personal problem about playing this kind of scene, and I . . . I think that as the person running this collective theatre, for the good of the production, you ought to replace yourself . . . get another actress who won't be so nervous about getting her hair mussed.'

Jack stopped him there. 'Nik, you're being unfair and offensive to Gloria. Gloria can play the part, she just has got to get into it, and you're not being very helpful there. She is not yet where you are in this scene: you have to give her time . . . to develop it in her own way. Not try to bludgeon her into it. She's underplaying it, but you're overplaying. But we'll work it out, and she'll do it beautifully. With the great style that she has, and that the part needs.'

By the time he'd finished speaking, Gloria was on her feet and in full control of herself, and once more asserting her authority as the boss of the enterprise. Calmly she said:

'I'll . . . think seriously about what you said, Nik. And if I decide that I am wrong for the part, I promise I will fire myself, okay, and get another actress. I'll let you know what I decide.'

11

After Nik had left, Gloria remained seated in her chair, staring ahead, rigid except for a very faint trembling that ran through her from the neck down.

'A drink?'

'Nik's right,' she said, 'I should replace myself. I'm not cut out to be an actress. I should quit. I have too many.'

'Nik's a selfish actor, a selfish human being. When something doesn't suit him, he lashes out. At anybody in his way.'

'He's a good actor.'

'When well directed. He overdid it today. You were nervous about the scene, and he made no effort to help you. The opposite.'

He could see that there were sobs forming at the level of her diaphragm and pushing their way up through her chest, and that she was trying hard to hold them back. The effort was making her shiver.

'Don't know why I should feel like this,' she said angry with herself. 'It's not very professional of me.'

'Nik's an invader. It's all "me, me". Doesn't matter what anyone else feels.' He shrugged. 'But you're right: he's got all the basics of a good actor. Maybe a great one.'

'That drink,' she said.

The downstairs bar was very packed and very noisy. Gloria ordered a vodka Bloody Mary for herself. 'I take certain things too seriously,' she went on picking at the wound. 'I should be able to be lighter. I am quite a light person in some respects. It's a part, I should be able to play it without feeling personally involved. Bet Lila . . .'

'Some women don't mind a bit of rough handling. Some even like it.'

'The sort you know? You do hang out with some weirdos. That hood Eddie Max and his floozies. What's the name of the little blonde?'

'I call her Slither Slither.'

She laughed. 'Can't imagine why.'

'Because she *slithers*. She's a beautiful slitherer. Her thighs slither against each other and hum a tune.'

'And that appeals to you?'

'Sometimes.'

'And other times?'

'Other times my ideal of womanhood is . . . someone like Gloria Vanderveld.'

'I'm flattered to be anybody's ideal, even a kidding one.'

'I wasn't kidding.'

He had a sense of the strangeness of the enterprise they were engaged in and he could see Gloria also was questioning the value of putting life on a stage to be observed rather than lived. He saw Lila come in and look around for him. She was wearing a short black sheath dress with a wide big-buckle red leather belt that emphasized the roundness of her hips and buttocks.

'Looks like you're going out,' Gloria said with a smile that couldn't help being superior. 'I have to admit, she is a gorgeous creature. Slither-slither type or the ideal woman?'

'Just for a bite to eat. Lila's not too great at cooking.'

'You didn't answer the question.'

'She's ideal in some respects, Gloria. Not in all.'

Lila had now reached them, and after a coolish exchange of hellos between her and Gloria, asked with a slight frown: 'Jack, are you going to be long?'

'The're one or two things still.'

'Another half hour? Or what?'

'Something like that. Why don't you get us some Chinese food . . .'

She looked disappointed and annoyed. 'You said we were eating out. I got dressed.'

'Sweetie, I'm rehearsing a play. You can't do that to a strict timetable. Things emerge and have to be followed through.' He gave her a five-dollar bill and a kiss and a pat on the behind. 'Get the Chinese and some wine,' he said. 'And don't wait for me if you're hungry.'

'How long d'you think you'll be?'

'I can't say, Lila. Let's just say I'll be back when I'm back.'

'When's that going to be, roughly?' she insisted.

'Don't fret, you'll have him very soon,' Gloria promised her. 'We're almost through.'

'Don't be too long,' she said pleadingly to him. 'I'm lonely when you're not with me.'

'I'll be as quick as I can,' he promised her. When she had gone, he told Gloria: 'Sorry about the pressure. Lila gets more demanding every day. The moment you give 'em a pillow on which to lay their little head, they've got a piece of territory staked out and start putting up fences.'

'That's a very big generalization to draw from one small girl. I imagine you're pretty demanding yourself, Jack. You certainly are as a director . . . you demand more than I am able to give, and that makes me feel . . . very inadequate.'

He told her that was nonsense. She was so hungry for reassurance, it would have been needlessly cruel not to provide it. It was now too late to find another actress for the part, with the opening in just over three weeks. To get an established Broadway name was not feasible financially, and in any case would be against the spirit of collective theatre, whose whole raison d'etre was to develop 'unrecognized' talent. However inadequate Gloria might be, in some ways, for the role of Camilla, she was the best choice they had. And his job, in Carl's absence, was to build up her fragile, bruised ego and her sense of possessing the womanly allure for Camilla.

'Well, we're not going to solve that in the next ten minutes,' Gloria said, 'and Lila'll be fretting. I better go home and learn lines.'

'You'll be all right?'

'Yes, I should think. Strasberg teaches us: Use it! Use the hurt. Use the wound.'

'That's it.'

'I'll try.'

Her voice had a break in it that he found troubling; he couldn't be sure if she was okay, or too proud to admit that she wasn't.

'Let me put you in a taxi,' he offered, and when they had found one he still felt uncertain about her condition and said he'd feel better if he saw her home.

The taxi went up through the Village and then across Broadway, and she was silent most of the time, window open her side, letting some of the free-floating energy of these lively streets flow over her. The building in which she lived was a five-storey walk-up that had seen better days, a lot better days. It was now in multiple occupation but still with the tattered dignity of former times clinging to its crumbling facade, where a battered sign plainly announced: 'Rooms'. The wind had piled up the dirt and litter against the sagging stone steps where neigbourhood drunks sat holding bottles in brown paper bags. It could be a pretty rough street, he knew from previous visits, and he saw that the entrance door of her building hadn't been closed properly by the last person to leave and so any street lout could go in and take up overnight residence on the dark stairs. He thought it best to deposit her safely in her own apartment, and once there she said to come in, she was going to phone Carl, and he was sure to want to know how the rehearsals had gone today, and she didn't trust herself to give an unbiased account. Carl had gone to Sag Harbor to rest, but wasn't in his room, and she left a message for him to call her back.

'Want to wait for Carl's call? Or you want to get back?'

'I'll wait a bit.'

Though he had often been to this apartment, when he was hanging around them all the time, he had never been there when Carl wasn't there too, and now there was a totally different feel to the place. It was her place, he could see that clearly now. It was marked by her style: one big studio room, with rusty old steel tie bars holding massive roof timbers in place, room divider bookcases . . . kelim scatter rugs . . .

He said: 'This apartment's like you. Elegant-simple.'

'You mocking me?'

'Not at all.'

He was looking around the whole time, as if he'd never been there before. The walls were of red cedar wood tongue and groove boards which in parts served as a bulletin board on which press clippings and photos and other matters of current interest had been pinned up, creating a proliferating collage.There were piles of books and magazines and newspapers and files all over the floor.

'I wouldn't say elegant,' Gloria corrected him. 'I'd say messy. Carl just left everything as it was and went off, mad at us all, I guess, and I haven't had time to clean up after him. Carl's not a very tidy person, he just drops the thing he has finished with on the floor and picks up the next thing . . . that's people who live inside their heads for you!' An indication of some irritation with the beloved.

She slumped down in a big old sofa and lit a cigarette, not

bothering now with the crystal-filter lung protection system. 'Do me a Bloody Mary, Jack dear.'

The drinks were on a long marble butcher's slab supported by furnace-blasted steel brackets. Carl's work space consisted of a trestle table with a Remington portable typewriter, and scattered around variously coloured notebooks bent back on their spines, the pages densely covered with Carl's sprawling handwriting. Carl's desk was like an archeological dig with the different layers representing different periods of his recent activities. At the top of the pile were drafts of his latest notes to the cast. The trestle table was nowhere near big enough to hold everything that was currently engaging Carl's mind, and the overflow had spread in all directions.

'Carl doesn't want to stay, you know. Has he told you? He wants to get out of America, thinks it's going fascist . . . also, I expect he must be pretty fed up about not being able to make a living in the land of opportunity.'

'You going to go to England with him, if he leaves?'

'How can I? I can't abandon the Tramline now. I can't throw that up, we've only just got started. There's also the long-term personal aspect: Carl and I. How that will work out in the end. Carl's doesn't believe in binding relationships. He says it's part of the property system. People should be free. Which I can see *in theory* is true.'

'But?' He walked to the window and looked out, bending up the slats of the venetians. He watched bums taking up residence for the night in doorways that were not barred to them by grilles and padlocked gates.

'I hate being alone in this place, even for a couple of nights,' Gloria said. 'I get physically sick. Have to pack pillows around myself, not to feel that I'm in an empty bed. Don't know who I am when I'm alone. That's when I don't exist. God, why am I going on like this when all you want is to get back to your Chinese and your beautiful Lila. Sorry, sorry. It's overflow. With all those winos and weirdos in the street, you can't even go out if you need a breath of air. You're stuck here. Think I'll check into a hotel for the night.'

He brought over the chrome jug in which he'd made the

Bloody Mary and poured a good-sized measure for her through the strainer. The telephone rang and it was Carl. She carried the phone over to the part of the open-plan where the bed was and lay back against the cushions, holding the speaker stand close to her lips and talking softly into it. He couldn't tell whether it was work talk or private talk — but whichever, she seemed settled in for a long conversation. He watched her on the phone: her swept-back hairstyle, her wide open porcelain-fine face showed him generations of glimmering Vanderveld profiles. Pure and simple. When she and Carl were finished talking she got up from the bed and, dragging the long telephone lead after her, carried the phone to the sofa. 'I'm going to put Jack on,' she told Carl. 'He'll tell you how the rehearsal went today.' She gestured to him to come over and he sat down beside her and took the phone stand and earpiece out of her hands.

Carl sounded calmer today and rested. 'I had a moment of sheer paralysis back there,' he said. 'Must have been over-tiredness, but I've bounced back now, I'm full of ideas. I've been making extensive notes for the cast which I'm sending back to Sheila to type up. Just keep them working, Jack. Don't let them argue. How was it today?'

Jack reported on the day's work, without referring to changes he had made. He simply said that they'd done the café scene in depth and that it looked good, and that he'd gone through the seduction scene with Nik and Gloria, and though it was still pretty rough, he thought the ice had been broken now, and that the way was open to getting it right. They talked about Carl coming back the day after tomorrow, towards the evening, and that he would personally take over rehearsals the following morning, starting with a complete run-through. 'Just keep them in line,' was Carl's instruction. 'Don't let them get the bit between their teeth. You know what actors are like!'

'Yeah, I know what actors are like,' he said, shooting a sideways glance at Gloria. 'Carl sounded good,' he told her when he'd put down the phone. 'What he say to you?'

From the chrome shaker, Gloria added substantially to her Bloody Mary, the level of which had got too low.

'You make good Marys. Peppery. Plenty of vodka, not too

much tomato. Just right.' Her face seemed more flushed than before. 'Carl? Oh, he said . . . that actors were like children, they had to be told what to do and mustn't be allowed to argue. The author was the creator; the actor, the interpreter. So he's got to remember his place. No arguing with his creator. The actor knows that his role is an ephemeral and secondary one and so he feels inferior to the author, and that causes battles of egos . . . that was his in-depth analysis of what happened.'

'Did that make you feel good,' he said, 'being an ephemeral interpreter?'

'Yeah, great!'

'How you feeling now?'

'Ephemeral. You want to go, huh? Oh, I'm okay.'

'Really? Or you covering up for yourself?'

'I'm just tense about the role,' she admitted, 'my body's very tense. Full of protest. I've got no business being an actress. For I rebel against my creator! Don't want to speak his lines, play his scenes the way he's written them. There's a prudishness in me, I know. I know all of that.' She laughed hoarsely at herself. 'Scared of my sexual feelings, Carl says.'

He assessed her flushed, troubled state and picked his words with care.

'Gloria, you have so much style, I don't know anyone who has such style . . . but I think you need help with this part, and I don't know if Carl can give you that, the phase you two are in.'

'What phase is that?'

'I'd say, a questioning phase . . . is that right?'

'Questioning is dead right. Questioning but not answering. God! It's just the beginning of rehearsals, and already I'm exhausted. How am I going to get through it?'

'Like you always have done,' he said. He put a consoling arm around her. 'Ease into it, you got to steer into the skid . . . Nik was a big strain today. He's got to be held back, so you can grow into it at your own speed. I'd know how to help you do that, now — if I was directing you.'

'But you're not,' she said sharply. 'Carl'll be back in a couple of days, and then it'll be back to the way it was. He won't like what you've done with the café scene, though I think it's brilliant. But he'll think all that business on stage distracts from the words.'

'Carl's wordy, can't help writing parables. He wants his message to get across. What he doesn't realize is . . . take out the message, it gets across better. Carl's gonna fuck it up. For himself. And everybody else.'

'That's the knot we've got ourselves in.'

'Cut it.'

'I can't. I don't have the courage.'

'So let me cut it.'

'Carl's your closest friend.'

'It'd be for him too, even if he doesn't think so.'

'Oh God! I don't know any more. I just know that all this agonizing tires me out, when I need all my energy.' He moved closer to her and nudged her head onto his shoulder to let her rest. She accepted the prop gratefully, breathed in deep, and seemed to grow less tense: her breathing became so steady he thought she'd gone to sleep. He let three or four minutes go by without budging. Let her get un-tensed. Then she stirred, and he said:

'I better go now. Let me drop you at a hotel . . . why don't you stay at a hotel a couple of nights, till Carl gets back?' Without moving her head from his shoulder she asked in a voice into which there had entered a note of quiet wilfulness: 'Jack, would it be a terrible imposition for you . . . not to leave just yet. I'll be all right in a minute or two, I just need to . . . get myself together. Is Lila going to get very het up?'

'I can phone her and say I have to stay with you, that you're not feeling too great . . . and . . .'

'Will she believe that?'

'If she doesn't, that's too bad!'

'How bad is too bad?'

'I'll survive it.'

She reflected for a moment. 'The girl at the switchboard at Carl's hotel, she said *they'd* gone out to dinner. You think he's gone there with someone?'

'Oh -- could mean anything or nothing.'

'Yes,' she agreed, then added without looking at him: 'Same goes for you staying, if you stayed . . . could mean anything or nothing.' Her head was still on his shoulder, and he felt the faint trembling of her body being passed on to him.

'What d'you want it to mean, Gloria?'

'Not being anybody's property cuts both ways, wouldn't you say?'

'You're not too happy, are you? With the way things are.'

'Oh, I'd like to be happy. I really would. But I'm not very good at it. You saw,' — she gave a self-mocking laugh, and was lightened by it — 'no good at sex scenes.' She lifted her head from his shoulder and looked him full in the eyes. Hers were brimful and abnormally bright, with a touch of panic in them. His were without qualms. 'You think I'll get better at them?' she said. 'Or am I a lost cause?'

'No, you're not a lost cause.'

'I love Carl,' she said, 'but . . . who knows what may happen. Carl may go back to England.'

'Can't go by what *may* happen,' he said.

'What can you go by?'

'What you want to happen.'

'Don't know that either.'

'I know.'

'Yes, you know what you want.'

'I want to direct Carl's play,' he said matter-of-factly, 'because I know I can do it better than he can. That's nothing against Carl. He's a writer, not a director, and writers are the worst people to direct their own work.'

'Well that's straight out.'

'There's something else I can do better than Carl — again, nothing against him.'

'What's that?' She couldn't bring herself to look at him.

'Make you happy.'

'How's that nothing against him?'

'Things change. People change. I don't want to lose Carl's friendship. Trouble is, there are other things I want enough that I'll risk it.'

'You want it every way.'

He put his hand on hers. 'It's what you want as well. Be honest, Gloria.'

'You're someone who takes what he wants.'

'Shouldn't I?' he asked her innocently, and she didn't answer or take her hand away from his.

There were stages that you went through, and once one stage had passed you had to go on to the next one, otherwise you got stuck where you were, and he was not going to get stuck. There was always some destruction involved in moving on. She was very tortured about it, but that made the sensations all much stronger. Everything had to be overcome in her first, and there was a bright shiny sharp taste to that. She wanted to know joy, without the hangups, and he could give her that. He knew she was the person he had to have in his life, not only because he was in love with her, and had been for the past year — which for him was a long wait — but also because this was what was due to him now.

12

Carl's return from Sag Harbor coincided with the move from the rehearsal room to the theatre itself. The run-through was going to take place on stage. Though the set was by no means finished there were one or two props in position now. One of these was the chaise longue on which the seduction in the opera box was to take place. Stage costumes were not ready, but some of the actors had attempted to dress for their parts out of their own wardrobe: Rothschild was in a dark suit with waistcoat, bow tie, a flower in his buttonhole; Oskar was wearing a long overcoat with fur collar over his corduroy slacks and carrying a cane and a homburg; Gloria had provided herself with a Chinese-style jacket for the café scenes, and for the Opera seduction scene a strapless evening dress with a voluminous skirt made of white tulle and green satin decorated with white violets. Eichmann was in black leather motor-bike outfit, and the Old Pianist in his worn velvet jacket. Only Nik, evidently requiring no external aids to characterization, hadn't made any attempt to dress for his role and was still wearing a pair of old slacks, mud-spattered boots and a lumber jacket.

Carl, who had not told the cast when he'd be back exactly, slipped into the theatre unnoticed, and quietly took a seat at the back of the auditorium. The actors were gathering on stage. Only when they were ready for the run-through, and Jack had activated the provisional light grid, did Carl make his presence known, coming slowly forward, almost like an outsider wandering in where he had no business. He was not immediately seen by those on stage and had to clap his hands to let them know he was there.

'I expect you've benefited from my absence,' he said to them, 'to make huge steps forward, while I have taken advantage of the break to have some fresh thoughts about the production and draw up notes for each one.' There were some mock (and not so mock) groans at the mention of notes. 'I won't give them to you now,' he said, which aroused a burst of hoorahs. 'I'm going to watch the run-through and update my notes in the light of what I see.'

Then he sat down in the second row, four seats in, and gave a gesture for the performance to start. He had not asked any members of the production team to sit with him, and so sat alone. The run-through moved uninterruptedly — since he did not see fit to interrupt at any point — towards the seduction scene in the Vienna Opera house at the end of Act I. Jack had gone over the scene several times with Nik and Gloria since the first rough and violent attempt at it, and it had been improving steadily.

At the end of the run-through Carl remained seated in the dark, saying nothing. Seconds and minutes went by without him giving any reaction — he seemed to be quietly making notes. The actors were beginning to talk animatedly among themselves. Finally, there came that odd, curiously imperious handclap that was meant as a call for silence. Then he got up slowly and spoke to them in a low voice:

'I see that there have been changes. Textual cuts, rearrangements of speeches, and in some cases the complete abandonment of stage directions. Where the play has not been changed, perform-ances have grown.' He looked down at his notes. 'The opening café scene has become very bitty, and the rhythm of Oskar's monologue has been lost by all the needless movement, as if this were a musical comedy. I imagine that Jack was trying to get some movement into a static scene. But the scene in the café should be static, *frozen* — until Oskar brings the characters to life with a sweep of his hand. Here and elsewhere we shall simply have to go back to the way it was done before. There are other things that have gone wrong in individual performances. We'll take a break and I will prepare new notes, and then we will seek to get the production back on track . . .'

Nik had come forward, holding up a hand to cut in, and Carl gave way to him.

'Yes, Nik?'

'Carl,' he said shaking his head up down for some seconds, 'we got a problem here.'

'Well, I'm here to help you solve problems.'

'Our problem is, Carl, we don't think you're the best person to judge how this play should be directed — fact is, we don't want you to direct it. We think that Jack did a good job in your absence and we want him to continue. This was voted unanimously by the entire collective.'

Carl stood for a while silently absorbing the full import of what Nik had said. He seemed grimly calm, whatever he was feeling reined back.

'I don't want to criticize what Jack has done in my absence. A different director will naturally approach the text in a different way.' He paused, holding himself tightly in check. 'But this play originated in my head, out of my experience, and only I can know.'

'Carl,' Nik said, roughly cutting him short, 'we decided that either we get another director or we don't do the play.'

Carl looked straight at Gloria. 'You agreed to this?'

'Carl, this production needs an outside mind.'

Carl's look was blankly uncomprehending. Speaking directly to Gloria, making it a personal matter between him and her, he said: 'Gloria, it amazes me, darling, and throws me completely, completely, that you — that *you* — can talk this way.'

She replied grimly, determinedly, her mouth tight as a wire: 'I have to address myself to our situation here. Another failure would likely finish off this theatre and all our plans and hopes, and I can't let that' — her voice had become implacably firm — 'I can't, I *won't* let that happen.'

He responded to her unbudging stance by becoming equally unbudging. 'It is my play, Gloria,' he said very quietly, 'and I do think that I am entitled to have it produced the way I wrote it, so if you and the rest of the cast refuse to perform the play I wrote, I have no alternative but to . . . withdraw it.'

He had said his last word and turned around and began walking away down the side aisle towards the exit, withdrawing himself. On the stage the actors were talking among themselves in low voices. Finally, everybody became silent, just as Carl was about to go out the door. An exchange of looks indicated that it was agreed Gloria should speak for them all. She had to pitch her voice more strongly than when she had spoken to Carl before, since he was almost at the exit now and had his back to her.

'I'm sorry but you can't do that, Carl. People other than you now have an interest and an investment in this play. You can't withdraw it, I'm sorry. The management has a legal option on producing it, which it is able to exercise, and it also has the legal right to change the director if the one engaged is thought not right for the production. We, the collective, are the management, so we have those rights, and are exercizing them.'

Having had to say the public part of the speech to Carl's back, since he had not turned around, she now started to run after him, as he was leaving through the door, calling to him in a much softer and more private voice: 'Please, Carl . . . please! Wait for me. Darling, we have to talk.'

Next day Carl did not appear at the theatre. When Gloria arrived she said he had not come home last night, had not telephoned or left any message for her. She had phoned the hotel in Sag Harbor where he sometimes stayed; they'd said he was not there. She had tried one or two other places — the cafés and diners to which he sometimes went to work, but he had not been seen in any of them.

'When you spoke to him, after . . . how was he?' Jack asked her.

'Angry, of course. But it was that very controlled anger of his when he doesn't so much as raise his voice. Just the tone gets more and more ironical. He didn't really say much at all. I thought he was going to . . . have a few drinks, that he'd probably come back pretty late, but that he'd be back. But then when he didn't come back, and there was no word from him. Jack, we've done a terrible thing to him. I don't know if we had the right. I don't even know if we have the legal right. It's a standard of all play production contracts that the management is not allowed to change the author's work without his consent.'

'He left no indication where he might have gone?'

She shook her head. 'I knew he wouldn't take it well, you couldn't expect him to, but I was counting on him making the best of it, in the end. I said you would listen to all his points and not go against anything of fundamental importance to him. But he simply wouldn't discuss it. He's washing his hands of us — in disgust. I'm so worried, Jack.'

'He's punishing us. You didn't say anything to him to make him suspect?'

'No. No.'

'Carl has a sixth sense for bad news. I have a feeling he knows.'

'How could he?'

'I think he knew before it happened.'

'How?'

'He lies awake nights imagining these things. Sees the whole story unfold.'

'And — what? Goes to Sag Harbor thinking those sorts of thoughts? Deliberately leaves us to. . . Oh, I can't believe that.'

'Something he used to say: imagination begets the event. Oh, Carl can be pretty strange sometimes, you know.'

'That's what scares me.'

'Yeah, me too. But there's not one damn thing we can do,

except get the play on as best we can now.'

Although there were things that he would have done differently had he directed the play from the beginning, he knew what could and could not be done in the time left before the opening night. The actors would have to perform the pictures in his mind. These pictures were very detailed, and he was not sure how he had come to construct them: it seemed as if he had 'remembered' them . . . or dreamt them, at any rate he had not laboured over constructing them, they had simply come to him with so much conviction that he was sure they were right. His task was conveying them to others.

The day before the opening, there was still no sign of Carl. He'd been missing now for nearly three weeks and all the grimmest scenarios had been entertained. The police had been informed. Checks of hospitals and morgues made. They'd even telephoned his old mother in England to ascertain, in a roundabout way, without letting her know their inquietude, if she'd heard from him. She hadn't. Nik's theory was that Carl had simply washed his hands of them — walked away: that was his style. He wouldn't want to hang around and watch his play being wrecked. He was angry and bitter and wounded, and phoning up to put their minds at rest was the last item on his agenda. Maybe he was taking legal advice and would arrive, at the last minute, with a court order stopping the opening. Or he was just mulling everything over, and Carl took a long time to mull things over.

With the play's opening on top of them, all such speculations had to be put aside. Jack had been working twelve, fourteen hours a day, kept going by jugs of coffee and bennies and scotch. From the day he had taken over, the entire cast had become aware of an unusual force coming from their director, and it had animated their performances. In places he had made them break up sentences into beats and given separate emotions and thoughts to each beat. He was talking cinema to them. He told them: 'Forget about set speeches, exits and entrances . . . no set-piece scenes. Think of it as constant movement.' And directing the actors wasn't the only thing he was doing: while an actor tried to implement a particular instruction, while scenes were being run through, Jack was listening and watching and also doing twenty other things: he was lighting the stage, getting the look of it right, assessing the effect of lighting changes and then making further changes. 'Double that one. Halve that one,' he was telling the electricians. He was telling the set designer that the banquettes must be deep red plush. 'Get velvet, not the imitation stuff. It has to be velvet. I don't care what it costs. Find some old velvet somewhere.' To Old Pianist Doblitzsch he said: 'I want you to tail off the *Tales of the Vienna Woods* into dissonance . . . and then pick up the melody again.' He told Rothschild to wear a bow tie. And spats. Never mind what he actually wore, that was the picture in Jack's mind which had to be fulfilled. Eichmann's shoes must shine like mirrors, he said, because 'he's an obsessional . . .' He told the lighting director: 'Follow spot tight on Oskar, all the time.' He called out to the electricians different lighting combinations: 'Reduce 13 by 2 . . . okay, try reducing it by 3 . . . let me see what that does . . . yeah . . .'

Things were brought to him for his approval. The photographic copies of Austrian newspapers of the period, in cane frames, for the café scenes. The Austrian bank notes. Nik, his hair dyed the colour of dead leaves, wanted to know: 'Is it okay?'

'It's fine,' Jack said. And his uniform, eggshell blue? 'That's fine too.'

Camilla's clothes, the dress she wore for the seduction scene. He gave his approval. As long as something corresponded to the picture in his mind, it passed.

The night before the opening, when everybody else had gone home, he stayed behind with the lighting director, continuing to work on the lighting. At the beginning, in the café scene, the set had to be bright and rich and red and gold and blue. And then gradually the tone darkens, the shadows deepen. 'It starts out MGM, and then gets to be vintage UFA Fritz Lang.'

During the full dress rehearsal, next day, catching sight of Lila in the auditorium had an adverse effect on Gloria; she had dried several times and her performance had lost finesse. He called a fifteen-minute break and talked to her alone.

'Got a problem?'

'It's Lila,' she said. 'Seeing her there disturbs me, can't you do something so I don't have to see her? Tell her it's over between you?'

'Haven't had the time.'

'When're you going to tell her?'

'I was going to tell her after the opening.'

'Tell her now. I'd feel better if you told her now, and she wasn't around.'

He could not let anything affect her performance so her demands had to be met.

'I'll see what I can do about that, Gloria. I want you to be happy.' And straight away he went down the aisle to the row where Lila was sitting and signalled to her to come out.

Apart from Stella's, where they wouldn't have been private, there was no place nearby to sit down and do this in a civilized way, and he hadn't the time to go further afield, because it had to be done fast. He walked with her by the trashcans and the padlocked iron doors of tall bleak storehouses with their weather-gnawed iron pillars and grimy windows and rust-eaten friezes. A smell of oil and gasoline and axle grease came from an open bay where trucks were unloading metal-bound cardboard cartons stamped with the trade-mark of a Chicago meat canning firm.

'Got to tell you something,' Jack said with slow, paced diction, taking Lila's hand in his, but not looking at her, looking instead at the big Negro in the sweat-stained T-shirt pushing a trolley of canned meat up a well-worn metal ramp to the loading platform of a goods elevator. 'Don't want you to take this wrong, but . . . your presence is disturbing Gloria.' He gave a shrug of not being responsible for other people's hang-ups. 'So, might be best if you didn't stay around during the rest of the dress re-hearsal. And you better not come tonight . . . we can't go giving our leading lady a crisis of nerves on opening night.'

Lila turned to look at him hard, with her dark heavy question-ing eyes. She had to wait until the clatter of the trolley going over the metal ramp had stopped. 'What about if I have a crisis of nerves?'

'You're not opening in a play tonight.'

'You mean my having a crisis of nerves doesn't count. Why d'you suppose I'm so upsetting to her? Listen: she was upset the first time she . . . you . . . set eyes on me. What's it got to do with her? She's going with Carl, not with you. Or am I behind the times?'

'There isn't time to work out reasons,' he told her. 'It's just best if you don't come.'

'But I want to come. I'm entitled to come. It's your work . . . I want to see what you've done.'

'Come another night.'

'I don't want to come another night, I don't want to be left out of the first night like I'm nothing to do with you.' Her voice had become high-pitched and petulant. 'I'm not supposed to come to the dinner at Sardi's either? In case I disturb her. I'm with you, aren't I? Aren't I? She's supposed to be a professional actress, why can't she bear to have me around?'

'You're right about that,' he conceded. 'That's why it's probably going to be simpler if you're not . . . with me.'

She couldn't believe what he was saying, and was, at first, · more incredulous than aggrieved, until the full import of his words had sunk in. 'What! Are you saying you're ditching me? Is that what you're saying? Because she objects to me? What's it to do with her?'

'I think it's come to the end of its natural life with us, Lila.'

'Well, I've heard of getting the kiss-off, but this is the quickest ˎ coolest kiss-off I ever heard of. I don't get it. We've been making out pretty good together.'

He looked at his watch. He had to make this quick. 'Lila, we said it lasts as long as it lasts. No ties. It was good while it lasted. Sometimes it was very good. Sometimes great. Things change, that's all. People move on.' His voice became brisk and precise and formal. 'I'll help you professionally any way I can. If I'm in a position to help. You can always call on me. Let's stay friends.' He looked at his watch. She emitted quick bursts of hoarse, disbelieving, painfully dry laughter. Her rat-a-ta-tat laugh. As if trying to dislodge something stuck in her throat, the tears she wasn't permitting herself.

'You're really giving me the brush-off,' she said, shaking her head disbelievingly, her face beginning to break up; he had to move fast to block the tears before they got started.

'Lila. The play opens in less than four hours. We need to get certain things straight. Okay? About the room: you're welcome to stay until you've found somewhere else for yourself, and got on your feet. Only don't expect me to be there much, I'll just be in and out.'

'You'll be at Gloria's, is that it?' Her voice had gone bitter. 'Well, that figures. Gloria Vanderveld. Rich. Mother, the great Louise Vanderveld; stepfather, the powerful, influential George Jakes, connections everywhere. That figures for a young hot-shot director on the rise.'

He shook his head sadly. 'You got it wrong, Lila. Gloria is with Carl,' he said firmly. 'So don't get things mixed up in your pretty little head. We're all out of time, Lila, I really have got to go. There's a hundred things still.' His voice went lower as he pleaded with her. 'Don't give me a hard time. Do what I ask.'

'What choices do I have?' she asked dazedly.

He kissed her with finality. 'This is nothing against you. You're a terrific girl. It's just that things change.' She was looking away towards the river — the mass of tears was just behind her eyes.

'The stupid thing is that I love you,' she said, looking up at him.

'You'll get over it,' he told her with the softest smile he could muster.

'Anyway,' she said, 'don't get to be too much of a Hollywood heel before you've even got there, huh? That'd be a shame, because you're a nice person really. Or were.'

He turned and started walking away from her. She wiped her eyes.

'Just remember what they tell you in this business.'

'What's that?'

'They say be nice to people on your way up, because you'll meet them all again on your way down.'

'What makes you think I'm on my way up?'

'Anybody can see that.'

'If you really want to know — I only manage to keep my head above water, that's all.'

13

Any chronicler of Jack Strawley's life is bound to be struck by his great self-belief at this point, as well as his lack of scruples in attaining what he wants. It's as if he knows that he's going to become 'Genius Jack', and that therefore everything is permitted. Self-delusion fulfilling itself?

The complete autodidact, he hadn't gone through any kind of apprenticeship in the theatre (unless the fifteen months sweeping floors and moving scenery counts): he seemed to have just absorbed everything out of the air around him. Directing his first full-scale play, he took charge of professionals far more experienced than himself (Gloria, Nik Ransom and others, including technical experts such as those who had charge of lighting, set design, and costumes), and in some way exerted an authority he did not yet have. Was it all gigantic bluff, was he bluffing himself as well as everybody else? Or was it 'genius'? Or, a less glorifying explanation, did he possess an extraordinary flair for artistic — and other kinds of — theft, for 'seeing out of the corner of his eye' and absorbing everything of any use to him, including other people's work (past and present), and seamlessly making it his own? I suppose it could be said that this is precisely what the *auteur* film director — as which he was later to be acclaimed — does.

He must have long ago, when still a child, understood that every new step involved some loss, and every win was predicated on somebody else losing. You had to clear a path, and that involved destruction of what stood in the way. You couldn't let sentiment slow you down. And he came to understand that as talent grows, the heart dries up.

SEVILLE TAPE 14(NIK SPEAKING 003 TO 045)

'From the beginning, the way Jack used actors was manipulative. He laid you on his canvas—in the case of women, literally. He used you as his colour. It was all for his glory. He'd call on you to give him some red or some blue or dark or light. Whatever. As an actor you're just raw material to him. You try to give him what he wants because he has the devil's own charm in getting stuff out of you. But he's doing the painting, not you. He uses you. If you really want to know what I thought of him, from the beginning I thought he was a very talented shit, which is better than being an untalented shit but is still being a shit. I know people say the same about me.'

While I cannot totally dismiss this point of view, it is an actor's view, and a very special actor's view at that, and was not by any means shared by all the actors who worked with Jack Strawley. Some found that he brought out marvellous things in them.

My own mixed feelings about him underwent further modification from the time that I began conducting all those hours of taped interviews with him. I began then to have a sense of what it meant to be inside his prickly skin. From his perspective, things did look different. That he was capable of behaving very badly, nobody can deny (and he did not deny it); that he was willing to sacrifice friends and lovers and fellow artists to advance his purpose is unquestionable, but it has got to be remembered that he was equally ready to sacrifice himself, and one has to understand that at bottom he was always staking his life for a cause, which may have been purely his own, as many would say, but could also be said to have been whatever film he was making at the time, into which he always put everything of himself. If that is the tapeworm of talent devouring the body from within, then it was a price he was willing to pay.

14

Throughout the whole of the performance he was moving about in the auditorium, constantly shifting his position, changing his sightlines. Unable to sit still for a minute. Making notes.

Noting the way it all fitted together — or didn't. He saw what was working and what wasn't. The opening café scene was slow, even with the changes he'd introduced, even with big chunks of Oskar's monologue turned into small scenes. *Must speed up here. How? Start scene in middle. After action has begun, not before. That'll speed it up. Eichmann the faceless man in the dirty raincoat is walking over their graves. Convey this. How? In his bitter bureaucrat's face. Hiding behind the aspidistra — sheer farce! — spying on Rothschild flirting with Camilla.* He noted that Gloria was getting all her laughs, whereas Oskar was not getting all his. Why? Because Oskar the dealer bargaining with Eichmann for the lives of Jews was humour so black the audience had to be given permission to laugh. *Okay, give them permission. How? Have Oskar laugh at himself, with grisly gallows humour . . . Laughs to freeze the blood. Show it: laugh/ freeze/laugh/freeze . . . Seduction scene good. They brought it off. A shocked gasp went through audience. There were no laughs on Camilla's sexual cry. The crimson joy! The rape of Austria! Worked. Gloria did it superbly, with such an anguished foreshadowing of the catastrophe coming that the audience couldn't laugh. God, she's good now. Not frightened of the sex at all. The love scene in Act III wasn't right, though. Not enough intensity, wrong to do it without any physical contact between them, without that we don't believe Camilla's 'I can't,' when she says she can't give him up. Correct this. How? Final curtain ('She couldn't sing to save her life . . . and didn't.') good and moving. Some wept.*

He was pushing his way through the crush, against the flow of people leaving. Oh, that sweet audience buzz. They liked it, they responded. Oh yeah, oh yeah, oh yeah! His head was high above water for the moment. He felt an insistent tap on his shoulder, and turning as much as he could within the press of bodies saw with the edge of his eye someone else pushing against the flow, coming after him. He was leaning across the solid block of backs, long arm extended like the arm of a grab crane with its claws rummaging in the prize pot. 'Sydney Carver.' A razor sharp smile. 'Met at George's party.' This was shouted through the buzz, past the heads of those who uncaringly stood in his way. 'Last year. Remember? I'm gonna try and look in at Sardi's, but don't suppose we'll get much chance to talk *there*. How about we share a cab? I'll have it wait out front. Want to talk to you, Jack.' More people had come between them. The undiffident young man pointed to where they were going to meet and then with an 'Excuse me a sec, Jack,' went off tunnelling into the crowd surrounding a man called 'Lenny'. Grabbing 'Lenny's' hand, he reminded him above the buzz which had become a roar that they'd met at Aaron's. 'I . . . just wanted to say . . .' What he wanted to say was lost in the buzz, and presently he was tunnelling back again like some earth-moving machine. When he'd elbowed enough people out of the way to be able to shout in Jack's ear, he shouted: 'Lenny loved it, thinks it's the best new production on or off Broadway this season.' He continued shouting conversationally: 'It *should* transfer. If there's any justice in the world, it will. But don't count on justice. I don't. Make your next move . . . *now*. If you want my advice.'

Hanging onto Jack, the young man with the far-reaching arms had arrived with him backstage in time to grab Nik Ransom as he was coming out of the dressing rooms.

'Got to tell you,' Carver yelled in his ear, above the din, 'you're the best new young actor to emerge since Brando and Dean and Clift . . . I'm not kidding you, Nik. *Very* terrific.'

'Who is this jerk-off?' Nik demanded.

'I met you at George's party. The delectable Maureen? Forgettable as she is on screen, nobody who has known her on her back ever forgets her, huh?'

With rare good humour Nik told him to fuck off. Which did not disconcert Sydney Carver: he was used to to being told to fuck off and took it in his long stride. 'What a character! What a joker! What an actor!' he enthused. 'Jack, I have to tell you this in all honesty: you did a great job with this piece, and a great job with Nik.'

Jack went into the dressing rooms and spoke to those in the cast who were not going to be at Sardi's, since it was a private dinner that Gloria's mother and George Jakes were giving. He congratulated everybody, said the performance had gone well.

There were places where the playing needed to be tightened up. He was issuing a call for tomorrow morning, 11 a.m. Then he talked to one or two of them individually. Several said what a shame Carl had not been there to see how well the play was received. He would have been gratified by the response. Mention of Carl brought back the persistent nagging worry that the pressure of getting the play on had pushed into the background. Jonas Logar, the Viennese actor who played Oskar, had known Carl a long time, longer than any of them, having been to school with him in Vienna, and he said it was Carl's style to 'pull out' when things went against him: he had this passive but highly effective, in fact devastating, way of expressing his disapproval, his scorn, by walking away. It was the world-weary cum worldly-wise Viennese shrug of contempt raised to the level of action. He just removes himself from you, Jonas Logar said.

'The question is, how far does he go in that?'

When Jack finally was able to get out of the theatre, and was looking around for a cab, he heard a voice call to him: 'Here! I'm here, Jack.' And so he was: smiling, long-armed Sydney, standing by the open door of a battered old Yellow Cab.

'You kept the cab waiting all this time?' Jack asked, trying to work out who this joker could be.

'I said I'd meet you here,' Carver said, hurt at having already been forgotten.

In the cab, to place who this man was, he asked him: 'How d'you happen to know that our friend Maureen is so talentless? Except on her back.'

'Only roundabout knowledge of the latter, regret to say.' He laughed thickly. 'But I have it on good testimony. As to her lack of other talents, that I can vouch for personally. Since I represented her one time. When I was working in the George Jakes office. Set up on my own now. Sydney Carver & Associates.' He handed Jack a visiting card upon which his name was boldly engraved above the words, 'Theatrical, Cinematic, TV, Radio, Vaudeville and Literary Representation'. The agency address was crossed out. 'We're moving,' Sydney explained, 'to bigger premises. Not quite ready. You can get me at the number on the back, meanwhile.' There was a phone number pencilled on the back. Every time the cab went over a pothole, it started to take off on its broken suspension and then came down with a bone-rattling, metal-shaking crunch. 'Want you to know,' Sydney was shouting in Jack's ear against these crashes, 'whether the critics recognize this or not — you never know with them — *I* know what a terrific job you did, Jack, because I saw an early rehearsal, when Carl was directing, and there is no comparison with what it is now. Just out of curiosity, who's your agent?'

'Vincent Waterhouse.'

'That's a solid agency. You couldn't do better. Vincent doesn't hustle, he doesn't oversell, he doesn't ask for the moon. He's not a bluffer, you know what I mean? He represents long established quality that he doesn't need to sell. And doesn't. Goes off and plays golf and takes his calls at the clubhouse bar. Clever stuff. Very subtle. You ring up with a hot deal and they tell you he can't come to the phone, he's playing golf! Let people say what they like — that he's not working hard for his clients — point is he doesn't have to work hard, so why should he? He's a rich man and a lovely old guy. Stick with him, he'll build up your career slowly but surely . . . if he lives that long,if you live that long, hah-hah! — excuse the sour grapes, I'm just green with envy that *he's* got you.'

The cab had arrived at Sardi's, and Carver had leapt out, in the abrupt way he had of doing things, and was patiently explaining something through the driver's window,

'No cheques, mister. I don't take no cheques,' he was told.

'Well how much is it?'

'Fifteen eighty-five.'

'How can it be that much, Jesus!'

'I was waitin' for you outside all that time.'

'I don't have it on me. Why won't you take a cheque, for Chrissake?'

'I don't, bud, that's all. Fifteen eighty-five on the clock.'

'That really inconveniences me.' Sydney Carver went through all his pockets, gathering together bills, quarters, nickels and cents and counting out the total on his palm. It came to six dollars and sixty-five cents.

'Can't do it,' he informed the cab-driver.

'How much is it?' Jack asked feeling in his pockets.

'Fifteen, eighty-five. Say eighteen with the tip, though he doesn't really merit a tip, but I like to be generous.' He put his own six dollars sixty-five cents back in his pocket, since his contribution appeared to not be needed now, while Jack paid the cab fare.

'Listen, I got to run,' Sydney Carver announced. 'I'm gonna give Sardi's a miss tonight. It's a place that gets to be boring when you go there too much. Really I just wanted to congratulate you and to say . . . if I can be of help any time, I'm an admirer, just give me a ring. Number's on the back. Nothing involved. Anything at all that I can do, on a purely friendly basis, I'll be glad to do it, because I care about Talent. And you have it! Listen, just out of curiosity . . .' He had started off on his precipitate way when he swung round. 'You thought at all about what you want to do next? You thought about cinema? You have a very cinematic talent.'

'I thought about cinema.'

'Well, listen. Oh, I'm convinced Vincent is going to come up with film offers galore for you to choose from. Now you mention it, didn't see him there tonight. Was he there?'

'No, I didn't see him.'

'Maybe he went on one of his long weekends up to his dacha. Vincent doesn't like the city when it's too hot. And who can blame him? Since he doesn't have to like it. Give me a ring any time. Always glad to help Talent.'

As Jack entered the restaurant, he felt the excited buzz rise to his face like the welcoming warm wet lick of a dog's tongue. Beaming Gene Sardi escorted him to Louise Vanderveld's table. One or two people clapped him as he passed, and he smiled and gave little humble bows of acknowledgment.

'Come and sit here,' Louise Vanderveld called to him, patting the empty chair at her side. She waved her finger at him in rebuke. 'What have you done to my little Gloria! Little Miss Priss. You've made her sexy — you wicked man! How you've done that I'll never know.'

'She gets it from you, sweetie,' George Jakes told her with a sour grin of adoration.

5

'Certainly doesn't get it from you,' Louise responded snappily and confided to the company. 'George doesn't like sex. He hasn't fucked *me* for ten years. And he only does it with Maureen Talentless in order to keep up with the boys, which takes some doing in her case.'

Before Louise Vanderveld stood a bottle of gin upon which substantial inroads had already been made. Next to it there was a bottle of scotch from which she poured Jack a generous amount, half filling his water glass. By his glass there was an envelope with his name on it. He recognized the handwriting immediately. He poured himself another scotch and then opened the letter and read:

Dear Jack,

I know it's inexcusable but I couldn't bring myself to speak to *anyone* — just wanted to disappear. I have that desire at times. I have come out of it now. I slipped in to see the production tonight. I didn't want to make my presence known, expecting to loathe what I saw and was going to return immediately to my bolt-hole. (Where would one go if one didn't have bolt-holes to go to?) Then, as the play unfolded, I began to realize that you have understood it better than I. You have directed it brilliantly. We will discuss what you have done in greater detail one day, but for now I just want to tell you that I wept with the audience when Oskar pronounces his epitaph for Camilla, whereas when I wrote those words my eyes were dry. I think it is not too much of an exaggeration to say that you have saved the play when I was in the course of ruining it. I know that now. You've taken a piece that was full of monologues and essays and lectures and turned it into a play of human passions. I don't know how I could have been so stubbornly unseeing. (I have this theory that we all commit 'invisible mistakes': i.e., mistakes that are invisible to us but all too visible to everyone else, and, of course, you saw what I did not see . . .) Tell Gloria not to worry, that she's wonderful in the play, sublime, and so is Nik. I'm okay now, but I am going to be absent a while longer, after which I will make my way back slowly. Tell Gloria I will phone up soon and regret having caused her anxiety, and that I love her. Love, Carl.

He handed the letter to Gloria, and she read it with a mixed expression on her face that reflected relief, bewilderment, resentment.

'Why doesn't he write to me? And what's it all mean? Where is he? What bolt-hole?'

'You know Carl. He has a taste for mystification.' He was grinning now with happiness and relief. 'I'd think it means nothing. Just his Old Viennese way of saying if things are bad they are very, very bad, and if they're good they can only get worse.'

Before midnight Gene Sardi came in with the *Times* and *Herald Tribune* under his arm and started handing out copies. Louise Vanderveld was first to find the review in the *Times*. 'If it's good,' George told her, 'read it out, darling. If it's not, we don't want to hear it.' It seemed a good sign when she started to read aloud in her resonant stage voice:

'The best way I can describe *Hotel Metropole,* an extraordinary new play by Carl Schmidlin at the little Tramline Theatre in Greenwich Street, is to ask you to imagine something written by Arthur Schnitzler in collaboration with Vicki Baum, in other words an intellectual *Grand Hotel.* Viennese-born playwright Schmidlin has exploited for his own clever ends the Vicki Baum formula of criss-crossing destinies converging in a single setting.

'The true and essential irony on which the play is founded is that Vienna's grand hotel, complete with pianist playing Strauss waltzes in the palm court, became after Hitler had taken over Austria the Nazi headquarters of one Adolf Eichmann, in charge of the Jewish Bureau, to which wealthy Jews went to bargain for their lives.

'The Vicki Baum formula becomes in Mr Schmidlin's hands a vehicle for black comedy and stark atrocity. The cross-section of characters that he puts on stage includes Baron Rothschild, one of those who were able to buy their way out, and the horrible and macabre and comical, yes *comical,* Nazi bureaucrat of death,

Adolf Eichmann, as well as Camilla, a witty and tragic Jewish journalist, who is seduced by the brutishly attractive "romantic Nazi" Wirthof. The play is by turns erotic (the seduction of Camilla in a box of the Vienna Opera during a performance of *Tosca*, with her sexual cry symbolically echoed by the arpeggios of Tosca's suicide aria), psychoanalytical (Camilla's drive towards self-destruction), and morally horrific (Eichmann selling the lives of Jews through the art dealer Oskar). It is a black fable told with intellectual verve.

'Out of this sprawling material director Jack Strawley, whose first full-length production this is, has fashioned a theatrical tour-de-force that puts a Viennese grand hotel and the Staatsoper on the Tramline's tiny stage, and also brings off the transformation scene when the hotel becomes the Nazi HQ — with the Old Pianist still playing Strauss waltzes. Not only has twenty-two-year-old director Strawley obtained stunning performances from Gloria Vanderveld and Nik Ransom as Camilla and Wirthof, but he has made of the play — which sometimes gets perilously close to becoming overtly preachy and, what's more, to losing the thread of its sermon — a dynamic and moving experience. Young Mr Strawley clearly possesses a flair for creating extraordinary imagery. If *Hotel Metropole* does not rapidly find a home on Broadway, the outlying Tramline theatre (with only 150 seats) will be full for some considerable time to come.'

Louise put down the paper, and there was a round of applause from others in the restaurant who had listened to the review being read out. Turning to Jack, she said in her sharp and knowing voice:

'Well, my dear. Isn't that *nice?* A nice review, isn't it? Nice to get the midnight hags on your side giving you all that lovely encouragement, telling you you'll be king. Want to listen to an old hag who knows a bit about this business? Oh, it's lovely to get the acclaim. But that's just the first step, Jack dear. The second is the cash register which has got to ring loud and clear and long. And then you have to do it again. And again and again. *And* on top of that, you need . . . glue. Something Gene O'Neill said once. That man is born broken, and the grace of God is glue. You've got to have glue, Jack dear. That sticks good. Oh, don't worry: *nobody* gets it all together. Except, sometimes, when they're dead.'

'Don't know that I can wait that long,' Jack said to her.

15

Next morning, at 10:00 a.m., the phone rang in his room, and the voice that was waking him up said: 'If it's awkward right now, just say and I'll ring back later. After a triumph like last night, it's a cinch you're not sleeping alone.'

'Who's that?'

'It's Sydney,' Carver said with a note of grief in his voice that it had not been immediately recognized. 'I expect you're not properly awake yet.'

'What's the good news, Sydney, for which you're waking me up this early?'

' . . . I was just ringing up for *you* to tell me the good news. After those reviews! Exactly as I predicted. I expect Vincent has been burning up the line with offers from Hollywood.'

'You're the first to call this morning.'

'I'm frankly amazed. You mean, he didn't even ring to congratulate you on the reviews? Well, I expect he's out of town, he'll ring you with the offers as soon as he gets in. Listen, Jack. I wouldn't want to pre-empt Vincent, but you know, dearly as I love the old guy, he *is* slow, so I just mention this in case it's of some interest. I had to talk to Dore last night — Dore Schary — in connection with a client of mine, and your name came up and I mentioned about the great job you'd done, and about your interest in directing films, and he was interested. That was before the reviews. Then I read the reviews, and I called Dore again, I woke him up, I said , "Listen Dore, I've just read the reviews, and purely as an act of friendship,

I don't even represent him, I tell you this: you should move fast, if you're interested, because this guy's going to have offers coming out of his ears and nostrils. Not to mention other orifices. I told him to ring you direct, not to go through your agent, I wanted to give Dore a slight edge, so I gave him your phone number, since he's a friend . . . hope you don't mind that. I'm having lunch with Sam Spiegel, and I thought, with your permission, I'd suggest he goes and sees the play.'

'You don't need my permission to send people to see the play.'

'It'll be booked out, can you arrange seats for Sam, if I can get him to go.'

'Sure.'

'I'll let you know. Enjoy your triumph. You deserve it.'

Jack spent the morning giving the actors his notes and tightening up scenes.

There were several phone calls from Carver that Jack did not take or return. After the fourth, he gave Sheila a message to give to him: 'Say I'll talk to him at 1:15.'

She came back. 'Mr Carver says he'll be having lunch with Mr Spiegel at that time, but he'll try and take five minutes to call you. And can we put aside two seats, for Mr Spiegel and Mr Spiegel's date, for this evening, in case Mr Carver is able to arrange for him to come and see the play.'

'Do that, Sheila.'

There were no other phone calls during the morning — nothing from Vincent Waterhouse, nothing from the Waterhouse Agency — and at exactly 1:15 p.m. he took the call from Carver.

'Can't talk to you long,' he said, 'I'm at "21" having lunch with Otto . . . he's right here next to me . . .'

'I thought you were having lunch with Spiegel. Otto who?'

'Preminger. We're expecting Sam any minute. He's gone to pick up his date. Now what I want to tell you is this . . . I've been thinking. Forget MGM, forget Twentieth. Forget Warners. Otto agrees with me.'

'That I should forget them?'

'Yeah. This is the Age of the Indies coming . . . go with one of the independents.'

'Like who?'

'Like Sam, or if not Sam what about Ray Tangy?'

'He makes shit films.'

'That's one way of looking at it. Another way of looking at it is — he makes commercially successful films. The fact that they are not very highly thought of gives you an edge, Jack. Not everyone wants to make a film for Ray Tangy. Sam, let's be frank, can get Huston, or anybody else he wants. Otto can get Otto. But Ray . . . with him you have an edge. I'll fix up for you to see him.'

'I hate his films.'

'Why's that a problem? Ray hates his films too. He's got better taste than that. Does Barbara Hutton buy her jewellery at Woolworth's? So don't turn up your nose. Look. I don't want anything out of this. What you got to lose? Just go and see him. Jack, I'm doing you a favour. Purely as a friend . . . and admirer. I have no pecuniary interest. I won't even be there. Go and see what he says. Can't hurt you.Can it?'

'Okay,' he said to bring an end to the conversation. 'Let me know if . . .'

'No if. 3:15 p.m. At his office. Give you the address. It's . . .'

'Today?'

'Sure today. Who d'you think I am, Vincent Waterhouse? When I do something I do it today, not tomorrow. When I have a hot property, I run with it, and you're a hot property today — tomorrow who knows? — even if you're not my hot property — okay, that's my misfortune, I'll try to bear it. I'm doing this because I like you and believe in you.The address is 711 Fifth Avenue. 12th floor. Suite 208. 3:15 sharp. I got to run. I can see Sam and his date. Oh, this'll kill you. You know who his date is? Maureen. Maureen Talentless. Come to think of it, that's how Sam prefers his actresses. Nothing on the screen, great on their back. Bye for now. Call me to say how it went with Ray.'

In the lobby of 711 he took the elevator that went directly to the 12th floor, where signs directed him to Suite 208/ Tangy Productions. He went into a reception area furnished like the hall of an English country house with an open fireplace in which an imitation log fire flickered. There was a long line of somebody's ancestors on the walls: forbidding Edwardian ladies in long tailored jackets with velvet collars and cuffs, ankle length skirts, long-veiled black hats. There were bronze elephants either side of the fireplace and smoked glass mirrors complete with mottling that gave back a darker, handsomer version of yourself. He'd been waiting for a couple of minutes when a well-preserved grey-haired woman in her fifties appeared, wearing a tweed box-pleated skirt and pearls, and asked in an overstrong British accent if she could be of any assistance to him, and Jack said she could indeed, he had come to see Mr Tangy, and she said, without needing to consult any list, 'Mr Strawley? Let me take you in to him.'

Inside, behind a burr walnut Victorian partners' desk, sat Ray Tangy, a large man, chubby about the chin, in white shirt with button-down collar and striped Yale tie and blue double-breasted blazer with white buttons. In front of the desk two antique globes of the world were being pensively spun by a studious Sydney Carver.

'Just stopped by to make the introductions,' he explained. 'Since I was dropping Otto off . . . so happens he's in the same building. Ray, baby, I'm . . . I'm just being the Jewish match-maker here and bringing you two kids together, and then I'm gonna leave you to it .'

'Stay a minute, Sydney,' Tangy invited. 'If you're not too pressed for time. You could maybe be of some help to us. Like you could light our cigars. Huh?' Tangy pushed a box of Hoyo de Monterreys towards Jack Strawley. 'Take a cigar, Mr Strawley. You, too, Sydney.'

'Oh, he's such a kidder. Love ya, Ray!'

Jack had not availed himself of the offer of a cigar and Sydney Carver reached across him with his long-reaching arm and selected two, expertly rolling them between his fingers to test their quality. 'Taking one for you for later,' he explained to Jack.

Tangy must have pushed a bell for a young man with blond crew-cut hair put his head round the door, and Tangy said: 'Come on in, Doug. Want you to meet Doug Bodworkin, my invaluable assistant. Doug, bring us three Hines. You drink cognac, Mr Strawley?'

While the cognacs were being sipped there was polite, and impolite, chatter about Otto and Sam, and Maureen the Talentless, who provided two or three minutes of ribald diversion; and the globes of the world, which once had belonged to Captain Cook, it transpired, were spun to and fro with increasing speed by Sydney Carver; and the film producer's horse paintings were admired, and reference was made to the impressive world grosses of the three films he had on release that year.

'Mr Strawley,' he said, 'if I've learned one thing in my years in this business, I've learned about survival. This is a rat race and you can't be a mouse in a rat race. In the past I've employed genius-boys and I learned my lesson. I learned by losing money. You want to know why are you here? Good question to which I don't have a real good answer. Let's say Sydney here twisted my arm, Mr Strawley . . . and he's a good arm-twister.'

'I don't know why I'm here either, Mr Tangy. Expect we both got our arms twisted.'

Ross Tangy indicated a Wedgwood jar on his desk, 'Have a chocolate, Mr Strawley. Now that you are here. They're Belgian. The best. Sydney tells me you want to make films. He says you're good, he says you're going to be one of the best. I'm a man who likes to have the best. Just look around. I'm a man who likes to have quality. Quality at the right price. It's got to be at the right price. When you have a story for me that you can bring in for under a hundred and fifty thou, come back and we'll talk again. Have a chocolate, Mr Strawley, Sydney. There's nothing to beat Belgian chocolate . . . Let me tell you something about myself: for me, money has no meaning except the beautiful things it can buy.'

'Ray,' Carver said taking three chocolates, eating one and placing two in reserve before him, 'you should go see *Hotel Metropole*. It's a marvellous play, it's quality. But it's also *Grand Hotel,* and *Grand Hotel* worked once, worked more than once, and can work again.'

'*Grand Hotel?* With the heroine dying in a concentration camp? Do me a favour, Sydney!'

'The script's going to need some work, what script doesn't?'

'Mrs Tangy and I will go and see it in due course,' Ray Tangy

said with a properly respectful note entering his voice when he
spoke of Mrs Tangy. 'Mrs Tangy likes that sort of thing, where
you have to sit on uncomfortable seats in a room in a warehouse,
she likes it . . . that sort of thing appeals to her . . . I'm not
saying I won't enjoy it myself, but . . . please, Sydney, a picture
for today's audiences it is not. If Mr Strawley has something a bit
more . . . punchy — you know? — come and see me again.'

'As a matter of fact, Ray, Jack *has* got a subject for you. He
was telling me about it the other day, and I thought straight away
that's a Ray Tangy pic. Of course it's not fully developed . . . but
I should think we could get something down on paper for you, in
the next day or so, a two page outline . . .'

'What's the subject?' Tangy asked.

'It's a New York picture,' Carver said, 'two principal male
parts, the criminal and this other . . . fella. There's an escape in
it. Couple of murders. Low-life settings.'

'Something like *Cry of the City?*' Tangy asked, showing a
modicum of interest.

'Something like that,' Carver said, looking to Jack for verifica-
tion. 'Jack, tell Ray a little bit about it,' Carver said coaxingly.
'Give him a taste.'

'Yeah, tell me something,' Tangy said.

'Which subject you talking about, Sydney?'

'You know the one,' Sydney said, 'where there's this killing
and the chase.'

'That's a good subject,' Jack conceded. 'I wouldn't want anyone to think because I talk about it in public it's in the public
domain, Mr Tangy.'

'Ray doesn't do that,' Carver said. 'We all know there are
producers who steal other people's ideas and stories. They're
thieves, nothing less. Common criminals. Ray is an honourable
man, and a gentleman — I can vouch for that. Apart from which,
even if you're not my client, I'm going to protect your interests,
aren't I? Go ahead. You can feel free to tell him the subject,
Jack.'

'It's about this hitman for the Mob who says he's really an
artist at heart . . . and that he only blows away them that's got it
coming.'

He remembered something Carl had said in warning him about Eddie Max. 'The film's called *Killers Kill,*' he told Tangy.

Out in the tumult of Fifth Avenue, after the sound-proofed calm of the 12th floor, Sydney Carver said: 'You sold him on it. He liked it. I could see.'

'Sydney, this is crazy. The story, it's not even mine. I've got no story . . . I just made that up. I don't know where I got it from.'

Carver stopped him right in the middle of all the noise and bustle of Fifth Avenue, standing over him, very tall and long-armed, his face solemn and prophetic.

'Doesn't matter where you got the story. Nobody owns a story. It's yours now. Where d'you think Shakespeare got his stories? Listen,' he said, holding up traffic, 'nothing and no one is beyond your reach . . . it's all out there for you. You just got to reach for it. Jack, I don't see any reason why you shouldn't make a career as glittering as Kazan's. You have the talent, all you need is some luck.'

'Where do I get that?'

'You got it. I'm your luck.'

'How did you get into my life?'

'I just did. That's how luck happens. Unexpected.'

'What's in it for you? You're not even my agent, you won't even get 10%.'

'Like Ray says, money means nothing to me except the beautiful things it can buy. '

'What d'you get out of it then?'

'A little tiny piece of your future. Nothing in writing, just a friendly understanding between you and me.' He extended his open hand, and, after a moment or two of hesitation, Jack took it, and they shook. He wasn't quite sure on what, but since he wasn't committing himself to anything in writing, he didn't think it could matter that much.

PART II

TOWARDS THE CENTRE

16

My rash use of the epithet 'genius' in reviewing *Killers Kill* did not have any noticeably immediate consequence for Jack Strawley's life and career — reviews in highbrow magazines do not determine what happens in the movie business. The effect was more insidious and took time — more than a year — to develop, and then it required a growing underground buzz, followed by one or two chance combinations of events, plus Jack's indefatigable self-belief, for the mythic overnight success to finally happen. The first somewhat doubtful step in this sequence was Sydney Carver getting Strawley a contract with MGM. It was by no means a big deal. Jack was paid $150 a week in the first phase of a seven-year term. He saw the studio chief Dore Schary just once, and after six months of frustrating inactivity, during which he was offered nothing of any interest, broke the contract and returned to New York. His future did not look very promising. And then, in the odd way in which things come together, a couple of other threads in his life became fortuitously intertwined. In Paris a young film journalist by the name of François Truffaut saw *Killers Kill* and wrote a highly laudatory piece for *Cahiers du Cinema* , talking of 'a secret masterpiece'.

As a result of Truffaut's enthusiasm, the film was chosen for a festival of *cinema maudit,* devoted to films overlooked or damned by mainstream opinion. There it won other admirers, and a bandwagon effect began to develop. In this atmosphere, someone from United Artists' European operation saw the film, discovered that it could be bought cheaply and snapped it up. It might have lain unshown on their shelves for a long time but for the fact that attendances for one of their big-budget films which was slotted into a tight release schedule, unexpectedly collapsed after one week in the London West End, and some other film was urgently needed to fill the gap. And so the unscheduled *Killers*

Kill was quickly pushed out. The underground buzz was astutely amplified by the U.A. publicity machine, and it fell on receptive ears, since an anti-establishment mood was gathering pace, and outsiders were now in. An opening existed for an overlooked young genius, preferably with glamour and dash, and Jack Strawley fitted the bill. In these circumstances, the fact that one critic had employed the term 'genius' (however loosely), and another 'masterpiece', in writing of the film, and that it had been acclaimed at some French festival that nobody had ever heard of before, was enough of a hook to whet the appetite of the popular press. It made a good story that the 'genius' had walked out on a 'million-dollar MGM contract', telling the studio chiefs to go to hell (it was not said that a million dollars was what the contract could theoretically have been worth over seven years, if it were to have been renewed with incremental salary increases and bonuses year after year). The fact that the principal role in the film was played by a new vibrant young actor, Nik Ransom, who was now wanted by all the studios, and that it introduced a slithery new sexpot by the name of Lila Karr, all helped to contribute to Jack Strawley's sudden celebrity, albeit that he was still to all intents and purposes unknown. This contradiction had never been a problem in the film business before and it wasn't on this occasion. Thus the cocktail reception for *Killers Kill,* held in the River Room of the Savoy, brought out the full panoply of the British press.

The new celebrity had a crooked grin and a mocking air, as if to show how little he considered all this to be worth. I remember also that he appeared to share with Pete, the photographer hero of his film, a freakish fastness of vision: he seemed to see everything in a fraction of the time others needed to register the same event, he took things in with a single look of his overly bright eyes. I had the impression of a mind driving too fast.

After we'd been introduced — this was our first meeting — he took me aside briefly to speak into my ear, asking that I join him and his people for dinner afterwards. 'Private,' he warned. He gave me a look in which a menacing smile uncurled on his face, and quickly disappeared to be replaced by sweetness, as if to say, 'only kidding'.

One moment mocking, the next tender, I found his rapidly fluctuating attitudes disconcerting. It was difficult to find the right tone in which to respond to him. If I spoke seriously, I was thrown some piece of barbed banter, and, when I participated in the banter, his eyes froze over. He could kid, but others couldn't. I felt at that first meeting of ours constantly in danger of being wrong-footed by him. One minute I was made to feel pretentiously intellectual — 'Yeah, I know, that's the way you and the French boys see it,' — and the next, when in self-defense I had perhaps been a little flippant, I would get the frozen-over look. All through the Savoy press reception and during my subsequent evening with him and his 'people', I was entertained and stimulated, but my smile was sometimes strained as I tried to accommodate myself to his changing mood and register. I saw the way his eyes framed you in their sights. *Tchkkk, tchkkk.* The way they looked around and recorded everything. I remember him saying in the course of the evening that he had never been a child, and I could well believe that: I had the impression that for him life had been a serious business from the start. He'd had to start winning straight away, nothing was ever just a game. Because if you didn't win you were dead.

A partial explanation of how he affected me, that night, must derive from the fact that once a man has been called a genius (and believes it, as I think Strawley believed it, at the beginning at least), he can no longer remain the same man, he cannot help but take on a certain aura for himself, and then, by a process of transference for others. Even though it was I who first had used the word 'genius' in relation to him, my subsequent attitude to him was affected by my own hyperbole.

It was enthralling, and very tiring, to watch him. One minute he was spilling over with exuberance, with love for you, and the next he had retreated within some prickly inner core. I cannot remember now who all his people were that evening, but they included Gloria, of course — he was married to her by then, and they were expecting a baby. I saw how she watched over him with tender concern. Of all the people there, she was the only one who could actually control him to some degree, and was permitted to criticize him (up to a point) without incurring instant retaliation. Even she didn't get off entirely scot-free.

I would look at Gloria questioningly when I didn't quite know how to take something he had said, to establish whether it was said seriously or kiddingly, and she would act as interpreter, so that I did not get him wrong. 'Jack doesn't mean that the way it sounds,' she'd explain quickly. 'He appreciates enormously what you've written about his film. Jack says what passes through his mind, he has almost no capacity for self-censorship. So you have to excuse him when he says things like that. Don't take any notice. Please?'

Turning to me with a New York street expression of 'it's in the bag' and an accompanying thumbs-up gesture, he said with an air of letting me into the secret of how things work: 'You know, if I didn't have Gloria, I don't know what I'd do. She's my saviour, that woman. Because she's wise and true and good and beautiful. And loves me. That's what women do. They love you, goddammit. So they can save you, see? And that's how they get you in their clutches. Hah, hah, hah. You see? You see? Now if you're talking about Gloria, it's worth being in her clutches. They're such beautiful clutches, who wouldn't want to be in 'em? Hah, hah. Hah-hah! The trap, that's the trap! Oh, I'm very picky about the traps I fall into. I only fall into the best, and this woman saves my soul.'

'And that's not easy,' Gloria put in, with tacit permission from him.

'I know it's not, I know,' Jack agreed with her. 'But being me isn't that easy either.'

He had drunk a considerable amount by then, and that was when he believed with the greatest certitude in his own genius.

At one point in the course of the evening, when Jack had made some remark about being crowned with the crown of thorns by 'the French boys', Gloria interpolated the information that he was largely self-taught, and for reasons that no doubt would cost him ten years of psychoanalysis, couldn't bear teachers or being taught by others.

'What Gloria's saying,' he explained, 'is that I'm a savage whom she's been educating up to her high level, so I'll be worth saving.' He gave his hard double-edged grin, and I remember thinking that there was something frantic about it, as if his life depended on it.

There were times that evening when Gloria looked pretty unhappy with this constant kidding banter, but she took it all. I was to discover that people tended to take things from Jack Strawley that they would not have taken from someone else. 'Could you please cut that out, Jack,' she pleaded with him, at one stage, 'it's really very wearing. What's wrong? Your film's been accclaimed, you've got lots of offers, you've got me — for God's sake, what more do you want?'

'You really wanna know? To piss at the moon,' he replied with the hard, fast glitter in his eyes.

17

He had first gone to the American bar, bright thin images, no contrast, no *thickness*, his life thin as a thread, which was strange with all the good reviews and things happening fast now. After all the waiting. He sat drinking by himself, waiting for the *click*, knowing there was a crowded room of people waiting for him to appear. But he had to get himself balanced out, couldn't go into the press reception in this thin weightless state. He sat up at the bar watching the girl in the strapless black cocktail dress sitting by herself in an alcove, waiting for someone but meeting his eye now and then, and he thought that would work too, that would give him some thickness, some vein of feeling, if it were quick and rough and dirty. That would provide the thicker pulse. Get some flow started. The click. He needed the click. Hadn't happened yet, but he couldn't wait any longer now.

The River Room was packed, brightly lit, none of that low-key lighting here, it was all pink and yellow MGM over the rainbow, and the press with their grey-red faces slopping around the pastel walls, slap-slap, swirls and eddies, champagne in hand, gins and Dubonnet, neat scotches. Mouths wide open, shovelling in hot bacon-wrapped little livers on toast, and other savoury tid-bits on sticks. He spotted Lila surrounded and talking fast. One film, and she was giving press conferences: her lacy red dress gripped her so tight below the knees that she had to hobble about as if crippled. 'Give us a slither, Lila,' the photographers were begging and she obliged with a slithery walk before sitting down again and continuing her life story so far. ' . . . men can be so cruel, life can be so very cruel, but I think you have to keep on and break through, fight, I'm a fighter . . . and I'm going to get there . . . I'm very determined.' Nik, unshaven, wearing a canvas and leather windcheater, stoned, arrogant, was standing with head cocked to one side snarling answers to questions and yawning. Gloria was talking to a bunch of women journalists, girls' talk by the look of it. Baby talk. The grey and red journalists didn't have notebooks, they had backs of envelopes and inventive memories. He was getting paced now. A bright, smiling girl carrying a bundle of handouts approached him.

'Hi, Mr Strawley. I'm Moira Goldberg from the Savoy Press Office? Let me get you a drink and introduce you to the U.A. people here. You've probably not met them yet, have you?'

She had a bright chirpy voice, very upbeat, American accented, with a nice quick trill to it. 'They're over there. If you'd like to come this way, I'll take you over. By the way, congratulations on all the marvellous reviews. All merited. I saw the film, and it's *so* good. It's one of the best films I've seen in ages. It's so fresh and new. As if you're re-inventing movies from the beginning.'

'Stay around,' he told her. 'You're just what I want to hear — *and* see.'

'Oh, I will,' she promised with polite flirtatiousness. A nice, enthusiastic sort of girl, a bit gushy maybe, but that was part of the job: full of vim and drive, and pretty too, with that sort of sparky New York outgoingness.

'What you doing in England, Moira?'

'My mother's English, it's my Dad who's American. When they split up she decided to go back to England, and I went to live with her. Don't any more. I live on a houseboat — on the river near Battersea.'

'Sounds romantic.'

'Oh, I love it. I love rivers.'

'Me too.'

'This is Lew Silver,' she said, introducing him to a portly man with bushy, chuckly eyebrows. 'He's the one's going to be looking after your press relations.' Having delivered him into the right hands, she added: 'I'm sure Lew'll take good care of you, he's a sweetie, but if there's anything at all I can do, just call the press office and ask for Moira. Now watch this guy,' she added quickly, lowering her voice, 'he's poison.' She was indicating an approaching journalist with camel-hair coat draped loosely over his shoulders and a long black cigarette jutting from the steep slope of his face. 'Rex Race of the *Daily Express*. Circulation four million plus. Do not be fooled by the cheery manner. A venomous pen has Rex the Race. Hello Rex, you gave me a good laugh last week. You always give me a good laugh, provided you're not writing about anyone I care about.'

'Moira, my sweet,' the columnist told her, 'that guy really needed taking apart. Had a little fun with him, that's all.'

He swivelled stiff-necked, directing the Sobranie cigarette with its gold tip filter in the general direction of Jack Strawley.

'Haven't seen the film yet, but heard the ballyhoo. Doing any business, is it?'

'Broken every opening day record since . . .' Lew Silver began.

' . . . last week? I know, I know. You know what worries me about your film,' Rex Race said swinging towards Jack Strawley, ' — at the same time as it intrigues me — though I haven't yet seen it, as I say, but I do know what it's about.'

'Might help to see it.'

Rex Race brushed this suggestion aside. 'Oh, I will. I certainly will try to get to see it, when I can. But there's so much . . . Jack . . . I can call you Jack? Call me Rex.' He spoke with a slight slur perhaps due to the fact that he kept the long black cigarette in his mouth all the time. 'This hood in the film, I'm told is somebody you know or knew? Was a pal of yours. A contract killer, is that right?'

'Can't make films about people who go home and mow the lawn.'

'Oh, I realize you've got to have action . . .'

While he coped with the questions, he could see that Gloria was having a nice chat with the girl in pearls. Woman to woman. Babies and families and clothes. Carl was standing alone, his fine brow furled in worry for the world, a vodka glaze over his eyes. Nobody talking to him. He waved to him to come over while fending off questions from Rex the Race and others. He was being asked about his announced next project: *The Deafness of Ludwig van Beethoven.* He explained that there would be no large-scale musical performances in the film, that it was princi- pally about Beethoven's deafness to the world, about his failure in human relationships. About the coldness of genius. The theme was taken from something written by Balzac — that genius was a monster which devours all feelings.

Trays with drinks were appearing under his nose every other minute. The clicks in his head were getting faster. Out of the crowd that had formed around him, a member of the press asked if it was true that *Killers Kill,* when it first opened in New York, had been totally ignored.

'Yes,' he said. 'It was spotted, in the first place, due to one of your critics, your Stephen Dall. Then . . . next step was that the French boys took it up. They have this festival of *cinema maudit.* Damned films. *Killers Kill* took the prize. We were the king of the Damned. And there were some fellows from U.A. around, looking for bargains . . . and some others from Germany and Italy. And suddenly we weren't the Damned, we were the Loved, which goes to show — that you can go from being the Damned to being the Loved in one leap. And I should think back again just as fast. Because once you've been called a genius what else can you be called, except a fake genius? It's like you're driving around in a high-powered car never knowing if you've got any gas left in the tank.'

'Afraid you may be running out of gas, Jack, after just one film?' Rex Race inquired, putting in the needle.

Jack nodded his head slowly up and down, up and down, seemingly deliberating the remark, during which time Gloria was looking at him a little anxiously, and the man from U.A. was looking at him, putting on his most beaming public relations smile, and the girl from the Savoy press office was also looking at him, and for her sake if no other reason, this slimy journalist should be put down, he thought.

'Where you journalists have the advantage,' he told him, 'is you got nothing to run out of.'

Next day, just before noon, the girl from the press office, Moira, phoned through to say she had a whole set of his clippings, and did he want to stop by to pick them up, or she could have them sent up to his room. He said to send them up, and ten minutes later there was a knock on the door and she had brought them herself. He wasn't out of bed yet, and Gloria was in the bath. They had just finished breakfast, and there was coffee left in the silver pot: he poured the girl from the press office some and told her to sit down, indicating a tub chair by the bed, and hastily started going through the heap of clippings she had brought him. The reviews of the film were all good, the gossip column stories mixed: some gushing, others with an edge to them. Nik was reported as being uninterested in money, saying that it was a crime for an actor to be rich, a statement that the columnists took with a large pinch of salt. Gloria was interviewed mostly about the baby she was expecting and how it might affect her life and career. 'Your husband has been called a genius. What's it like to live with a genius?' Her discreet answer was: 'Not always easy but very rewarding.' Rex Race's column was headed: '"GENIUS JACK" IS AFRAID OF RUNNING OUT OF GAS.' The story was full of sly sideswipes with a prediction of comeuppances to come. If you considered what Hollywood had done to Charlie Chaplin, Orson Welles, Erich von Stroheim, Clifford Odets, the odds were stacked against so-called geniuses.

'Rex Race . . . oh, God . . . he's such a mediocre man,' Moira Goldberg said. 'He just resents anyone of talent. He has got to deride. He's known for that. Don't take any notice. But I'm afraid you may find yourself stuck with the "genius Jack" tag . . .'

'Which case I'll have to live with it,' he said, not making it sound too punishing a task. He was skimming through some of the other stories. Gloria called through the bathroom door: 'Have we decided where we're going to have lunch?'

'I'm waiting for Sydney to call. Are you nearly ready?'

'I'm doing my hair . . . fifteen minutes.'

'My God, did I say that?' he asked Moira Goldberg, his eye having come upon an unlikely sounding quote. 'You were standing right by me.'

'That's press interviews for you.'

'They make them up?'

'They're inclined to be inventive. They didn't get you at all.'

'What didn't they get, in your opinion, Moira?' Her dark hair was gathered away from the face, done in a french pleat at the back: a neat and practical style for the working girl. She had her legs crossed, one twisted under the other complicatedly. Very complicated legs. A complicated girl, no doubt, under that fresh cheery American career-girl complexion.

'Oh, they got the tough, ambitious New York savage OK. What they didn't get is the rest of the story.'

'What's the rest of the story?'

'Sounds corny but . . . well, the vulerable side.'

'You think I have a vulnerable side?'

The phone rang, and he picked it up swiftly, saying nothing, not even Hello, just listening. After a couple of minutes of listening, he snapped into the receiver:

'Sydney, tell Dore I love what he did at RKO and couldn't be happier that he wants us. But the six months I was at MGM he didn't come up with anything for me and now he wants to say he *discovered* me? And I have some moral obligation of loyalty to him? Because he paid me a few hundred bucks to hang around. Other things being equal — namely, the money — I'd rather accept Zanuck's offer. Darryl's a fire-eater, Schary's an Alka Seltzer-eater, that's the difference between them. It's true that Schary's read books, but on the other hand he gets backaches at critical moments . . . which can be more of a disadvantage than not having read books. Tell him that if he can't meet our price — and you better up it by a few thou — it's off, I'm not going to trade dollars for nostalgia . . . that I'm not very nostalgic about. You want to have lunch, Sydney? Come here at quarter of one. We'll go down to the Grill. I have to be here.' He put down the phone. 'You were saying, Moira. About my vulnerable side?'

She laughed. 'Maybe you have to look hard for that. You don't let anything stand in your way, do you? You're very determined to be . . . *great*. And why not?' She wore a slimly cut blue suit: cool, neat, professionally correct.

'Don't sound too attractive — huh?'

'Somebody wanting what you want, and going for it hard, lot of people'd consider that attractive in a man.'

'You one of the lot of people?'

'Why d'you wanna know what the heck *I* think?'

'You must be quite an expert — on men going for it hard.'

She gave a little laugh. 'I have come across the type,' she acknowledged, 'and a lot of them are nothing to write home about as human beings. Or as men, for that matter. But I wouldn't say, from what I've seen, you're one of those.'

'What makes me different?'

She thought about this, as if it was a brain-teaser, a half-smile on her face.

'I guess what makes you different,' she said eventually, 'is that you really do have some genius, I'd say, and that's where your first loyalty lies. I'm not so sure about your second loyalty.' She smiled with bright eyes.

'You're very astute, as well as flattering. A little less public-ity gush, please. You're giving me a lot of insights into my character. I don't imagine that's normally part of the job of press officer.'

'Hey, I'm not the press officer. I'm a little young to be press officer of the Savoy. I'm one of her assistants.'

'How old are you?'

'Twenty.'

'What does being an assistant press officer at the Savoy entail, Moira?'

'Oh, handing around drinks and bringing celebrities their press clippings in bed. Being agreeable to slimy journalists on the phone. That sort of thing. It's a start.'

'For what? That coffee must be cold . . . let me get them to send up some more.'

He reached to pick up the phone. Flesh-coloured seamed nylons. Restless knees. That constant crossing and uncrossing of legs, indicating energies difficult to hold down.

'I drink too much coffee. Makes me jumpy . . . I've got to get back. Lot of important people arriving today. Who have to be cossetted.'

He put the phone back in its cradle. 'What's it a start for? You said it was a start.'

'I haven't worked that out exactly. After my parents got the divorce . . .' She stopped herself. 'Oh, you don't want to know about me.'

'Yes, I do.'

'It's nothing special, up till now. But it will be.'

'Yeah, I have a hunch it will. I'd guess you're very able.'

'That's true. I am. I can do the press officer's job better than she can. You mind immodesty in a woman?'

'No. I find it rather attractive, if you want to know.'

On/off bursts of the hair-drier from within the bathroom indicated that Gloria was in the course of setting her hair.

'You have an American cigarette, by any chance?'

He gave her a cigarette and lit if for her.

'I've got to go,' she said again, not making any sign of moving.

'We could go and have coffee somewhere,' he proposed, 'since this has all got cold.'

She hesitated, and then said: 'You have a lunch date with Sydney. Your wife's drying her hair. And you're not exactly dressed.'

'Won't take me a minute to put something on.'

'Okay. Coffee then.'

He threw off the sheets and got out of bed. His clothes were on a chair by the one on which she was sitting and he had to pass in front of her. For an instant she turned her head away slightly, smiling, but then considering this a little coy, and not being a coy girl, she allowed her eyes to pass glancingly over him. When he had dressed, he called to Gloria through the bathroom door: 'Darling, I have to go and do something for about ten minutes.'

Waiting for the elevator to arrive, he said to Moira Goldberg: 'You drink too much coffee. You said.'

'I do, that's right.'

'So why don't we skip the coffee?'

'If you like.'

'Instead of coffee, why don't you show me one of the other rooms here? For when I come back next?'

'What sort of room you interested in?'

'One with a view of the river. High up. I like to be high up.'

For about half a minute she stayed looking at the geometrically-patterned bronze elevator doors, not saying anything. She seemed to be wholly concerned about when the elevator was going to be there and did not look at him at all. When it was finally there and the doors had opened, she said, still without giving him a glance:

'Wait for me on the top floor. I'll get a key.'

He let her take the elevator down, and got into one that was going up. He waited for her on the landing. She arrived a few minutes later with a key, saying nothing. She opened the door of the room she had chosen, and said: 'You have a good view of the river from here.'

He went to take a look from the window while she remained in the centre.

'You like this room?' she asked him. He didn't answer, but walked slowly over to her. 'Assistants to the press officer have to do a lot of menial things,' she said smiling, 'but showing rooms is not normally part of the job.'

'Well, I do appreciate you doing it for me.'

There was a silence that was getting long.

She asked, 'You like the view?'

'The view's great, Moira. A very beautiful view.'

'I'm glad you like it. We aim to please at the Savoy.'

'And you do. You do. Very much so.'

Absent-mindedly he hooked one finger around a large mother-of-pearl button on her jacket, tugging lightly, very lightly, on it. Her body was in tense equilibrium between the tug of his finger and her own weight. He was little by little drawing her towards him by the finest of threads.

'You're going to pull that button right off.'

'Not if you come a bit nearer.'

'You've got to remember,' she said, 'that I work here, and this being the Savoy, we can't go around with buttons missing.'

'I understand that,' he said, letting go of the button, drawing her by the waist instead, and then letting his hand slide downward.

' . . . we're . . . expected to be well . . . turned-out,' she said. 'And unrumpled.'

'You're very clear-thinking, Moira,' he said withdrawing his hand and letting go of her. 'Now — if you hung up your clothes, they wouldn't get rumpled.'

'Very true,' she allowed.

She did not look at him while she quickly took off the jacket and hung it on a wooden hanger, and then the skirt which she hung up on hooks, and then pulled the knee-length pale peach satin petticoat over her head, and though she was fast, he was faster than her.

She looked at him wonderingly, amazed to find herself — and him — both naked like this.

'So what now?' she asked twiddling her thumbs. By way of answer he lifted her up at the waist, and she said, 'Oh, I see. I see. They're gonna have to call you Jack-in-the-box, huh?' As he lowered her bit by bit, she accused breathlessly: 'Oh, I can see you like to torture . . .'

'Feel free to scream.'

'Yeah, I will.'

'What are you thinking?' he asked her, a while later, observing the distance spreading out between them, which had been down to nothing just a few moments before.

'I'm thinking Gloria will have finished drying her hair and be wondering where you are, and that you're late for your lunch date with Sydney.' She was swiftly getting dressed. 'Well, if you really want to know what I was thinking, I was thinking . . . what am I doing here? Because, while I enjoyed that, for what it was, I don't really know what it was. Don't you think you should get dressed?'

'You're a lovely girl,' he told her. He pulled on underpants and trousers.

'Woman,' she said, buttoning her blouse. 'I wish you wouldn't call me a girl. I'm not a girl, you know. Even though I'm pretty young. OK. So I'm a lovely woman, yes? And now what?' She looked at her watch.

'I'm not going to give you any story. I don't think you'd want that. Gloria and I are very close, it's a good marriage. And necessary to me. If anything came between us, we'd come apart torn and bleeding.'

She nodded understandingly. 'So this was just — a little light day music. Nothing wrong with that.' She was completely dressed now, except for her shoes.

'It was very wonderful,' he said formally.

'Yeah, it was for me too,' she said, her voice becoming formal too. She sat on the bed and put her shoes on. 'Shame about the "torn and bleeding" angle, because it might have been nice to know you more. But I'm a pragmatist, so I understand. You better decide where you've been . . . ' she looked at her watch. ' . . . for half an hour. In case Gloria should ask.'

'Gloria doesn't check up on me.'

'Well, if she does ask, you better say you came down to the press office. There were some clippings I'd forgotten to show you. You were reading your clippings?'

'You're foresightful and efficient as well . . . you're going to end up running MGM.'

'It's on my list.'

'What else is on your list?'

'To be happy with a man I love, who loves me.'

'That might be harder. Not because you wouldn't be easy to love, but because . . . men are such wild beasts, aren't they?'

'Are they? You love Gloria, don't you?'

'Yes.' He puckered his brow. He now was fully dressed too. 'But it's more complicated.'

'Yeah, I can imagine.'

'Maybe you can't.'

'So, this is where we say goodbye?'

'You ever come to New York? Because if you do, give me a ring and . . . '

'No, I won't give you a ring,' she said. 'It's not my nature to hang around hopefully. And I wouldn't want to cause any of that torn and bleeding.'

He kissed her strongly.

'Yeah, that felt very final,' she said. He said nothing while she examined his face, placing it firmly in memory. They went to the lift. They had it to themselves but didn't speak.

At the third floor, she said: 'This is your floor. Go on, get out . . . and be great.'

'You too.'

Carver's overlong form was curled up tight as a metal spring inside the narrow telephone booth in the Savoy lobby. The smoke from one of his foul little Dutch cigars made the cubicle look as if it was in the course of being fumigated. Seen through the glass of the door, he appeared to be shouting. He signalled to Jack that he was nearly through and, opening the door and venting some of the foul smoke into the lobby with vigorous hand movements, was heard to say before he hung up: 'Charge this to Room 304.'

'What you charging to my room this time, Sydney?'

'Been trying since last night to get through to Darryl, finally got him.'

'Why were you shouting at him?'

'The line was bad. Also, he was shouting at me.'

'I thought he was pleased we decided to go with him instead of MGM.'

'It's nothing to worry about, Jack. Have no fear.'

'Sydney, the one thing panics me is you saying nothing to worry about.'

'I told him it was totally ridiculous.'

'What is ridiculous?'

'The Winchell smear.'

'What Winchell smear?'

'That you're involved with the Commies.'

'Is that what he said?'

'He dropped one of his ton-heavy hints.'

'Saying?'

'He says your closest friend and collaborator, Carl Schmidlin, is not only the present Mrs Strawley's previous big passion but a red-hot Red-lover to boot. Signs off, "So ain't that cosy for Mrs Strawley and the Ruskies".'

'Zanuck's influenced by that garbage?'

'I think I was able to put Darryl's mind at rest.'

'How'd you do that, Sydney?'

'I told him: "Jack's no more of a Red than you are, Darryl." I said there was no truth in it. "Forget it, Darryl," I said.'

'What he say?'

'Well, he didn't say. More like . . . screamed. If there's no truth in it, where did Winchell get that stuff from? I told him how should I know what garbage bins Winchell gets his stuff out of, and I took the opportunity to remind him, delicately, that on the strength of his offer — his word on the phone "which I know is your bond," I told him, — we had turned down Schary, who had been bitterly disappointed. So we expected him and Twentieth to honour the agreement, even if nothing is actually signed yet.'

'What he say to that?'

'Said he wanted to sleep on it.'

'Let's go back to MGM. Let's go back to Schary and the bad back.'

'Not on. I called Dore before I called Darryl. I didn't tell Darryl that, of course. He told me MGM had regretfully withdrawn.'

'They were so eager just yesterday.'

'Yesterday the Winchell column hadn't come out yet.'

'Schary's . . . a man of honour, a Democrat, a liberal . . . a humanist. Schary's not a man to be influenced by gutter gossip. . . .'

'Of course Schary wouldn't be influenced by that shit. His reason — is you're too expensive.'

'Tell him we'll give him a little price-cut.'

'I think a hundred bucks a week'd be too expensive right now, what with his bad back and all. My reading is: spare me the *tsuris*! Look . . . don't give it a thought. It'll clear itself up. I put my trust in Darryl. He doesn't knuckle under to anyone — what Darryl will do is he'll check into your background and provided you're clean — which I have assured him you are, 100% — he'll come through, no problem . Just have to sit this one out for a while. Here's Gloria.'

Gloria was coming out of the elevator, looking ravishing: being pregnant gave her an extra glow. She had the beginning of a question on her face, and he saw her glance at the clock. She was on the point of asking what had occupied him so long, then decided not to ask.

She said, 'I'm starving. I have to eat for two now.'

'Yes, you do.'

She looked at him sharply. 'Something wrong?'

'Nothing Sydney can't fix, he says.' He reached for Gloria's hand and held onto it tight, experiencing a sudden sensation of falling. That really would be a record: to fall before he'd even risen any way.

She saw him grin as if his life depended on it and said: 'Jack, there always are problems. I know that from Mother. Even when things are going fantastically, there's always a catch. Always. Whatever this one is, you'll overcome it. Because you have made a good film, and you have talent . . . and that gets you through.'

18

It was the sudden come-down after all the highs: that was what made it so hard for him. When he'd least expected it. Fitted in with his theory that catastrophe approached out of the corner of your eye . . . no build-up shots. No progression, no Max Steiner score. You couldn't plot its course. Wham! It was there. On top of you. It was getting him down because he hadn't been prepared for it. Had thought he was there, and then suddenly . . . this. When they wanted you, the studios phoned and cabled five times a day, *and* in the night, but when they were off the boil there were a hundred reasons why they weren't able to get back to you. And they were definitely off the boil now. Zanuck had put *The Deafness* in turnaround. Gone cold on the material. Even apart from the clearance problem. The moment you were in question on one level, everything else was put in question as well. Suddenly it no longer seemed like such a good subject, a film about a deaf old man with sublime music in his head and bitterness and animosity in his heart. Suddenly Jack Strawley didn't seem to be such a genius on the basis of one low-budget crime picture.

'It'll take a little time,' Sydney told him on the phone from New York, 'because they got to check through all the stuff in the investigators' report.'

'What fucking investigators' report?'

'Yeah, they do that now. The studios. They hired a private investigation company, who specialize in this kind of research work, to look into your record and write them a confidential report. I haven't seen it, but there are three categories, and you didn't come out in the right one, which is "See", meaning "could find nothing". You came out between "Bee", which means questionable, and "Very Que", which means very questionable.'

'What am I supposed to be very questionable about?'

'I don't know. I'm trying to find out. If I can get hold of a copy of the report I'll send it to you. Meanwhile enjoy yourself. Take a vacation. Whatever you do, don't come back — they're liable to serve a subpoena on you, and that we don't want. I have feelers out . . . something'll emerge. What I said in the beginning holds — I *know* I can get you everything you want. This is a temporary problem. I'm not back tracking one step, I have total belief in your future, Jack, only you're gonna have to postpone it a little.'

'Am I blacklisted?'

'You're sort of graylisted. I don't think they got anything on you personally. My hunch is it's all to do with Carl and Gloria.'

'To me that's pretty personal, Sydney.'

They'd had to come down abruptly from the high expenditure bracket that they had got into during the euphoria surrounding the London opening of *Killers Kill*; euphoria for which United Artists had picked up the tab while the film was being launched.

Now he and Gloria were on their own, having to pay for everything themselves, and he had long ago gone through the small sum he'd been paid for directing *Killers Kill*. He was earning nothing, and Gloria was earning nothing; they were living on her capital, and there was the baby on the way. Obviously they couldn't go on living at the Savoy and had started apartment hunting for something that was right in terms of locale while also being affordable. Eventually they'd found a place in Bolton Steet. It was on the fourth floor, without an elevator, and a bit dingy, with offices below, but the location couldn't have been better — between Curzon Street and Piccadilly, with Green Park just five minutes' walk away. Perfect for when the baby was born, perfect for access to the places he needed to have access to.

It was a mad thing for him to have done. They had no money and he'd gone out and bought a Jaguar XK150. He'd bought it second-hand for only £350, which he considered a great bargain. It was a superb car, with that quick surge of power at your fingertips — and the perfect colour, too, racing green — and so he had to have it, even if it was extravagant in their present circumstances, even if its petrol consumption was horrendous. He'd bought it on the spur of the moment, although he had no money in his account, and Gloria had had to cover the cheque.

'You realize,' she told him, 'that's one year's rent you've just blown.'

'I had to have it,' he said, uncontrite. 'Listen, two weeks ago I could have earned that in a couple of days.'

'That was two weeks ago.'

He reproached her: 'Oh, ye of little faith.'

On Sundays, when the telephone in Bolton Street was not ringing so much, and there was no need to run up and down the four flights of stairs every couple of hours to look in the mail box, they got into the XK150 and zipped out to Hampstead to spend the day with Carl. They usually left the car in the car park opposite Well Walk and set out to follow Carl's regular morning tramp on the Heath. The walk took them across wild grassland with sizeable areas of marshy ground, past oaks that were 250 years old, down into steep hollows, up over mounds of stones and dead branches and fallen trees. They tramped through a springy compost of pine needles and decomposing leaves. There were asphalted footpaths by which to get to Kenwood, but Carl showed them where he walked when he was alone, and on those occasions he enjoyed the solitude of the less explored paths and the mystery and dimness of areas where you had to find your way by orientating yourself in relation to the sound of traffic coming from the main roads.

Usually, the one-way tramp was enough walking for Gloria in her condition of advanced pregnancy, and she stayed at Kenwood House, had a coffee and looked at the Rembrandts and Constables while Jack and Carl walked back across the Heath to where they'd left the car.

Today Carl was following a newly-found path through a dim copse. He didn't look round at all for orientation, seemed to know where he was going. It was a narrow path that had to be taken in single file. Carl was in front, speaking almost to himself, in the way he sometimes did when trying out lines to hear how they would play, although he was not a good actor of his own lines, and others could lend them greater credibility. In his slightly stilted way, head tilted marginally to one side, he was speaking over his shoulder to Jack, who followed close behind. Perhaps it helped not being face to face.

'. . . I've made him a young American poet in the play, utterly without scruples — women seem to find that erotic.' Swallows dived and screeched above the matted branches. 'It's a good part, the poet, he's very clever, something of a charlatan, and a thief — at any rate he steals other men's women and wine, petty crimes like that, and other people's work, which is more serious — genius steals, he says, echoing Stravinsky — that's his approach . . . that capitalist society is really an open invitation to the thief. As well as being a thief, he's extraordinarily talented . . . or a complete fake. I haven't made up my mind which.'

They had come out of the copse and into a wide stretch of grassland, with the car park straight ahead.

'Sounds as though I'm the person to direct it,' Jack said.

'Yes, I think you probably are. And there's a good part for Gloria. But don't tell her just yet. It's not finished, and I don't really know how to end it. One of them will have to die, I suppose, I can't think of any other way of ending it, but I haven't yet decided who . . . or how.'

Gloria appeared to need a great deal of sleep since becoming pregnant. A lassitude had come over her; it was as if the baby not only fulfilled her physically but also arrested all desire to assert herself in other ways. It seemed quite sufficient for her to simply pay heed to the needs of the growing new life within her without thinking of anything else. She was less interested now in 'the crimson joy'. Its purpose having been achieved, there was no longer any need for love's frenzies; it could be calm and soft and at convenient times, instead of in response to some sudden overwhelming imperative. She urged him: 'Gently, gently . . . the baby, the baby.'

'He's not watching us, you know. Not yet.'

'But he is. They know everything that goes on. It doesn't have to be so rough . . . it's also very nice gentle. Shhhhh! Go easy, darling.'

As if in anticipation of her new little lover due to arrive shortly, she seemed to obtain her most intense joy at her breasts, now splendidly lush. At her climax there was a taste of milk in his mouth.

He looked at her asleep and found her beautiful, more beautiful than she had ever been, but in a different way, it was the beauty of a Lippi Madonna, with a quality of virginal purity, self-sufficiency . . . and complacency. 'Oh, I do love you, I love you so much, darling,' she told him over and over again while he collapsed within her. And then she asked with wide innocent eyes: 'Oh, but what happened? That's not like you.' And he had to blame it on the whisky, of which he was drinking a considerable amount now. When she asked him to go easy on it, he snapped back: 'I know. Go easy. Go easy. His majesty . . . is watching. I'm going to go so easy, pretty soon I won't need to breathe.'

Half of him was not there. He was using only half his mind,

half his body, living only half his life — the husband, the
father-to-be, the alien who had to have his Registration book
stamped by the police every few weeks. Who had to have a
work permit and a residence permit. Perhaps also a permit to
exist. He was slowing down to the point where he risked coming to a complete stop. 'You see, Gloria, you get on a train and
then you can't get off . . . you can't get off the fucking train,
that's the problem about trains. That you can't get off them.
They won't let you.'

She came straight out with it then, feeling the confinement
that he felt and his resentment of her for confining him.

'Pull the emergency cord, buster!'

But how could he pull the cord, dammit, with a baby coming
and the money problems. They were living on Gloria's money,
Gloria had paid for the car, Gloria paid the rent and his restaurant
and bar bills at the end of the month. And lately it wasn't even
with her money, because that had run out too, but her mother's.

Carver's covering note was brief and noncommittal. He wrote:
'I've succeeded in obtaining the Hartwright Research and Secu-
rity Corporation's report on you to Twentieth, which has probably circulated throughout the industry by now. Here it is. Call
me and we'll talk.'

He read it pencil in hand, making notes in the margin:

'For identification purposes: this report is on Jack Strawley,
born Jan. 31 1930, at Haversville, Massachusetts, son of Alfred
(Fred) S. Strawley, insurance adjustor and Benita Fay Thurley,
spinster, without occupation.

'Nothing known prior to October 1949 when he took up
unpaid employment as an asstistant stage manager with the
Tramline Theatre Co., in a former tram depot/warehouse building situated on the West Side at Greenwich Street below Canal.
Company run as a Communist-style collective by Gloria Vanderveld, actress, daughter of the well-known actress Louise
Vanderveld (married to influential movie and theatre agent
George Jakes) and her first husband, Hubert Vanderveld, stage
designer.

'In Sept 1949 Gloria Vandervelde was co-habiting at her apartment on West Tenth Street, Manhattan, with Carl Schmidlin, born Vienna, March 9, 1922, of Israelite persuasion, a refugee of Austrian nationality, previously resident in London, England, who was issued with immigration visa no. 4766 at the American Embassy, London, in December 1946. Schmidlin was at that time a member of the British Communist Party (not declared in his visa application).

'Schmidlin befriended Jack Strawley some time in 1948/49. They lived at that time within ten minutes' walk of each other and both frequented Lower East Side Austrian, Polish, Russian and other Eastern European cafés and restaurants, as well as artists' bars in Greenwich Village. They regularly patronized cinemas such as the Academy of Music, on East 14th Street, where foreign films were shown, including Russian films; the Thalia cinema, which has held festivals of films by the Russian director and friend of Stalin, S. N. Eisenstein, Loew's Sheridan on 7th Ave, and the 8th Street Playhouse. They also patronized Womrath's bookstore on 8th, where Communistic literature is sold. In 1951, Schmidlin signed a petition appealing the sentencing of Julius and Ethel Rosenberg convicted of espionage in behalf of the Soviet Union against the United States. He was a member of, or had present or past connections (in some cases liaising from Britain during the war), with the following 'front' organizations in the US:

National Citizens Political Action Committee
American Committee for the Protection of the Foreign Born
Joint Anti-Fascist Refugee Committee
Civil Rights Congress

Schmidlin was the principal organizer of the Tompkins Square film society, which made a speciality of showing Russian films and included in its lecture programme lectures by Communist party members or fellow travellers including Hollywood screenwriter W.V. Kyser (one-time associate of Russian director Eisenstein, the friend of Stalin.) In his evidence before the House Un-American Activities Committee, in June 1952, Kyser named twelve people whom he had personally recruited into Communist front organizations in the Los Angeles area, and stated that, in New York, meetings of the Tompkins Square film society's film appreciation seminars (organised by Schmidlin) were a cover for planning Communistic infiltration strategies. He stated that Gloria Vanderveld and Carl Schmidlin had attended several such meetings, and Jack Strawley at least one.

'As the lover of the woman who ran the Tramline Theatre, Carl Schmidlin was influential in directing the theatre's policy towards staging so-called 'progressive' plays, including two of his own, and works by Bertolt Brecht with music by Hans Eisler (both now resident in East Germany). He was instrumental in obtaining employment for Jack Strawley at the Tramline and in giving him the chance to make his debut as a director of works that he, Schmidlin, had written, namely: *Suicide Note,* and *Hotel Metropole.* Schmidlin is also the author of an unpublished short story, *The Death Artist,* from which Strawley derived the idea (though this is nowhere indicated in the credits) for his film *Killers Kill.*

'In view of the foregoing, we suggest that Carl Schmidlin be listed as "Very Que", and Jack Strawley and Gloria Vanderveld (now Mrs Strawley) as somewhere between "Bee" (questionable) and "Very Que". While we have not found direct evidence so far of Strawley's Communistic affiliations, his and his wife's strong personal links with the Communistically affiliated Carl Schmidlin render Strawley's position questionable. Unless able by personal testimony to clear up the questionable points in his record, we feel that his employment might be highly embarrassing to the Studio.

Best wishes,

Hubert Frinkley, Snr. investigator'

Over a very crackly fading/surging line to L.A., Carver said:

'Their attitude is that these things may not be a crime but that they're suggestive of certain orientations, and all they're doing is issuing invitations, that's all, not warrants for arrest, invitations to come on down and see them and talk it over. Explain yourself. Say who you are. Where you're pointing. They want to be reassured that you're a loyal citizen and love the United States.'

The crackling had become particularly bad. It was like shouting into a howling gale.

'They want me to crawl . . .' Sydney interrupted him, but what he was saying wasn't clear with the bad line. 'Sydney, I can't hear what you said. I can't hear you. Call me back.'

'Jack, you hear me? Listen, Jack. What I said is *there is another way.*'

'What? Sydney, can't hear a word you say, all I can hear are echoes, call me back . . .'

'I said there is another way that doesn't involve crawling.'

'What's it involve?' he shouted back. The line had suddenly become clear and the peristent echo that had been punctuating Carver's words with ghostly reiterations thankfully was gone, and now his voice was crystelline in its clarity and logic and mastery of tactics.

'Involves money.'

'How much money?'

'Twenty-five grand or thereabouts. Maybe a little more, maybe a little less.'

'I don't have a little more or a little less, I don't have anything. I'm broke, Sydney.'

'Borrow it.'

'Against what?'

'Against your future, Jack. Against your glittering future . . .'

'Who's going to lend me against my glittering future?'

'I am.'

'Where you going to get it from, Sydney?'

'Don't worry about that. It's just money.'

The line had become echoey again and was rather ominously reiterating Carver's words.

He'd become a father now, and this was a factor he hadn't as yet fully integrated into his life. It was something to do with him but he did not know exactly what. It was outside the subject of his life, a kind of diversion from the main way. He adored the baby, a pretty little girl they'd decided to call Anna: she seemed straight away to have fallen in love with her father, and while other people's babies made his skin crawl, it was clear that he was totally smitten with this dazzling little cocotte while at the same time resenting the further curtailment of his freedom of action that her arrival imposed on him. It was another tie. The flat in Bolton Street had only two rooms, there was nowhere to put a nanny; so one of them had to always be there to look after the baby, or they had to employ baby-sitters, which meant being home by a certain time of night, normally before midnight, and he couldn't conduct his life in such a strictly ordered fashion. He took the restrictions badly, refused to adhere to them: it was necessary for him to 'make an appearance' in certain places in order that people would be aware of his existence, otherwise you were dead. You were very quickly dead in this business . . . and when he went to make an appearance somewhere, to show that he was not dead, he often went by himself and, not having to be home by midnight on such occasions, sometimes stayed out till three or four in the morning. Gloria resented the fact that he allowed himself such freedom of movement while she was obliged to stay home and look after the baby. In their present circumstances, without any help, there was no point in her even trying to get work, and the fact that she had not received many offers prior to the baby's birth did not lessen her sense of grievance at having to sacrifice her career as an actress for the sake of her marriage. 'What about me showing myself, to show that *I'm* still around? That I still exist?' she demanded.

To which he had replied: 'All right. We can take turns.'

'You want me to go out by myself and get picked up?'

'I have complete trust in you, Gloria.'

'I know that's what *you* do.'

'I trust you, but you don't trust me.'

'You have no reason not to trust me, whereas I do have some reason not to trust you.'

It didn't make her more tolerant of their situation that it was she who footed the bills for his gallivanting, since they were living largely on her money, borrowed from her mother and George. Jack had no shame about running up huge bills in bars and nightclubs and restaurants, to which he invariably added extravagant tips — 20% or more. He said that he could not afford to be seen *not* giving large tips. As soon as he had a film to make they'd be able to move to a larger place, perhaps a house with a garden, and then they'd be able to employ a nanny, Gloria would be free to work again, and their whole lifestyle would be totally different. They wouldn't be so exhausted from being woken three times a night by the baby crying, they'd be able to get back to the married life they'd had before. Because at the moment their marriage was no marriage, he said menacingly. But he was prepared to wait for it to get better. He was working on it. What did she think he was doing? If he was out hustling, it was for both their sakes and for the sake of their marriage.

He had come to the conclusion, with some bitterness, that there was something about motherhood that rendered women asexual. They became smug and lazy with having fulfilled their role. Now it was all the baby, the baby. There was this huge difference between being two and being three. It meant he was not the only one anymore. There it was, another life, with its insistent needs and demands in direct competition with his own needs and demands. The rival. And Gloria now had the motherly self-satisfaction of having brought a new life into the world. No more crimson joy. They were the parents now, not young lovers with boiling blood, and so had to be 'parental' even when they fucked. She held him to her, passively, calmly, as if she were feeding him at the breast too. Now he sometimes could not muster the drive that had always been omnipresent before, and this she took as a sign that he was getting over the frenzies and was becoming more 'mature', more caring, while he took it as a sign of physical decline.

One day, seeing how much he had been drinking and how angry he was because the producer he had rung hadn't rung back all morning, she said, attempting to soothe him down:

'You think you're the only one who wants success. You think I don't want it just as much.'

'Well, you're keeping pretty calm about it, in that case.'

'Darling, you can't force it to happen, nobody's all-powerful. I'm also ambitious.' She was wearing box pleated tweed skirt and twin set. She dressed like some lady of the shires these days. Sensible shoes. Wore her reading glasses. Hair cut short . . . practical. At least she didn't sit around in curlers and dressing gown, like some. 'We've got everything we need to be happy,' she told him. 'We *are* happy. You just don't realize it.'

'Well as long as you realize it, then that's all all right, isn't it?'

'Throughout the credits', he told Carl, 'the telephone is ringing and not being answered. It's an insistent, panicky sound. We get some jazz and some modern dissonant music behind the ringing. Sometimes it sound like cats. Sometimes like a baby bawling and sometimes like fucking. We'll play around with the sound. Then we go close on Harry Stonier holding the ringing phone, and it's still not answering, and he's sweating and thinking . . . imagining things. And then the phone is picked up, we don't see the person at the other end, we only see Harry, and Harry says: "Where were you?" and at the other end, in Baden-Baden, Leonora replies, only we don't see her or hear what she says, the POV is Harry's, and he says, "You were stuck in the elevator? My God, for how long? That's a disgrace, in a five-star hotel. Were you very frightened?" Are you with me this far, Carl?'

'Go on,' Carl said noncommittally.

'Okay, now comes the scene in the elevator. Leonora and the poet screwing. Cut back to Harry Stonier, holding the phone. The scene we have just seen has passed through Stonier's mind . . . so is it his jealous imagination, or did it really happen? Or both? Both jealous imagination and real. These are questions we are never going to conclusively answer. We want to leave it open to the audience's imagination.'

'And what has really happened?' Carl asked.

'I don't know. How should I know? I'm just making the film. And even that hasn't really happened . . . yet. But it will.'

'Will it? My plays tend not to happen.'

Carl was such a fucking pessimist, as always. When Jack's mind was taking off, Carl was pulling him back down. Carl had come close to having a success with *Hotel Metropole*, Kazan having been interested in doing it on Broadway, but Kazan had wanted to change too many things, and Carl had said he'd think about it, and while he was thinking about it Kazan had decided to do something else instead. Carl had absolutely no feeling for the main chance. Came from examining everything from every angle to find the catch, instead of just plunging in. In New York, when he'd first known him, Carl had possessed a Bohemian glamour. Jack had been bowled over by him, but later it had all gotten more and more difficult for Carl. In London, living in that gloomy basement flat, alone, with the old ladies in the upper rooms, no woman in his life, the habitual tone of irony in his voice was sounding more and more like bitterness. Gallows humour.

'Carl, if you write it the way I'm suggesting, it'll happen. Have faith in me. I can make it happen.' Carl was shaking his head doubtfully. 'It's your story, Carl. I'm just giving it a framework that makes it a film. You want to tie up all the loose ends, I want to leave them loose.'

'In a murder story, the author, if nobody else, must know who did it.'

'In a conventional murder story, yes. But I want it to be a murder story in which the author doesn't know. A murder mystery without a solution.'

'It's a smart idea but unworkable.'

'Carl, you just have to write it. I'll make it work.'

It was a cold blustery day, with kites being flown. Some of them, seized in powerful air spirals, were soaring up on a sudden gust, making everybody run and pull hard on the strings; and then someone pulled too hard, and the weightless skein of canvas and balsa wood came crashing down.

19

The phone call from Carver as usual required careful decoding to separate the over-statements and the under-statements, the true from the almost-true, the almost-true from the damned lies.

'Jack, I talked to Burton. He says he saw *Killers Kill* and liked it a lot and would love to make a film with you. I've talked to him about *The Interloper.* No, he hasn't read it himself, but he knows what it's about and is intrigued. What? He's intrigued by the concept. He doesn't want to do another epic. The question is do we want him? Look, I'm not pissing on Burton, but the question in my mind is how much does Burton *really* mean in box office terms. I don't even know how good an actor he is *on the screen.*'

Decoded, this meant we can't get Burton, his reader's report pissed on the script but don't worry, we don't want Burton anyway.

'So where are we, Sydney?'

'Schary is very interested. He's high on it. Provided we can get clearance for you from the Committee, and provided we can give him a star name to hang it on and do it for a budget of under half a mil.'

'Those provideds are mutually contradictory, Sydney.'

'I know. I'm working on that.'

'Has he read Carl's script?'

'Officially, no. He can't have read Carl's script because of Carl's "Very Que" standing with the Committee. Unofficially, I can tell you he likes the concept.'

'The concept?'

'The bottom line is he wants to make a film with you, if we can line it up right.'

'How?'

'Be patient. I'm working on it for you. I guarantee to come up with something.'

His lunch appointment with the producer Herbert Moneypenny — or Hubert Honeymoney, he could never remember which — wasn't until 1:00, but he wanted to arrive a little early at the restaurant in Curzon Street, to see who was there and to show that he was there, because if you were not there, where were you?

Although the restaurant was only ten minutes away, on foot, he took the Jag, since the high-powered dash up Curzon Street might boost his morale somewhat. It was raining heavily, and

Brian the doorman protected him with the green umbrella for the three steps to the canopy. Inside, there was a small blockage around the cloakroom counter. The girl with the steeply piled hair had taken off her ocelot coat and was waiting to deposit it on top of an assorted pile of minks and assorted lesser furs and macs. She looked back over her shoulders at Jack, and uttered an enthusiastic 'Hi!', while clearly not quite able to place who he was, and he said 'Hi!' back, as enthusiastically, without any idea who she was.

'Cold enough for you, Mr Strawley?' Giovanni wanted to know. 'And who are we having lunch with today, Mr Strawley?'

'I'm meeting Mr Moneypenny.'

'Mr Honeypenny, yes of course,' Giovanni said. 'Do you wish to go to the table straight away, sir, or wait at the bar?'

'The bar.'

At the clamorous bar sat Rex Race like a bronze sculpture of The Drinker, buttonhole, white silk tie, crocodile cigarette case.

'Not a bad selection of fillies today,' Rex Race told Jack Strawley. 'I'd be ready to put a coupl'o'bob on that one over there.'

'Which one?'

'With the Borgia brothers.'

The filly's eyes were not too firmly fixed on the race she was running in and eventually they encountered Jack's. It was the redhead he'd seen around: the one in the jersey jumper through which the sharp points of her stiffly brassiered breasts thrust out like spearheads. Three barmen in orange bolero jackets worked with accomplished swiftness, reaching for bottles on the mirrored shelves behind them, pouring, shaking, mixing, stirring and garnishing while grinning and chatting at the same time. As he reached the point of ordering, one of the three, Franco, pouring vodka into a glass sparkling and crackling with ice, called out over the high electric hum of interleaved conversations: 'A long time no see, Mr Straw? At least a week. What happen to you?'

'Siegi and Mario also have to live, you know. Whisky, Franco. Just a dash of soda.' He gave a wide grin. 'And the name's Strawley, Franco.' Franco laughed, threw up his hand. 'Mr

Strawley, yes sir. Sorry, sir. How you keeping, sir? And the beautiful Mrs Straw?'

'Very fit.'

He looked around. Pretty young women in the company of not very pretty but very sleek older men. Well-known faces whose names he had forgotten. Or never known. People you saw in this place and in other places. Men in drape jackets. Girls in hissing silk. A tingling eroticism in the smoky air. An inflammatory mix of the beautiful and the moneyed. The bar was filling up fast; he saw Moira Goldberg come in with Bruce Tucker, and all eyes were on the American star. Moira was looking cool and crisp in a cream suit with a tailored jacket, sloping pockets that drew your attention to the hips. And why not? Her hips were very worthy of attention. She looked good in suits. She didn't seem to notice him as she and Tucker were being steered through the crush towards their table. For some reason seeing her made him want to weep. He realized that he had been wanting to weep all morning, ever since waking up. He called out to her: 'Hello Moira!' She stopped and looked back, and he went up to her.

'Thought you'd gone back to New York,' she said. Crisp.

'Looks like I haven't.'

'Well, nice to see you, Jack!' Bruce Tucker hadn't slowed down his loping stride and was waiting for her at his table, which the waiters had pulled out. 'Talk to you sometime. *Ciao.*' Brisk.

'How things at the Savoy?' he called after her.

She turned around with an air of having to make this brief. 'I'm no longer at the Savoy,' she said smiling. 'I got fired.'

'I didn't know that . . . I'm sorry.'

'No need. Got a better job. With Lester Crabtree. Personal public relations.' She let the smile become momentarily warmer. 'All due to you really, come to think. Getting fired, that is. Give my regards to Gloria.'

'I will.'

'Take care.' Cool again. Crispy cool. That was how it went on the Big Wheel. One minute you were at the top, the next at the bottom. The wheel turned, and the bush drumbeats sent out the news fast. Those in the know knew. Moira looked as if she'd be in the know . . . as if she had her finger on the pulse of celebrity, knew where it beat strong and firm and where it was just a feeble, thin flicker. The tables to the right of the bar were beginning to fill up as people started going in to lunch. 'Give me another whisky, Franco.'

'Right away, Mr Strawl. Squirt of soda?'

'Strawley, you squirt!' He smiled ferociously. 'No soda. Straight up. Just ice.'

'You a character, Mr Strawley. You really are.'

Seeing his Rank producer come in, he drank the whisky at a gulp. He was half in his skin, half out. Another couple of whiskies and he might be able to get back in completely. At present he was at risk of falling into the fiery lake.

Herbert Honeypenny was a large portly man with a red cynical face. He was carrying a copy of Carl's script for *The Interloper.* Jack could see that he had placed a bookmark about a third of the way through the 180 pages.

'See you haven't quite finished reading it,' Jack remarked, seated opposite the producer. He gestured urgently to a waiter to bring him another whisky before anything else. Place not your trust in the sons of men but in whisky!

'Oh, near enough, near enough. Just a few pages perhaps. It's been a very busy period, you should see the stack of scripts on my desk! So, well, you want to know what I think? What I think, yes.' He pondered this for about a minute, not having had the time in his busy schedule to do so earlier. 'It is,' he finally decided, 'remarkable. No question. *Remarkable.* Could be a very outstanding film. The idea is . . . well, remarkable. A wee bit esoteric, perhaps? More like one of those Italian films, rather than something for Rank. And a bit near the knuckle. Those scenes in the elevator. I don't think we can get away with that. Between floors? Is that feasible?'

'I'm willing to do a feasibility test myself.'

Mr Honeymoney gave a hee-heeing chuckle. 'To be absolutely serious for a moment,' he said, 'I would have to say that *The Imposter . . .*'

'*The Interloper,*' Jack said.

'. . . . is perhaps, remarkable as it is, a tad difficult as a subject, for us, right now, in the present climate of the industry . . . like to keep an open mind about it. Could perhaps be your second or third film for us. Start with something a bit more . . . shall we say, accessible? For the ordinary filmgoer, you know.'

'What d'you have in mind?'

'Well, we have this murder mystery. *Encore in Hell*. About a series of murders at an end-of-pier Brighton theatre. I sent you the script, didn't I?'

'Yes. Of which I read all 105 pages, and not a page too short.'

'It's a journeyman job,' he said, 'not perhaps one that would stretch a man of your capabilities, I know, but it's in the honourable tradition of the English murder mystery. And there are parts for some of our most attractive contract artistes.The director's remuneration is a wee bit on the modest side, since it has to be a low-budget picture.'

'How modest is modest?'

He was scoring the white tablecloth with the point of his steak knife.

'I think we could go to around seven hundred and fifty.'

'Pounds?'

'Oh absolutely.'

'Per week?'

Hubert Honeymoney or whatever his name was gave the good-humoured chuckle of one being outrageously teased. 'That would be the director's fee. For directing the film. We could perhaps wangle a small percentage of profits in addition.'

Then he attacked his fillet steak and salad with his steak knife, while Jack continued cutting up the tablecloth with his.

When the waiter inquired if they would like a dessert, Herbert Honeypenny said that Mr Strawley would no doubt wish to have another whisky, and to bring the bill.

'Coffee, Jack? You haven't eaten a thing.'

'No, I don't eat much for lunch,'

'Drink it mostly, do you? I don't think there's any point in drawing this out, since there would appear to have been a misunderstanding. Your agent told me you were interested in working for us, but evidently that is not the case.'

The waiter who brought the coffee spread a napkin over the cut-up tablecloth and confiscated the steak knives.

Jack was looking around for Moira in the cream suit that sloped so amazingly over her amazing hips. Gone. Gone. He had a sense of desolation and felt tears prickling his eyes. He could feel himself shaking all over and wanted to lay his head on Herbie Honeypenny's lap, but did not think this was a good idea. As an urgent matter of self-survival, it was necessary to get out of the fiery lake before he got all burnt up.

Outside it was raining even harder than before. He stood in the rain, waiting for the Jag to be brought to him, and noted that he was breathing too fast. The moisture-laden atmosphere did not contain enough oxygen, and he was suffocating. He had a pain in his chest and down his left arm. This can't be a heart attack, he told himself. You don't get heart attacks in your early twenties. Unless you are Jack Strawley, who does everything quicker and younger than anybody else. Since he could no longer stand up straight, because of the pain and the dizziness, he sat down abruptly on the kerb, feet in a puddle.

Presently he saw Moira emerge from the restaurant with Bruce Tucker. They were very close together, intimately close. That made him want to weep again. Seeing him sitting in the gutter, getting all wet, she gave him her hand to help him up.

'Had a little too much, Jack?' she inquired, smiling.

'I think probably not quite enough,' he said, accepting her hand and getting to his feet unsteadily. 'Need quite a bit to cope with our Herb. What d'you say to a booster shot? Or are you in a desperate rush?' He gave a quick glance in the direction of fleeing Tucker while perilously swaying, as if about to sit down in the wet again, and she had to take his arm to steady him.

'Bruce, you know Jack Strawley?' she called to Tucker, who was already some way ahead. He turned, irritated to have to do so, being accustomed to women following him around and to not having to check to see if they were still there. Moira put a cigarette in her mouth and asked sweetly: 'Give me a light, Bruce. I expect you saw Jack's film, *Killers Kill?*'

'No,' Tucker said, making a big effort to be sociable, 'I didn't get to see it but I heard about it.'

'Who've you got in your new picture?' Moira asked Jack.

'Nik Ransom'll be in it, and there's a part we're talking to

Burton about.'

'Good actor,' Tucker said.

'Who? Burton or Nik?'

'These new young actors,' Tucker said with an all inclusive tight smile. 'Talented bunch.'

'Remind me of the story again,' Moira said. Jack was swaying, and she took hold of his arm to hold him up.

'It's about . . . a happily married woman, nearing forty, who meets this penniless poet — and thief — in Baden-Baden.'

'Sounds in'resting,' Tucker said, starting out towards the taxi that had drawn up. His appetite for showbiz chat was all abated. 'Moira, you comin' or stayin'?'

'You go ahead, Bruce. I don't think there's anything else we need to discuss right now. I'll see you . . . later.'

'Okay, dear.'

'How are you, Jack?' she asked when Tucker had gone off in the taxi. 'You okay?' Her face showed concern as he swayed again. 'You don't look too great. Want a brandy?'

'Yeah, a brandy.'

They went back inside, and Jack ordered brandies at the bar. He drank his swiftly.

'You look very good,' he told her. 'Things going okay for you now?'

'Oh, sort of. Fine. Fine. Though it gets wearisome — all those big star egos . . . I want out. Soon as I can.'

'My, you move fast! How long is it since you left the Savoy?'

'Almost nine months.'

'Already!'

'PR's not for me. I have the need to do something a teeny bit more creative. I'm working on it. I'd like to get into producing.'

'Is Bruce going to be a help there?'

'Bruce is a sweetie-pie. And an egomaniac, of course. At the moment we're getting along fine.'

'Giving him the full Moira Goldberg cossetting?'

'He's nervous with the British press, it has such a very bad reputation. Needs somebody to hold his hand all the time.'

'And who better than you?'

'Yeah,' she said with a sour grimace. 'So what's the deal with Rank?'

'No deal, Moira. They want me to do some crappy end-of-the-pier murder mystery. Not interested in my project.'

'And MGM?'

'Schary wants a big star name. On a budget of half a mil.'

She thought for exactly half a second. 'Bruce is a big star name.'

'It's not a Western, Moira.'

'Bruce has done lots of films that are not Westerns. He's a good actor and he wants to change his image. He's very interested in youth.'

'I can see that.'

'You could do worse.'

'He wouldn't want to do it. It's a part that goes right against the Bruce Tucker image.'

'I'll let you into a secret. Bruce Tucker goes right against the Bruce Tucker image.'

'And he'd want too much money. Metro want a star but they want a cheap star.'

'I can talk to him, if you like. You never know. I could give him your script and then . . . You really aren't well, are you? I thought you'd just had a bit too much to drink, but I can see it isn't that. I think we should get you to a doctor. You have trouble breathing?'

'A bit.'

'I think you should sit down, and I'm going to call a doctor.'

'No doctor,' he said, 'doctors are killers.'

'C'mon, Jack.'

'No doctors.'

'So what we going to do? Where are you living now? Look, I better get a taxi and take you home.'

In the taxi, when she asked for his address, he shook his head. 'No, no . . .'

'You're being unreasonable, Jack. Why don't you want to go home?'

'I'll be all right in a while. It'll pass.'

'So where do I tell the taxi to go?'

'Anywhere.'

Through the fog in his mind he was aware, at a certain moment, of crossing the river, of a change in milieu from the smart Chelsea Embankment to gloomy, desolate streets lined with derelict Victorian warehouses. Even in his present condition, his eye went on functioning independently, noting the delicate pilasters framing the boarded-up windows, the loading bays with their iron pulley-wheels and chains, the wharves with iron capstans and sand dumps, and the tied-up barges. He was only partly inside his own body, which was sick with some unknown sickness, the other part was engaged in a cinema of the mind. One acutely angled shot climbed like a nimble steeplejack up the high-rise council flats, with their menacing windows of net curtains; another shot tracked around a builders' depot with its piled up marble and granite slabs, past a coach works, a dingy corner pub, narrow pedestrian walks splitting off to the right. He could smell the blackened brickwork of the wharves and the river slime. The taxi drew up at right angles to a narrow alley with a sign saying 'Riverside walk,' and Moira got out and paid the driver, after which she helped Jack to get out. She said:'It's about ten, fifteen yards, can you make that?' and gave him her arm to hang onto. They walked along the alley, with frequent stops because of the breathless state he was in, until they came to a stretch of embankment where there were some withered shrubs in concrete tubs and backless concrete benches. From a gap in the embankment wall a gangway went down to the moored boats. She helped him along the slippery wooden planks and onto a boat, painted green with red trim, that was firmly planted upon a dry section of the river bed. Going down the gangway, he stopped again, and it looked as if he was unable to go on, but what he was doing was looking around, across the river and along it to the curve of a low-slung bridge just ahead, and he said: 'I do like rivers. Something about rivers . . . moving water. I don't know what.'
  'I remember you liking rivers,' she said.
  He seemed to revive a little. With her help, he managed to get himself below deck, using a narrow iron ladder. He was stum-

bling along a gallery to a cabin with bunk beds either side. She helped him onto the one with the porthole offering a glimpse of the river, and he fell back exhausted. She told him to close his eyes and rest, and he did what she said, and gradually his breathing became less strident. He had begun to doze off when suddenly he sat up straight, his face very white, shaking and sweating. He was holding his hand to his chest and taking violent gulps of air.

'What is it, Jack? What is it?' she asked alarmed. She took hold of his hand. 'Yes, hold on to me,' she told him. 'Oh, Jack, hold on, hold on. Don't let go. Jack.'

He was shivering and shaking so much, with his teeth chattering noisily, that she brought a blanket and wrapped it around him. There was some imposter living inside his skin who was sick as a dog and screaming and perhaps dying; hitting him over the head with the whisky sometimes worked, sometimes the whisky knocked him out, but this time it hadn't, perhaps the motherfucker had grown resistant to it and, having got himself invited in, was staying put .While this desperate struggle went on with the intruder, in the cinema of his mind he was watching life go calmly by: the heavy rain on the river, the barges loaded with gravel, the lights across the water. A police boat searchlight slicing through the trash illumined long, braided strings of river scum and picked out miscellaneous floating objects in its random sweep; and then, in its slow revolve, passed over Moira's boat and lit up Jack Strawley's face, down which tears were streaming.

'Listen, I'm going to call a doctor.'

'No doctors,' he insisted.

'Then what should I do, Jack?'

'Lie next to me,' he said. She came and lay next to him, and he held tightly on to her, still shaking but slowly drawing heat from her body. It was not enough, he needed more, and sought to intertwine his limbs with hers, to which she consented freely, and when it seemed that he could not stop shaking, he undid her blouse and pressed his face deep into the flesh of her breast, breathing hard. Then — and since it seemed like a matter of life and death, she could not refuse — it was essential for him to be inside her. Sick as he was, he was forceful in baring her body, and though she would not have thought it possible from the state he was in, he was potent for the brief moment that the frenzy lasted, after which he seemed suddenly much better and almost immediately fell asleep.

An hour later, when she looked in, he was awake and staring out at the river. He could smell the green slime lapping against the rotting wood of the jetty. He could smell the rust on the hulls of the sand barges. The smoky acrid mist lying, totally still, under the iron bridge; the oil spills, the gravel, the dead fish and a faint touch of sea brine. Inside, he could smell hot cocoa, and Moira's warm moist skin. She asked him how he was. He said he was fine.

'You really better? That's amazing.'

'You did it, Moira. You cured me.'

'Well, I've heard some lines, but this beats them all.'

'Wasn't a line.'

'Well, a very unusual sickness, in that case.' She laughed. 'Anyway, whatever it was, I'm glad you're better. You had me scared for a while. Want some music?' He nodded, and she started going through her LPs. 'Lena Horne?' He nodded. 'How about Julie London? You like her?'

'You choose,' he said, 'just play whatever *you* like.'

'Sammy Davis?'

'Okay.'

He saw that among the signed celebrity photographs on the cabin walls there was one of Sammy Davis Jr., dedicated to her with a playfully intimate message, and another signed, 'with love, Bruce'.

'You also went out with Sammy Davis?'

'Oh, once or twice,' she said dismissively. 'They just like to have some presentable person to go to the theatre with them.'

'Is that what they like?'

'Yeah. That's what they like.'

'You're moving in a very starry world.'

'Yeah, and I want out 'cause . . . it's not what I want.'

'What is it you want?'

'I want to do something more creative, not just . . . Let me ask you something. Since you're better now. You are better? If I can get Bruce to read your script, and if he likes it and wants to do it, and if it happens . . . will you give me a job on the picture?'

'If it happens, you can ask Bruce for a job.'

'I don't want that kind of job.'

'What kind of job d'you want?'

'Assisting you.'

'Why assisting me?'

'Because I want to learn from you.' He reached for her. After a minute, she disentangled from him. 'For a convalescent, you're unusually hyper-active. Didn't we just do this?'

'Sort of.'

'This may not be such a good idea,' she said as he started drawing her towards him. She held him off. 'I thought we'd worked that all out. How you and Gloria mustn't have anything come between you, because you'd come apart bleeding.'

He was avoiding the daunting directness of her look. 'Hold it. I need to get one or two things straight in my mind first.' But he was not in a mood for discussions. 'You're amazing,' she said, doing nothing to stop him now. 'Not only do you make lightning recoveries from heart attacks you haven't had but you take whatever you want. When you want. I can see I have a lot to learn from you. You going to let me?'

'You're pushy,' he said.

'Look who's talking.' His fingers and hands were all over her, everywhere. 'Is it a deal?'

'Provided you remember the small print.'

Twisting about under him, her hair had fallen across her face, partially covering it up, and he cleared her hair away, digging her out with rough determined fingers, so he could look into her Persian cat's eyes, which were green and slanty, with enlarged pupils, and showed him everything. He wouldn't let her hide: took hold of her tossing head and held it still. He made her look up in his eyes the whole time, so that he could see all her sensations, and when she saw that this was what he wanted, she let him see everything, keeping her eyes wide open to his.

'The way you look into me. It's like you're doing it to me with your eyes . . . bastard! You want to see it, don't you? You've got to *see* it, God you're such a voyeur! I've never seen anyone look like that into anyone, it's weird. Can you see it in my eyes, what you're doing to me?'

'In your beautiful big cat eyes.'

He watched her shaking and saw the plot unfold in her fierce, angry expressions — the body being torn — the living and the dying — all the things that happened at once, in a compressed way, during love. He had the presence of mind — the coldness of heart — to make mental notes: if you're doing a love scene, remember this, remember this expression. Remember it — her eyes, like in that Ingres painting. Then the dim angry look, the puzzlement — what am I doing here? What am I *doing* here? With this man! And then the shaking which wraps it up — the wrap-up, the drowning. The descent. The dying fall. It's always a fall. Followed slowly by the surfacing, and it's a different person. Different voice. Different eyes.

'That what you wanted to see?' He didn't answer. 'Why d'you have to see it?'

'Things only are real to me if I see them.'

She wanted to get out now, the narrow bunk bed not being suitable for psychological enquiry into reality, or the savouring of after-glow. He let her go. She felt around on the floor for cigarettes, and when she'd lit one she went to change the LPs on the automatic change.

'How about Art Tatum? For that touch of "after-gloom"?'

'That'd be good.'

She put on the record and he lay still, absorbing the lament.

'Want to know how you fuck?'

'No. I have enough critics.'

'Like somebody getting his revenge. His sweet revenge.'

'You mind?'

'Did I look as though I minded?'

'I don't know. Women always look angry during orgasm. Murderous sometimes.'

'Must be the things you do to them. I thought women looked happy. Didn't I?'

'Yes, but other things as well.'

'At one point, I don't really remember, but I think I may have said something that is . . . outside our agreement, I believe.'

'What was that?'

'That I love you? I think I may have said that. Slipped out. Sort of in the heat of the moment.' He nodded noncommitally. 'Well,' she explained, 'if I did say it, and I'm not really sure, I may just have thought it—for a moment, you know—well, if I did, I don't want you to get panicky. I wouldn't want to bring up something that's a deal-breaker.'

He laughed. 'I'm glad you're not fragile, I'm glad you're this pushy, ambitious New York Jewish broad.'

'Yeah, I'm fairly robust. But you're not, are you? What was all that before?'

'You can see I have a need of robust young women.'

She listened for the record change. 'I think this is going to be the Julie London now. Oh, I love that song. "Cry Me A River". You know it? Speaks to me, that song — it's a scene I know well. Oh, do I know it! Yeah, I do love that song.' She lit another cigarette thoughtfully and sat with her back against the bunk bed, her face turned away from him, listening intently to the sugary lament.

'I never told you I was married, did I? Yeah, I was married when I was eighteen.'

'Didn't last long. You're only what now?'

'Twenty-one. It lasted just about a year. Oh, he was charming, my husband. But he didn't believe in stuff like paying the rent. Or working for a living.'

'That's a certain type.'

'There was a child.'

'You have a child?'

'He was an adorable baby. So beautiful.'

'I can imagine.'

'He was retarded. I nursed him for eighteen months. Did nothing else. Then he died. I would love him and love him, all the time knowing he was going to die. That he had to die. That it was best for him. If need be, I was going to help him.' She sat with eyes closed, listening to Julie London singing about lost loves. Then she looked up sharply. Her body rocked back and forth. 'Want to know why I push hard? You know what my

161

mother does? Her work? She's a saleslady at Selfridges. Men's shoes department. All day long she's on her knees lacing up shoes, unlacing shoes, and smelling their feet. You can see why I'm motivated. How old is Gloria?'

'How old? Why d'you want to know? Oh, she's thirty-three, thereabouts.'

'Okay, one day I'm going to be "around thirty-three or thereabouts," or maybe even forty-five or thereabouts, and I'm going to be going with this young fella who's, let's say, a few years younger than me, and he's going to start noticing the lines around my eyes, and that I've got a little bit too much flesh around the middle, it was nice and sexy, one time, but now it's not elegant, and when I'm not there he's going to be looking for reasonably pretty girls of around twenty-two with good chemistry. That's when I don't intend to be dependent on any man — anyone — for my reason to exist. That's why I'm pushy. And that's why I plan to learn from you, Jack. Everything you can teach me.'

20

The tall, rangy figure of Bruce Tucker was extended on a sofa, his long legs reaching far beyond it, with the heels of his antelope boots resting on the glass top of a low coffee table. He was on the phone. 'Hiya Countess, what's new? Oh, sure am . . . sure . . . yep . . . nope . . . no, sure I feel good, never drink too much. Always stop between drinks.' He gave a broad wink in the general direction of Jack and Sydney. Moving the heel of one soft boot so that it rested balanced delicately on the toe of the other, he sank down deeper into the sofa and laughed silently, his large nose crinkling up in the seductive way that it did on the screen. 'How's the Princess?' he inquired giving another wink all round, accompanied by a schoolboy grin. 'Great . . . great . . . you do that, honey. Call me, huh? Give my best to the Princess.' He hung up, daintily unwound his long legs, at the same time shifting his weight to his left elbow while, with his right hand, he refreshed the tall ice-filled tumbler from the bottle of Nicholoff vodka. He was wearing fawn gabardine slacks and a checkered wool lumberjack's shirt with a Paisley patterned silk scarf knotted at the side of the neck.

With a conscious effort, he turned his attention back to the matter under discussion.

'It's *different,* all right,' he said. 'Script's a bit talky, but the talk's good. Darn unusual film for Bruce Tucker to be in. Be takin' a risk. Daughters of the American Revolution won't like it. Could get banned.' He frowned down into his drink. 'Audiences are used to seeing me win through in the end, whatever I'm up to my neck in, and in this film I don't win. Nobody wins. But, hell, I liked the script. I found it true to life and I think Jack here's a talented young director and, you know, I believe in going with the young, keeps you young . . . young in body, young in spirit . . . that's why I said to Moira — nice kid, Moira, very bright — that I'm in'rested and let's talk. It's a fine *acting* role, the husband.'

With an apologetic gesture for interrupting him, Sydney intervened to say: 'Bruce, for you it's gonna be nothing less'n a Oscar-winner!' He spread out his arms as wide as they'd go to show the full extent of his conviction. 'People don't always realize what a very fine actor you are. This is the role in which you show 'em.'

Bruce Tucker scratched the side of his nose and grinned with modest pleasure, his famous lazy, amiable grin. 'You may not think so from some o' my films, but I darn well learned some stuff about acting,' he admitted. 'Remember once John Barrymore saying to me: "You skinny so-and-so, wish I could do the things you can do." That kind of made me feel good.'

Sydney Carver cut in: 'Bruce Tucker *and* Nik Ransom, permit me to say, that is great casting.' He jabbed his finger in violent warning to anyone with the temerity to disagree. 'That is screen chemistry!'

'Provided you c'n get it past the censor. Some of that stuff in the script is . . . pretty close to the bone. In places, it's right through the bone. I'm not objecting to that. It's honest, and I think I've served my time in the clean-livin' department, upholding the Code and all that. Actors have got to be in the business of interpreting life as it's lived.'

'You're so goddamn right, Bruce,' Sydney Carver said.

'Where d'you fellas see yourselves going with this project? Is this going to be a studio picture or an independent?' he asked them.

'I am this close,' Carver showed an immeasurable distance between thumb and forefinger, 'to closing a deal with Metro. Dore *loves* the material, he just loves it. And he's wild-crazy about Jack as a director. Dore was the first studio chief to have the insight to see Jack as a major talent. The first to give him a contract. What he insists on, and I agree with him 100%, is that the elements've got to be right, it's got to be cast right. Moment I say to him we got Bruce Tucker and Nik Ransom, we're in business.'

'Now whooaah there, Sydney! I said I'm in'rested, I didn't say I'd do it. Gettin' a picture off the ground is a lot of accidents coming together at the right time . . . we still have got a distance to go. Who d'you see playing the wife?' He turned to Jack Strawley. 'I see Ingrid in the part.'

Jack Strawley began: 'Bruce, I'm thinking in terms of Gloria playing the part . . . she's right for it . . . and she's a very good actress.'

'I agree she's a good actress, very good stage actress,' Bruce Tucker said slowly. 'And I can see your reasons for wanting her.'

Carver stepped in swiftly to mediate the situation: 'What Jack wants to say, Bruce, is we're going to do whatever is best for the picture. In the first place, let's build this up around you — and Jack. And Nik. As the main elements. And *then* see who else'd fit into that set up.'

Bruce Tucker rose from the sofa, stretching himself to his full disentangled height.

'Okay,' he said, 'you fellas gonna have to be leaving now,

'cause I have a lady coming to see me who's a little shy about being reco'nized. Be in touch.' He gave them an intimate wink and flapped his hands upwards, shooing them out.

Because of the bad weather a lot of flights had been cancelled, and the quickest way of going turned out to be to fly to New York and to take a train from there. He met Carver at Penn station. Sydney was not saying much for once, didn't discuss details until they were alone and warmly ensconced in the train's observation lounge, whiskies in hand, looking out across the white countryside, the freight yards of New Jersey resembling a vast plain of igloos, fields and forests under snow, lakes and ponds all iced up.

'Didn't want to say too much on the phone because you never know who may be listening. This is delicate, Jack. This is very delicate. And I have to tell you it isn't 100% certain. What can I say to you? All I can say is we took the best advice, we paid our dues, we *should* be out of the woods.'

'How much is this costing us, Sydney? That we're not 100% sure is going to work.'

'It's like owning a yacht, you don't ask how much it'll cost.'

'Where we getting the money to go sailing?'

'Jack, these are Cayman Island deals, Dutch Antilles deals, Bahamas deals. They write it off. Put it this way: the government's paying for it in the end . . . it's like drilling for oil. The duds they write off. One in ten, one in a hundred, turns out is a gusher.'

'And I'm supposed to be the gusher.'

'Naturally, they're hopeful it'll turn out to be a good investment for them.'

'How much?'

'Jack, I went to the very best. They're the top experts in the field. I got us the best deal I could.'

'What you sign away, Sydney? What did I sign away?'

'A tiny little percentage of your future, Jack. With the future you're gonna have, you won't even notice.'

At the Delaware river the train took its long exhilarating leap over the packed ice floes, and Jack Strawley felt Sydney was right, if you were going to fly high you couldn't think too much about the cost.

Outside Union Station, the golden eagles atop the black columnar lamp-posts had extended wings of sheet ice. The dome of the Capitol, partly hidden, showed dully in the distance like a quarter moon seen through cloud.

As arranged, he arrived alone for his appointment with the subcommittee of one, consisting of Congressman Delbert Wanger, sitting in executive session, attended by staff senior investigator Howard Bradlaugh.

'You appear to have hung out with just about every Communist and fellow-traveller in show-business,' Congressman Wagner declared, slowly turning the pages of a file before him.

'About three to be exact, Mr Chairman. If that's "every", I don't see what you've got to worry about.'

'Your wife has been a prominent campaigner for Leftist causes, she has signed protests and declarations like she's giving away autographs. Your best friend, Carl Schmidlin, is or was a member of the Communist Party of Great Britain and lied to US immigration authorities about that. You know or knew W.V. Kyser, a very suspect person. By his own testimony, you were part of Kyser's Communist cell in New York.'

'If I may correct you on one small point, Congressman. It wasn't a Communist cell. It was a film society discussion group.'

'How naive can you be! Didn't you ever suspect that the film society was a front?'

'As far as I can remember, all we ever did was see film classics and discuss montage.'

'Russian film classics, weren't they? Eisenstein, wasn't it? You seem to have been extraordinarily innocent, Mr Strawley.' He shook his head with much sadness. 'However, it is my opinion that while you may have been innocent or foolish in your choice of friends, you were never a Communist yourself. That's what you say in your letter. Upon which I commend you. A very good letter. A fine, well-written letter. But it's easy to speak in generalities. As I say, that's all very commendable. But what we need is evidence of a willingness to act in protection of your country's vital national interests. For this we need names.'

'I believe you already have a lot of names, sir.'

'We have some, but nobody can be sure of the full extent of the threat. The crucial question is do we have all or most of the names, or are there a lot of these Reds still out there being protected? Before you answer . . . we're going to do this correctly.'

He handed Jack Strawley a long typewritten list of names and while Jack was glancing down this list, Congressman Wagner banged his desk with a gavel and mumbled very fast: 'I declare this sub-committee of the House Un-American Activities Committee in executive session. Congressman Wagner in the chair. Now, Mr Strawley. I'm going to put you under oath.' He reeled off the words of the oath at top speed.

'I do, Congressman.'

'Sir, will you be so good as to cast your eyes down the list that I have handed to you and tell us, remembering that you are under oath, if you are able to add any other names to the list before you?'

He glanced swiftly down the list and said: 'I cannot.'

'Please state to the Committee what your connection is or was with Carl Schmidlin.'

'In my late teens I knew Carl Schmidlin in New York, we shared an interest in cinema. We became good friends.'

'Did you ever discuss politics with him?'

'No. Only films.'

'You were not aware of his activities in behalf of the Communist party?'

'I know nothing of any such activities.'

'Are you presently in contact with Carl Schmidlin?'

He hesitated. 'We are both presently living in London. We sometimes run into each other. The film world in London is a small place.'

'Then you have not broken off your connection with him?'

'He's a friend.'

'Do you presently have any professional connections with Carl Schmidlin?'

'No, sir, I do not at present.'

'The Committee thanks you, Mr Strawley. You may step down. I declare this executive session closed.'

Congressman Wagner stood up.

'My daughter Amy is a big fan of yours, Mr Strawley. She saw your film *Killers Kill,* says you're a genius. May I suggest to you that you use the talent with which God has blessed you to be vigorous in support of the democratic American institutions we all respect and love.'

'I certainly will, sir.'

'Amy said if I give you a hard time she'll give me a hard time. I haven't given you a hard time, have I?'

'No, you haven't.'

'Good. Because I don't want my daughter to give me a hard time, you know.'

'Well, give her a big kiss from me, Congressman. Tell her that I thank her . . . and you, sir.'

He felt that he was on a winning streak and that he had to keep going while he had the hot hand.

Schary was enormously busy. There were producers who had to wait four or five weeks to get fifteen minutes with him, and Carver said he wasn't sure he could get Jack in immediately. 'That may have to be another trip.'

'Tell him we're coming to see him *first.* Because he's our first choice. Because we respect his artistic judgment and his fearlessness in tackling difficult subjects. Like anti-Semitism. All the stuff he did at RKO. And juvenile delinquency at MGM. Lay it on! The way only you can do, Sydney. If he doesn't want to see me *before* my other appointments, hint that could be his loss.'

'We don't have any other appointments, Jack.'

'Sydney, I hate to teach you your own business, but he doesn't know that, does he?'

Next day, at 3:30 p.m., Strawley and Carver were ushered into the presence of the large, friendly labrador grin attached the large, friendly labrador nose of Dore Schary.

'How are ya, doll?' Schary demanded, swivelling between Carver and Strawley and figuratively embracing both at the same time while remaining stiffly seated, on account of his bad back, behind the L-shaped desk.

'Dore! You're looking great,' Carver declared.

'So are you, sweetie,' Schary told him. 'As for the youth, here,' he indicated Jack Strawley with the proud kidding fondness of a father for a son who has at last lived up to expectations, 'this son of a bitch gets better lookin' all the time, which ain't fair, you can't have his talent *and* looks. How're ya, doll?'

The pleasantries took a few more minutes. You would not have believed that there was a six-week waiting list of people to see Schary which they had succeeded in jumping. Without actually moving his upright back or creasing his suit, he told Carver:

'You know what I love about this boy? He reminds me of myself when I started out. I also was full of pride and passion and idealism, which I had to temper *a little,* not too much, I hope, in learning that first and foremost a picture has got to entertain its audience. If you do *that*, heck! after that you can do anything you like, but you got to do that *first of all.* All the Hollywood greats, people like Huston, like Ford, like Stevens, like Wyler, possess that combination of integrity and entertainment value. Without integrity, entertainment comes out looking shoddy, and without entertainment value, integrity comes out pompous . . . unwatchable.'

The homespun reflections continued to flow a while longer, until the business in hand was finally got down to.

'I like your script,' he told Jack Strawley, 'I like it a lot. It's a work of art.'

'Carl's written a fine screenplay, with some help from me.'

'Carl? Carl?' Schary asked. 'I don't know who that is. I think you must be talking about this fellow . . . what's his name? Harold?'

'Harold Heath,' Jack said.

'Right. Right. Harold Heath. Well, you and Harold Heath have done a fine job of work. Bruce Tucker wants to work with you, I've talked to him. Bruce is an actor who wants to go with the young and the new . . . and with Bruce in it, this picture, though very unusual and not really what you'd think of as an MGM subject, can be a success. L.B. of course hates it, let me tell you. And there's a lot of opposition to it throughout the studio, and New York too is against it, in fact it's *generally* detested. L.B. says to me, "I wouldn't make this picture with Sam Goldwyn's money, but if you want to burn your fingers, immerse our audience's face in filth, go ahead burn your fingers." I told him I liked it and that I was going to do it. It's modern and it's adult, sexual without being salacious: it's about *passion,* a woman's passion. This woman is like Anna Karenina, like Madame Bovary. She has romantic and sexual yearnings, and, if this subject can be handled right, we can get a present-day woman's audience for it, identifying with her, because women are changing. I'm not afraid of tricky subjects. I wasn't afraid to tackle anti-Semitism in *Crossfire,* and I'm not afraid to tackle modern marriage in the case of *The Interloper.* Provided that it's done in good taste.'

Carver said: 'I can guarantee you, Dore, that it will be. It will be very sexual and it will be in very good taste. You can rely on it.'

'I'm pleased to hear that.We can shock our audience provided we do it with good taste. Now there are a couple of other things as well. Jack has got to get clearance from the Committee. Without that, we cannot get to first base.'

'I can confidently predict, Dore, speaking from knowledge that I have in my possession, that Jack will have full and complete clearance within fourteen days.'

'Pleased to hear that,' Schary said. 'I have full confidence in Congressman Wagner. He's expensive but trustworthy. My second thing is this picture has to come in at under half a mil.'

'Dore, sweetie, Tucker's fee alone is two hundred thousand. How d'you expect us to make the picture for what's left?' Carver protested.

'If he wants to be with the young,' Schary patiently explained, 'Bruce has got to make some sacrifices. He'll have to take a deferral. We'll cut him in on the gross, but he has got to do the picture for fifty thou up front. At half a mil I can make a profit with this picture, over half a mil and I could be a dead duck.'

'What happens if he won't do it for that?'

'Get another star who will.'

'And if we can't get a big American star at that price?'

'We'd have to think again. Who've you got in mind for the wife, Jack?'

'I want Gloria to do it.'

Schary gave Jack a look of total candour. 'I know she's a good stage actress. That talent goes in the family. As a young man, I had the privilege to work on a couple of pictures with her mother when she was in her heyday. I think Gloria has some of the same quality and I am sure will be as big a star one day as her mother was. But . . . in my opinion, you need someone in that role that the audience knows and will accept as doing what she does. I thought Ingrid. Bruce is of the same opinion. What she's lived with Rossellini gives us a tantalizing real-life parallel that is very helpful to us . . . done in a tasteful way, naturally.'

Jack, under scrutiny, took time to reflect before replying: 'Of course I'd be thrilled — thrilled — to work with Ingrid, Dore, but my fear is that she's too great a star. She loses reality because of being Ingrid Bergman. The moment her name rolls on the titles you know the story. The other factor is that if we have Ingrid, no conceivable way could we bring in the picture at under half a million. You see what I mean, Dore?'

'In her present situation, I think Ingrid might be inclined to be reasonable.'

'Not that reasonable.'

Schary sighed philosophically. 'The bottom line is you want Gloria.'

'Yeah, I want Gloria. She's right for it.'

'It's perfectly understandable that you should want Gloria, Jack.'

Jack gave a private smile, shyly admitting his understandable preference for Gloria.

He said, 'This is going to be an unusual picture, a very personal picture, and I know what I can get out of Gloria . . . whereas anybody else would be an unknown quantity.'

Schary was silent, his paternalistic grin fixed stiffly on his face. His big head nodded, his suit did not budge. 'Okay, you got your darlin'. Provided you've also got Bruce. And can bring it in for under half a million.'

Breakfast in the Bruce Tucker suite was at noon. This time

Tucker wore a red satin dressing-gown and was pyjama-less underneath. On the glass coffee table there was a breakfast tray with a coffee percolator, a jug of milk and brown eggs on a saucer. There was also a glass of water in which Alka Seltzer tablets were fizzing.

When Jack Strawley asked him what he wanted to do first, Tucker replied, 'Sleep.'

'And second?'

'Second I want to sleep too.'

Jack apologized for cutting into his sleeping time. 'That's okay,' Tucker said, drinking Alka Seltzer and sipping coffee, in alternation, 'since we got to do this, let's do it. Just a few little points.' He put on a pair of heavy horn-rimmed eyeglasses, which made him look what he was, a man in his middle fifties, and his face crinkled up with the effort of concentration as he slowly turned the pages of the script.

'It's a good script,' he said, 'has some problems, but what script doesn't?'

With an expression of getting down to serious work, he started turning pages, looking for the scene he wanted. When he couldn't find it straight away, he shook his head and put the script down.

'Can't find it right now but, in any case I want to talk about the script overall. There is some heaviness, you know, in some of the scenes. Some of it seems heavy to me.'

'Where, Bruce?'

'Oh, it's just all over. Places where it should be light, it's heavy.'

'Could be because you've read it too often?'

'I read it once. I only ever read a script once . . . if that. That's what stayed in my mind. That it's a touch heavy,' he said a touch tetchily.

'The writing is not feather-light, but nor's our subject,' Jack pointed out.

'This Harold Heath fellow,' Bruce corrected him. 'He's got a heavy hand at times. Here's the thought I had. What I think you oughtta do is get David Cawley. To put some polish on the script. I'm told he's good . . . has got a light touch *and* prestige. I don't think it calls for anything major. Just a general lightening . . . making it just generally lighter and inserting humour wherever possible. Also it needs to be about twenty pages shorter.'

'If we're going to get some truth into this picture,' Jack started to reply, but Carver cut him short.

'Truth, truth! Who knows what is truth? The truth changes from minute to minute.'

21

Gloria was always tense when getting ready to go out. Putting on a face was anxious-making: first Estée Lauder, a gossamer cushion to work on with chisel brushes and eye definers — great play of the eyes always. She used brush lipsticks, and face shapers and floats of colour . . . made much of bones. Hers being so good. Thick lashes. Blot-out to neutralise lip colours. She worked with concentration.

'My skin gets so dry and pale. I hate my skin.'

'You have a lovely skin,' he called back to her from the shower. Gloria was greatly dissatisfied always when making up to go out.

'I should have had my nose done.'

'You dare!'

The telephone rang, and he ran dripping out of the shower to answer it. She threw him a towel, screaming: 'For God's sake! The baby-sitter!'

He called over his shoulder: 'She doesn't look at naked men. She's only interested in sticky Italian cakes.' To appease his wife he placed the towel unconvincingly about his middle and picked up the phone. The baby-sitter, Patrizia, hovered briefly into sight licking her sticky fingers, and then disappeared again. Uninterested in men in towels.

'Sydney,' he told Gloria.

'So?' She was re-checking nails and face and hair and eyes and bones.

He hesitated about telling her, since he was expecting that she would get furious, but if that were going to happen, then the immediate problem of what to wear might provide a valuable diversion. The mirrored sliding doors of Lady Greave's Heal's wardrobe, circa 1937, had been rolled back, and she was contemplating her choices. Angrily she went through her wardrobe. 'I've got nothing to wear,' she said taking out a long black crepe evening dress and immediately rejecting it. She considered a velvet skirt with silk chiffon embroidered top. 'Makes me look old,' she said. He was glad she was using up some anger in this way.

'We've hired someone to do a polish on the script,' he told her.

'Oh, I bet Carl was thrilled about that!' She was so preoccupied with her choice of clothes that she had hardly registered what he was saying.

'He doesn't know yet.'

Now she registered. 'He doesn't know! You're doing this behind his back!'

'Gloria, I'm under a lot of pressure from all sides. Tucker *demanded* a re-write . . . a polish, that's all. He's a big star, has a lot of clout. Sydney and I decided the best thing was to head him off.'

'Who've you got?' Gloria asked taking out lustrous gold velvet evening trousers with notched ankles to fit over boots.

'David Cawley.'

'It figures. That's why we're going to his first night. I thought there must be some reason, since we never do anything without a reason.'

'The play's amusing, you'll enjoy it.'

'How d'you know?'

'I've seen rehearsals. He's a wizard with words.'

'What's the wizard with words going to polish up, exactly?'

'The bits that are a bit heavy.'

'You can't do this to Carl. He's your friend. You're not the sort of Hollywood rat who does that. That is not who you are. I hope.'

'I am whatever I need to be to get this picture made.'

She started pulling on the trousers. 'Is this too much? Will everybody else be wearing duffle-coats and corduroy?'

'Duffle-coats are not your style.'

While tying his tie, he examined her in the mirror, weighing up the seriousness of her disapproval. She was going to be carrying one of the three main roles in the film. In the battles to come he needed some people to be on his side. She was pulling on the gold trousers and suddenly stopped. 'I really don't feel like going. I think I'm liable to be sick all over the wizard with words. I'm not coming . . . you can go by yourself.'

'Finish getting dressed. You're coming, Gloria. It's necessary. Oh, for God's sake! Cawley doesn't want to do it either.' He smiled slyly. 'Only reason he agreed was because he wants to meet you, he's wild about you. Warned me he intends to get you into bed.'

'And you took him on!'

'See what risks I take for all our sakes.'

'Rat!' she said in a softer voice, tying the belt of the trousers tightly.

At dinner he asked Gloria what she had thought of the play, and Gloria said:

'Some good jokes.'

'Is he good for *us*?'

'Depends if we need good jokes.'

'Tucker wants to introduce more humour . . . he's scared to death of portentousness.'

'Well, Carl's humour *is* pretty portentous.'

'Needs a David Cawley shine and polish. A touch of English playing down.'

'How are we supposed to learn our parts if we don't get the finished script until the day before we start shooting?'

'That's not going to be a problem. Start of shooting is postponed.'

'So David Cawley can put in his jokes.'

'No. Because Tuck has got another film to make first. A big production for which he gets a hell of a lot of money. So we have to wait.'

'At this rate it'll never be made. Maybe it shouldn't be made. With all the compromises, and the Cawley shine and polish, it won't be what it was going to be, will it?'

It was always a sign of deep-rooted dissatisfactions when Gloria started smoking before the first course. When it arrived she tasted a couple of spoonfuls of the lobster soup, and then continued smoking. He didn't touch the soup at all. Drank neat whisky instead.

'The money we spend on restaurant meals we don't eat,' she said.

'Why is that?' he asked.

'Because you are profligate, you spend wildly. You have no sense of economy.'

'You saving my soul again, angel?'

'Somebody's got to, since you don't take the trouble.'

'What you don't understand, Gloria, is that you've got two hundred years of solid stable Americana in your bloodstream, gives you a set of well-disciplined genes that never step out of line . . . whereas I'm an upstart savage, and my genes don't know any better.'

'That's true,' she said. 'You have no moral sense. But with this film you're giving turpitude a whole new twist. Carl's your closest friend . . . probably your only friend, if you don't count me, and you don't count me your friend. Your burdensome wife, your sometimes joyful lover. But rarely if ever your friend.'

'That's not true.'

'You never listen to me. About anything important.'

Opposite them sat a stout dandy in his late forties, with a pale face, a red carnation, a small quantity of slicked down hair back and sides, and two girls. The girls were pretty, vivacious, and blond, smartly turned out and friendly; they laughed a great deal at the stout dandy's jokes, intimately touched his hands, his cheeks, the back of his neck. Playful little things. The stout dandy seemed to know Jack Strawley and beamed greetings to him from time to time, and Jack beamed back noncommitally. Eventually he remembered who the man was.

'He writes for one of the American cinema trades . . . Box-Office Report. Something like that. What d'you suppose is his appeal to the chicks?'

'Complimentary cinema tickets?' Gloria suggested.

'You only get one for the free seats. To get two you'd have to provide choc-ices as well.'

'Unless you're a demon in the sack.'

'Don't see him in the role.'

'The answer is that he takes them out to places like this, and famous, up-and-coming film directors nod to him, which suggests to these girls that he can do things for them . . . ,' Gloria offered.

'My theory is that he's impotent — or queer — or both — so they feel safe with him, and they can get around without risk. Free transport.'

'Why are you envious of a fat, impotent queen?'

'I'm not envious of him. I'm curious about his appeal.'

'Every time you see a man with a pretty girl, there's a lamentation in your heart that you have the misfortune to be tied to me.'

'You're becoming very persecuted, Gloria.'

'No, just psychic. Like I had the feeling you were going to do this to Carl, and you did.'

He stopped drinking whisky and addressed the question with as much sobriety as he could muster. 'Gloria, we need this film badly. It will re-start my career. It had, let's face it, come to a halt. After one fucking film. Tucker agreeing to do the film is what enabled us to set it up with Metro. Everybody there except Schary hates the project. The only way Schary will do it is with some insurance, like the name of Bruce Tucker and a low budget. If Tucker walks away now, everything collapses. You know how much we're spending every week while I'm not earning anything?'

She gave a sour laugh. 'Yes. I do know, darling. Since I mostly sign the cheques.'

'It's a loan,' he said. 'From first day of shooting I get eighteen hundred dollars a week.'

'Which we are spending before we've got it. And which, furthermore, you may never get, since at this rate the film's going to get delayed until Tucker's too old for the part, which he is already.'

As often happened, they left the restaurant having eaten practically nothing.

'I don't know why we do this,' she said, as he tipped the cloakroom girl lavishly.

'To see who's there?'

'The people who were there you didn't want to see. The ones you wanted to see didn't want to see you .'

'Yes, but one day they will.'

'That's when you won't want to see them.'

'That's when you know you've arrived.'

'Some arrival.'

She didn't want him to drive, saying he'd had too much to drink. Gloria driving, they took the slowest way, going by way of Curzon Street, where traffic was reduced to a crawl. Glowing cigarette ends drew attention to the dim forms in every dark doorway. Brazen white faces with set expressions. He noted one or two new girls amid the regulars. Cheap fur coats of mid-thigh length were being worn on the pavement tonight. Under the furs, some of the ladies of the night were in black underwear, which they displayed in the sudden flame of cigarette lighters.

'There was no need to go this way,' Jack told her. 'You could have gone along Piccadilly.'

'I like to see the night sights,' she said, 'don't you? Along here's where you perceive the real truth about married life.'

All along Curzon Street cars were stopping, windows were being wound down, and prostitutes were entering into discussion with potential clients. If agreement was reached, the girl went round to the other side of the car and got in. 'That one there's quite pretty,' Gloria said, indicating a young girl with light coloured hair. 'How much does one like that cost?'

'Four, five pounds, I imagine.'

'Less than the dinners we don't eat at Les A. Not dear.'

She threw the car violently forward, pulling screechingly around one of the stopped cars, where negotiations were taking place. When they'd reached Bolton Street, he said: 'Let me park. Calm down, will you?'

'Can you tell me something, Jack? Why d'you make calls from phone boxes when we have a fully working phone at home?'

'Could be a call I forgot to make.'

'That you have to make from a phone box? Can't make from home?'

'We into tapping phones now, Gloria?'

She wept for about ten seconds, then recovered determinedly, lit a cigarette, and said: 'I'm tense. And tired. We're spending all this money, and none coming in. And I see you refusing to anticipate . . . *anything*. You don't make any plans for eventualities. You don't care what's going to happen *if* . . .' she said shrilly.

'That your grievance, Gloria? You're bursting . . . with grievances. What is it?'

She gave the question careful thought and a restrained reply. 'When Anna was born,' she said in a quiet voice, 'you were bedazzled, Jack. I have never seen anyone so bedazzled. In love with your baby girl. It lasted about three weeks . . . and then . . . some other dazzling plaything entered your life. You're a man of great intensity, and you focus all of it on one person *for a while*, and then you've had enough and you focus it somewhere else. And the person who was a little while before the apple of your eye is let drop with a great thud.'

'I know I do that with some people,' he admitted, 'my interests change, but I don't do it with you. I have some good and permanent fixtures in my life, of which you are the main one, Gloria. You and Anna.'

'Am I? I wish I felt that.'

'You can. I promise you.'

In the apartment they heard from Patrizia that the baby had been very difficult, had been crying a great deal, but was finally asleep. Patrizia was paid, and left. They undressed in silence. In the bed he drew up her nightgown. She said she was very exhausted, and he said he would be gentle and that it would calm her.

'We have too much anger floating around. And I don't even know what about,' he said.

She touched him tenderly. 'I do appreciate you, Jack. Even when I don't go out of my mind, I am appreciative of you, you mustn't think I'm not, it's just that I'm in a period . . . when there's a limit to how much upheaval I can take. I need to be calm. Acting is always very stressful for me, and this part especially. If this film ever gets made, I have a feeling I'm going to be made to look at things we've managed to avoid looking at up till now, and it scares me . . . It scares me, Jack. I almost hope it won't get made.'

He told her: 'Save the fear. You'll need it. Because the film will get made. And actors who get scared give the best performances.'

22

In the end, it was another full fourteen months before *The Interloper* could start shooting. Tucker's big-budget picture in Africa had been delayed, as a result of which Jack's film was further delayed, and then Tucker's film went over schedule and over budget, and after that he was needed for re-takes, and long before all of this, MGM had undergone a palace revolution, and Schary had been deposed as studio chief. The old brooms were out, the new brooms were in. By the time all the dust had settled, Bruce Tucker was *really* too old for the part, but the pulling power of his name was such that this could be overlooked, and provided they could wait for him — there was still some post-synching he had to do, and then he needed a holiday — their film was going ahead.

Carl had been certain it was not going to happen, and when finally it was happening, Jack was determined to cast off in style. And he wanted Carl there, that was essential to the celebrations: get him out of his grim basement flat with the grimy net curtains and the gas rings and the plastic shower unit and the pervasive smell of boiled cabbage percolating down from the old ladies on the floors above. He wanted to flaunt before Carl's eyes that he had made it happen, even if to that end some compromises had to be accepted. It had taken him almost two years, but in the end he'd pulled it off! And it was an achievement to have got this unusual film off the ground, and there was the sensation of flying high. Let Carl have a whiff of the perfume of success. Get him out of his bolt-hole. Let him see what it meant to get a picture like this rolling. Let him witness it with his own sceptical eyes.

There are bronze statues in niches in the entrance hall and mahogany wainscoting all around the walls, and a baronial carved oak staircase. And in the bar, women's bared shoulders are reflected in mottled mirrors with giltwood frames pendulous with golden grapes and pomegranates.

He says in Carl's ear: 'Don't put it down straight away. Breathe it in first, before you spit it out.'

It is still early for a place such as this, and in the quiet, which is like that of a great library, an Italian prince with brilliant black hair is drinking red vodka Nicholoff, and standing by his side is a stunning girl in a dress that descends to a dizzying V-point at the beginning of the buttock cleft. It requires a strong hard look for Jack Strawley to establish for certain that this is Maureen Talentless, metamorphosed from New York blonde to black-haired Roman butterfly, much photographed companion of stars and princes at Giorgio's and Capriccio's and Alfredo's and Hostaria dell'Orso, and Biblioteca and Bricktop's, of course. Her eyes are belladonna bright, and Jack Strawley, though he has his lovely Gloria by him, as necessary to him as breathing, is once again captivated. She meets his eye, recognizes him and gives him a long slow smile and a little intimate shrug of a bare white shoulder blade, signalling *that's life*. She says something about him to the Roman prince at her side, and he looks up at Jack as if he is a cockroach who has just crawled out of the woodwork.

'Well,' Maureen says to him as they brush shoulders within the smart throng going in to dinner, 'haven't you come up far from sweeping floors.'

'Not as far as you've come from whatever it was you were doing, Maureen.'

'All distances are comparative,' she says.

'Compared to?'

'Where you're going.'

'And where are you going, Maureen?'

'Far,' she says. 'Far.'

'And where have you got to, would you say?'

'Only London, and only for one day. Tomorrow we go back to Rome.'

'Bad timing again.'

'We'll get it right one of these days. Are you doing a film?'

'We start day after tomorrow.'

'How exciting! Who's in it?'

'Oh . . . , there's Nik, Nik Ransom — you remember Nik? She laughs. 'Do I remember Nik? Yes, I remember Nik.'

' . . . and Gloria. And Bruce Tucker. Yeah, I guess you do remember Nik. He's over there.'

'Say hello to him for me.'

'You mind if I don't?'

'No, I don't mind one bit, as a matter of fact.' She gives a laugh that is still delicious to his ear. 'I like the way you say "and Bruce Tucker." You must be very successful, Jack.'

'Things are happening now,' he concedes, and adds: 'Even though we didn't really get to know each other that time, I've often thought about you, Maureen.'

'Have you, Jack? As a matter of fact, I've thought about you too. I do remember our conversation very well. Might there be a part for me in your film?'

'Up till this minute there wasn't,' he says. 'But let me put my mind to it.'

'You are sweet, Jack. I'd be so thrilled to be in a film directed by you. Even if it was only a small part. The things I've been in so far haven't exactly shaken the world.'

Around them a variety of foreign accents coalesce into a chic babble. They are going to be seated at their respective tables and so have to part. He gives her a lingering look that Gloria cannot fail to see. And when he has sat down at their own table, Gloria cannot fail to see how his eye keeps going back to where Maureen is sitting.

Carl is putting it all neatly down. Oh, he knows about this

place. The epitome of gangster chic. Nightclub in basement. Private rooms upstairs. For quick wife-swaps among the Smart Set. Done in the best of circles these days.

'Want to ask you something, Carl,' Jack says. 'About the script. The scene where he comes back, Stonier — and finds Leonora and the poet in bed together, and he walks away from it — says nothing. I'm not too clear what's going on there. Why's he walk away?'

'In the Cawley version? The wizard with words becomes cleverly speechless there, doesn't he? When there is a banal explanation, leave it out, and the scene looks more profound. Cawley has mastered that art.'

'What's the banal explanation?'

'Even I, Jack, know when to leave some things unsaid.'

Jack has drunk enough to come out with it: 'We used to say things to each other. We no longer do.'

'Saying things is not always useful.'

'Why write at all?'

'Cawley would say — to seduce actresses. But then he's a wit!'

'What would you say?'

'Not being as witty, I'd say . . . I don't know.'

In the inside room a thickset singer with the three-piece band is singing 'Volare'. The head waiter comes to tell them that there is Partridge à la Something-or-Other on the menu tonight. Orders are given, costly wines commanded. Jack appears distracted, keeps turning in his chair to see what is happening in the international set. Nik has become monosyllabic with ennui and alcohol, while Gloria's face becomes more and more tightly drawn as Jack keeps turning around, making no secret of where his interest lies, and Carl has an air of being grimly content for once.

'Isn't that Talentless Maureen?' Gloria says eventually, 'that you are so conspicuously besotted by? I seem to remember her being a blonde at one time. When she was plain Maureen Fisher, and George used to screw her if he could bestir himself. So now it's the 2,000-year-old prince. I expect *he* bestirs himself rather more often.'

23

The production had to work around — or with — Tucker's long-established habitudes. He didn't like to rehearse because rehearsals made him 'fake it'; he gave his best performances when they just happened. If a line or action did not come out sounding right, where Tuck was concerned, he'd crunch up his forehead and say: 'Looks to me somethin' wrong there. Got to change that. How about if he . . .' It was not a question of the actor changing his performance to fit the role, but of the role being changed to fit the performance. His marvellous instinct for what 'worked' had been vindicated over a period of thirty years, and it was difficult to argue with that kind of success.

Gloria had done very little filming in her career, and to let her warm up Jack started her with a shot that was not in any of the scripts or re-writes. This shot simply showed her walking by the Thames — returning home after having been to the cinema by herself. His instructions to her were: 'You're still half in the story. Walking along following your thoughts.' That was it. He had set up the dolly tracks on a stretch of the Embankment under the big chestnut trees, with the thick interweaving cables of the arc lamps trailing back to the generator truck in the road. Police were directing people and traffic around the taped off area. First of all, the camera moves were rehearsed using Gloria's stand-in doing the river walk, while Douggie Byron ran around with a light meter fine-tuning his lighting plot to meet Jack's demands: he wanted colour to be used to get an *almost* black and white effect — and there should be no fancy framing, nothing 'painterly' about the scene. He wanted the light to be grainy, becoming harsh as the street lamps came on.

When Douggie called, 'Ten minutes', Jack told Gloria:

'Darling, just walk it for me a couple of times. Without working at it.'

Her walk and pace were different from the stand-in's, and the grip pushing the dolly had to re-adjust himself to her movements. Jack had taken the operator's place behind the camera for the walk-through. He wanted to see exactly the way it was going to look on the screen: the jerky camera moves to left and right, to show Leonora reacting to sights and sounds . . . river traffic, road traffic . . . the chimney stacks of Battersea Power Station . . . the wharves on the other bank; then back again to her walking and looking straight ahead, and then the camera going away from her, a fast backward movement widening the picture, to show now the full bustling street scene in which her 'solitary' walk was taking place. He wanted to do it as a single shot — which called for some nifty pushing by the dolly grip. At the end she was to gradually catch up with the tracking camera and walk into a head and shoulder close-up under a street lamp, and the audience would then see her state of mind. Following Gloria's walk through the camera's viewfinder, he found he was looking to see if she really did have bags under the eyes, as Douggie Byron had implied when proposing to use the 'Magic Max' make-up. Jack-the-camera saw only what the camera saw, and had to accept that she did indeed have lines, didn't have the smooth, tight-skinned complexion of a twenty-two year old. Looked at like this, so coldly, she bore all the signs of a woman in her mid thirties. It wasn't that she looked *old*, but the youthful bloom had gone. It had been replaced by something else, maturity, character, a real person whom he loved, and these aspects created their own picture in his mind, but his mind-picture was different from the picture that the camera saw: the mind picture was affected by his feelings, his recollections, an entire library of images from the past, whereas the camera only saw what was before it at that moment. For the story they were doing it was right that Gloria should look her age, and even a bit older, since it was supposed to be about a woman approaching forty, with all the fears and insecurities of reaching that hazardous threshhold — this was the basis of her wild behaviour with the poet. The lines and small flaws in her face would make her look more real and make the sexual scenes stronger. So clearly he'd been right to rule out recourse to the Magic Max. At the same time, he was depressed to think that she now needed such aids to look her best.

When Douggie Byron had called out, 'Okay for lighting', and all the others had indicated that they were ready too, Jack, crouching on the dolly platform next to the camera operator, called 'Action' very softly, in an intimate whisper to Gloria, to cue her to her interior mood. As the camera was tracking alongside her, he felt he was seeing into her as never before. Never did you look at another person with the fixed intensity — and objectivity — that the camera brought to it. Oh, in life you did not dare to look at anyone in that way, it was too devastating, but he was having to, because he was the director and had to see what the camera saw.

The first take was nearly perfect, but he did two more to cover himself, and then they moved the entire convoy of trucks to the house where he and Gloria were now living, in Paulton Square, to get a shot of her coming home, putting the key in the door, and then of her leaving the house, turning into the King's Road and looking in the window of an antiquarian bookseller while watching the phone box across the road.

The decision to use the outside of the Paulton Square house, and its immediate surroundings, had been taken partly in order to save production costs but also to get that extra degree of verisimilitude which came when an actor was moving around in a locale that was his own. It was a way of taking the story even closer to home, and, while this entailed some risks in terms of touching emotional nerves, he felt that the benefits for the production outweighed those risks.

Altogether he managed to get six different continuity shots of this kind, which, together with the river walk, added up to about two minutes of screen time. He thought that was pretty good going for a first day of shooting, and it had served at the same time to get Gloria used to the camera without challenging her too much straight away.

At the end, when they were finishing up, and Moira was making her entries in the log that she had elected to keep, in order to have a complete technical record of the production, she asked him about the shot of Gloria walking by the river.

'Why'd it have to be done in a single shot?'

'I wanted that feeling of coming out of a film and being still in the story, not yet readjusted fully to the outside reality. That's her state throughout the film, between fiction and real life.'

'Why couldn't you have got that if you cut?'

'Cuts break the spell. Indicate a changing viewpoint — ie., going out of the subject's head. Whereas in the long take you're with her all the time and it's clearly her POV. Some of it is going to be completely silent, not even any music, at other moments we'll have traffic sounds, a driver shouting at her, but I'll stop the sound in mid-shout, because she's not there, she's in her mind, I wanted everything to look dull and wintry — and not quite to add up.'

'So getting Douggie to use the amber gel is to . . . ?'

'To dull down the colours, to give us a listless feeling. Which is her state.'

'Why'd her hair have to be uncombed?'

'She forgot to comb it coming out of the cinema. Too preoccupied. You ask too many fucking questions, Assistant. What you trying to do? Learn my job?'

'Sure.'

The move from the Bolton Street flat had been both desirable and necessary: with both of them filming they needed a larger place so they could have a full-time nanny for Anna, and that meant a house where they were not all on top of each other. The house in Paulton Square being on three floors meant that the functions of the household could be compartmentalized: he liked to keep things separate, didn't want the pram in the hall, or business being conducted from the bedroom. His life was getting to be complicated, and he needed to keep the main threads apart. From the square down to the Embankment and Battersea Bridge was only a short walk, and on the opposite side of the bridge Moira had her houseboat. On that particular stretch of mudbank she was the only resident, the other boats that tied up there were barges and tugs and pleasure cruisers and were not lived in. With its bright orange trim, Moira's boat was distinguishable, even from the Chelsea shore, and he liked the feeling of having his women close by, accessible, but on separate sides of the river.

Gloria was bringing to her performance as Leonora aspects of herself that she had never fully revealed to him before. Carl's writing of the part was so close to her character that she couldn't help digging deeply into herself. Jack was drawing the performance out of her, fearful of what he was going to find out, since it was so much about their life together. It was like playing some very dangerous truth game. Part of what was coming out in this game was her deep-down stubborn American puritanism, which accounted for her terror of the big sex scene coming up with Nik. Jack had written into the script lines taken directly from their own intimate life. You had to steal from life. In her acting of the part, she was rendering her painful account of breaking off with Carl and taking up with him. Was confessing her guilty self-abandonment to the 'crimson joy'. And her subsequent sense of having been tarnished by it. These things were coming out in her performance, and some of it was a shock to him. It was the shock of not knowing the person you were married to. He sensed that the excitement of her performance was going to be in proportion to the risks they ran, and he wanted that excitement on the screen, and so was ready to push Gloria to the limit. If what came out risked stripping themselves so naked that they might not be able to look each other in the face again, that risk had to be run. In life you could get along never showing the whole of yourself, maybe that was the smartest way, maybe that was the only way, keeping inside your secret enclaves, but in a dramatic film, in *his* film, the masks had to come off. Well, so be it! He was also, in the way he was directing the film, exposing his own most intimate nature. Your character depended on the person you were with, and with Moira he could be the 'savage', didn't have to make excuses. He needed her around. She was fast becoming indispensable to him. She didn't mind his 'sweet revenge'. Okay, so everybody had to get something off their chest in the love act. Okay, so there were always ghosts. You couldn't get rid of the fucking ghosts. Had to live with them. She knew he had plenty . . . so what? There was the tough raunchy side to Moira that could take all that from him. With Moira he didn't have to be on good behaviour. Because she'd seen him in the gutter sobbing and she had seen him with all the masks off wanting what he wanted, and, as far as she was concerned, it was all okay, as long as he let her learn from him.

She didn't demur when he said: 'Okay, I need cigarettes. Americans. A bottle of J & B. A thermos of very very strong coffee. And you.'

'I don't seem to get much time to myself.'

'Are you complaining, Assistant?'

'No. I know pushy ambitious Special Assistants aren't allowed to complain. You won't catch me complaining.'

'When did you get to be a *Special* Assistant?'

'Just now. I got promoted, right?'

The interior of the Stoniers' house had been built by the art director to match with the facade of the house in Paulton Square. Approaching the set, the outside presented an unprepossessing aspect of rusty iron scaffolding and lath and balsa wood walls, but for the interior, art director Percy Drummer had created a house in keeping with Jack's idea of elegant rich living. The couple had become rich in the course of David Cawley's script re-writes because Jack had felt that the rich afforded more visual opportunities and gave him more scope for trenchant commentary. And he wanted to oppose the Bohemian poet-thief to the bourgeois life of the successful author in his Hampstead house.

Jack had told Percy Drummer he wanted lots of mirrors everywhere. There were convex Regency mirrors in the entrance hall and on the stairs and a mirror opposite the bed in the guest room. The sex scene between Gloria and the poet was going to be filmed as a mirror shot. Out of consideration for Gloria's uneasiness about this scene, Jack and the art director had chosen a George III oval giltwood mirror in which the seduction scene would be seen. With its mottled dark plate enclosed by flame motifs and an elaborate crest of scrolls and leaves, the picture in the mirror was going to have the character of a Fragonard painting. The mottled glass would darken and blur Gloria's nakedness. Finally, the scene was going to be carefully edited so that the audience would only see a woman's glistening back, her head thrown back with passion, hair streaming. He had promised Gloria that there was going to be nothing in the scene that millions of people had not seen and accepted in paintings. They'd have to film more than was ever going to be used so as to give him enough footage to edit down to what he needed, but finally the shot would not play longer than five or ten seconds on the screen, and they'd be able to darken it further in the lab, if she wasn't entirely happy with it.

Despite these assurances Gloria was panic-stricken about doing the scene. He offered to cut it down to a conventional shot of her in bed, covered up, and the poet standing naked by the window. That would indicate what had transpired without any physical intimacy having to be shown, but she considered this to be opting out. She thought it was essential for the story that the audience should have a glimpse of Leonora in the grip of the 'crimson joy', the performance would be incomplete without that.

The day they were due to shoot the scene she was shaking with nerves, and there was nothing he could do to calm her. Moira, in her earnest, eager-to-learn manner, asked him on the set: 'How do you intend to handle this with Gloria?'

'What are you talking about, Assistant?'

'She's scared to death.'

'What do you suggest I do, Moira?'

'I don't know. Maybe . . . try to discover what lies behind her fears?'

'No,' he said, 'that won't work. Go to the bottom of the class! It's back to making the coffee, young lady.'

'So what *will* you fucking do?'

He liked that she stood up spiritedly for herself.

'Use it,' he said. 'I'll use what the scene brings out, even if it wasn't in the script, because that's what's there underneath. Yeah, even if you find out things you don't want to find out.'

'That's smart,' she said at once.

'Yeah. If it works.'

24

When Gloria came out onto the set, she was in a long voluminous Japanese silk robe which she held tightly to herself; her
shoulders were hunched, she was shivering, and the expression
on her face was of someone preparing herself for an ordeal. She
mounted the Georgian staircase and when she reached the top
straight away hit her marks, sat down on the edge of the bed and
lit a cigarette. She was trying to cut off from all the activity
around her and concentrate on the scene. The focus-puller was
measuring the distance between her and the mirror and between
the camera and the mirror, and Douggie Byron was fine-tuning
the lighting plot. He directed the grips, getting them to fractionally shift the positions of the heavily gauzed arc lamps and the
reflector panels held in tripod stands. In the story, the room was
in darkness with the only light coming from the landing as the
door is opened. There is the shock image in the mirror, and then
the door is closed again. The lights were tested while readings
were taken on Gloria's face. A girl from make-up, in a white
smock, carrying a box of Kleenex, a bushy brush, a jar and a
comb and hairbrush came and sat next to Gloria on the bed, and
Gloria lowered the Japanese robe to her waist and placed herself
in a position for the girl to apply fine brush strokes to her bare
back, to make it glisten as if from sweat. Douggie Byron put his
meter on Gloria's back and took a new reading. Immediately this
had been done, Gloria pulled the robe back up around herself
while Nik, without any ado, stripped down to his briefs and lay
on the bed beside her.

Tucker had taken up his position at the bottom of the staircase.

Jack squeezed past him and ran up to the bedroom. He kneeled
between Nik and Gloria on the bed. He checked the alignment
with the oval mirror and showed Gloria the exact movements he
wanted from her. Keeping her robe on, continuing to take drags
on her cigarette, Gloria took up the demonstrated position crouched
over Nik, very close to him but avoiding any bodily contact with
him. Gripping her by the arms, Jack slowly twisted her round to

give him the exact posture he wanted. When he received the signal from Byron, he got up and swung across the gap by the side of the stairs and onto the camera platform and looked through the viewfinder himself. After a minute he murmured, 'Looks good,' and then called to Gloria: 'Take off the robe, darling . . .' Gloria took the cigarette from her mouth and held it out to the props man standing by the bed. Despite the heat of the film lights she was shivering.

Jack said to her: 'Gloria, throw your head back, darling, throw it right back, right back.' He peered intently through the viewfinder as she followed his instructions. 'That's good, that looks good,' he said again, encouragingly. 'I like that. Okay, let's do it. Quiet everyone.' Then: 'Action.'

The camera on the crane was starting level with Tucker at the bottom of the staircase. The script called for him to take off his raincoat and throw it over the banisters. And then, unsuspectingly, but touched by some subconscious unease, he starts up the stairs, the camera on the crane moving alongside him. He goes to switch off the light that has been left on on the landing, sees that the door of the spare bedroom is ajar and goes to close it — and sees the scene in the mirror.

The first four takes were all ruined due to Gloria's false movements. She was becoming more tense with each spoilt take and angrier with herself. On the crane, Jack saw that Tucker was playing the scene beautifully, not 'acting' it at all, but showing everything on his face. He was doing it just right. One of those times when he was able to simply pluck the performance out of the air. At the top, as he opened the door, the grips working the jib arm of the crane abruptly hoisted the camera higher, and at the same time the operator rotated dizzyingly to fix on the glistening image in the mirror: Gloria, head thrown back, hair streaming, in the throes of the crimson joy. Gloria was doing it fine now, pouring herself into the part with perfect control. Self-consciousness all gone, her embarrassment consumed in the heat of the scene, she was using everything that had been stirred up in her, her dread and her shame and her distaste overcome by a streak of sheer exhibitionism which made her careless about how she was exposing herself to all their eyes, and to the camera.

From his position at the top of the stairs Tucker suddenly said: 'Goes on too long. Tuck can't be standing here half an hour just *watching*.'

Jack quietly called, 'Cut'. With an effort he held down his anger. The scene had been playing beautifully, and Tuck had ruined it by his intervention. It was unprofessional, and it was a betrayal. And it was what stars did, if they didn't like the way something was going.

'Okay,' Jack said, holding his voice steady, treating the incident as if it were some minor technical hitch. He spoke swiftly and in a low voice, trying to preserve the strong emotions that had built up in the actors— of which Tuck's breaking up the shot was probably a manifestation, he told himself.

'Perfect, Gloria. Nik, great. It was beautiful that time, though, as Tuck says, a *little* on the long side, so let's do it this time speeded up a bit. Okay, Gloria? Tuck from the bottom of the stairs, please.' He was trying to get in another take swiftly, before the mood was completely dissipated. But Tucker wasn't moving towards his marks. 'Whenever you're ready, Tuck.'

Long slow thought processes were unfolding in the star's troubled brain, and he wasn't ready yet to move. Finally he said: 'It's not gonna work, Jack.'

'Take ten,' Jack called. 'And . . . Nik, Gloria, everybody . . . nobody move, hold on to the mood. Keep focused.' Putting an arm around Tucker's shoulders and steering him away from the others, he said: 'I know what you mean about its being long, Tuck, but we can always trim it down in the cutting. Otherwise, it was just beautiful, and your reaction to the mirror shot was abolutely dead on.'

'What bothers me,' Tucker said slowly, 'is I'm standing there starin' at them . . . not doin' anything while they're going at it like rabbits .' He shook his head, solemnly tightening his lips over his teeth. 'What it looks like is that he's getting off on . . . his own wife being laid by this good-for-nothin'. Well, that's sick, that's real sick . . . and then,' he shook his head again several times, 'he turns around and . . . walks away from it, goes back down the stairs and out the house, saying not a word, which makes him not just a voyeur but also a worm.'

'It's a complex scene, Tuck . . . a lot of different strands of feeling are coming together there . . . and you got it all, the way you did it. I don't know how but you did. So don't try to break it down.'

'It's not right,' Tucker said, uncomfortably cogitating, wincing, his weather-beaten face crinkling up with honest-to-goodness effort. 'Not right. He sees the woman he loves jerkin' around with this guy, this thief he's taken into his house and he turns away from it. He oughtta smash his face in . . . the audience has to get some release for its emotions, it wants to see the guy's face smashed in.'

'It's not that kind of a film, Tuck.'

Tucker was shaking his head slowly, grappling with heavy thoughts. 'I dunno, I dunno.' He scratched the side of his nose in his endearing way while his eyes fumed. He shook his head making little tchk tchk sounds with his teeth. He was spreading his hands indicating that he'd been left no alternative, and this was what was going to have to happen.

'Got to do it . . . different. Can't make Tuck look like some fairy. Like some'un can't get it up with a woman. Turns it into a Claude Rains *character* part. Where he's getting his kicks in other ways . . . sick ways . . . know what I mean? Tuck's not yet ready to hang up his six-shooter . . . and watch. Got to do somethin' about that scene.'

'What do'you want done, Tuck?'

'Got to find a way round it.'

'You have any suggestions?'

'I'm not the writer, I'm just the actor. Ask our writers to come up with something.'

In the afternoon there appeared on the set two men in sober dark suits who were unknown to Jack. One was in blue, the other in charcoal grey. The older and taller one was about fifty, thin, balding, had a beaklike nose and wore rimless spectacles and a button-down striped shirt and striped tie. The younger one, in his early thirties, had all his hair, which was dressed with hair lotion and clean cut round the ears and had a side parting. 'Who are the zombies, Sydney?' Jack asked his producer between shots.

'New brooms. They're part of the team that came in when Mayer and Schenck and Schary went. They're there to sweep up the mess. The balding guy is Vic Stiller, Senior Vice-President, Europe, and the guy with the slicked down hair is Bill Gayley, Assistant Chief Executive Officer, International Financements. They're the shape of things to come, Jack. The czars are out, the accountants are in.'

'What the new brooms sweeping around here for? Our budget is about the size of their cigar bill.'

'Cost control is the new buzz word. Nickels and dimes. Everything counts. They want to know why we're six days behind schedule and 8% over-budget. And why we have a scene of Gloria walking by the river in which nothing happens and which was not in the approved script.'

'What you tell 'em, Sydney?'

'I told them that we're getting great production value on the screen.'

'What they say to that?'

'They want to know why was the scene shot in such a dull way, why was it so dimly lit like we couldn't afford the arc lights. They say it looks as though it was shot in black and white.'

'You tell them it was meant to look like that?'

'Yeah, I did. But they're not Warner Bros, they're MGM, and at MGM, even without L.B. Mayer, they like nice, bright, vivid colour. Also, they want to talk to Tuck. They want to know if he's happy with how things are going so far.'

'What if he isn't?'

'If he's unhappy enough, they get a new director.'

'How can they do that!'

'Easily. That's how.'

Douggie Byron was lighting the other wall for a reverse shot on the poet, using Nik's stand-in. Nik was in his dressing room. Tucker was in his dressing room. From the look of it, Douggie Byron could be quite a while before he had got all his lighting done. Could be another hour. A dangerous period during which the actors weren't doing anything, and the greysuits could get to them.

'Delay them getting to Tuck, Sydney. Say I have to talk to him about a difficulty we've run into in his next scene and that Tuck can't be disturbed right now.'

When Carver had left to try and head off the new brooms, Moira asked: 'Can I say something?'

'No.'

'Why can't I say something?'

'Because you're always wanting to say something,' he said, irascibly. 'Stop pushing so hard, Moira, stop pushing. Sometimes it just gets to be too much.'

'I have an observation to make. Listen to me, Jack. The problem is Bruce, and I know Bruce better than you .'

'I don't want to know about how well you know Bruce.'

'Here's what I know,' she persisted determinedly. 'He's an old-style star who expects to look good on the screen. And in that scene he doesn't look good. He looks like shit. It's an image-thing, it's a machismo thing. He told me once about how he was due to play in a Western where he can't shoot a gun. It was a great script. He talked to his pal De Mille about it, and De Mille told him that a Bruce Tucker who can't shoot a gun was letting the kids down. He didn't do the picture.'

'We're not making a Western, Moira.'

'Jack, he's a star. A big star. One of the biggest. He's a king, it's a question of his dignity. They used to put people to death for insulting a king.'

'He's supposed to be acting a part.'

'Stars play themselves, Jack. Which makes everything personal, it's *his* manhood that's on the line when he walks away from that scene.'

'What am I supposed to do, give him a gun?'

'Yeah.'

'What are you saying?'

'Whatever it may look like, at first, he's still the fastest draw.'

He saw what she was saying now, and it was smart. It was very smart.

'Okay, Assistant. Go to the top of the class!' he told her. 'Now, take this down. Cable Maureen Wynner in Rome. Reads: CAN OFFER YOU SMALL BUT VERY NOTICEABLE PART IN SCENE WITH TUCKER ONE OR TWO POSSIBLY THREE

DAYS' SHOOTING. FOR WHICH YOU ARE PERFECT CAST-
ING. HOPE TIMING IS RIGHT THIS TIME. LOVE JACK.'
   He got a breathless stop-less cable back the same day.
   'JACK DARLING TIMING PERFECT AM HONOURED AND
FLATTERED TO BE ASKED WHEN WHERE HOW DO YOU
WANT ME LOVE MAUREEN.'

When Gloria heard that Maureen Wynner was being brought out
from Rome to play a small part which Jack had written in for her
himself, necessitating a whole new scene not previously in the
script, requiring twenty extras and a three-piece rhumba band,
she looked at him as if he had gone mad.
   'You have two MGM executives here checking the nickels and
dimes, and you're going to hire this untalented starlet that everybody knows is only hired when somebody wants to screw her.'
   'That's what she's going to play in the story. Herself.'
   'We all seem to be playing ourselves in this picture. Especially
you.' He saw the anger rising up in her dangerously. The brimful
woman who one day was going to overflow. 'All of a sudden you
have the money to bring Maureen out from Rome, put her up at
the Dorchester for three days, hire extras to play party guests.
Are you going out of your way to make these people fire you? I
don't get it. This film's supposed to mean so much to you . . . to
us. And you're risking all that because you want to fool around
with this little tramp who's been had by everybody in the business who can move her up a rung or two.'
   He was calm and unwavering. 'It's not what you think,' he told
her. 'Trust me, Gloria. It's a vital scene which the story needs.'

The scene for which Maureen Wynner had been flown over from
Rome required her to listen captivated while Tucker, as author
Stonier, tells her about the enemies of promise in a writer's life.
   The first requirement of her small role she fulfilled without
difficulty: she looked stunning in a high gloss chintz evening
dress that was like molten zinc moulded to her body from neck to
ankle.
   For the first set-up she was required to be standing all alone at
the party, looking lost, and author Stonier comes up to her, fills

her champagne glass and starts telling her who these people are that she doesn't know. They're the enemies of promise, he says. She doesn't understand this, and he shows her. Over there is money-on-the-nail, an editor at *Playboy*. The woman talking to him is Leonora, another enemy called marriage. His marriage. Closely associated to an enemy called the pram-in-the-hall. The place is full of enemies. And you, he tells her, are the greatest enemy, and the most enticing, the charlock's shade. Sex, the corrupter of the writer's will to work.

That was the end of the first party set-up. After six takes, Jack Strawley was satisfied and gave instructions to prepare the next scene.

Maureen hadn't had a chance to talk to him yet in private and she tottered towards him in her shiny tight dress. Seeing nowhere else to sit, she asked 'Can I?' and, without waiting for permission, sat herself down on his knee, just lightly, while waiting for someone to bring her a chair.

'How'd I do?' she asked him. 'Did I say the line all right?' She had had to say: 'Why am I an enemy?' Had she said it provocatively enough? He said she didn't need to make any big effort to be provocative. She shifted her weight around on his knees, and he said, 'Let's aim to have a drink together, we can talk about your part then. Suppose I come round to the Dorchester after rushes.'

'What time'll that be?'

'Around nine.'

'What'll I do until then?'

'Think exciting thoughts,' he told her.

Considering that she had perhaps sat for too long on her director's knee, she asked Moira, standing nearby, to bring her a chair. Moira made a face but did it, and Maureen said sweetly: 'Oh, thank you, honey, thank you, what is your name?' and then added quickly: 'If it's not too much trouble, Moira, could you get me some cigarettes? I'm right out. American ones. Marlboros or Pall Malls . . . and matches. Oh, and coffee, very black.'

Moira shot Jack a sharp questioning look.

He told her: 'Get the cigarettes, Moira. Would you please? And bring some coffee for me too.'

Later, going over the next day's scenes with her, he mused out loud: 'The scene with Maureen has got to be very light . . . she isn't worth . . . well, anything . . . it's a quick little fling with somebody of no . . .' He was floundering. 'Hell, it's not even a one-night stand, a five-minute stand. For his ego more'n anything. That was your idea, right? To make it a Bruce Tucker part and not Claude Rains.'

'Jack, I don't think it's a light scene at all. It's only light on the surface, it's heavy underneath. Underneath he's ruining his life.'

'That what he's doing?'

'Figure it out for yourself when you see her tonight.'

After the rushes, he was flying high. First he phoned Gloria to say he was going to be held up. There were problems that he had to deal with. To expect him when she saw him. Then he phoned Maureen. He was just leaving the studio now and would be at the Dorchester in an hour's time.

'Oh, Jack,' Maureen said sleepy-voiced, 'when you hadn't called by nine I took a pill. I thought I ought to get a good night's sleep, so I'm in good shape for my big scene tomorrow. We'll have our drink tomorrow night, Jack. When it's all over.'

He said, 'Okay,' and though he felt angry and frustrated and disappointed, he knew she was right. What he'd been planning was crazy in every way, especially in view of the scene she had to play tomorrow with Tucker. He didn't want all the sexual tension dissipated, he needed it for the scene. Save it, save it. Don't use it all up beforehand. Get the value on the screen.

25

The set that had been built gave author Stonier a workroom with a double expanse of soundproof plate glass overlooking the living room area, so that he was insulated inside his eyrie while at the same time able to watch what went on below in his household. This fitted well with the character of Stonier, someone who wanted to be isolated and alone and at the same time in control of the people in his life. The scene for which Maureen Wynner had been brought over from Rome would take place in the dark workroom, patchily illumined by light coming from the party below. There was going to be the rhumba band playing silently, and the 'enemies' swimming about like golden carps in a fish tank . . . and to the side of this picture-framed scene, the charlock's shade, luscious Maureen. Jack explained the set-up to her: the left side of the screen was going to be filled by the swirl of guests, drinking, eating, wise-cracking, flirting. This was the Stoniers' rich, fashionable existence, money-on-the-nail smoothly mingling with praise-on-the-nail and the slimy mallow and the nodding poppies. The whole blighted field.

'Down there it's the comedy of manners, up here it's the hard stuff . . . What d'you say, Maureen? You game?'

'It's going to be a good scene, isn't it? You're going to do it stylish?'

'It's going to be stylish,' he promised. 'And real.'

'Okay. As long as I don't have to do anything gross. I wouldn't want to do anything *gross*.'

'It won't be gross. It'll be stylish.'

'Okay.'

He suggested that she and Tucker get to know each other.

'Discuss the scene, spell it out, get rid of any hangups you may have — about anything, at all — so that you're comfortable,' he told them both. Meanwhile, he was going to go down and direct the party guests. Though the POV was from the soundproofed writer's office, and what the party guests were saying couldn't be heard up there, Jack had worked out a whole series of conversations and scenes going on below, to make the party scene really alive. He'd worked out how these conversations progressed and interlocked with other things going on. Movements were carefully blocked out. He told a girl by herself that she was trying hard to get into one or other of the tight groups, but was being ignored, kept out, until money-on-the-nail lets her into his group and quickly seeks his reward with her, while his wife, trying hard to keep up her side of their open marriage, flirts desperately in the next group. By the end of the morning everyone at the party had been given his movements and his subject of conversation. Working with Douggie Byron, Jack had arranged the lighting so that the writer's unlit workroom was like a dark cave that the guests could not see into, though somebody standing in it could see out. To introduce an additional element of danger, he had a *Tatler*-type magazine photographer going around below, with a press camera, taking flash pictures of groups and individuals, and whenever the flashes went off, the white magnesium flare for a split second threw some light into the dark space above.

Lunch in the studio restaurant was at long tables, with no reserved places, everybody sitting where they liked. He arranged it so that he was sitting across from Maureen and he put Moira next to her, for Gloria's benefit.

'So how you and Tuck getting along?' he asked Maureen.

'Like a house on fire.'

'Not *too* much on fire.' He made an effort to keep his smile light.

'You wanted it to be a fiery scene, you said.'

'Just for the scene, you know.'

'Tuck's really an attractive man.'

'If you like that sort of thing.'

'What sort of thing you talking about?'

'Oh, you know. These Hollywood old-timers.'

'Tuck's not old, not what I call *old*. Not in his interests.'

'You been finding out about those?'

'We've been working on the scene. You know, how we're going to — uh — fit together, him being so tall and all, and me being kind of on the small side. I asked him if he was going to lift me up, but he said the doctors don't allow him to lift. He said they allowed everything else.'

Maybe it was being insecure, but he reminded her of their date.

'We're seeing each other tonight, after rushes?'

'Oh, sure.' Eyes playful and bold. 'I'm going to be thinking about that.'

'Okay, let's get to work.'

In the upstairs part of the set, representing the author's workroom, Jack put Tucker and Maureen side by side against the dark wall and gave them directions. 'Don't think they even kiss. It's that out of control. They've just come in here to do it.'

She had her serious working face on now, digesting his directions.

'Okay, Maureen?'

'Okay.'

He told them to go ahead and take a shot at it. It was a rehearsal, but he was going to have the cameras running because sometimes the first try turned out to be the best.

He gave a sign to Dave Collins, on the lower level of the set, to get the party guests moving around, talking animatedly, and he waited while the scene was livening up there and getting a natural swing to it — the rhumba band playing, the hustlers hustling, the dealers dealing, praise-on-the-nail waxing fulsome, the photographer moving among the guests — and then he gave the signal for the camera to start the slow pan to the charlock's shade. The two of them appeared to have done their preparatory work well. Tucker was dipping his hands freely into the molten zinc, and the high gloss dress was catching the bounced light as Tucker dragged it up her body, over thighs and hips — she helping him with a nice sense of urgency — and then both of them were tugging underneath. Jack was right by the camera lens, close behind Tucker. He saw Maureen's face cut vertically in half, her gaping mouth, one swimming eye and, below, the swirl of party guests. Maureen was giving herself up to the scene, not holding back, and Tuck was improvising freely — very freely — as instructed, with Maureen being very accommodating. The problem was that she had the fixed facial expression of an inflatable plastic doll and he had to stop the take, it was so bad.

'You were doing great,' he told Maureen, 'but try not to "compose" your face, you're doing it as if you're posing for a pin-up, you've got that sexy pin-up expression . . . I want it to be real and hard, not soft and cheesecakey. Forget about how you look. You're in the dark, by yourselves, nobody can see you. Let yourself go. Let me see that in your face, Maureen. Remember, what he's doing is crazy — risky as hell, self-destructive. You're the "enemy of promise", one of the destroyers . . . it's not "sugar and spice everything nice". Okay, let's go again. Action.'

They started up again. Although the glittery dress was soon bundled up almost to the level of her crotch, and she was being bruisingly banged against the wall by Tucker's rough-riding love-making style, her expression remained resolutely plasticated.

Jack had to stop the scene again, and spell it out once more. He took her aside, and while she was tugging down the clinging material of her dress — she was a bit bruised and dishevelled, but smiling bravely through it all — he told her: 'For Christ's sake, Maureen, is this how you are in real time?' Trying to think of a way of getting through to her, he thought, she's like one of those loose-jointed dolls that you can twist this way or that, joints everywhere, and whatever the contortions, always has the same fixed expression. He got very near to her, so near she was relaxing her knee against his and breathing hotly into his mouth, and he said: 'You do the body movements fine. But we won't see much of that, what we'll see is your face, and your face says: oh, isn't this *nice*! And that's exactly what it isn't. It isn't nice at all. That is not the feeling of this scene . . .'

'I'm trying, Jack. I'm doing my best . . . I'm acting my head off.'

'That may be the trouble. Stop acting, Maureen. Just do it.'

She listened to these instructions and tried again. It was no good, and now he stopped her after a few seconds, saying bluntly: 'Again. Without acting.' They did five, six, ten takes, and still it was no good, and for each take the whole elaborate business of the party guests following their different courses — mingling, developing their storylines — needed to be set in motion, everything had to be re-started again and again. Between takes, while the make-up department worked on restoring her face, and the wardrobe people fixed her dishevelled dress so that the dishevellment could begin anew, Maureen was near hysteria, biting her lip, fighting the tears, the rage, the panic.

Jack told her: 'When the camera's not turning you're good, you're real. Then the moment I say "Action", you freeze-up, you get actressy, you want to look *nice* . . . and it's no good.' He tried to get the camera turning secretly so that she wouldn't know she was being filmed, but she knew each time and went straight into her dolly look. After the fifteenth dud, he blew his top. 'I guess they're right when they call you Maureen Talentless . . . only we now have got to add, *including* on your back.'

'You do love to put women down, don't you!' she shouted back at him. 'You're a sadist, that's what you are! If you think you're seeing me tonight, think again!' Her gorgeous face was turning blotchy and hard and snarly, and she was good, you could see some real emotion at last. If only she could do this on camera. He didn't care what emotion she showed — let it be hate.

'The hate's good, Maureen. Let me see the hate . . . You're right, men put you down. Because you're so gorgeously easy to put down. Go on. Give me the hate, Maureen. Give it . . .' She was sobbing spasmodically, her eye make-up running, and she looked crumpled and beat-up, and he was not letting them repair her face or fix her dress, was letting the camera turn, because this mess she was in was a sign of some human life going on somewhere within the all-plastic body frame. Automatically she arranged herself for another brutal assault from Tucker the bronco-buster, and while she was doing this, Jack took Tucker aside and told him: 'She can't act it because she can't act to save her life. Just go ahead. Just go ahead. Just do it. Any way you want. Do it any way. I don't care what. Just get some expression out of her.'

Tucker said with his sly, lazy, slow grin: 'It's her face that's the problem. Everything else works just fine.'

'Whatever you want, Tuck. Just get me something I can print.' He called 'Action' again, and Tucker was shuffling forward softly, secretly, going in close, up against the cringing form, his hands fumbling between them, and then Jack was seeing a sudden surprising flow of real life seeping through the high gloss of her beautiful wrecked face. It became contorted and she was letting out a real-life gasp, a real-life sob, anger and pain and humiliation and something that was not quite pleasure mixed up together. And then she went limp, gave up, allowed it, except in her eyes, which were full of rage, and only when it was over and Jack Strawley had said 'Cut and print!' did she have the full hysterical fit.

She wouldn't see Jack or Tucker in her dressing room, or any other man; the only person she'd let near her was Moira, and when Moira came out her face was grim.

'She's going to the cops.'

'Stay with her, Moira. Tell her we're all very sorry, things got out of hand, we lost control, say we'll make it up to her.'

But there was no shifting Maureen: she wanted revenge for the way she'd been humiliated in front of everybody, used like a cheap prostitute . . . They'd undertaken that there'd be nothing gross, and they'd lied to her and abused her, and she felt dirty, and she was going to get her own back by dragging them into the dirt with her, she was going to talk to the press, mire Tucker's image, ruin his career.

Summoned by Moira, the doctor arrived to give Maureen an injection and doctorly advice. His report was not encouraging: she was a very hurt, very determined little girl, he said, and she was going to get herself together and then she was going to the police.

'You go with her,' Jack told Moira. 'Stick with her. See what you can do. We got to do something, otherwise . . .'

She cut him short. 'Yeah, I know. I know what "otherwise" means. I've gotten to be quite an expert on "otherwise" since working on this movie.'

They watched the rushes in sullen silence. By 9:30 there was still no word, and he put through a call to the Dorchester and asked for Miss Wynner's room, and Moira answered — cryptically.

'Can't talk right now.'

'What's going on?'

'She's giving a press conference.'

'*Fucking hell!* And what are you doing?'

'I'm . . . acting as her PR. Doing what I can, Jack.'

'What you can! Meaning?'

'I can't talk,' she said and hung up.

He drove back to London fast, drove right up to the Dorchester and let the doorman park the XK150. At the desk they said that he couldn't go up to Miss Wynner's room, she was with the press still, and nobody was being allowed up who hadn't been approved by the public relations lady, Miss Goldberg. They would give Miss Goldberg the message that he was waiting downstairs. He went and sat in the bar and ordered a whisky. It was half an hour before Moira finally came down.

'What's going on?' he demanded.

'The last of the press have left now, they all came at different times . . . it got long, with her repeating it all, each time,' she said wearily.

'Repeating what each time?'

'I stopped her going to the cops.'

'But she's been talking to the press.'

'Yeah.'

'That's as bad.'

Moira said in a low exhausted voice: 'Actually, it isn't. I got you off the hook.'

'Can you make yourself a bit clearer, Moira. She's talked to the press?'

'You want the whole scenario blow by blow?'

'Yes.'

She took a deep breath followed by a long gulp of whisky. 'Okay. I'm going to make this quick, because I'm whacked out. Scene 1: I send a taxi with the stills — Larry's photos are just sensational — to all the nationals. She'll be on every front page tomorrow. Scene 2: Interior. Hotel bedroom. She's fuming and screaming blue murder . . . then she starts getting all these phone calls — from the papers — they've seen the photos and they all want to send reporters. I tell her yes, see them, can't hurt.'

'You told her to see the press! Jesus Christ, Moira!'

'Wait for it!' She took another gulp of whisky, draining the glass, and signalled for refills. 'I have experience of the Maureens of this world. Publicity has a calming effect on their nerves. Especially when combined with suitable quantities of the hard stuff. And Moira's Sob Sister advice column. We get round to exchanging girls' stories. About what pigs men are. And I tell her the best revenge is don't get mad, get even. And the way to get even is cash in on the publicity. It took some doing, but however bad an actress she is, she's not dumb. So finally it clicked.'

'What she tell them?'

'What her public relations adviser Moira Goldberg advised her to tell them. That while it was a small part, it was her most challenging acting role so far, and that you were this genius of a director who had got out of her things she didn't know she had in her to give. And that Bruce Tucker was wonderful to work with . . . a perfect gentleman.'

'You're a great girl Moira Goldberg.'

'Yeah! Like Sydney says, the truth has a funny way of changing from minute to minute.'

A lot of his most fraught conversations with Gloria seemed to take place when he was driving dangerously fast. That was when Gloria chose to put the banderillos in his neck.

She had watched the rushes of Tucker's scenes with Maureen in silence. A silence that had gone on after the projection was over, and became heavier all the time, until finally, in the car, he demanded:

'So what did you think of the scene?'

'Since I know how it was obtained, what I think of you is not expressible in my normal ladylike vocabulary.'

'You are always so fucking moralistic, Gloria.'

'That's just your way of discounting what I say in advance.'

He was overtaking, going up to ninety, split seconds in hand, oncoming cars hooting.

'You cut it fine,' she said calmly.

'You talking about the film?'

'I was talking about your overtaking. But it applies to the film too. Most of what you shot you can't show, can you?'

'We can show enough. We'll end up with around ten seconds

of showable footage, and the audience'll believe it's seen the lot. Wait till you see it cut. It's going to cut beautifully.'

'That was a pretty lowdown thing you did to her, you and Tucker.' He was staring into the dazzling lights of oncoming cars; the dazzle drew his eyes, blinding though it was. Gloria looked away at the English countryside flashing by in the dark.

'You have a taste for dangerous driving,' she said.

'It got out of hand,' he admitted. 'She didn't help. She flashes go-stop, go-stop. And Tuck's brakes, from long disuse, are not in such good working order.'

Rain pelted the windscreen in sudden torrential bursts. When he overtook lorries it was like going through a car wash of muddy water.

'You couldn't have her yourself, so you . . .'

'However you want to analyze it, Gloria. I was trying to get a scene that's vitally important to the film. We were desperate — because she can't act. I didn't plan it . . . it just got to an explosive mix, and . . . happened. Look, it's not the worst thing that ever happened to our Maureen. In fact, it merely anticipated by a few hours something that it would seem was already scheduled . . . according to Tuck.' They were sealed inside the fast car with hardly any sense of movement, as if their frantic speed amounted to no more than standing still. 'And I tell you, those ten, fifteen seconds of screen time are going to do her a lot of good. More good than all the little walk-ons for which she has so willingly sacrificed her all in the past. In that scene she looks as though she can actually act. She'll get lots of offers after this. She's not even mad at me any more. But you are . . . for reasons I find hard to understand.'

'I don't like what I see in you sometimes.'

'Gloria, it works in the story. It works. It shows what thin ice their marriage rests on. That it can all just blow up in their faces . . . for something trivial, like the Maureens of this world.'

'Is that what our life rests on?'

'We're talking about a film story. Our life is somewhat different, I'd say.'

'But also somewhat similar. No?'

'Happy marriages don't make film stories . . .'

'Is that supposed to mean that we are or that we aren't happy?'

'I think we are, Gloria. Insofar as that's possible for me. At any rate, you're the most important thing in my life. You and Anna.'

'But it's one of the enemies, isn't it? Marriage?'

'Like the man said, it's better to marry than to burn.'

'You're not too sure about that, though.'

'As long as I've got you to be sure for me . . .'

Later, when they were home, and the speeding in his head had stopped, he said: 'Gloria, there's this wild savage you've got yourself landed with, and you've got to give him some moral direction. Because he hasn't got any. Being this savage . . .'

'He has talent.'

'I don't know. He's a good thief. He sees what he needs and he takes it. With or without permission.'

'He has some other qualities as well.'

'Like what?'

She thought for a moment. 'He tries hard,' she said. 'And keeps on trying, whatever happens. Doesn't give up . . . pushes the rock up the hill.'

By the time the shooting was over, and the looping and the mixing of the music and the editing — which took him altogether four months, working twelve hours seven days a week — by the time all this was done, and he had a film to show, he was completely exhausted mentally and physically, and his doctor said he ought to do a cure, get off alcohol for a while, get off the pep pills and the sleeping pills, clear out the system and start afresh. The doctor sent him to a fashionable health farm in East Anglia. The place boasted masseurs and nutritionists and dieticians and hydrotherapists and physical educationists and a hypnotist as well. It was said that, in another wing, there were also psychiatrists on call, should they be required. Since so many varied ailments were catered for — including, the prospectus said, the pernicious ills arising out of the modern-life struggle — it seemed possible they might have the right cure for him.

For the first few days he simply slept and read and savoured

the surprisingly warm March days with light mists straggling
across the flat countryside. After the high-speed months, it was
good to drift about in slow motion, to wind back the reels, to eat
healthily and drink nothing but fruit juice and mineral water all
day. Delicious, also, to eat alone and not have to converse. At the
end of the first week, Gloria came with little Anna, and he took
some heed of his offspring for about the second time since she
was born. Fatherly emotions stirred in him, to his amazement. It
seemed you were programmed to feel these things. The pram in
the corridor was the enemy too, but it seemed you couldn't
wriggle out of your biological inheritance.

While wheeling Anna through the meticulously manicured
grounds he talked to Gloria about the life they were going to
have soon, just as soon as things got settled. They talked of
buying a house in the country. She said she could not see them
living in the country — she could do it, but he was too urban a
person. It was all right for a couple of weeks' health cure, but on
a permanent basis, she thought he needed the hum and bustle of a
big city. He said she'd be surprised but there was a reclusive side
to his character, and there were times when he wanted nothing
and nobody except her and Anna. 'You two fulfil my life totally,'
he said. 'I don't need anything else.'

The day after Gloria and the baby had visited him he received a phone call from Carver saying that their film had been
chosen as an official entry for the Cannes Film Festival, which
was in just over a month's time, and so it was going to be
necessary to get a final cut ready fast. The reaction from Metro
to the 'director's cut' had indicated that they didn't know exactly what to make of the film but, in any case, considered it
was too long by about twenty minutes. The sorts of scenes they
wanted to cut, like Gloria's riverside walk, which they said
didn't advance the action of the story — they wanted to eliminate scenes in which 'nothing was at stake' — were in his view
essential to give the film its character, pictorial mood and style.
Metro also objected to his 'dull use of colour' and wanted the
colours brightened up in the lab. He told Carver: 'Over my dead
body.' Another 'editorial comment' was that 'in those scenes
where we don't know what's going on exactly, the music needs

to be more pointed, to give us clues about the characters' states of mind.'

A good reception at the Cannes film festival was going to be of tremendous importance it would provide them with world-wide advance reviews and, if these were good, they would strengthen his hand in resisting Metro's crass ideas. So, even before his health cure had reached its second week, he was having to whip himself up for more battles.

Carl came down to see him in the second week. His forehead was getting loftier as his hair receded further at the temples, and he had let it grow long around his neck. In his palely beautiful face the eyes had the quietly burning inner light of the unrecognized prophet. At first there was a remoteness about him that Jack found unsettling, but little by little, as they walked and talked, some of their former closeness returned.

'Is this place doing you any good?' Carl asked him with suspicion.

'I'm on the mend, I think . . . oh, I don't know if it's the place. It's probably England's green and pleasant land. The Carl cure. Worked once before, remember. I was just totally exhausted. Fuses all blew at once.'

'You had, of course, been overloading the system rather heavily, from what I hear.'

'Yes. I had . . . I know, I know, but I needed the lift, Carl. I actually need to be a bit *maniaco* to be at my best and then, of course, I come down with a thud.'

'So much striving for. . .?'

'I can't live in my little burrow in the wilderness like you, Carl.'

'Even if it's a worthless glory?'

'Yes. Like certain kinds of women — the more worthless they are, the more I have to have them.'

'The Maureens of this world.'

' . . . the Maureens. Exactly. Exactly. Even if they do sort of vanish into thin air when you try to actually get hold of them. You know, I didn't even make it with her.'

Suddenly it all seemed so ridiculous, what people did in their lives, that they both burst out laughing simultaneously, until their eyes were streaming, and they had to put their arms around each other for support. When some gravitas was eventually restored to the conversation, Carl asked:

'What about you and Gloria these days?'

'Good, and not so good. Gloria is very precious to me, Carl, but I seem to need the other, too. Oh, I know what risks I take, and that it's not worth it, I know that. But I have to do it. I wrote in "the Maureen scene" because I wanted to show a man risking ruining his life — for nothing.'

'Yes, that *is* your scene.'

The long alley of chestnut trees went on and on like the final walk in a Chaplin film.

'"Though the play may begin as an amusing comedy," Carl quoted, ' "the final act is always bloody".'

'You rather relish the idea of that, don't you?'

'Whether one consoles oneself with truisms or with the Maureens of this world . . . comes to the same, I suppose.'

They laughed conspiratorially, joyfully, and it was good to be joyful together again.

While they were waiting for the bus to take Carl to the railway station, Jack told him about the film having been invited to the Cannes film festival and, in their renewed spirit of closeness, said he wanted him to be there.

'Even though we can't put your name on it, I want you to be there, Carl. It's your story, your subject, your words.'

'Some of my words and a lot of David Cawley's.'

'It's your concept. And we might even win something — which I know would ruin all your pessimistic scenarios.'

'Even when you win, you don't win,' Carl pointed out. 'Isn't La Wynner the proof of that?'

Jack laughed, with a touchy kind of agreement on the subject of Maureen Wynner — the unwinnable Wynner! And Carl joined in, laughing gloomily alongside him. How all those girls, so desirable from a distance, evanesced into nothingness as you tried to seize hold of them: these vanishing bodies, *trompe l'oeil* creatures of the screen.

PART III

GLORY'S WAY

26

Sydney Carver knew in his gut when a place and an occasion had been made for him and his style of operating and, as soon as he got to Cannes, he saw that the Festival was his sort of place. Driving along the Croisette in the aromatic spring air, the sweet smell in his nostrils was not of mimosa but of deals. The lobby and terrace of the Carlton were already a ferment of wheeling and dealing, and before Carver had got as far as the desk to register, he was fervently embraced by an impeccable Italian called Renzo, who was wearing a Swiss voile shirt open to the navel and a wafer thin Cartier gold wrist watch. The polished mahogany face crinkled into a mock-guilty grimace, a loose hand fluttered in the air alluding to some indescribable experience of the night and, in a heavy aroma of Italian male perfume, he announced: 'I hear only great things about your movie, Sydney — what is called?'

'*The Interloper.*'

'Great title. Unforgettable! Gre-a-t. *Faab*ulous, I hear it is *faab*ulous movie. This new young director you haf discover? Strawssland? And the all-time great Bruce Tucker.'

'Strawley.'

'Yes?'

'His name is Strawley. The director.'

'You are so right! Strowlly. *Faaab*ulous!'

'Coming to our showing, Renzo?'

'I keel myself, but cannot do . . . I must see Darryl. I haf promise him.'

In his first-floor all-cream suite, Carver noted with satisfaction that his balcony was overlooking the beach — and an American frigate at anchor in the bay. The suite was appropriate to his standing, and so he would not have to make a row, for which he had been preparing himself, should they have given him an inferior suite. He knew that in Cannes you had to battle and was ready for the fray.

On the coffee table there was a glossy book giving, after many pages of advertisements, the list of jury members and the official Festival programme. Flicking through these pages he assessed the competition. It included a Japanese film about rape, impotence and voyeurism, a Greek film extolling the life of the prostitute, an Indian version of *The Government Inspector,* an Italian film about the rich, full — and hollow — life of present-day Rome, a Swedish film about death and a Canadian film about incest among Eskimos. He studied the names of the jury members with their capsule biogs. A well-known Italian film director; a great French cinema actress of a certain age; an English critic; an American cameraman who had worked with Wyler, Hawks, Curtiz, Siodmak and Wellmann; a Syrian documentarist; an American film archivist and historian; a Swedish scenarist who had worked with Sjoberg and Bergman; a French Marxist intellectual; and a German novelist.

Trying to figure out how *The Interloper* would strike this motley crew, he came to the conclusion that no more than two of them, at most, would agree on anything, and that the bestowal of prizes would be decided in the usual manner by horse trading. He grasped at once that there were enough second and third and fourth and fifth and sixth prizes in the offing for the dealing to be lively and complex. The jury members would have to be of unshakeable certitude — *and rectitude* — if they were going to remain immune to outside influences. They would have to be inured to the ballyhoo, the cocktails, the intimate dinners, the gala receptions, the blandishments of vested interests, the favours of the powerful, the beautiful bodies, the bookmakers' odds, the critics' opinions — expressed not only in their printed reviews but also conveniently polled by one of the trades, so that the line-up of popular and highbrow views could be seen every day at a glance. All in all, Carver concluded, to expect impartiality of a Cannes jury was too much to ask for. A quick look through the trades brought to light no reference to *The Interloper* as a possible contender for a major prize. The film had not yet been shown anywhere; the director's final cut had been finished only a few days before the Festival began, so there had been no chance to hold previews and generate advance word-of-mouth. They were coming in unknown and unsung. There was much to be done.

By the time he had changed into white slacks tied with a rope belt, a red silk polo shirt, espadrilles and yachting cap, and made his way down, the pre-lunch cocktail frenzy was in full swing. Every table on the terrace was occupied and a pack of killer-photographers were on the loose scrambling back and forth between the beach restaurant and the terraces and lounges in search of well-known faces and/or bodies to photograph. Finding these in short supply just now, they were snapping recklessly at anything that moved. Since the terrace was full, Carver took up position at the bar, from where, by means of a regular swivelling movement of the neck, it was possible to keep an eye on what was going on at the café tables, the restaurant entrance and in the wide corridor, with seating on either side, along which came a continuous flow of people looking for some person who was nowhere to be found. Finding, instead, somebody they had no desire to find, there followed a great deal of unenthusiastic hand-shaking, embracing, cheek-kissing and bear-hugging, done with eyes constantly on the move. Carver's eyes moved faster than anyone else's. There were lots of people here that he had no wish to see, and the sight of such individuals caused his eyes to go instantly blank. The people brushing by, squeezing his hand in intimate under-the-counter salutation, were all freeloaders and sharks and parasitic rats who wanted to use him, while being of no use to him, and he disposed of them swiftly by means of the blank eye. He spotted Renzo hovering momentarily between difficult choices — there was the dark-haired beauty sullenly flashing signals at him from within the Greek delegation, but there was also the delicious teenage rape victim, with downcast eyes, of the Japanese entry who, while less apparently accessible, offered more exotic, more indescribable prospects. Seeing Renzo's indecision, Carver preempted matters by offering him lunch, which the Italian accepted, saying sagely: 'Yes, you are so right, haff got to get back my strength.'

With his instinct for essentials, Carver had understood at once that Cannes was made up of two categories of people: those who were looking for somebody and those who could not be found, and it was disastrous to belong to the former category, you had to be one of those who could not be found. On this basis he went to have lunch with Renzo on the beach, leaving it to MGM to find him. The first showing of *The Interloper* was tomorrow morning and was to be followed by a press conference. The second showing was a gala performance at 22h30, preceded by a cock-tail reception at 18h30. Carver was supposed to go over the arrangements with MGM's publicity and advertising man and they had made a lunch appointment at the Carlton. Since he had not turned up on time or specified at which of the three Carlton restaurants they were to meet, Carver considered the publicity man dead. It was one of the Carver's strengths to know immedi-ately when somebody was dead and should get himself buried. He bought Renzo — and the two girls, one in toreador pants, the other in short black leather skirt, that Renzo had invited to join them — a handsome lunch, which he charged to MGM, signing the bill in the name of the publicity and advertising director, who was by now so dead he was polluting the atmosphere. He con-fided his problem to Renzo. 'Dick Stiller's a deadbeat, doesn't know anybody. Doesn't even know me.'

'I know you and I know everybody, even Dick Stiller, and he's not worth knowing,' Renzo said. Going by the number of em-braces, handshakes and kisses of all kinds that Renzo exchanged with the passing crowd, Carver calculated that the Italian's claim to know everybody must be at least partially true. Film producer, scenarist, professor of cinematography in Rome, contributor to cinema journals, representative of Hollywood studios, stringer for highbrow and lowbrow newspapers and friend of the famous, Renzo wore each of his many hats with dash. Carver proposed that he should work for him during the festival, and Renzo, unsurprised, raised five fingers of his left hand, plus three of his right, by way of specifying his fee. Carver grasped the three fingers in his palm, and it was a deal. His first deal of the festival and, he thought, a good one.

On Renzo's advice, Carver did not join the afternoon rush towards the Palais des Festivals to see the Indian production of

The Government Inspector. Renzo had an unerring nose for the films that one had to do one's utmost to miss and usually succeeded in missing most of them.

Instead of going to the movies, they went in a motor-boat, with the two girls from lunch, to Sam Spiegel's yacht, moored off Cap d'Antibes, where the guests included Georges Simenon, Maria Callas and the distinguished French cinema actress and Prèsidente of the Cannes jury, Florence Duthey. Carver at once told Madame la Prèsidente of his enormous admiration for her as an actress, his youthful infatuation with her as a woman, and his present desire to know her better. In his eagerness to show he was on her side, he referred to how unjustly the French had treated her immediately after the Occupation, in the matter of the German soldier with whom she had been romantically involved. She explained: *'Mon coeur appartient à la France, mais mon cul appartient à moi.'*

'Ah, now, if you'd've got Tucker here,' said the MGM publicity man who had eventually found them — one day late — and was making himself deader by the minute, 'I could have done something with Tucker. And I could maybe have done something with Maureen,' he offered with a half-leer, driving the spike through his own heart.

Carver told him: 'Whatever in your base mind, Mr Stiller, you think you could've done with Miss Wynner is not what you're being paid to do, Mr Stiller, and besides you couldn't't've . . . 'cause yours ain't big enough for her.'

Dick Stiller emitted a low hee-heee-hee that seemed to come all the way from his intestines.

'Now Mr Stiller,' Carver said, 'what I think you need to tell yourself and, if it's not too much bother others as well, is that our film's gonna win the Palme d'Or.'

'It's what I always say, each time,' he assured Carver.

'This time,' Carver told him, 'try to look as if you believe it.'

The morning screenings at the Palais des Festivals were informal, and people turned up in jeans and shorts and beach wear, the journalists carrying their bulging leatherette Festival portfolios.

The hyper-excited Festival buzz ceased as the lights went down and the credits came up. There was some isolated clapping when the director's credit appeared on the screen, followed by attentive silence. Several times in the course of the film the audience broke into brief applause for a particular shot or scene: once or twice there was whistling at a line of dialogue. Jack Strawley could not assess what these reactions meant in terms of the overall response to the picture. There was a short burst of applause at the end of the screening, and as they got up from their seats a large bearded man with an Eclair newsreel camera and a lighting rig walked backwards ahead of them, filming them going out. There were people standing up applauding: one or two shouts of 'Bravo' from close by. He took Gloria's hand in his and, maintaining his public face for the cameras, said:

'Think they liked it?'

'I think they did but you can't be sure.'

'They better have,' he said. 'Fucking French.'

'The French love you,' she said.

'That was last time. Bet they hate me this time.'

'Stop being so paranoid. Of course they won't hate you, it's a good film.'

'I know. But watch out for me. Don't let me get out too far.'

'You okay, Jack?'

'I don't know, Gloria. Truth is I don't really know.'

He could feel the sweat cooling on his skin. They were being steered to the Salle de Conférence and onto the brightly illumined platform where there was a long table with microphones and pitchers of water and glasses. The questions began slowly, ponderously. Some were in English of varying degrees of fluency, others in French or other languages that had to be translated by an interpreter. Then the replies were translated back into French. Where had such and such a scene been shot? With what sort of camera? Why did he use such long takes at times? 'Reaction against Eisenstein who wanted everything done by cutting. And to get the claustrophobia,' he said.

A French woman journalist asked what was the significance of the fact that the love scenes in the film were all either interrupted by something or somebody—a lot of unintentional coitus interruptus going on — or else ended badly in some other way. 'What do you wish to say by this?'

He seemed not to know what he wished to say by this, was looking puzzled, as if it had not occurred to him up to this minute that all his characters had been left in such unfulfilled states.

'Perhaps is that you have a grudge against women?' a woman journalist from Italy asked.

'Do I have a grudge against women? Is that the question? Ask my wife . . .' Laughter. 'Oh . . . , you think she could be biased? Then ask Carl. Carl?' He looked around for Carl, and spotted him sitting towards the back. 'My friend Carl. Known me a long time. Knows me better'n I do. Also — had a lot to do with bringing this film about. Knows its whole secret armature. Carl, what d'you think? Why's everybody in the story so unfulfilled?' Carl was shaking his head and holding up his hands, pleading to be left out of this. But Jack was insistent, his voice hitting a note of stridency. 'Come on, Carl. Give us your theory on it? Am I against women?' Carl was smiling and declining to reply.

Gloria spoke tensely in Jack's ear: 'Jack, don't stir it up.'

'My wife tells me not to stir it up. She thinks I go too far out,' he told the audience over the microphone, grinning, 'but going too far out's what I do best. My film goes too far out, I know . . . I know. I shouldn't stir it up? C'mon, Carl. Come on, stir it up a little. People here seem to think I'm getting my revenge, my sweet revenge, against women in this film. So, what's your opinion? You haven't even told me yet what you think of the film. C'mon, be honest.' He was going on with relentless provocation, the hard dark glitter in his eyes.

Since it seemed Jack was not going to let go until he'd got an answer out of him, Carl said slowly: 'All I can say, Jack, is that whatever you touch, you make unmistakably your own. So I expect . . . ,' — he turned to the journalists — 'I expect Jack has some very good reason for everything in the film . . . including the fact that the love scenes don't have any . . . outcome. So you really must ask him about that.'

Coming out of the cool dimness into the sudden glare of the midday sun streaming into the Grand Palais foyer, Jack Strawley seemed dazed. Photographers and TV cameramen positioned themselves to get shots of the director and his group. There was a burst of applause as he was spotted, and some shouts of 'Bravo' from those lining the marble stairs on both sides. People were trying to shake his hand. He was being hustled and pushed about by the excited crowd pressing in on him. There were muttered questions. Requests for private interviews. People wanted him to read their scripts, to discuss their projects. The journalist who had suggested he might have a grudge against women, said: 'I'm sorry I have put you in a spot, it's a very good film, I like it very much.' He started making his way down the steps, holding tightly onto Gloria's hand, which was all that was keeping him upright. They were all following him, sticking tightly to him. He felt a rush of elation, followed by nausea. He got to the exit doors gasping. The band of followers were with him still. They started out into the white dazzle of the street with its slashing sunlight, and the crowd of adherents stuck with him, hanging onto his words.They were all pushing to hear what he was saying, to see where he was going. The bearded man with the Eclair camera had got himself inserted into the thick of the crowd and was pointing the camera straight into Jack's face and walking back- wards. Couldn't cover his face like a criminal: had to make the best of the situation. He heard himself answering questions into the thrust-out microphones as if it were someone else speaking. Some imposter. Renzo was trying to fight his way through to them. He pointed to the beach. 'I haf book a table.'

The small but determined crowd around Jack was refusing to disperse, it was following him along the Croisette and it fol- lowed him across the road, bringing the traffic to a halt, and then down the steps to the beach restaurant where Renzo had booked the table. The crowd that had gathered sprawled on the sand or sat down at adjacent tables or turned their chairs to see better: they now numbered fifteen or twenty and consisted of press men and photographers, young would-be movie makers, publicity seekers, groupies, sightseers, locals, and unidentifed others. Renzo kept telling them to go away: 'Basta, basta!' But they didn't seem to understand Italian any better than English. 'They can smell success,' Renzo said, putting a cheerful interpretation on things. A biplane did show-off manoeuvres in the sky, trailing a long banner for a film called *Love Inferno*, and, as it dived and twisted, the girl on the banner plunged in a frenzy of loose-limbed convulsions. A woman came up to Jack and asked him: 'Who are you, young man? Are you somebody famous?' And when he wouldn't tell her who he was — claiming not to know, which didn't fool *her* — she gave her opinion that he wasn't anyone.

There was no sun umbrella where he sat, and the sun beating down on his head was making him feel light-headed, not enough sugar in his blood, not enough blood in his brain, and he could feel himself drifting up towards the loose-limbed logo-girl of the *Love Inferno* when he spotted Carl coming towards him, smiling gloomily.

'You really fucked me up back there,' he told Carl, his face grey, waiting for the click that the whisky should have produced by now but hadn't. It was clear he needed another and he banged his glass, signalling to the waiter to refill it.

'No, you fucked yourself up, Jack. You were determined to stir it up.'

'You put the knife in, Carl.'

'All I said was you have a knack for making things your own.'

'*I know what that's supposed to mean.*'

'You're being ridiculous. I didn't want my name on the film.'

'You made that pretty obvious. As a so-called friend, couldn't you have lied a little?'

'I think you already have enough people lying to you, Jack.'

With the second whisky he'd reached a point of free-momentum, where his words were coming out unchecked, driven by mechanisms he knew nothing of. 'You're starting to talk as pompous as you write. Thou shalt not alter the words of the Prophet Carl! We changed some of your lines! Have I earned the vengeance of the Jews for that? Your Jewish God going to strike me dead?'

'I suspected, but never wanted to believe, that you have that streak in you,' Carl said going very white.

'What streak? What d'you mean? Oh, c'mon. Oh, c'mon, Carl. Don't be such a fucking persecuted Jew all the time.'

He made a violent movement of getting up, in doing so knocking over a bottle of wine on the table. He was casting off from Gloria's holding hand, turning his back on wine-stained Carl and starting to walk away: from them all, his newly acquired fans and the press and the photographers,and the curious onlookers, and the ivory jewellery vendor and the bearded newsreel man, all these maddening people. He was striding furiously towards the sea when he felt the glass hit him on the head and shatter. He could feel the blood trickling down from his scalp He was staggering, partly because of the blood and partly because of the sun. And the damned crowd And the nausea. And the *Love Inferno* girl diving towards him out of the sky. But mostly because of Carl. Having done this — having thrown the glass. Carl drawing blood! He could feel it on his fingers. He sat down in the sand, or collapsed, he wasn't sure which, and told himself: go slow, slow, otherwise it's all going to blow up in your face, just when you've practically got it made.

27

For the gala at 22h30 he wore a silk dinner suit with satin cowl collar and upturned cuffs with satin facing. Gloria was in a strapless black evening gown, with blades of satin hanging down over the narrow skirt. The crowds were held back behind police barriers manned by gendarmes in dress uniform.The film lights came on whenever somebody slightly known descended from a car, and the arrival of a star name produced a sudden electric storm of flashbulbs.

During the *séance* the bursts of applause were stronger and more prolonged than at the morning show, and, at the end, when the spotlight fell on the handsome dazzling Strawleys in the front portion of the *balcon*, the applause went on and on. There were some isolated 'boos', but these were quickly drowned out by the rising volume of 'bravos'. Looking into the stalls, seeing the rapt upturned faces directed towards him, he felt a sudden wave of panic: they were going to find out that he was an imposter and a thief, and he was going to be exposed. He disguised his panic as best he could, smiling all around, raising one hand in humble acknowledgment of the applause. They started to make their way out, the portable light rigs moving with them, the news cameramen walking backwards up the steps, and there were people standing in the aisles and on their seats applauding the magic couple blessed with so much talent and happiness. He kept his easy smile going while fighting the heady cocktail of elation and dread. Seeing his grin get wilder and wilder, Gloria told him to hold on to her and he whispered back: 'Oh yes, darling, oh yes, I have to. Don't let go of me. Don't, don't whatever you do.' Outside, at the top of the stairs, there were more lights and a battery of press photographers and radio broadcasters with microphones and TV cameras and people pressing in on them from all around. They spotted the upsurging Carver rise out of the waves of bobbing heads, his long power-ful arms cutting through the crowd as if it were water. He drew alongside and said in Jack's ear: 'The word is we'll get some-thing, maybe Gloria'll get best actress, but the Palme is going to the fucking Japs.'

'Who told you?'

'Renzo.'

'How does he know?'

'Renzo hears these things. He has his ear to a lot of pillows.'

The crowd of onlookers on the Palais steps were all the time seeking to get closer, to brush against the winners in life's race, and there was a very pale-faced girl with staring bright eyes squeezing up against him, saying how wonderful his film was, how wonderful he was. The fervent fan followed him closely down the marble steps and, at the bottom, wedged herself between him and the rest of his admirers. She produced a copy of *Cinemonde* with his photograph in it and asked him to sign over his photo 'with a personal message for Sal'. Since there was no suitable surface on which to sign, she offered her back as a desk, bending over slightly, and while he was signing on the glossy paper her hand ran up the inside of his thigh to touch the magic.

On the red-carpeted sidewalk, in the crowd that was waiting for cars to take them to the party being given by the Italian delegation, Carver was in action, arms flailing, elbows jabbing left and right. About to get into one car, they saw Sydney pointing in front of him, indicating not that one, *that* one. He bundled them quickly inside. At first it seemed that he had insisted on this particular car just because it was ahead in the line — since he could never resist anything that was ahead. But it wasn't only that, on this occasion: it transpired that this limo contained Renzo and the Director-General of the Festival. Carver at once apologized for filling up his official limousine. 'Hope we aren't taking anybody's place,' he told the Director-General, without looking unduly concerned at this possibility.

'Not at all,' the Director-General assured them, 'my wife, I expect, will make her way in one of the other cars . . . they are all going there.' Renzo made the introductions, and the Director-General said in his mandarin French manner that he certainly remembered Mr Carver, they had met on Mr Spiegel's yacht, and he was delighted to meet Mr and Mrs Strawley. He had found Jack's film most interesting and hoped 'our estimable jury members will perceive its merits.'

The party for the Italian film was being given at a private villa about 10 km from Cannes, and once out of town the Director-General asked if anyone would object to the windows being open, since it was such a soft and balmy night, redolent of bougaenvilla and pines and the sea. Such a good idea of the Italians to give their party in the countryside, away from all the Festival madness.

'I was saying,' Renzo reported back to them, 'how iss amazing the Japanese can make their fine films for so little money . . .' Everyone joined in praise of the clever Japanese and their economical work methods — few shots, in total, intensive rehearsals keeping the numbers of takes drastically down, low salaries for leading actors and, of course, Renzo said, very little expenditure on advertising and promotions. He imagined that an American company like MGM would spend on advertising *The Interloper* far more than the entire budget of the Japanese entry.

'For such a great American company, MGM have not spent very much in Cannes,' the Director-General permitted himself to remark drily.

'Very shortsighted,' Carver agreed at once. 'The lamentable mentality of these *salesmen* and accountants who run our big studios now! They're such cheapskates. They say to themselves, we never win prizes at foreign festivals, so why bother to spend the money? That's so narrow-minded.'

'It is an understandable point of view,' the Director-General conceded. 'Believe me, I am trying to get our juries to adopt a less chauvinistic outlook. But we too have our national attitudes to contend with.'

'Couldn't agree with you more,' Carver said without specifying on what exactly they were agreeing.

'If only we were able to persuade you big American producers of the real value of coming to Cannes with your films, and of bringing your big stars like Bruce Tucker . . .'

'If Tuck felt really appreciated here, hell! If he felt he *had a chance to win* — oh, he'd be here, I guarantee you,' Carver predicted.

'You guarantee it?' the Director-General mused into the delicate South of France night. 'I know your time here is very occupied but would you happen to be free for lunch tomorrow, Mr Carver?'

'Unfortunately I have a lunch appointment that I can't change but I could manage breakfast.'

'Then, let us say breakfast, shall we?'

The private villa near Grasse that had been taken over for the Italian party was built in grandiloquent 1920's style. It was approached by a long straight drive lined by spring-fed marble fountains that descended in terraces to a marble swimming pool, the four corners of which were ornamented by plaster Venuses rising from the waves. Green floodlights illumined selected trees and shrubs, while alleys and grottos and arbors had been left unlit, producing a chiaroscuro effect for the eye as well as dark leafy recesses for strolling guests seeking privacy. If it all looked rather familiar, this was because the Italian film company throwing the party had sought to reproduce the setting of a party in their film, which was all about the hollow pleasures of the rich. Already, in keeping with the Fabrini film, several glorious girls had fallen fully dressed into the illumined swimming pool, and the girl who had been wearing a billowing white ballroom gown had succeeded with one try, in freeing herself of it, and now was floating nude on the surface, while a frenzied burst of photo-flashes lit up the pool like a film set.

Fabrini was surveying his glittery domain, surrounded by journalists and photographers and admirers.

'I am like a deep sea diver,' he told them. 'I must go down to see what is below, and there I see many marvels, strange fishes, secret caves, monsters of the deep and beautiful mermaids. Because I am artist I come up to report what haff seen. Danger is to one day get tired, to don't come up, to stay down.'

Inside the house a string band played *Tales of the Vienna Woods* for one middle-aged couple dancing like competition dancers. French windows opened onto a loggia where a guest in a white dinner jacket was putting handfuls of cigarettes from a box of Abdulla No 37s into his pockets. On a densely packed platform hung with Chinese lanters, the Cha Cha Cha was being danced with zest to the energetic playing of a four-piece dance band, Renzo and an ash-blonde prominent among the dancers. Waiters dressed as Spanish grandees came with champagne. Buffets had been set up in marquees. Word spread that the Beluga caviar had run out, causing panic. 'These Italian cheapskates,' said an American lady whose bosom resembled a Cartier counter.

'I can't get over Carl throwing that glass at me,' Jack said as he walked with Gloria. 'I just can't get over that. Carl! Non-violent Carl. The pacifist. The guy who walks away from bad scenes.'

'You spilled wine over him. It looked as though it was deliberate — you provoked him, Jack.'

'What d'you mean I provoked him? I said he'd fucked me up

at the press conference, and that's true. I have to be so careful about what I say to Carl? He's my oldest friend, I should be able to say things to him.'

'You called him a persecuted Jew.'

'That's what he is.'

'Well, he did lose most of his family in concentration camps. You didn't let him answer. You walked away. You turned your back on him, having said something about the vengeance of the Jews.'

'Christ, I don't know what I said. But he didn't have to react like that.'

'You've got all this success coming to you now, and he has nothing, not even his name on the screen, and it's his work.'

'In addition, he gave you up for me. Well, I sometimes get a bit pissed off with everything Carl's sacrificed.'

Around 2 a.m., Carver came back from scouting out the scene and reported with some disgust:

'Mostly Italians and French and some Germans. On the other hand there are girls.'

'. . . falling into the pool.'

'Oh, they'll fall into anything you say,' Carver said without enthusiasm.

'Like the hollow pleasures that they are,' Jack added.

Renzo joined them with the ash-blonde who it turned out was not a hollow pleasure but a police psychiatrist. Renzo, when there was a break in the conversation, took them aside and gave them the latest info. 'Here is the present line up,' he announced. 'Three for the Japanese, two for the Fabrini, two for us. The Marxist dithering between the Cubans and the North Koreans. That leave Madame la Présidente. The unknown vote. Which the Italians hope to get, and that make it three/three/two, leaving the Marxist the deciding vote, if he want to use it. Or he can waste it. The best for us would be if Madame la Prèsidente come to us, then we can maybe get the Marxist to switch, since Gloria is in good standing with the Left. But is very unlikely darling Florence will come over to us. She and Fabrini go back long way. She was in one of Fabrini's first films, and he was one of her big loves . . . so that is where is her heart.'

'Maybe so,' Carver said, 'but where her heart is ain't necessarily where her ass is.'

It was beginning to look as though the party might come to rival the party in the film: guests were drifting off into the dim areas away from the Chinese lanterns and the photographers. Near the swimming pool, Jack saw his starry-eyed fan from the Palais des Festivals steps. She was turning her head in all directions, as if looking for somebody. He told Gloria that he was going to get himself a drink and he'd be right back. After the bar he took a sharp turn towards the pool and bumped into Fabrini, who had the graciousness to stop and utter a few flattering words.

'Good luck, *cher collègue*. Your day will come. If not this time, another time. I wish you the best luck. You are a true poet of the image. You will have the glory . . . one of these days.'

While Fabrini was speaking, Jack had seen the excited fan with the glistening face and overbright eyes, and she had caught sight of him too and was looking at him with a fixed, intense expression. Having found him, her eyes did not let go of him, and he cut off Fabrini, saying: 'I am one of your greatest admirers. Thank you for saying what you said, I appreciate it a lot.' He added, confidentially: 'The word is that it's between you and me, and I got to tell you . . . I don't believe in winning next time.' He slipped away in the direction of the fixed glowing eyes. She had an Australian accent, mousy brown hair, pale flesh. Her eyes were agitatedly moving about all the time, and her hands too — finger stiffening and twisting and clenching. She couldn't seem to keep any part of herself still.

'You must have made a lot of effort to get into this party,' he told her. 'Is it up to your expectations?'

'Oh yes, yes. Yes. You're so . . . dazzling, so brilliant.'

'I think that's the light of the pool,' he said and started to lead her away from the lit-up area, steering her between illumined trees and shrubs into the vibrant night with its secret arbors. He was looking around for somewhere to go with this dazzled crazy girl with the agitated knees. He drew her behind a tree.

'People may see us,' she said. 'It's not very private here.'

But this didn't stop her from running her hand lightly along the inside of his thigh to touch the magic again, and, with the bodily contact her nervousness about being seen disappeared.

Voices aproaching, voices receding. Approaching.

Presently he saw Gloria, alone, in the brightly lit part of the gardens, turning slowly through 360 degrees, evidently looking for him, and he drew back from the glistening demanding eyes, the agitated hand.

'Jack? *Jack?*' Gloria was turning and calling inquiringly into the dark, as if sensing that he was close by. He could see her looking straight at him and quickly separated himself from the girl.

'Jack . . . there you . . .' she began, seeing him standing, unmoving in the dark, and then she saw the jumpy form behind him, adjusting her clothes: the edge of a face that the light caught.

'What are you doing there with my husband? Who are you?' she asked the girl, with a sense of the absurdity of that question — it was quite obvious what they had been doing. 'Oh, nobody,' the girl said, 'I'm nobody.' To Jack she said quickly: 'Bye, Jack. It was really great *really* meeting you.'

He and Gloria walked back to the marquee in silence, past the violently shaking dance platform, where Carver was determinedly dancing with Madame la Prèsidente, who was receiving his, for once, undivided attention. There wasn't any whisky at the buffet tables, and Jack said he was going inside the house to get some.

'Don't you think you've drunk enough, Jack?'

'Not quite enough, darling. If you really want to know.'

'I think we should be going . . . this party's getting very sordid, wouldn't you say?'

'Depends what you think of as sordid.'

'Isn't up against a tree with a girl, whose name you don't even know, sordid?'

Trying not to scream, she couldn't help sounding prissy. He would have preferred for her to scream.

'You go looking in the dark, you see things you don't want to see,' he told her.

'Oh! so it's my fault for looking for you? I shouldn't look?

You asked me to hold on to you,' she reminded him. 'I can also let you go, you know,' she added warningly. 'I really can. But you said, "Hold onto me, Gloria. Don't let me go off." And you sounded as though you meant it.'

'Obviously you didn't hold on tight enough.'

He drank another whisky in silence. She saw his eyes become incandescent. 'It's . . .' He shrugged and rocked back and forth on his feet. 'That sort of thing, Gloria, believe me, while it's oddly compelling in the moment, leaves absolutely no trace . . . as if it hadn't happened at all.'

'It leaves a trace, Jack. In me.'

'Well, it shouldn't because it's nothing. I know what's important. You and Anna . . . and winning this fucking Festival. Because I *can* win. I know it. I'm going to win this thing, Gloria. You'll see.'

'Winning's the worst thing that could happen to you,' she told him softly. 'Why d'you need to win all the time?'

He didn't answer at first, was looking away. Then he said softly with a half-shrug: 'It's a question of recognition.'

'Is that worth what you put yourself through? And put others through, those who love you?'

'Sometimes you're a pain in the ass, Gloria.'

'I know that. But I keep you alive, and that takes some doing.'

Next day, speculation about the awards became heated when it was learned that Bruce Tucker had flown in from Los Angeles. Various reported sightings of him on the Croisette created outbreaks of mass-hysteria among the photographers, but all these reports were wrong. He spent the entire afternoon sleeping in his hotel room, from which he did not budge until it was time for him to go and pick up his best actor award at the Palais. For this grand occasion he was suitably tongue-tied.

'This is somethin' really scares me . . . well, see, I usually have a script and I don't have a script . . . for this . . . but what I wanna say . . .' He mumbled and stumbled on for about five minutes without ever finishing a sentence or saying anything coherent, and at the end everybody in the audience said that what they had seen was real star quality.

The Japanese film won the award for best director, and the Fabrini film won the jury prize for outstanding film, and also for best actress.

Gerald Longley had been asked to present the principal prize, the Palme d'Or, but the distinguished old English director had got the wrong idea, due to alcohol or age, or because his French, which he insisted on speaking, had a way of breaking down at crucial moments: he seemed to think that he was getting some sort of prize himself and began a speech in French saying how deeply honoured he was and how he loved France and the French, and how the French had always loved his films. When the applause had died down, an official came onto the stage and muttered something into his ear, pointing to the as yet unopened envelope in Longley's hand. Looking peeved, Longley tore it open and announced without further ado:

'The Palme d'Or is awarded to *The Interloper.*'

Going up to receive the prize, Jack Strawley's face was set and sombre. His acceptance speech was brief and suitably modest. 'I owe this prize tonight to many people, from among whom I single out my wife, the wonderful actress, Gloria Vanderveld, who gives such a marvellous performance as Leonora, to my producer, Sydney Carver, who has striven so hugely — far beyond anything anyone could have asked of him — to make this happen. But above all, I owe this prize to the man who taught me to read books, to think with my head as well as with my eye, and who . . . is the real *auteur* of *The Interloper,* and of many other fine, although insufficiently recognized, works. The screenwriter Harold Heath.'

28

The winning of the Palme d'Or at Cannes at age twenty-nine
was the consecration of 'genius Jack'. Greatly helped by the sex
scene between Bruce Tucker and Maureen Wynner, which for
those days was considered exceptionally *sexual*, *The Interloper*
went on to gross $6,000,000 at the box office, and for the studios
that was the ultimate consecration. Now they all wanted this hot
young team; Strawley and Carver. They wanted them with Wynner
again, because Wynner had been so sensational in her small part
in *The Interloper.* At first Strawley resisted. 'She can't act,' he
said. 'And screwing on camera is a trick you can't do twice . . .'
Who said you couldn't? they said. And, in any case, they believed she had star quality. What he wanted to do, he said, was
Heart of Darkness, based on the Conrad story. It was Carl's idea
and he had come up with an intriguing modernization. There
were other subjects that the studios would have preferred him to
make, but they accepted that being one of these genius boys he
wasn't going to do a Doris Day picture for them and so they
made a bargain with him: provided he agreed first to do a picture
with Maureen Wynner, they'd finance the script and the explora-
tory work on *Heart of Darkness,* and if the script was okay, and
could be brought in at an acceptable budget, they would let him
do it. But first Wynner. It didn't have to be a piece of shit, they
had nothing against quality . . . but quality with sex. Bring us a
subject, they said. And he had brought them an astringent comedy called *Polly & Jane*, about two identical twins, to be played
by Maureen Wynner, one of whom is a sexpot and the other a
'professional virgin' — a category of woman that existed at the
time — and what happens when through force of circumstance
they are compelled to switch clothes and roles.

The film was being made on the French Riviera, and I had
gone out to cover the shooting. I found Jack Strawley in aggres-
sive good form, alternately coaxing and whipping a sizzling
performance out of Wynner, I came on the set one time and found
him yelling at her with a grin down one side of his face that said,

according to how you read it: 'I'm kidding you,' *or* 'I'm only kidding that I'm kidding, I mean every word.' And the words got pretty hard. 'Now c'mon, ugly face,' he was yelling. 'Behave naturally. *Naturally.* Is that what you call naturally? Listen. Listen. Listen, darling. I don't want you to think. Thinking is not what you do best.' His face broke into the kidder's wide grin. 'Look, I'm kidding you, but please. Please, will you do me a big favour? Don't act. Your acting is not what audiences are paying to see, okay? Just *be*. Be yourself. Be beautiful. Be what you are . . . and, listen, why'd you stop before? I know it was no damn good, but let *me* tell you that, it's not for you to cut the scene. Don't ever, *ever* cut the scene. You carry on until *I* say it's no good. Or you drop dead. Now again from the top.'

She took it all. He had turned her into a hot property, and you didn't say no to Success, if you were Maureen Wynner, whatever it might cost in terms of a little ritual humiliation, which she said he only did because he had to discharge his nervous overflow somewhere, and in any case he was only kidding. They were having a bubbling hot affair all through the shooting, and she let on that she liked a touch of roughness in a man. Even if he did make her cry quite frequently. It made the making up stronger.

Gloria was staying with Jack at the Hotel du Cap, which determined his field of action somewhat, but not to the point of significant self-denial; it meant he had to confine his flings to the set, where he was in control and could shut himself up in his trailer with Moira monitoring all access to him — and that applied to Gloria too if she should turn up unannounced, which she had the elegance not to do. He was also still involved with Moira — on the basis that she made way for others who came along. It was being said that she sometimes arranged other women for him: anything to make him happy, to hold on to him, since she loved him. Others said, no, it was because she was so goddamn ambitious. People were calling her 'the gal with the most upwardly mobile ass', and there were those who claimed she did it because she had perverted tastes and liked to watch her lover perform with others. Whatever the truth, and maybe it *was* changing from minute to minute, you could see that Moira was invaluable to him; she arranged his life and work efficiently, covering up for him when that was required, apologizing for him handsomely with flowers and champagne when apologies were called for, which they quite frequently were, stalled for him when he couldn't make up his mind, lied for him when there was no other alternative, and kept Gloria away when she had to be kept away.

Strawley seemed to charge up on the stresses and strains of production and his complicated private life. The nervous tensions he generated all around him produced crackling energy sources that he drew on for his creative impetus. He didn't seem to ever get tired. At the end of a stressful day, he would take a large group of people out to dinner at the Colombe d'Or or the Bonne Auberge and be in top form. People said he must be dosing up on amphetamines. His own explanation was that he had a faster normal heartbeat than others. 'Instead of a resting rate of sixty, mine's a hundred . . . that's why I'm racing all the time.' This was also, according to him, why he needed so little sleep and was going to die before his time.

Polly & Jane was an even bigger success than *The Interloper*. It grossed over $10,000,000, which put it on a level with Wilder's *Some Like It Hot* and inevitably caused Wynner to be talked about as another Marilyn Monroe. I thought, then, that it was a very slight piece, made to cash in on Wynner's publicity, and my review was somewhat faint in its praise. Later, much later, I and others came to see it as a delicate, clever, stylish film: one of his best: it was Strawley being cynical and sophisticated and very funny and, although not apparent on the surface, serious. At the time it was said to be exploitative because it did blatantly exploit Wynner's sexuality (it also showed her very unsexy as the plain Jane twin), and didn't seem to be 'about' anything, but in retrospect it came to be seen as a comedy of the new sexual mores. The sixties were upon us, and things were changing. In any case, it mattered little what the critics said, the public flocked to the film, and he was on course for solid, big-time success.

His rise, reaching its acme, in conventional terms, with an Oscar seven years later for *The Policeman,* was helped along by historical factors: it was the period when the Hollywood studio system finally broke down under the impact of television and the parallel rise of the independents. Louis B. Mayer and Harry Cohn were dead; Darryl Zanuck had quit direction of 20th Century Fox for France, Juliette Greco and independent production. The most successful American film company, United Artists, was based in New York, owned no studios and had no contract artists on its payroll. It was evident that UA was much leaner and lither for going into the TV era than the old majors tied to their obsolete dream factories. In the first place, these had been built by the movie pioneers to supply a steady stream of films to the cinema chains that they themselves owned. After the war, the US government had brought in a 'divorcement' bill that compelled owners of studios to give up ownership of cinemas, and, as a result, the need to supply their own cinemas was gone. In any case, film attendances were plummeting and the kind of standardized entertainment formerly provided by Hollywood was now being offered free by television.

In these changing times, United Artists pointed in the direction in which the film industry would have to evolve. By confining itself to the business of financing films, UA was able to pick its projects throughout the world, take advantage of the lower costs of making films in England, Italy and Spain and, having no expensive artists under long-term contract for whom work had constantly to be found, could move fast to snap up the hot property and the hot talent of the moment. United Artists did not concern itself directly with production, leaving the film-makers virtual freedom to make their films as they wished, which was another bait for the top talent. Control was exercized, albeit from a distance, through a new faceless breed of money men, who for the film-makers often were no more than voices on the telephone.

What had replaced the studio system was 'packaging', putting together an enticing package of story, director and stars. The money men consulted their little black books in which were entered the box office returns of every film made during the past few years, and on the basis of these figures decided whether the package they were being offered was likely to make money or not. A particular star or a particular director, or a combination of the two, would be considered bankable or not according to their track record, and the art of being a producer was to deliver a package that would appeal to the men with the little black books. If the business in general was in crisis, a handful of films were making more money than ever before, and since the fate of a studio like MGM or Columbia sometimes rested on a single film, all the companies were looking for the genius who would hit the jackpot for them. The constant scramble to find such magicians gave rise to the master wheeler-dealers — men like Sam Spiegel, Joe Levine, Samuel Bronsten, the Mirisch Brothers, Dino de Laurentiis, Sydney Carver — who could convince enough people that they were the ones who *knew,* had access to the magic. A director like Jack Strawley, with a couple of films in the little black book showing good returns, was a name to conjure with, and Carver had become a master conjuror. Thus the partnership Strawley-Carver became one of the success stories of the sixties. Carver seemed to know more often than not what the public would want to see and, more importantly, had the gift of convincing the heads of film companies of this, and Strawley had the talent. With this combination they couldn't go wrong.

At the same time, in the way in which such movements tend to occur, box office success was producing a shift in critical opinion. In the sixties, Jack Strawley was making films that were too popular for him to be considered *truly* serious, and the high critical regard in which he had been held at the beginning gradually turned to carping and then to downright denunciation. The trendy journalists who made a speciality of going against the tide five minutes before it was about to turn, were coming out with vitriolic attack pieces, saying that the genius was a fake dreamed up by one Stephen Dall and a bunch of French movie intellectuals with weird views about the film director as *auteur.*

I had myself become less convinced of Strawley's genius and offended him with my quibbling, my nit-picking . . . my damning with less enthusiastic praise than before. I did think that I had been guilty of hyperbole at the beginning and that I had carelessly helped to create a blown-up, artificial reputation. With that one-skin-missing temperament of his, he was sensitive to every thought that was passing through your head and reacted in his kidding/not kidding way. I became one of the 'equivocating hags', 'the eunuch in the harem', while he, dammit, was the *auteur*, the creator. What right did I have to criticize, to 'have reservations' about a film into which he had put so much? For he did indeed expend himself totally on every film he made: it was each time a tremendous struggle with all the forces arraigned against him, which had to be defeated not just once but again and again. And I was saying that the work was derivative — one of those critical clichés that he dismissed with utter contempt — that it lacked real originality and freshness. 'You take what you need and you make it what you need to make it. You make it your own. Nobody creates out of nothing. No work is unique. You feed off others . . . it's the food chain.'

Somehow — perhaps because it had come to be accepted, erroneously, that it was I who had dubbed him 'genius Jack' — I played a role in his life which went beyond that of critic and publicist: I was someone on whose praise he had come to depend, and therefore its (partial) withdrawal made him angry and resentful. I was placed in the invidious position of being the judge of Jack Strawley's worth as an artist, perhaps as a human being.

My relationship with him went through the vicissitudes that all his other relationships underwent, but while it was sometimes touch and go between us — he always maintained, mysteriously, that I had once done him a great injury, and this would be brought up from time to time without the injury ever being specified — we remained on reasonably good terms, and I (unlike others to whom he had once been close) continued to be invited to his house. I saw him fairly regularly throughout these years and he continued, at certain moments, to confide in me, almost as if, already then, he had decided that I was one day going to write the story of his life and should therefore witness certain aspects of it.

Hence I was at the house-warming party in 1968 to celebrate the Strawleys' move 'across the road' from Paulton Square to Carlyle Square. Although, indeed, only a few minutes from their old address, their new house was a much grander place; a splendid Georgian stucco and brick edifice with pillared entrance and high sash windows giving onto a long balcony. They had bought this house whereas they had been renting the one in Paulton Square. Their new place had six bedrooms, four bathrooms, a library, offices, a staff flat, a wine cellar and a small, elegant garden. It was not just a beautiful, comfortable house: it was evidence of the 'recognition' that he had craved and now obtained, at least from the powers of the commercial world. His household was now spread over four floors. Anna, who must have been eleven or twelve by then, was on the top floor, in her own quarters, well out of the way; Jack had his offices with phones and telexes on the floor below and then, on the floor below that, there were the guest bedrooms and, below that, the master bedroom flanked by 'his' and 'her' dressing rooms. The drawing room stretched in an L-shape across the whole of the first floor, with the dining room and kitchen on the ground floor.

It was after moving to Carlyle Square that he started to go in for collecting art, at first on a modest, practical scale — having so many walls to fill. Pretty soon he had caught the bug and begun to collect seriously. I think what had got him interested in the first place was *Cahiers du Cinema* writing of him, in a review of one of his films, that 'like Klee and Mondrian he fines reality down to a clean hard core, within which lie untold complexities'. There were situations and relationships in his films, said this French critic, of 'pure geometric abstraction'. After that, he started buying art on a regular basis. An added incentive for people in his earnings bracket was that art works could be bought with money paid under the table. It was common for directors to receive part of their fee in executive attaché cases stuffed with banknotes. Art was a safe untraceable home for this ready cash, and hence quite a few film people started to go in for collecting art. As a result of the article in *Cahiers du Cinema,* he had taken a good hard look at Mondrian and Klee, and he liked Klee very much, liked his references to the inchoate within a formal pattern and he liked Mondrian too. Quickly his enthusiasm spread to Magritte and Max Ernst and Edward Hopper and Jackson Pollock. And thence — in a broad backward movement in time — to the German Expressionists, and to the *fauves*. There is no doubt that his film-making was influenced by some of these artists. As in other areas, he simply took from them whatever he found was of use to him. He liked the ambiguities and the word play and the eeriness of Magritte, the urban desolation in Hopper, the erotic surrealism of Fini . . . But he would also unashamedly borrow from Delacroix and from Ingres. He once said to me that he was trying in his films to show in images more than the eye could see, more than the brain could grasp. He wanted people to be moved against their will, for unknown reasons. In one or two of his very best films, which I have analyzed frame by frame on a Moviola to try and discover the secret of the emotion generated, he made use of near-subliminal shots, that is, shots that last for less than three or four frames, approximately a sixth of a second, which is at the very limit of what the brain can take in and record. It was his claim that when he was in 'fast gear', his brain worked normally at this sort of speed and could take in those sorts of visions. This was when he saw what he referred to as his 'witches and devils'.

He was collecting paintings on the basis of what he could afford, which meant, on the whole, paintings in the £5,000 to £8,000 price range. In the sixties, for this sort of money, he was able to make some important purchases: a beautiful small Paul Klee that was a vibrant exposition of rendering visible what the eye cannot see and, a year later, a striking Magritte.

In this period of high earnings and high expenditure he was at his most enticing personally: running hard, of course, battling against the bastards and the shits and the motherfuckers, but superbly resilient to all their real or imagined put-downs. A frantic sort of charm imbued all his activities. If there was sometimes a somewhat crazy glimmer in his eyes, it was quickly masked by his extraordinary smile which mended all fences at a stroke, if you had it bestowed on you.

And so it came as a big surprise when, in 1970, a film he was about to start was called off because he was suffering from 'exhaustion' and had to go to a health farm in East Anglia for a period of complete rest. I quote from a piece I wrote at the time:

'The whole business of being a genius has suffered a severe setback, let's face it, as a result of the announcement that Jack Strawley's new film has been put in turnaround, which is the movie business term for called-off, cancelled, shelved indefinitely, because the director is 'tired' and needs 'a long rest'. Now geniuses are not supposed to get tired like the rest of us: they are expected to be endlessly, inexhaustibly creative . . . and certainly this image has been borne out by the career of Jack Strawley, who had seemed to be able to fly as close to the sun as he liked without getting his wings singed. But apparently he gets tired too. The truth is that Jack Strawley is now forty (which is a dirty trick to play on a wunderkind), and this is the age when you come to realize that while being a Boy Wonder may be wonderful, there's no future in it. Audiences don't want to be entranced by the same old wonders, they want new ones, and to appease them you have to keep dancing faster.' The article, although rather flip at the start, actually went on to say that maybe losing some youthful fire wasn't necessarily such a bad thing, that it permitted a more mature and reflective talent to emerge.

When he came out of the health farm he was sullen, dark-faced, brooding, and my guess was that his nervous exhaustion was at least partly connected with marital problems. His relationship with Gloria had always been, as far as one could tell, very dependent, very close and very fraught. On the whole, the tensions between them were kept well hidden, but there had been, in the spring of 1970, just prior to his 'tiredness', one grisly flare-up which I witnessed. At the time, I attributed it to his having had rather too much to drink that night. But in the light of his subsequent stay at the health farm, which I knew to possess a psychiatric wing, I began to see that the incident must have been related to some more fundamental disequilibrium in him.

It had begun, as things with him usually did, out of the blue. Suddenly there had been that 'kidding' menace in his voice and eyes that I knew well, and it developed from there. The incident occurred at his Carlyle Square house, at one of those smart little dinner parties the Strawleys often gave at that time. Gloria had said what a fine and important and shamefully unrecognized writer Carl Schmidlin was — he was not present that night — and how much Jack owed to him, as a writer and as a friend, something that he was always ready to acknowledge. There she made a mistake, for Jack was not ready to acknowledge it on this particular occasion, even if he had done so previously.

Apparently he was angered by something that Carl had supposedly said in an interview. According to the article, Carl had said that Jack was a 'savage' who had never read a book until one summer he succeeded in 'swallowing whole' the Twenty Greatest Works of Literature in the space of a few weeks, after which he'd never read anything again unless it had the possibility of being turned into a film. The interviewer had left out one crucial detail: the fact that in saying this Carl had prefaced his remark with the phrase, '*Jack would have us believe that . . .*' that is, Carl was quoting Jack talking of himself in an exaggeratedly self-disparaging fashion, *in order to rebut this story.* But the way it came out, it seemed to be Carl saying it, and Jack, very quick to resentment, considered it a betrayal, even if he had indeed said such things about himself. Carl had actually done the opposite: had gone out of his way to dismiss the story of the 'uneducated savage', saying that Jack possessed an extraordinary instinctive culture, had the ability to take in things in the blink of an eye. But on this particular night Jack chose to believe that Carl had betrayed him to the gutter press. I could see that he was speeding up, drinking far too much, and that his kidding bellicosity was getting out of control.

It started with the lopsided grin that gradually took over his whole face to say I'm-kidding-but-I'm-not-kidding. 'Gloria,' he told the dinner party guests, 'if you happened to observe her about the house, you'd see is only happy when she's cutting . . . cutting carrots, cutting potatoes, cutting cucumber, cutting roses . . . cutting off balls, anything like that makes her happy, and as a matter of propinquity they tend to be my balls she cuts off. It's her little hobby, and she's even ready to go higher up the tree of knowledge and eliminate the entire offensive trunk at a chop! Her colluder in this tree surgery is professional refugee-victim-tree-surgeon Carl Ignatius Schmidlin, who tells you wittily, *wittily*, why life's not worth the candle . . . your life, mine, his. Anybody's life. Therefore, logical thing to do is, end it. That's his message to the world.'

At this point, Jack was on his feet, swaying, waving the carving knife about, and his voice had taken on an ominous sing-song note as if he was working himself up for some sacrificial rite. The sacrifice of St. Gloria.

'C'mon here, darling. Show you . . . what I mean . . . *Come here.*' The timbre of his voice swung from sweet to violent, back to syrupy sweet. 'Angel face,' he purred coaxingly. 'Pussy, pussy, pussy . . .' — and then back again to kidding-serious-hard: *'Bitch! Cunthead!'* She had a fixed smile on her face as she sat there white-faced, unbudging, staring at him with grimly enforced calm.

'Darling, I think your performance tonight is just a teeny little bit over the top,' she told him when there was a gap in the tirade.

'You're not going to come and give me a kiss, then . . . let everyone see how you keep me alive with your devotion and your self-sacrificing and your missionary skills with *savages.*' A big, ostensibly disarming grin. 'Come here, *cunthead*!'

She backed him up in front of their guests. 'Believe it or not,' she told them sweetly, 'that term is an exotic form of affection in Jack's vocabulary.' She got up and started going towards him, smiling tightly. 'Jack,' she said coming to his side and putting an arm around him tenderly, while smiling reassuringly around the dinner table to tell us not to worry, it'll be all right. 'Jack, take it easy, darling. How about a little white one to bring you down, you're swinging a little high tonight, honey, let's have a little white one, shall we, and come down . . . what d'you say? Everybody here's your friend, Jack.'

I don't know what else she said to him, but she handled him with consummate skill that night, soothing the savage beast in him and then feeding him little white ones with quick flashing smiles around the table, and, in a while, his face fell out of its provocative-kidding mould, seeming to sag like artists' clay that has lost its plasticity, and you could see the high-flying energy drain out of him and the slow, hard, miserable expression of someone coming down to earth fast.

For the rest of the dinner he was quiet, well-behaved, almost as if he were not there, eyes moist, eating little and drinking only mineral water.

I remember their daughter Anna making an appearance at one stage — she must have been about fourteen then — and the frightened, tense looks she gave her father, and how his spirits seemed to improve briefly as he hugged her, and then fell again.

I had had a little glimpse of married life with the masks off. It was no more shocking than similar scenes in *The Interloper*, except for the fact that this was really happening. Gloria, fine actress that she was, managed to keep up appearances of course, but I thought I had seen how she was losing heart behind the bright outer mask and I was afraid that, strong as she was, one day she would crack. He had been using up people at a tremendous rate — a lot of his friends had fallen by the wayside (I was often amazed I had survived), and I thought that she might be next on the list.

The persona that Jack presented to the world was generally upbeat, of a man in charge of himself and his destiny. The 'other side' was seen only in isolated incidents such as the one I have described. He took pains to conceal his 'downside', and Gloria and Moira, in their different ways, helped in this, sheltering him from prying eyes and intrusive questions. But there were times when, for one reason or another — because he was feeling so good, or so bad — he let small cracks be seen. It happened once during a television interview with Dick Cavett in New York. Cavett had led up to it gracefully, saying: 'Jack, we've had a lot about the "ups" of your life, dazzling and well-merited, but I know there have been "downs" as well, and I wonder if, to balance the picture, you'd want to talk about those a little bit.'

Invited so charmingly, he had responded with frankness and zest. 'Yeah, my "black dog" days, as Churchill called them. He had them too. When I first came to London and was having my problems with the Un-American Activities Committee and couldn't get any work, despite having had a big success with my first film . . . one day I came out of a restaurant, Dick, and it was raining, and I just sat down in the street in the rain and the traffic and started, you know, shaking and weeping. Couldn't stop. I couldn't walk, I couldn't breathe. Thought I was dying of a heart attack. Felt very sorry for myself dying so young . . . I was twenty-five or six. Fortunately, somebody came along, a girl I knew, who picked me up out of the gutter. And sure, I still have my "black dog" days. And weeks. I have to live with that. I identify a lot with something Lowell said — about seeing too much and feeling it with one skin layer missing.'

Such public admissions of frailty were rare and only made from a position of strength — as in this case, during a major TV interview occasioned by his fame and successes. He'd won an Oscar the year before. There were the periodic stays at the 'health farm' in East Anglia, but it was a fashionable, expensive place to which eminent people went to recuperate from the strains and stresses of flying high and living fast, and the overall impression he conveyed was of someone suffering mainly from an excess of success. His marital problems were due to him being too successful with women, and his 'exhaustions' were the result of too many demands being made on his time and talents. If he had break-downs they were, like everything else in his life, the best.

This was how it looked from the outside. While I had had one or two glimpses of him with the mask off, I didn't, at that time, know the real truth of what was happening to him.

29

The way he'd planned it was to go out there with his team, take photos, have some script discussions in the settings they planned to use — places helped his visual imagination to flow — see one or two bullfights and then get back and work closely with Carl on the final shooting script of *Heart of Darkness*. United Artists hadn't been too keen on what they'd read so far, and Jack had had to fend them off by saying that what they had read was a very early draft that was going to be transformed once he and Carl got down to working on it together, which they had not done so far because he, Jack, had been too busy.

When Gloria heard of the plans to go to Spain she said she'd
like to come along. It sounded as though it was going to be fun.
This was not what he'd had in mind and he denied that it was
going to be fun. 'It's a location recce, you'll be bored. We're not
going to see galleries and churches. There'll be nothing for you
to do. I want to work on the script with Carl and go see some
bullfights, and you hate bullfights. They make you ill.' He had
considered three or four days away from the family setting to be
part of the well-earned break he was due and he didn't want to
transport the family setting with him.

'Who else is going?' she'd asked.

'Well, there'll be Sydney. And Carl. And probably Percy Drummer. And Moira, of course.'

'You're taking Moira?'

'She's organizing the whole thing. She's the only one who
speaks some Spanish.'

'Carl speaks some Spanish.'

'Yeah, but he doesn't organize things. He can't deal with the
mechanics.'

'Whereas Moira's good at mechanics, isn't she?'

'She's efficient. She gets things done.'

'Well, I want to come along. I don't see why I should get all
the boring trips . . . and when there's some fun going I'm excluded.'

'It's not going to be "fun", as you call it, Gloria. And you're
not excluded. I just thought you wouldn't want to string along
when we'll all be working.'

'Well, in that case, if I'm not excluded, I'm coming. Okay?
Unless you really don't want me to come.'

'Of course I want you to come if you want to come, I thought
you wouldn't want to.'

'Well, I do want to.'

'Then come.'

He thought, straight away, driving in from the airport, that this
was going to be a good place to recreate the heart of darkness:
the burnt ochre countryside, the dried-up rivers and streams now
gullies of dust, the wild orange trees with their shrivelled small

fruit, the slow, packed trains lurching alongside the dusty roads, the sense of provincial lassitude and decay, of rural rot and industrial overflow. Everywhere you saw signs of the Fascist state. Truckloads of bored Civil Guards being transported around, rifles over shoulders. Police hanging out at street corners and outside bars and *bodegas*, with unlit cigarettes stuck to their lips, wearing dusty uniforms, falling asleep on their feet. All of which was perfect for the setting of the film. On the roadsides there was the haphazard sprawl of primitively constructed and often unfinished buildings, with sudden patches of countryside flashing up like mirages.

'Hasn't changed much in all those years,' Carl observed.

'When were you here?'

'Just after the war. Before I came to America. At the time I thought about living here permanently. It was so cheap. And hot. And I liked the people and the wine . . . and the women. Altogether a pretty good place for a writer. Especially one not making any money.'

'Why didn't you stay?'

'Franco . . . that was the other side of it. Living in a Fascist country, although they left you pretty much alone as a foreigner.'

'You going to show us around?'

'The places I knew then are not on the movie-maker's circuit. Cheap bars and *bodegas*, cheap whorehouses.'

'You can show us anyway. I'd like to see how you lived.'

His first impression of Seville was of its different levels and its campaniles and elaborate ironwork balconies and the dramatic uniform whiteness of southern Spain, with cornices and pillars and pediments picked out in deep sand yellow, the hot strong colours offset by the cooling blue and white tiles of patios.

Depositing them on the broad steps of the Hotel Alphonse XIII, the taxi driver casually doubled the price on the meter, referring to something he called 'the airport tax'. Moira wanted to dispute this, but Jack said to pay him, they didn't have time to argue. He wanted to go out straight away and see the town, get that over with — he hated sightseeing but knew a minimum amount would have to be done. And so they did the Giralda in extra fast time. No point hanging around. This wasn't what he was going to film. What he was looking for was heat and desolation — and catastrophe coming out of the corner of the eye. Having done the Giralda, drinks were clearly earned. Carl took them to a little plaza, not far from the bullring, where eight narrow streets converged. They sat at metal tables and watched the slow re-start of the Spanish day. Within seconds they were being vigorously solicited by shoe-shine boys. After them came a succession of thin, sullen gypsy women with babies in their arms, who stood unbudging by their table, periodically clutching at sleeves, until given some coins. Then there was the legless man propelling himself along in a dilapidated wheelchair festooned with long strips of lottery tickets.

Jack turned to Moira: 'Okay, we've done the local colour. Tomorrow you and Percy hire a boat and start going downriver, see what you can find. We need wild shore, primitive-looking brush, rampant vegetation. Take lots of film, I want to see everything. Before you leave, find out when Antonio Miguel Francisco is fighting, and get tickets for all of us. Gloria'll come. Apparently this boy is just marvellous, has got to be seen. They say he's the new Litri. So what d'you think, Carl?'

'About the new Litri?'

'No. About Marlow, Carl. About what we discussed on the plane: making Marlow more substantial, more central.'

Carl gave his painful, understanding, ironical smile. 'Jack, Marlow doesn't have much character in the Conrad story, we just see the story through his eyes. Welles, when he was going to do it was going to do it with a first-person camera, so you wouldn't have seen Marlow at all, except as reflections.'

'Maybe that's why Orson's version never got made. We want to get this made, Carl. At least I do. I sometimes think to you it doesn't matter.'

Carl gave a sigh, followed by a sharp little stab. 'I don't know why you need *writers*, Jack. You're the *auteur*. What d'you need a writer for?'

'You may be right there, Carl. This may be the trip where we do away with the writer,' Jack said with a harsh little laugh.

Walking back to the Alphonse XIII, he let Carl go on ahead with Gloria, who was looking in her guide book and cross-checking with him about places to see. Carver put a hand on Jack's arm, holding him back so as to let the others get further ahead, until they were out of earshot.

'I don't want to be too brutal about this,' he began with eagerness, coming to a stop in the street.

'Don't deny yourself, Sydney. Be yourself. Who d'you want killed?'

'You're going to have to face up to it eventually. You'll never get this script of Carl's off the ground. You're going to have to bring in another writer. It's unfilmable as written. No studio'll go near it.'

'Why we here in that case?'

'I don't know. It's a waste of money . . . with the script we've got. I say dump Carl and get in somebody who knows about writing movies.'

'This picture is Carl's concept.'

'Maybe he's good on concept but he's shit at dialogue or movie scenes that move. He doesn't know fuck about action.'

'I'm working on that with him, Sydney.'

'He's not listening to you. He's on his own private destruction course. Pay him off, Jack. I like the guy, he has a deep mind but he's a loser. He wants to lose.' His mouth pulled down with the deep, visceral contempt that he felt for losers. 'You're spending all this time trying to coax him into writing a successful movie, but Carl's not interested in doing that. He's off on his own thing, which has nothing to do with making a film that audiences will want to see. I know you go back a long way. Okay. So let's pay him the full agreed fee and get shot of him. And we bring in a top, high-quality film writer like Pinter or Bolt.'

Sydney Carver hadn't changed in any essential respect with big-time success, and the passage of the years had just seen him become rougher in manner. There were fewer people he needed to flatter now, and many more that he could insult. A half-hour casting session with Carver left the ground strewn with the bloody remains of wrecked reputations. Stars, directors, designers and writers were casually demolished.' Look, I'm not pissing on him,' he'd say about somebody whose name had come up, and then proceed to joyfully do just that. This did not prevent him from embracing this individual with expressions of heartfelt tenderness five minutes later, his old habit of buttering people up operating in alternation with his later pleasure in pissing on them.

These days, his sharp thrusting nose thrust out further and further, as a result of his hairline having receded drastically, and people hesitated about getting too close for fear of cutting themselves.

'You know what I value about you, Sydney? That you're such a thug. When I need thuggish work done, you're the perfect man for it. But you don't touch Carl, understand? He's out of your province.'

'If you want to cut your own throat, be my guest.'

'I'll try to postpone giving you that pleasure as long as possible, sweetheart.'

Gloria was pale and feeling queasy in the thick of the heaving mass of people pouring into the bullring from all sides. Moira had got them best seats, in the *sombra*. Half the sky was black, while in the other half the sun blazed down. The clamorous crowd, propelled by pressure from behind, was bursting through all the arched entrances. Those with cheap seats scrambled up the steep amphitheatre steps to the upper tiers of the gallery, carrying their umbrellas and cushions and cameras and drinks and straw hats. Those destined for the *barrera* were elegantly dressed and moved solemnly to their expensive seats by the fence; the rest scrambled and clambered and shoved. In the passageway around the bullring, the sword-handlers waited with jugs of water and sponges and piles of folded muletas.

'I wish Moira had got us less good seats, further back,' Gloria said, squinting into the reflected glare of the sand. 'This is so near. We're right on top of it. We're going to see this *horror* from too close, and it's going to be unbearable to watch. And those photographers are going to be lurking around us the whole time, won't even be able to throw up in private.'

'You won't throw up. You'll love it,' Jack told her. 'I have a feeling it's going to be great. I'm so keen to see this boy they're all talking about.'

Carver was swivelling his long neck, looking over the massed spectators, counting heads in a small section, multiplying by the approximate number of sections and calculating receipts. 'This is quite an audience,' he said, 'quite an audience.' He was smoking a fat Havana cigar, and the smell of it was making Gloria's queasy stomach worse.

'A bloodthirsty crowd,' Gloria said looking around her.

Presently the first trumpet sounded and was followed by the parade of the toreros, a bustling colourful spectacle that helped to momentarily alleviate Gloria's apprehensions. Perhaps the spectacle would blind her to the horror.

30

It was difficult to come down after the great bullfight, with the feria mood spreading through the whole town, and the way he was falling in love with Spain, and all those amazing girls in the street with their fiery flirty eyes and their wild costumes, and the marvellous boy. Oh, he was in love with that boy. He'd made his first pass at a distance of fifteen yards, drawing the bull into a powerful charge of quickly gathering momentum. He had awaited it with cape lowered, perfectly still, and only at the last moment had he raised the cape to spin-turn the bull around himself with a minimal veronica, so tight and small it was like a contemptuous shrug of the shoulder. The boy's command was amazing. It looked as if he was turning the bull by the sheer exercise of his will. When he got to the bloody third act, the close work with the muleta, he was a thin wavering line of glittering gold and silver and glass, confronting the bull in a head-on power struggle: his litheness and command against its massive menace. He was leading the bull by the nose and the band struck up a gay joyful tune, celebrating his mastery. Again and again he had wrapped the huge beast around his slender form, leading it serenely through the death dance, patiently teaching it all the steps, letting the bull pass him so close that it left its blood as stains upon his jewelled belly. And at the end he had pointed his finger at it and called upon it to die, commanded it to die. 'You are dead bull, die . . . die!' It finally understood and its legs buckled, it sank to its knees, rolled onto its side, a great dead weight, and died.

As the carcase was dragged away, Carl, seeing the excitement blazing in Jack's eyes, had remarked: 'Have you noticed that when you see triumph, there's nearly always a dead body close by?'

It was the sort of thing Carl would say. Had to bring everything down. But Jack wasn't going to be brought down from his high.

'Usually yours, I guess,' he remarked with a hard edge to his voice.

Over the bridge, progress was slow in the ever-growing crowd heading towards the feria, and the taxi had to go at walking pace as they approached the film-set Moorish towers and archways at the main entrance, where the celebrants were streaming through in their dozens. The night was brightly lit with arrays of decorative lights strung out overhead. Waves of music came crackling and thumping and screeching through different loudspeaker systems, a great raucous medley in which now this, now that melody drowned out the rest. Threading through it all was the voluptuous wail of flamenco. Big waves of sound flowed over him, shaking him up, and there was the thumping and stamping in his brain. And the heavy heat. The roads were jammed with horse riders and horse-drawn carriages bedecked with flowers, and there were people on foot, of all ages, some in elaborate costumes, others in plain denims. The horse-riders were either stationary or moving in gentle to and fro promenades at a precise sociable trot.

The *casetas* were arranged in a grid pattern throughout the feria, dozens of them of varying sizes, some private, others open to anyone and everyone.

'Look at that girl in the red dress, what a fantastic dancer she

is,' Jack said. There were many of these great girls giving performances of the flamenco that in liveliness and passion sur-
passed anything you ever saw in professional shows. The girl in
the red dress was outstanding. He was falling in love with her,
with everybody, with everything, with the horses and the flowers
and the thumping music being pumped out by his brain and the
girls and the boys — following his nose through the exhilarating
night. Gloria was finding it difficult to keep up with him and kept
calling to him to wait for her, saying they would lose each other
in this dense crowd, but he seemed unable to slow down, kept
pressing hurriedly on through the costumed dancers and the
horse-riders, through packed marquees where the regular thump
of the music clanged on the ear with a sound like metal banging
on metal. He could feel the feria fever mount in him like a flood
tide. The dancing was spreading out from makeshift dance platforms to the places where people were eating and drinking and
right out into the clogged streets: they were dancing right under
the horses' hooves. These girls were so young and so beautiful
and so voluptuous, he couldn't get over how voluptuous these
young girls were in their dancing.

He was walking elatedly alongside Carl, and it felt like the old
days when they used to go on the town together in New York,
looking for girls, and Carl was the successful one then, with his
technique of sniffing a girl's perfume and trying to guess what it
was. Those girls went along with it, because he had something so
utterly appealing about him, so European and dashing and sad.
But he'd become worn down since then, and his long wild grey
hair made him look eccentric now, rather than dashing. A man
who lived in his own world and no longer went up to girls to
smell their perfume.

'Sydney talked to me,' Carl said.

'Don't take any notice of Sydney.'

'He said UA hated the script. That they will not make the film
in this form.'

'If UA don't want to do it we'll go to Fox or Columbia or
Warners. They all want a picture from me.'

'But perhaps not the one I've written.'

'I'll make them want it.'

'How will you do that, Jack?'

'You're going to make it so damned good they will *have* to have it — the way those big studios have to have something when they have to have something.'

'Jack, I'm not sure I can deliver what you and the studios want. It is clearly my failing, but I don't think I even understand what it is you want.'

'I'm going to tell you, Carl. Okay? You've written a great monologue. It's a wonderful soliloquy — notes from the under-world — but that doesn't make a film. Kurtz exists as a character. You've done that. But he's alone out there, talking to himself. The others are shadows. I want it to be at least a dialogue, between him and Marlow. Then we've got a film.'

'Marlow has no character in the Conrad story. He's the narrator who tells the story. It's Kurtz's story.'

'Okay, but this is a movie, so it's got to be *their* story. In the story you've written, Kurtz was a brilliant OSS officer working for Allen Dulles in the war. He had to test himself and come through . . . and he did that but he did some dubious things, as well, fell into the fiery lake and got all burnt up. Had to put himself together again. All that you've done, and it's good. Needs work but it's basically good. What's missing is a strong storyline. Here's the way to do it: when Marlow comes out with orders to eliminate him, what Kurtz sees is himself as he once was — he once had to do something like that. That's when he fell into the fiery lake. And what Marlow sees in Kurtz is the man he's going to be one day, when he falls in his turn. That's our story.'

'That's your story, Jack. It's not Conrad's, it's not mine.'

'Carl,' he said patiently but with some indication of exaspera-tion mounting up. 'Carl, you may have heard this before, so at the risk of being repetitive: movies are a collective art, and you and Conrad are going to have to share the credit with the rest of us worker ants.'

'Alternatively you may have to take my name off the credits, and Conrad's . . . and start again, as sole *auteur,*' Carl said, his face setting like concrete.

'Carl, you're being damned stupid, worse'n stupid . . . ridiculous! This can be a big film for you, an important film with your name on it this time! You've totally re-written Conrad already, so why scream about making Marlow the character we need to give the story dramatic tension?'

'I scream because I hear you talking like Sydney Carver. And, what's worse, acting like Sydney Carver.'

'Sydney may be the producer of my films, he may shout a lot but he has to do what I tell him — and does.'

'Then you must have told him you want me out of the picture, because that's what he conveyed to me.'

'Sydney thinks it'll be a better film — a bigger grosser, yes — if you have nothing to do with it, and he may be right. But I, for my own stupid reasons, want you to do it. I want to keep the intellectual quality that you can give it. But you have got to give me a storyline from which I can make a film.'

'Ah,' Carl said. 'When you want something, Jack, you can rationalize the devil's cloven hoof and make it smell sweet.'

'Carl . . . Carl, look. I am not the devil. I am not the Nazis. I am someone who wants to go on making films . . . good ones, if possible, with you writing them sometimes . . . or not, as the case may be.'

'Looks like it's going to be "or not"? Doesn't it?'

'That's up to you.'

'Is it? I think the decision's already been made. Few last the course with you, Jack. Why not just say it was a mistake and cancel the contract. I'll pay back the money I've received.'

'You are fucking insane. Apart from the fact that nobody in his right mind hands back money in this business, and you certainly are in no position to, don't you realize that UA has already sunk half a million dollars in this project in development costs and they're not going to just drop the whole thing because a writer won't do script changes.They just get another writer.'

'As you did with *The Interloper*.'

'We didn't do so badly with that. Won at Cannes, made money at the box office . . . got me some other films to make . . . worth having a glass thrown at you by an irate author?'

'Bravo!' Carl said very quietly. 'Now that's Jack-the-Talented-Shit speaking. He's the real thing, at least. Steals what he needs . . .

other people's ideas, work, women . . . without hesitation or scruple. I say bravo to that. What I admire most about Jack-the-Talented-Shit is that he has no qualms.'

'Even when you don't throw glasses your aim is still pretty deadly, Carl. When you want it to be. What are we talking about? My bad character? Or maybe some people are so eaten up with envy and rage and hidden resentments that finally all that seething stuff comes bursting out. OK, Carl, you threw the glass and got a hit. Congratulations. I think this time you may have got the bull's eye.'

He began to walk away, determinedly switching his mind to focus on something pleasanter: the girl in red who had so aroused his interest earlier. She was dancing with such verve and vivacity on the crowded wooden platform that the other dancers were gradually falling away and just standing still and looking at her. The red dress fitted her body closely from shoulders to just above the knees, precisely modelling her breasts, belly and buttocks, and below the knees the dress flared out into seven rows of lace-trimmed flounces. Her hair was deep black with a centre parting. She wore a rose behind the ear. Her eyes, intense and flashing, were laced with a touch of mockery. He watched her, enthralled by the ritual love play of the dance.

The others had found him now in the crowd.

'What's happened between you and Carl?' Gloria asked.

'Looks like Carl and I are through,' he told her.

'You fired him?'

'He fired himself.'

'You must have made him.'

'No. I did my best to get him to stay, but he wouldn't and he said a lot of things that now can't be unsaid . . . we both did. It's over, Gloria. There it is. According to him, I fall out with everyone in the end, and so it had to come.'

'What you're doing is going to destroy him, Jack.'

'I'm afraid, Gloria, I no longer care. He wanted it this way. I don't know why, he probably doesn't know why either, some perverseness of his. There it is. Nothing to be done about it now.'

He was staring intently at the girl in the red dress. Her forehead, her face, her arms and armpits were glistening from her exertions. The dance movements were boldly explicit, the girl offering herself repeatedly, provocatively, then drawing coquettishly back and then offering herself even more boldly, and the man moving convulsively forward in response, his body stiffly erect.

Gloria said coldly: 'Carl is right, you fall out with everyone. Who've you got left, apart from me? And how long will I last?'

'If that's how I am, that's how I am, Gloria. Jack-the-Shit. That's what Carl thinks of me and he may be right. Maybe that's what you think too.'

She saw the overbright light in his eyes, indicating the speed at which his brain was going.

'Come down, Jack, you're over the top.'

'No, I'm just having a good time. You want to bring everything down. To dullsville. You and the holy hermit of Hampstead, Carl.'

'Jack, I'm too tired to argue with you. How long d'you intend to stay, because I'm dropping?'

'Well, I'm wide awake, just getting into the swing of it,' he said. 'It's a shame. We don't seem to coincide about anything anymore.'

'You can stay, if you want,' she said. 'I'm going to go back to the hotel. I can't keep up with you, Jack.'

'Yes, you go,' he told her.

The girl in the red dress had finished the dance with her current partner. Abruptly all the frenzied foot stamping and head tossing was at an end. She had no sooner sat down than somebody else asked her to dance and unhesitatingly she accepted, and once more, with rising arms and stamping feet, was committing herself to the intense interplay of eyes and limbs, to the ravishment of looks.

The others were staying on for a while longer. Percy Drummer had that tight-lipped British stoicism about enjoying himself: he would stick it out to the end. And Carver and Moira were ready to try and keep up.

They strolled by the *casetas*. The spirit of the feria was everywhere in evidence, and in each place the flamenco was danced by people of all ages, with varying degrees of skill and beauty, but everywhere with enormous spirit.

'Cute little girls some of 'em,' Carver observed. 'Look at that one over there. Look at that ass!'

'Yeah.'

'I hear you and Carl had a standoff. What's the bottom line on that?'

'He wants to quit.'

'Now there's an offer you can't refuse, baby.'

'I didn't refuse.'

'Finally came to your senses. Congratulations.'

'Not so sure about that, Sydney. Every film I ever made, Carl's been there for me. One way or another. If not actually working on it, then as a friend. I've had a helluva lot of unpaid advice and support from him over the years. And ideas. Got used to having him there. He's a part of my moral back-up system. Don't know how I'll manage without him.'

'Jack, you can't afford to lose Gloria, or Moira, or me . . . we're your back-up . . . you can't do without *us*. But Carl you can do without.'

'Tell me what I need you for, Sydney. All you do is make deals with MGM and screw lady presidents of the jury . . . and fix the odd Palme d'Or for me. But can you get me that girl in the red dress back there? What do I need a producer for, if you can't even get me one these cute Spanish babes.'

'Jack, whatever you want. Whatever. Look at you. You're one of the dozen highest paid, most successful film directors in the world . . . in the world! Didn't I have something to do with that?'

'You had a lot to do with that, Sydney. I'm just not sure I should be grateful.'

The girls on their superb horses were all very smartly dressed in grey or black riding habits, white shirts and narrow black ties, and those wide-brimmed equestrian *caneros* that made them look so dashingly sexy. Most of them rode side-saddle, drink in hand, as if elegantly perched on the edge of a silken sofa. The ones who straddled their horses appeared incredibly wanton. Lovely young girls clasping the great beasts between their open thighs. With their knees and heels and hands manoeuvring and controlling the superbly trained animals. In the dense crush, with pedestrians brushing their flanks, stepping in front of them, behind them, the horses remained disciplined, responsive to their riders' slightest touch.

You had to let yourself be carried by the crowd. By 2 a.m. Carver had had enough and was ready to quit, and Percy Drummer, British grit notwithstanding, supposed that it might be time for him to turn in as well.

'You coming, Jack?'

'I'm not tired . . . I'm enjoying this.'

His brain was unable to stop. It had to keep running. To keep up with his fast heartbeat.

'Stick with him, Moira,' Carver said. 'Don't leave him by himself. Whatever he wants to do, stick with him. Okay? '

'May be places he wants to go where I may not be able to stick with him . . . or want to.'

'Moira, stick with him. He's flying too high. I'm counting on you, Moira.'

'Let's go find that girl in the red dress,' Jack impatiently told her as soon as Carver and Drummer had gone.

'Which girl in which red dress?'

'The one at the beginning.'

'There are a lot of girls in red dresses,' she pointed out, 'and I don't even know where the beginning is.'

'The one who's such a fantastic dancer. In the first place we stopped at.'

'They all are fantastic dancers. Which first place are you talking about? Jack, don't you think we should call it a day? I'm pretty tired.'

'Don't be so defeatist, Moira. The place where I was with Carl.'

'I can't remember where that was.'

'I can.'

Determinedly, he began to push back through the crowd, steering by some internal compass of his, driving hard, with Moira hanging on. Amazingly, he found the place. There were far fewer people dancing on the wooden platform now, and the girl in red was not among them. He looked around inside the marquee, pushing his way into every corner to see if she was

sitting at any of the tables, but there was no sign of her anywhere.
'I should think her Mamma came to take her home hours ago.
Long past her bedtime. And mine. What is this about her?'
'She's so incredibly beautiful.'
'You've seen incredibly beautiful girls before. Remember?'
'Not as incredibly beautiful as this one.'
'You're overheating, Jack. Come down.'
'Don't want to come down. Fine where I am.'
'Jack, let me take you home.'
'You can go home, Moira, if you want to welsh out. Nobody's
keeping you. Go home. Go home, traitor.'
'I can't go home while you . . .'
'You can. I don't need a minder. I'm fully grown up.'
'That's debatable, and, on top of it, you don't have a word of
Spanish.'
'I can make myself understood in essentials.'
'That's another thing I'm afraid of. You going to offer her a
part in your next film?'
'I'm going to offer her a part in my life.'
'Oh yeah? One or two other people already have got parts in
your life. You don't have much left to give away.'
'You don't know half the parts I have got, Moira.'
He saw the girl in red come back into the *caseta*, looking
around. Her eyes found him and she gave him a full dazzling
smile, as if she had been waiting for him all evening to come
back and offer her a part in his life. She sat down at a crowded
table with a group of her young friends, and at once somebody
wanted to dance with her. Before accepting, she looked towards
Jack, as if asking his permission. He nodded to her, smiling.
'You know this girl?' Moira asked him.
'Sure I know her, I'm going to marry her.' He was smiling
mysteriously to himself.
'Is that a fact?'
'Absolutely.' The crazy smile was stamped onto his face.
'Jack, come on. Let's go before you get in trouble.'
He wouldn't leave. He wasn't tired, he said. He moved closer
to the wooden platform and stood staring at the girl in the red
dress all the time she was dancing, and she, instead of peering

into her partner's eyes, peered into Jack's eyes, so that it was as if she was doing all those voluptuous movements for him. When the dance came to an end and the dancers broke apart, she stayed where she was, eyes downcast, waiting for him to make a move.

'Ask her to join us,' he instructed Moira, thick-voiced.

'You want me to get her for you, right?'

'Right.'

'She's very young, Jack. I don't think she's more than fifteen.'

'They mature early in these hot climes.'

'Jack, this is Spain. You have any idea what you may be getting into?'

'Don't argue with me, Moira. Just get her for me. Please, Moira. Do it, will you?' He and the girl in red were looking at each other intently.

'What shall I tell her?'

'You know what to tell her.' He shrugged. 'Tell her . . . that I'm in love with her, that I want to marry her. Tell her I'm a very famous film director. Tell her anything you like. Get her for me, Moira. I have to have her.'

Moira went over to talk to the girl. She did it smoothly. It was evident that she was paying her lavish compliments, conveying with words and gestures and facial expressions how utterly bowled over he was by her. Giggling between girls went on. Confidences were exchanged. Jack was being written up in all his aspects for the benefit of this young girl, his merits in different areas were sung. Moira praised him with womanly fervour, making it clear she spoke from personal experience. The little Spanish girl was drinking in the information avidly, her eyes brightening all the time. There was some problem that they were discussing. Moira proposed something. The Spanish girl looked doubtful and proposed something else. Whereupon Moira looked doubtful. There were more whisperings that had the young girl giggling again. Moira appeared to be giving her a lesson in the unopposable nature of men's desires. Finally the girl was brought over to Jack. He said one or two things to her, and Moira translated. The Spanish girl hung her head, then pointed to her left and started off, and Moira said: 'She wants us to follow. I don't know where she's going.'

'So let's follow her.'

They followed her through the thinning crowd, along paths laid with straggling cables, to a patch of waste ground beyond the last of the brightly lit *casetas*. Here, in the sudden gloom, there was a long row of trucks and trailers that contained the generators providing electric power for the loudspeaker systems and for the hundreds of brightly-coloured lights strung out across the fairground a hundred yards away. The music was down to a steady, rhythmic thump here. Some of the vehicles were caterers' trucks, and around them there were overflowing garbage bins that had drawn all the stray cats and dogs of the vicinity. Chicken legs and fish heads and the crumbling creamy remains of gooey cakes were being scrambled for around the bins. Further off there was the rustling of rats in the high grass. The girl in the red dress seemed to know exactly where she was going. Behind the parked service vehicles rose the dim towers and blocks of working-class habitations with inset balconies entirely given over to hung-out laundry. The long concrete facades were punctured by regular lines of small rectangular windows with their occasional vivid window boxes. From these windows a feeble light, filtered through grimy net curtains, fell on a line of dusty orange trees sprouting out of the paving stones. He was in the desolate outskirts of any southern Spanish industrial town.

The girl in the red dress, several steps ahead, was picking her way over the rough, litter-strewn ground. She stopped at a point on the outer edge of the fairground where the service vehicles were parked three and four deep. The second and third rows were gypsy-style caravans where fairground personnel lived during the feria. By one of these, the girl in the red dress stopped and turned around to give a smile that lit up the seedy area in her bright glow. She said something in Spanish, and Moira translated:

'She says to go in, that it's all right. Jack, she's awfully young . . .'

He didn't want to hear about this or anything else, and he followed the girl into the dim inner space that smelled strongly of unwashed clothing and unclean bodies and deep-fried food, and there was some other smell too. All of it was magicked away by the humid bloom of sexual ripeness that came from the girl. She stood waiting for him in the narrow space, blocking the corridor between low bunk beds. She was unfastening the buttons of her dress and opening the top part while speaking rapidly. Moira, standing behind Jack, translated: 'She wants you to give her a present. She says she has a sick mother and needs money. Since you're a famous and rich American and say you're in love with her, will you give her a nice present, she asks.' The Spanish girl's breasts were small quivering jellies, and he touched them. He rolled the perfect little nipples between his thumb and finger tips. She looked down, very proud of her stiff little nipples, and repeated her request for money: giving him a dazzling smile and at the same time rubbing her thumb over forefingers, which he could not fail to understand. When there was no immediate response from him, she went into a long histrionic speech in which smiles and tears alternated with references to what she liked to have done to different parts of her body.

'What's she saying?' he demanded when it seemed he could not go on ignoring what she was saying.

'She wants you to know that her nipples are so stiff because you excite her and because she has a very passionate nature and loses control of herself, and other things that my colloquial Spanish is not up to, and oh yeah! she wants you to give her the money *now*.'

'Tell her I'll give her a fine present, later.'

'She asks for something for her mother as well, and for her two brothers who are both out of work, and for her father too . . .'

'Nobody else?' he gruffly demanded.

'She wants you to look at her "little man in the boat" . . . she wants to show you how stiff it is.'

The girl had hoisted up her dress and pushed down the small undergarment. Swiftly and neatly she spread the petals of her sex with two fingers, exposing the hard little protuberance at the upper reaches of the glistening rosy pink slide. She was inviting him to touch and then smell his fingers, so he would know she wasn't faking. But he was put off by all the pinkness, wanting something darker, the pink was too candy-coloured, and, instead of doing as she asked, he spun her around, roughly and pushed her head down. Her buttocks were cold and smooth as polished stone and tightly clenched, and she was such a tiny girl he had difficulty heaving the polished stones apart. The girl was babbling the whole time, even while her head was held down, and twisting about with her rear, like a wriggly fish at the end of a spike. He was slipping and sliding about on her cold stony smooth surfaces unable to get in anywhere, while she continued with her hysterical babbling.

'Tell her I'll give her whatever she wants,' he shouted.

'She's got all these cousins as well. She wants a lot.'

He seemed not to care. He was battering against a stone wall, so tight was she. With her head forcefully held down, her face was full of blood and anger and wincing pain, but at the same time she was twisting round, her hand held out for money, money, she wanted her money first, this little whore, pay first, pay first, her grasping little hand was demanding while he pummelled at her determinedly, and then the surge of gory glory. Once finished, he didn't give a damn about her fucking cousins. They really were too much. What was she babbling about now? His voice was harsh and accusing and full of disgusted fury. 'What cousins?'

'It seems she's got all these unemployed cousins. Jack, she's asking for a lot of money. She's making threats . . . if you don't pay her. C'mon, Jack. Jack . . . let's go . . . C'mon.' Her voice had become agitated. She was looking outside and what she saw added a further stressful note to what she was saying. 'Jack, *Jack* . . . couple of her cousins or brothers just showed up, and I have to tell you, smallness does not run in the family.'

Holding back his anger, he told the weeping, cringing, stridently complaining girl:

'I'm very disappointed in you, I'm disappointed. You know, at the beginning I really thought . . . I'm disillusioned.' He pressed a bunch of tattered notes into her fist, and she screamed that it wasn't enough. As he and Moira stepped out of the caravan, their way was blocked by the big cousins who had the same rank semen-smell as the unwashed laundry inside. They had angry faces and were saying angry, accusing things.

'What they want?' he asked Moira.

'They say you dishonoured their little sister. They say you've committed a bad sexual offence. They say she's only fourteen, and you've committed a criminal act. You can be arrested and put in prison, they say. For a long time. They want money, plenty money, to salve her honour. Otherwise they'll go to the cops.'

'How much they want?'

She asked them how much they wanted and they said in English:

'Tousand dollar.'

He said: 'Tell them that whores, which they must know being in the business, cost at very most ten dollars in Spain. Tell 'em I already gave her fifty, I'll give her another fifty, and that's all.'

'It's not enough,' Moira translated. 'They're saying it's not enough.'

'Well, that's all they're getting.' He reached in his pocket and pulled out a bunch of notes and threw them on the ground at the feet of the cousins whose faces took on a dark melancholy aspect, and whose eyes and teeth had a dull shine.

'Now you've insulted them, as well as having abused their under-age sister. They want you to pick up the money.'

'Tell 'em to go fuck themselves in the ass, and their mothers as well.'

'I don't know how to say that in Spanish. And also I don't think I'd better.'

'We understood, Yank,' the cousins said and started pushing him back up against the caravan and grabbing him by the throat.

He yelled at Moira to go get the cops, and put his fists up to protect his face and they punched him in the stomach and, when he started to crumple, they spat in his face and kicked his feet out from under him, and they kicked him methodically while he lay on the ground, in the groin and in the face and in the stomach, and then they started to stamp on him. One of them had a knife. Seeing it, Jack grabbed hold of the foot that was kicking him and twisted it hard all the way round until he heard bones crack and a resounding scream come from the ill-smelling cousin and he twisted back the hand of the one who was holding the knife and repeatedly smashed the hand against the side of the caravan, until the bloody fingers had let go of the knife.

When Moira got there with the cops it took four of them to subdue Jack Strawley and put handcuffs on him, he had become so ferociously unreasoned, and in the police van he was ranting about Spain being a police state and that they were all filthy Fascists and war criminals and was shouting something about Guernica and Franco being Hitler's stooge, and they finally put an end to the unceasing flow of words by treading on his neck with their heavy boots and cutting off his air supply.

31

At the foul-smelling little police station, the narrow corridor leading to the cells was crammed, mostly with prostitutes and the bloody-faced, vomit-stained victims or initiators of street brawls. Policemen in shabby grey uniforms, ancient bolt-action rifles slung over their shoulders, guarded the night's haul while sloppily smoking. There weren't nearly enough cells to house everyone brought in, and prisoners and complainants were thrown together in an undifferentiated mass outside the charge room. Innocent or guilty, nobody could leave. Jack Strawley, semi-conscious, was simply unloaded like a sack of coals and left lying on the filthy floor. Statements might be taken tonight, or tomorrow night, or next week. Such matters were unforeseeable. They had wanted to throw Moira in with the rest, but fortunately one of the policemen remembered that she was the person who had come to fetch them, which seemed to point to her possible innocence of whatever crime had been committed, and so she was allowed to remain outside in the street where the beggars and cripples and gypsy women with children were hanging about, as they hung about everywhere.

It was at once evident to Moira that Jack, behind the pad-locked chicken-wire gate, whether crazy or quietened, conscious or unconscious, had zero chance of getting out fast. Nothing in Spain was fast, and justice was unlikely to be an exception. She considered phoning the consulate, but it was four a.m., and she wouldn't be able to get through until it opened in the morning, which might not be until ten or eleven, and the consul was unlikely to make himself available until after lunch, which in Spain meant around five or six in the afternoon. And Jack needed medical attention now, not only for the injuries he'd sustained at the hands of the cousins and the police, but also to bring him down, since he had gone *maniaco* while they were getting the handcuffs on him, and she knew that he needed his special medicines to get him under control, which no Spanish police doctor, if such beings existed, would know about. In his present state he was going to continue to be a danger to others and to himself. There was also the problem of informing Gloria of what had happened: she would have to be told something: the question was when, and how much. There was no possibility — given his battered state, and the fact that he was being held in jail on a string of charges, some of which related to sexual offences against a minor — that this particular episode could be concealed from her.

There was nothing to be achieved by just hanging about with the beggars outside the police station. The only thing she could think of doing was to go back to the Alphonse XIII, wake up Carver and get him out here. She'd come to the conclusion that he was going to be better at handling this situation than Carl, even though Carl knew Spain and spoke some Spanish, but what this situation called for was Carver, the earth-mover, not the moral debater Carl, who would start unnecessarily weighing up rights and wrongs.

When he'd been told the bare essentials, Carver said not to wake up Gloria: he would handle it. They took a taxi back to the police station, and he told the driver to wait there for him until he came out. Then he began pushing through the crowd in the usual Carver earth-clearing style. At the padlocked chicken-wire, he was confronted by grey-uniformed guards. Carver produced from his pocket a tattered bank note and, rolling it up into a funnel, pushed it through the chicken-wire into the backward extended hand of one of the guards, and soon afterwards the padlock was undone. While one guard held back the crowd — for which he, in his turn, received a tattered note — the other admitted them gloatingly to the melee. You want to be here, now you're here! Congratulate yourselves! Moira saw the chicken wire go back up again behind them and experienced a moment of panic. Now they were locked in too, and nobody on the outside knew, and, in a place like this, how could she call Gloria or anyone else? But Carver appeared unconcerned about such matters while he dug and shoved relentlessly towards the centre of power and influence, which according to his theory of society must exist, in some form or another, even in filthy Spanish police stations such as this one. In due course he got to a door, and ramming it open with one of his lighter touches found himself before a duty officer fast asleep behind his desk, flies buzzing around his face. Other policemen were seated at desks, smoking and playing cards, and looked up only to receive their allocation of tattered bank notes, which they pocketed in silence and without acknowledgement. In this way, Carver advanced. He gave the sleeping duty officer a dig, which produced a brief convulsion, and then drooping eyes opened suspiciously.

'Carver,' Carver said as if the name was legend around here.

While the name itself clearly meant nothing to the slumped cop, the manner in which it had been uttered signalled to him, through his sleep-fogged state, someone to be heeded. By dim circular logic he concluded that since the guards had let this man in to see him, he must be somebody who had the right (or the money, which amounted to the same thing) to see him, and that being so, he had better see him. Hoisting up heavy eyelids and scratching his genitals, he strove to focus his eyes. As soon as Carver saw that the cop was sufficiently awake, or as awake as he was likely to be in the foreseeable future, he told Moira to translate word for word everything he said and then started to speak. A grave error of justice had been committed by the Seville police: an innocent man had been arrested! The convulsively yawning duty officer seemed perplexed as to what was so unusual about this and continued to scratch himself. This man they had wrongly arrested, Carver went on, was a great artist of the cinema, a world celebrity, who had won the Academy Award — the Hollywood Oscar! — and was, moreover, a close personal friend of Maureen Wynner's. To this last item of information, the cop reacted with a moist widening of the eyes and a lubricious grin. 'This is true?'

'It is true!' Carver told him. And what was more, he needed urgent medical attention, he was an asthmatic, and in that stinking crowd outside, without air to breathe, he could suffer a fatal seizure. In which case he, the officer in charge, would be held responsible for the death of this world-famous man.

Slightly more awake now, the duty officer demanded of the card-players which of them had brought in the Americano and what he had been brought in for. Moira translated for Carver.

'They're saying that he committed a serious sexual offence against a minor and, even worse, insulted General Franco and the Spanish nation, broke one man's ankle, smashed another's fingers, and injured three policemen while they were struggling to put handcuffs on him. They're saying he's a madman.'

Carver at once demolished this evidence: he said that Jack Strawley was the victim, not the offender, in this case. He had been lured to the caravan by a prostitute of indeterminate age and there, when he refused her exorbitant pecuniary demands, had been set upon by her pimps. To all of which this woman, Moira Goldberg, had been a witness and could swear in court. The proof was that she had gone to fetch the police. Was that the action of somebody who was guilty? They were holding an innocent man. The night officer sat rocking his head and scratching his hairy nostrils. A slow thought process was taking place in his head, and at a certain point in the course of it, he unhooked the earpiece from the telephone stand, dialled a number, and pressing his lips close to the perforated mouthpiece, on which droplets of his breath were condensing into streaming rivulets, seemed to be seeking orders from somebody higher up. The words ' 'Ollywood Acaa-demy Avard,' and 'Oss-caar,' and 'Maureen Wynner' occurred several times, but Moira had difficulty in catching the meaning of much more than that. The duty officer then said '*si, signor*' a number of times before hanging up and turning his attention back to Carver.

'The arrested individual,' he declared, 'has committed a grave offence that carries a sentence of many years in prison. In addition to which there is the insult to Spain and the General Franco.'

'I appreciate that,' Carver said, recognizing the beginning of a negotiation. He offered the police officer a Romeo y Julieta cigar, and with his gold cigar-cutter cut the end for him when the policeman looked as though he was about to chew it off. He then lit the cigar for him with a gold Cartier lighter. He refrained from smoking himself.

Carver then explained: 'The reason we are here is to find locations for a major film. It's going to be shot entirely in Seville and the surrounding areas. That *was* our intention,' Carver said, emphasizing the past tense and the current problematic nature of the plan. He paused to let Moira translate and the cop savour his cigar. 'We plan — *planned* — to spend some 200 million pesetas in Spain. In and around Seville, for the most part. But to be able to film here we need the cooperation of a dependable local police force . . . if that can't be counted on, we'd be forced to shoot in Italy instead. I needn't tell you of all the benefits that accrue, public and private, in a locale where we're shooting a major film . . .'

The policeman had heard of such benefits but not actually experienced them personally: he rolled his lips appreciatively around the cigar in his mouth, which was already providing a certain foretaste of those benefits. Carver felt that he was getting somewhere.

'Respected Signor Carver,' the policeman said, 'there is the insult to Spain, to Il Caudillo . . . the injuries to two Spanish citizens and to my men and the grave sexual offence committed against a child . . .'

'A child-prostitute,' Carver corrected him. 'And swindler. She asked for a thousand bucks.'

When Moira translated this sum the card-playing cops let out yells of disbelief and stopped playing while they added their own animated opinions to the negotiation. Seizing this seemingly favourable moment, Carver instructed Moira to make an offer.

'Tell him we deeply regret the insult to Spain and General Franco. Signor Strawley had had a little too much to drink. He is also very sorry about the little girl. A mistake, a stupid mistake. He thought she was older. It can happen to anyone, no? Spanish girls being so mature and beautiful. Signor Strawley is an honourable man. A distinguished film-maker, winner of the Academy Award and the Palme d'Or at Cannes. He wants to make a contribution of $500 towards the little girl's re-education with the nuns and $500 to each of the policemen to compensate them for the injuries they sustained.'

'And the insult to Spain and the Spanish nation?' the policeman asked in a pathetic voice.

'Let's say $500 for that too.'

'In addition, yes?'

'Yes, all right, in addition.'

'And the insult to Generalissimo Franco?'

'Isn't that included under the insult to Spain, wouldn't you say, Captain?'

'No, I do not agree with you, respected Signor. The insult to Il Caudillo is quite apart — additional — to the insult to Spain. The Generalissimo Franco is a separate item. An apology to the value of, let us say . . . one thousand dollar?'

'All right, another thousand,' Carver said with an air of having his arm twisted by tough and wily men.

'Cash,' the policeman specified. 'Now. It must be paid cash before the signor can be released.'

'I have the cash with me and it will be handed over the moment I walk out of here and Mr Strawley is in the taxi which is waiting outside.'

'Just one last thing, Signor.'

'That is my final offer, sir. I will not improve on that.'

'Only this — a signed photograph. Of the beautiful Maureen Wynner. Inscribed to me personally.'

'I shall have that sent to you,' Carver said, shaking the policeman by the hand, and added: 'I think we can do business in Seville.'

32

While being kicked in the face by the cousins or having his face trodden into the ground by the Spanish civil guards, or even afterwards crawling on the filthy floor of the police station trailing blood, he had felt no pain or shame or fear. Just a kind of dark-minded exaltation. But once he was back in his suite at the Alphonse XIII, he hurt everywhere, most of all in his head. There were all these leaden waves that came out of nowhere, crushers of bones and being! These assaults upon his nervous system were followed by moments of respite when he was floating on a flat, windless, waveless, tideless ocean, with nothing stirring, heart scarely beating, blood barely flowing. Taking refuge in the body of his double, he watched the suffering of Jack the Strawman with an indifferent eye. The man without substance. His mind was alternately becalmed and racing, and, in the latter condition, there were those flashing, speeded-up pictures behind his eyes, pictures that showed things — and people — nobody else ever saw, like the air currents made by a speeding car, or the Fallen One on his throne in the fiery lake. He expressed a wish to die and had to be constantly watched.

When it was judged that he was capable of travelling, he was heavily dosed with Thorazine and put on an internal flight to Madrid, accompanied by Gloria, Moira and Carver, and from there the group took the BEA flight to Heathrow, where a doctor met the plane and drove him straight to the East Anglia health farm. They put him straight away in the psychiatric wing.

The first couple of days he was simply kept quiet with medication, and then on the third day he received a visit from a woman doctor with sympathetic sad eyes who said she was Dr Saltie. She asked him how he was feeling now and he said it felt as if he was living underwater, everything was distant, muffled, faint and appalling. Mostly, he was appalled by himself, he said. She nodded understandingly. She had a very understanding face: her smiles were wrested out of that understanding, and, when she smiled, her grey eyes, which matched the broad grey streaks in her hair, became pale violet. She was so deeply understanding that he was straight away a little in love with her. It seemed to him that she knew all about the states he had been unable to describe to her fully.

In the course of the next few days, in response to the regime of medication that she prescribed, his mood became blurred and diluted in a generalized torpor. It was a low mood and he felt awful, but he wasn't agitated or suffering physically; it was more a state of profound indifference, a deep stillness 'in which nothing moves', as he described it to Dr Saltie. The only vestige of 'movement' came during his informal thrice-weekly chats with her. She was finding out about his life and work and marriage and loves. When he asked what had been the matter with him in Seville, she replied with great gentleness: 'You went a bit mad, it seems.' Perhaps it was the tender, respectful way in which she said this, or else his state of indifference, but he was not horrified to learn that he had been 'mad'. He had already arrived at that diagnosis himself. He asked her why it was that it had felt good being mad, at least in the initial stage, and that being sane felt so dreadful, and she replied that certain phases of mania, before it became overlaid with agitation and terror, sped up the mind and made sensations more intense, producing a drug-like high. 'As if you were a god and pure genius flowed in your veins. Would you say that is how it sometimes felt?'

'How did you know?'

'Patients have told me.'

'You mean I'm not the only crackpot "genius" around here? There lots of us loonies?'

'You feel . . . you possess unique powers and your thoughts go so fast you can't keep track of them?'

'That's how it feels, yes.'

' . . . and that you can do anything.'

'All that's the craziness?'

'I don't know if it all is, Jack. Some of it, yes. But maybe not all. Great poetry has been written during what would now be clinically diagnosed as hypomanic episodes, great pictures have been painted in this state. It's possible that it has aided you in your film-making. I have to tell you that some patients, when they get better, miss their madness.'

He was still getting black moods but they were less frequent, less desperate. One day, walking in the grounds in a state of lethargic low spirits, he saw a rainbow. It appeared suddenly, perfectly formed, as if drawn by a compass, describing a complete half circle that extended from horizon to horizon, and he made out three distinct bands of bright colour — orange, yellow and blue — and realized that it was the first time he had seen colour since coming to the health farm. Looking around him he saw other colours now, the weblike browny-green of the copse beyond the outbuildings, the orange stab of late afternoon light on windows, the touches of red in hedges, and, accompanying this perception of colour, there was the awareness of a change of mood in himself, a lifting of the low-level depression, and it felt as if a curtain was going up on a lit stage.

Next time he saw her he told Dr Saltie that he felt he was ready to go home, that he wanted to talk things over with Gloria. Dr Saltie didn't agree: she didn't think that going back to Gloria was necessarily the best solution for him. She said that they had to face up to the possibility that Gloria might be at the centre of his sexual/emotional turmoil: that he had created a scenario for himself whereby he needed to become hypomanic in order to break out of the shackles of his marriage. Therefore, putting him back in shackles was not going to help; while he might accept that condition for a time, as a form of self-punishment and reparation, sooner or later he'd be compelled to break out again, and freeing oneself of chains called for a lot of violence. He might be more stable without chains. It was a point of view that shocked him, having always considered Gloria the protector of whatever was good in him. To be told that she might be the cause of his troubles was shattering. He did not know if he believed it. Dr Saltie was a very unconventional psychiatrist; at times, going by the violet light in her eyes, he thought that she must once have been something of a swinger, perhaps still was when she took off the doctor's white coat. She made references to R.D. Laing and to Lacan and to the fact that her ideas were not to the liking of the orthodox of her profession. She was considered 'too eclectic', she said once. In his present condition of 'sexual anaethesia', as she termed it — he had told her that he hadn't been getting any erections, lately — he was identifying with 'the reactionary little puritan' inside himself, which was the other side of the debauchée. Unorthodox Dr Saltie seemed in favour of overcoming the 'erectionless little puritan', who represented one of the poles of his condition. 'Cyclothymia,' she explained to him, 'in its mildest forms is simply an aspect of the human condition. One has high and low moods. Then as the swings become more extreme, at both ends, there is pain with some accompanying advantages . . . everything is lived more intensely. That's when you like it. When you are speeding up and at your most creative and most sexual. From there it goes on to its most extreme forms, where you are speeding so fast that life and sanity and other people's safety are threatened.'

Dr Saltie talked about Lacan's notion of '*le stage du miroir*' and of the false selves that people accumulated. Each one of us was a collection of such imposters, interlopers and pretenders. When he asked her why he kept having the desire to weep, she told him: 'Every instance of love failing is a reminder of a loss that nothing will ever be able to make good.' Although he was, she said, beginning to make progress in his recovery, he wasn't ready yet for a major step like facing Gloria and deciding his future.

He was happy to get a warm letter from Carl, wishing him well. There was no mention of their quarrel in Seville. Evidently that was being lumped together with his mental sickness, and could be excused as part of it.

'It is good to hear,' Carl wrote, 'that you are much better, and emerging. There are gains to be made from what you have been through. Many gifted artists have experienced similar episodes. There would seem to be some link between emotional and mental upheavals and creativity. It may be the price that has to be paid for "genius". In *The Phaedrus* Socrates says that madness is a nobler thing than sober sense, that madness comes from God. And this from soberly sensible Socrates! But remember you must come back to us, you must not stay down with Fabrini's mermaids and monsters, because we need your dangerous spirit on the surface. You told me once that you were born to tell the story of your life. One day you must do it. I myself incline more and more in the other direction, of simply being, which can take up so much time and energy there is none left over for *doing* anything much. You will make a wonderful *Heart of Darkness* one day because you have known the dark heart, so don't think any of it is wasted. Have you read Pessoa? Probably not, because not many have. A great mild man who died almost unknown, proclaiming his nothingness. That no woman had ever loved him, and once, when one did, it was very tiring. Oh, how I agree with him. He wrote these magnificent songs of despair which are the glory of Portuguese literature, working as a clerk, living a totally uneventful life and drinking himself to death . . . but writing this marvellous stuff, you see, in his quiet, secretive way.

Get well and come back to us soon because we love you and miss you,

Carl

Let me know if, and when, one may visit.'

About a week later, Dr Saltie having noted the return of some libido in his inner life — he was having dreams about her that she interpreted in this way — suggested that he could start having visitors. People who would not be too emotionally draining. Not, therefore, Gloria: he had too much to answer to her, and it was still too early for that. Although she telephoned him every two or three days, these calls were strictly formal inquiries about his health and did not broach on other matters. Nor was Carl considered to be a suitable visitor at this stage: from what he'd told her about Carl's letters, Dr Saltie concluded that Carl was himself deeply depressed and could not be relied upon for support. Moira wasn't a good idea either: he had not yet sorted out his feelings about her. What about starting neutrally — say with Percy Drummer? Start with him and see how it goes, she suggested.

So Percy Drummer was invited down, and the occasion proved unstressful. Never once did Percy make any reference to Jack's breakdown or to the fact that their meeting was occurring in a place that specialized in the treatment of well-heeled alcoholics, druggies, sex transgressors and manic-depressives. He himself sometimes went to a health farm in the country to lose weight and have a complete rest. Nothing better than to get away from it all for a while, was there?

'Mind you,' Percy said, 'you don't need to lose weight, you need to gain it.'

After that, it was all film business gossip. Who was doing what. What films had bombed at the box office. Which ones were raking in the big grosses. Who had taken over Paramount or Columbia, or was said to be about to do so. Who was divorcing whom. Who had died.

The next approved visitor, Carver, arrived wearing a cashmere sports jacket with a knitted grey tie. He was not, for once, smoking a cigar. What had happened to the cigars? He surely hadn't given them up? Jack asked him, and Carver replied that his current girlfriend, the Hon. Lady Georgette Stanley, known to everyone as 'Georgie', disapproved of them. She was a super girl and extremely loaded, although none of it was easily realizable since it was mostly in the ancient meadows of Mayfair, currently tied up in leases with peppercorn rents, but of course leases did finally expire, and in the next ten, fifteen years. . .

Carver reported that he could get Jack a deal with any studio he chose, as soon as he was fully recovered: they all wanted him . . . for the right project. There were numerous calls from stars eager to work with him. 'I'm keeping them all on hold, I want you to have a good rest and to feel 100%. There's no hurry. Let's get you the right project.' He had other projects on the boil with other directors. 'Not in your class, Jack. But talented. Young . . . *mouldable.*'

No reference was made to the events in Seville until Carver was getting into his car. The hood was down, the engine humming like a songbird.

'Sydney,' Jack said, 'just want to say this. I've been told I have you to thank for getting me out of that shithole Spanish jail. Moira told me how much I owe to your negotiating skills. I was a bit crazy there for a while. I guess I owe you two thousand bucks . . . and a lot more. The two thousand you can deduct from

receipts, as for the rest . . . I don't know how I can repay you.'
'Don't worry, you will,' Carver told him.

He was still shaky, still fragile, his mind turning over with
excruciating slowness. His eye saw only the palest colours, pale
blues and pastel greens and hazy pinks. He saw plants grow. He
saw the worm in the bud surreptitiously devouring its host, and
respectable women transported to slow-motion sexual frenzies
before his eyes. At odd moments he saw the prince of darkness in
all his evil glory, presenting his many-nippled body to all the
world to suck on. And he saw Eddie ('Eyebrows') Max blowing
somebody away with a puff of smoke. These images surged up in
him. Suddenly he had a complete picture of an empty room, its
floors and walls covered in thick blue felt. He saw heavy electric
cables writhing like snakes in a snake pit. He told Dr Saltie:
   'I know I'm not yet cured but still, I think I'd like to go home.'
   'All right — soon, soon: only you have to decide where that
is.'
   At any rate, he was ready to see Gloria now, he said, and Dr
Saltie agreed it was perhaps time for that.

Gloria, he decided, seeing her with new eyes that were beginning
to register stronger colours again, had a classical beauty that
didn't fade the way mere surface beauty did. It was deep down.
And moving because fragile, threatened . . . at the run-up to
fifty, inevitably threatened. Threatened or not, she looks sensational, he thought, and he was falling in love with her again. She
had a big smile prepared for him, the kind you had for convales-
cents who were on the mend but still in need of support: she was
looking tense and smart in a white Burberry raincoat and white
leather boots and a man's felt hat. He kept telling her how great
she looked and how much he was missing her, in every way, and
she kept asking him how he was, and he said better, a lot better.
Ready to come home, in fact.
   She said, lighting another cigarette from the one she was
smoking, that that was what they had to talk about, and her
voice was tremulous and she wasn't meeting his eyes at this
point but looking out across the flat, undramatic countryside

with its straggly lines of bare hedgerows going to the indistinct horizon.

'Let's talk about it, then,' he said with sinking heart. She said nothing, and he helped her out. 'You want to talk about what happened in Seville. Okay.'

'I need to talk about it . . . to understand. Because I feel . . . that I'm married to someone I don't know.'

He spoke to her quietly, matter-of-factly. 'It seems, according to Dr Saltie, that I went a little bit mad. Apparently it can happen. I'm better now. Fully recovered. Concerning the little whore, that was part of the craziness. I obviously had a vision of her that didn't correspond at all to the reality of what she was. It seems, according to Dr Saltie, that what I was chasing after was . . . a phantom of my imagination, not a real person. In other words, that I was *really and truly* mad. When the penny finally dropped, and I realized she was a prostitute — okay, a part-time prostitute — I got out of there fast . . . should have been able to handle the situation, but I . . . was speeding up and out of control. And when the cousins started pushing me around, and then the cops, I blew my top completely. Damned foolish, and the worst part of it is the deep-down dirty feeling you have to live with afterwards. There's a soiling that happens that you feel nothing will ever be able to wash clean.'

'I imagine you're speaking from previous experience . . . of that state.'

'Some.'

'Not all of it dating from "before we got together".'

'Gloria,' he said, 'there's nothing you need to know. I would tell you if there were. I love you and that's all there's really to be said. Anything else is *hors sujet*.'

'For you.'

'I wish it could be for you too.'

She had held herself back long enough, all those weeks when she'd been told he was not yet strong enough to talk to her and now that he was better, strong enough, she couldn't hold back her anger any more.

'Jack, you want to know what really appalls me, to my guts, about that whole Seville business, you want to know? Not that

you have a taste for buggering under-age girls, whether prostitutes, part-time, full-time or phantoms of your imagination.
That's not what throws me the most. It's that Moira fixes you
up — Moira, who is your mistress and obviously has fixed you
up before, fairly regularly, I imagine, and you've done these
things before *with her there*, that is the most sordid aspect . . .
while she looks on! That's what I mean when I say I don't know
you.'

'Gloria — nobody knows anybody.'

'You can try to know somebody. Okay, will you tell me
something? Will you tell me why she does it? If she's your
mistress and loves you — and you love her — why does she fix
you up with young girls? Why does she stay and watch? And
participate? Does she participate?'

'I suppose it must be due to her not having your moral convic-
tions. And that she likes to give me these "shallow and infantile
forms of pleasure". Okay, let's not bullshit around, call them
manias. Yeah, my manias. Which, like it or not, I have got.'

'And can't help,' she added sarcastically. 'What man can help
his manias, poor thing! So unreasonable of prissy wives to object
to some down-to-earth male manias! Lucky there's Moira, who
doesn't object. I wonder why. You know, I suppose, that she's
referred to as "Dark Ambition"?'

'No, I didn't know. Why would they call her that? Who calls
her that?'

'The "gal with the most upwardly mobile ass".'

'They call her that? Well, it's nonsense, because she hasn't
"mobiled up" that far. Hasn't got far at all! Makes a reasonable
living, is respected in the profession. But if you're suggesting
that she sleeps around to advance herself, she hasn't been very
successful at it so far.'

'Why does she hang onto you, and take the treatment you give
her, if she doesn't think it's going to pay in the end?' There was
an onrushing momentum in Gloria now, she could not stop, it
had to pour out of her, because she was full to the brim with all
the dark stuff that had been accumulating in her all these years
and now she couldn't absorb any more and had to pour it all back
into him. Suddenly she was weeping, with hanging head, a gush

of uncontrollable tears. He was at a loss how to respond to the stream, the racking painful sobs: she was tearing at her throat with her fingers, it had tightened so much that she had trouble breathing. When he tried to put his arms around her, she threw him off, unwilling to be comforted.

'I understand that you feel this way about Moira, it's only natural.' He tried to say it gently but he wasn't going to come out with a quick fix of lies. He closed his eyes, let his breath out slowly. Control. He'd told Dr Saltie he could control whatever came up with Gloria. He mustn't let Dr Saltie down. He gave himself the cue to disengage. Cut! Cut the scene. 'What can I say, Gloria? You're hurt, understandably, and so you lash out. You've been seething all the time they were pumping those drugs into me to quieten me down, and it took them a while, so you've had a long run-up to this moment, you were holding it all back, and now . . . now I'm able to take it, well, you let me have it, which is understandable, I suppose. I don't blame you, but you're assessing this all wrong. Yes, Moira's energetic, pushes hard, mostly on my behalf, not her own. She's very valuable to me professionally. Moreover, she completely accepts the situation *as is*, has no wish to push you out of my life . . . knows that you come first in all my considerations and accepts that . . . and always has. And she admires you tremendously. She goes in awe of you, Gloria.'

'Gee thanks!' Hackles rising, bile flowing — face all harsh-edged with her terrible wrath that nothing could appease, trying to get it all out between the sobs that she couldn't stop. 'Good old reliable Moira, hanging in there . . . That you need her so badly that you can't help yourself is so immature of you and so destroying of me. Can't you see? If you pretend to care about me, how can you subject me to such pain?' She was weeping bitter, dry, dredged-up tears that broke into the classic beauty of her face and made her look old and soured by life, damaged to the core, a ruined object. In the ruins lay ugliness and hate and danger.

'Gloria, you're making it very hard for us.'

'*I'm* making it hard for us. *I* am? Surely it's you who's doing that?' She was so shocked by this way of putting it, by his shifting of the villainy onto her, that she abruptly stopped sobbing.

'What is it you want, Gloria?' he asked. 'What can I do to make it up to you?'

'What do I want?' She seemed startled by this question.

'Yes, tell me what I have to do.'

'I don't know. I can't look into the future.'

'In the present.'

She considered the matter practically, wiping her eyes, getting her voice under control. Then spoke with definiteness. 'It's too humiliating for me to go on this way.' Sharp, hard, decisive: all cutting edges. 'You ask me what you must do . . . there's only one answer possible, you've got to decide between Moira and me.'

'A good old-fashioned ultimatum.' He laughed, disengaging. Disengaging. And thought it over briefly while she watched him with clear dry eyes. 'Well,' he said eventually, 'if you make it an either/or decision, it's going to have to be Moira, because Moira doesn't impose that kind of decision on me. And I'm no good in corners.'

He was surprised by his choice: he hadn't expected to be faced with it and hadn't worked out in advance what he might feel or say in such a situation. His answer surprised him as much as it surprised Gloria but it had come out with calm conviction. As if he'd known all along that he'd give that answer in such a situation, only hadn't been prepared to admit it before to himself. He'd planned to go back with Gloria to London: had planned to take up his married life with her, to be a loving husband and father, to the extent that this was possible for him. He might have even got around by himself to giving up Moira. But to have it imposed on him as a condition was unacceptable to him. If she'd let me decide for myself, he thought, I would have decided in her favour. But she had to put the fucking shackles back on. And given that, I had to cut them, I had no other option, so now I'm free of her.

Gloria's face had clouded with shock. She hadn't expected this simple, plain answer, had expected prevarication and fudging and half promises and half lies, but not this categorical choice, and it was too late to back track, her pride was too great to withdraw the conditions. Her dignity would not permit her to do that.

'Yes, Carl said you break with everyone in the end. None of us can keep up. There it is. I'm not going to try and influence you to change your mind. It's your choice. Leave it like that for now. The sordid details we'll have to work out later, when I've got myself more composed.'

33

Moving in with Moira was all very low-key: nothing decided — can I come and stay? — and then staying on, from day to day, never saying if it was for a weekend or a week or forever. He was mending slowly, the lithium and the other stuff he was taking kept him in balance, even if it did make him feel as if he was fighting his way through mud up to his neck.

The constant frenzy to *do* seemed to have left him. He was content to be quiet now. The mud kept him quiet. And the erectionless little puritan. It was amazing how unlibidinous you could be when up to your neck in mud. He didn't want to do anything. Was he testing her? To see how Dark Ambition would take to Lithium Man.

'This *is* a new Jack Strawley,' she said, finally having to acknowledge the change. 'Three weeks! Is it guilty conscience? Or what?'

'Must be all the medication.'

'What are we going to do about that?'

'Like the doctor said: play it by ear.'

'That's what you're doing with me.'

The diminution of desires. It wasn't just that his sex drive had diminished almost to zero, all his old compulsions had dried up. Including the desire to make another film. Why did he have to make another film? Why do anything? Like Carl said, *being* was quite enough to have to do. Took up all one's time and energy. Was his state of mind due simply to the fact that nothing Carver brought him had truly grabbed him? His life was flat and calm, dead calm, and that was fine by him. For now. Until something happened. He was waiting for something to happen. Whatever it was going to be.

'Carl's got the answer,' he told Moira. 'You have got to have the strength to live the way you want, not get drawn into crazy, frantic enterprises that kill you. Which is what 99% of the film business is 99% of the time. When it isn't waiting.'

'You can't live on the 1% that isn't, if there is 1% that isn't,' she told him. 'And you don't get points for waiting.'

'In that case, forget it.'

'Yeah? And what d'you do for eats? And other unavoidables.'

'Go and live in Spain. Used to be able to live on nothing in Spain, Carl says. And be free. Would you come with me and do that, when the money's all run out?'

'Is it a test question?'

'I don't know. Would you?'

'Let's say it's a test question, because a practical proposal it isn't. You want the truth? To the test question. Okay. I love you, Jack. Which I know wasn't our deal, but it's happened and I can't help it . . . and I know women in love are expected to follow their man. Only I don't think I could give up working. For me, that's connecting with the real world, and I couldn't give that up for lotus-land.'

'What d'you mean the real world? God, Moira, we live such unreal lives in this business, it's all business. Where's the real living? Carl has got something when he says. . .'

'Can we skip that one, please? I've got enough Carl quotes to last me a lifetime. What is he — your guru? Why don't we ever see him, if you're so in love with his quotes? Or is it with him you're in love?'

This was January now, freezing January. Every morning the portholes were frozen opaque by the watery fog, and he had to heat them up with the hair dryer to be able to observe the passing river traffic: the coal barges and sand barges and the gypsy boats that provided the only sense of movement in his frozen life.

'We don't see him because he doesn't approve of what I've done to Gloria — and Anna. Nor do I, if you want to know.'

'Gee thanks.'

' . . . he's very moralistic about that. He can get to be real Old Testament. I doubt he'd be willing to see you. You're the evil temptress in his script. Anyway, I think he prefers to write letters. Lately, he's not been over-fond of close contact with the shitty human race.'

'Is that what *we* are, the shitty human race? Thanks a lot. Sorry I'm depriving you not only of your darling Gloria but also of your beloved Carl. Go see him by yourself, you shitty human race.'

He turned it over in his mind. 'Maybe I should. Maybe . . . maybe. I don't know. I miss him. We go back a long way . . . but he hasn't suggested it. And I don't initiate things right now, as you may have noticed. I think that's still the illness. Or the cure. I don't know which anymore. I guess I'm waiting to see what happens. I'm treating you badly, aren't I? Like I treat everybody badly. I'm just so . . . undecided about everything at present. I'm sorry I'm doing this to you but I don't seem able to do anything else.'

He pulled her down onto his lap. She had a very easy way of fitting onto his body. Any time, any place. Easily adjustable Moira, the human Anglepoise lamp. So unlike Gloria who had her principles and her rules and her right time and place and a sense of what was elegant and what wasn't. Had to be courted and seduced all the time to get her to break out.

'It's going to get better,' he told Moira. 'Give me time. I'm still an invalid.'

'You're doing okay for an invalid. I'm not complaining.'

'Did you know that they call you Dark Ambition?'

'Ambition's always dark when female but white-hot if it's male.'

'Women are supposed to be the warrior's rest.'

'That's the old Jack Strawley, who was a macho pig. The new

one, I don't know what he is. He's playing it by ear and not saying much. But I'll take you as is,' she said chirpily. 'I've got you for as long as I've got you. I'll cry when I have something to cry about. Not a minute before.'

It was strange to be living on Moira's old houseboat — he'd never figured out why she was still living on the boat, why she'd never bought a house or flat. In her chronically impermanent life she seemed to have never got around to making such a monetary commitment, as she had never got around to making a real commitment to any man. Was she keeping all the doors open for him? He hoped not: that would have been a heavy responsibility.

With him not working and therefore not in need of a special assistant, she'd gone back to being a publicist, and the publicist's job it seemed involved a lot of overtime. Stars' egos had to be massaged at all hours, and their hands held through sticky interviews on late-night shows. It occurred to him, as he went on his riverside walks or ate an omelette by himself, that the publicist's job might sometimes involve more than holding the star's hand in interviews. He didn't ask about that. It was a mistake to extrapolate from the past. And anyway, their deal was that they were both free: no shackles. He couldn't hold it against her that she was involved with the world at a time when he had decided to withdraw from it. And so he did not ask questions when she came home late, sometimes well after midnight, even though this was happening more and more frequently.

The time she didn't come home until next morning, he did ask her.

'You want details?'

'I want to know.'

'The deal was we're both free agents.'

'You are. But you can tell me. I just want to know.'

'I don't want you to stop liking me.'

'C'mon, Moira, who'd you fuck?'

'Are you asking because you mind or because you're getting off on it?'

'I want to hear the news.'

'Okay. This is not in answer to your question. Because I'm not answering that. But I am spending a certain amount of time with

Tony. We have this project together. He wants to get into production, he's pissed off with not being in control. He wants to produce or direct or both and he likes this screenplay I wrote.'

'What screenplay?'

'You read it, you didn't like it.'

'Which one?'

'It's the Anais Nin. The one about her and the anonynmous collector of erotica who gets her to write erotic stories for him.'

'Right. So you have one-to-one script conferences, production meetings and other sorts of late-night sessions.'

'We're working on it together.'

'Has he bought the rights from Nin? They may be sold, and then you're doing it for nothing.'

'I checked that out. Rights are available.'

'Nin may have other plans.'

'I saw her a while back when I was in New York. We got on . . . she liked me. She'll let me have the rights . . . if I can get something set up. She's sort of given me a free option.'

'Which means you've given Tony a sort of a free option. On the rights, and on you.'

'Does it annoy you?'

'I don't like seeing you being taken for a ride.'

'Well, if we're going to be crude about this. The ride's not unpleasant. And unless you go on rides you can't know if you're being taken or not.'

'That's logical. Okay: being logical, why stick with me, when there are Major Stars in the offing? Who can give you better rides.'

Her eyes met his, and she said very coolly, very matter-of-factly. 'You want to know seriously why? Because you enrich my life, Jack. That's why. However this turns out with us, I'm a lot richer having known you. Any time you want to re-negotiate, I'm ready to drop Major Stars and Projects and come to lotusland. If that's what you want. But you haven't made up your mind, have you? And meanwhile I have to get on with my life. Don't I?'

'Yes.'

He didn't know what he wanted. It was on account of her that he no longer saw Carl. Carl was his oldest, closest friend. The occasional glass-throwing episode or slanging match didn't change that. But now Carl was entirely on Gloria's side: to him Moira was the marriage-wrecker. And that was certainly one possible reading. If it weren't for Moira he'd still be with Gloria, living at home in Carlyle Square, seeing his child who was growing up into a young woman without her father around, getting back into the swing after his enforced absence for reasons of madness, whereas what he was doing was vegetating, lying around on a leaky, cramped old Battersea houseboat, reading all day while his companion of the free spirit was having production meetings with Major Stars at all hours. She was free, he was bound. By his own indecision. And the mud up to his neck. He reminded himself that it was Gloria who'd said either/or. And it was he who had said to Moira: no commitments, all options open . . . now you see me, now you don't. So how can I blame Moira? How can I expect her to turn down Major Opportunity when any day she might come home and find me gone?

Early one morning, before he'd cleared the frozen fog from the portholes and seen what it was like outside, the phone rang and Moira took it, and after a terse exchange held the receiver out to him: 'Gloria.'

He had phoned her from time to time during these past months, to find out how she was, but this was the first time she'd called him. It wasn't even seven a.m. and there was not a glimmer of morning light over the river.

'Yes, Gloria?' he said briskly.

'I wouldn't have phoned,' she said, 'if I didn't think it was important.'

'Are you all right? Anna?'

'I'm all right, yes. Sort of all right. And Anna's all right too. It's not about us. I'm calling about Carl.'

'What about Carl?'

'He came for lunch yesterday, came to cheer me up, but he was the one who was low. I mean really low. I've never seen Carl so low before.'

'It's a system he has, called balanced melancholia . . . suits his temperament, it's the cheerful ones you have to worry about.'

'I am worried about him, Jack.'

'Okay, I'll give him a call. Today. I'll sound him out. You shouldn't worry about Carl. He hangs in there.'

Her voice was controlled but charged. 'I've been calling him since yesterday after he left. That was around three in the afternoon. He said he was going straight home. I phoned him at his flat but there was no reply. I phoned all afternoon and all evening and part of the night — no reply. And I phoned again just now and still no answer.'

'He probably went to a pub, picked up a girl . . .'

'He wasn't in any mood to pick up a girl when he left.'

'So she picked him up. Women are drawn to melancholic men.'

'I can't see it. Everything revolted him, all of human kind. He was so . . . so low. I didn't like to let him leave, but he said he'd take a taxi home and sleep it off. Somebody has got to go and see if he's all right. I'm scared, Jack.'

'I'll go.'

'I have to go too.'

'We'll go together.'

She must have seen the taxi approaching because she was outside the door when he got there, and he was shocked by her appearance: she looked all in pieces, faceless without make-up, racked by spasms of smoker's cough that left her drained and pallid and shaking. He tried to formally embrace her, but she made an awkward movement of avoidance that stopped him. She was all sharp edges.

'I didn't know who else to ring,' she said, placing their meeting solely on an emergency basis.

In the taxi, the conversation was halting since there were so many areas that had to be avoided.

'Is Carl working on something?'

'No. He's stopped writing. Says he can't find words . . . they don't come and that it's pointless anyway, nobody wants to hear what he has to say.'

'So what's he been doing with himself?'

'He goes for walks on the Heath.'

'And you, Gloria?'

'I sometimes go for walks on the Heath with him. Otherwise, not a tremendous amount. I've had a couple of small character parts in films that are not out yet. And you?'

'Likewise, not much.'

'And Moira?'

'Moira's very busy with her publicity jobs, and trying hard to get into production . . . she's out all day, I hardly see her.'

The streets were completely deserted this early Sunday morning, due no doubt to the intense cold. Railings rimed with hard frost. Parked cars with iced-up windscreens, and the wipers frozen to the glass. Street lamps with portcullises of icicles. The Heath, from the skirting road, looked like stretches of Arctic wasteland. Not a human being or a dog in sight.

They went down the dirty area steps and rang the bell of Carl's basement flat. No answer. The drab brown curtains were not fully drawn and they could see into the dim sitting-room which was empty and still, but with a gas fire flickering in the tiled hearth. Two more long rings of the bell brought no response. Jack banged on the window with his fist and called through the glass. No answer, no sound.

'What do we do?' She was biting her gloved fingers, and her pallor matched the dirty grey of the ice patches on the ground.

He could see that the window catch was not in place: Carl's theory had always been that the best burglar protection was to have nothing worth stealing. Which being his permanent condition, he had no fears of burglary. With the blade of a small penknife Jack was able to prise up the sash-window and slide it open. Shifting aside the window box with the dead flowers, he climbed in over the cracked cill.

'Stay outside,' he told Gloria, but she wouldn't stay outside and scrambled in after him. The sitting room was empty and tidy. He walked quickly to the door that connected with the bedroom, hesitated for a moment before opening it. Gloria followed him in. The bedroom was empty too, with the gas fire lit. The room was very warm, suggesting that the fire had been on all night. On the roughly made bed were indentations indicating that someone had lain down there without getting under the covers. The portable radio was on, emitting the ecclesiastical tones of a Sunday morning. He went out into the corridor, opened the bathroom. Empty. He looked in the kitchen and that was empty too. Having established that Carl was not in the apartment, they started to look around for some indication of where he might be. In the kitchen, a packet of fish fingers had been taken out of the fridge and had defrosted, dripping onto the floor, without the packet having been opened. It looked as though he had started to prepare a meal for himself and then changed his mind. There was an empty vodka bottle on the drainer. Empty wine and beer bottles on the floor.

'The booze was all finished so he went to a pub,' Jack said.

'Pubs close at night.'

'He'd had a few vodkas by then, got a bit more cheerful, went home with a woman. Or a man. That's the only explanation, Gloria. We're going to be accused of prying into his private life. Not to say breaking and entering.'

'Why didn't he answer the phone?'

Jack found two used earplugs on the bed.

'He was resting. Put these in his ears.'

Gloria nodded, her face grey, her heavy-lidded eyes dim. They went slowly round the room, searching for something. She saw what she was looking for, lying on the floor by the bed. A small pill bottle. She went and picked it up and held it up to the light. There were some capsules remaining in it, and she emptied them onto her palm. Five of them.

Jack said: 'If they're going to do it, they take them all to make sure.'

She dropped the capsules back in the bottle. On the side table there was a glass of water, half full, standing on a pile of *New Statesmans*. Back to the sitting room. The desk by the window was austerely tidy, the Remington portable devoid of any typing paper. The wastepaper basket contained some old newspapers but no crumpled-up sheets of paper indicative of a writer at work. A padlocked metal trunk by the wall. The flat had a feeling of emptiness and stillness about it, like a place that hasn't been lived in for months. The shelves of the G-Plan room divider contained long overdue books from the local public library and a large number of paperbacks. The books were all in place on the shelves, none lying open on floor or surfaces. No sign that Carl was currently reading anything, or judging from the barrenness of his desk, working on anything. He turned around and saw that Gloria was wringing her hands, her mouth open.

'Jack, I've got such an awful feeling.'

'D'you know something I don't?'

She shook her head, fighting back her distress, not trusting herself to speak. 'What do we do now?'

He spoke with determined calm. 'Remember he disappeared once before. What I propose we should do is leave a message for him to phone as soon as he gets in, and we'll ring every hour to check if he's back. If we still have no word by, say, eleven or twelve, we come and talk to the old ladies. See if they know anything. I don't want to create embarrassment for him. There'll be some simple explanation, you'll see.' She was weeping quietly without tears. 'You act as if you know something, Gloria.'

She shook her head again, her lips tight. She was trying to take charge of her voice. 'Only the state of mind he was in when he left yesterday. There is one thing I want to do before we go back. It's a longshot, but I want to check it out because of something he said yesterday. I think he may have gone for a walk on the Heath, he always goes in the morning, and . . . and maybe he's had a malaise. I think we should look.'

'The Heath is big, Gloria.'

'He always does the same walk. To Kenwood and back. He goes on that walk every morning in every kind of weather. He says that's how he keeps in one piece.'

'If that's what you want, let's do it.'

Starting out from Gospel Oak Station, and then crossing the stark open sports area, which was under deep, hard-frozen snow covering, they felt the lash of Siberian winds that came in abrupt pounding bursts, turning their faces raw red and making their eyes water. The sky was low and grimy with massed clouds in which there was not a chink of an opening. Ugly municipal buildings acted as occasional wind-breakers.

'I can't believe he'd go out in this,' Jack shouted through the howling wind.

Inside her Russian-style long, brown suede coat with fur lining, Gloria was shivering. Jack had put up the collar of his sheepskin aviator's jacket and buttoned it in front to keep it upstanding and tight about the ears, but even so they were anaesthetized by the cold. His head felt like a block of ice. The tarmac footpath along here had become surfaced in a laminate of hard black ground frost, making it treacherous to walk on, and Gloria's shoes having insufficient grip, she was obliged to hold onto him, their closest contact in quite a while. Presently the tarmac gave way to rolled gravel which enabled her to walk unaided, and she at once let go of his arm. After the exposed, featureless slope, they entered an area of grassland and hedges and tree clumps, where the footpaths were unsurfaced, random, meandering, and there was no clear and obvious path for Carl to have taken.

Where paths split, they tried to remember the route that Carl usually took, since he hardly ever looked where he was going, was entirely inside his mind on these walks and simply followed the path he had always taken before. Where they felt unsure, they scouted out the alternatives, looking into hollows and ditches and by the sides of rotting tree trunks, and peering into the undergrowth, in the grey light, for darker shapes.

'We're doing this,' Jack told her, 'purely to cater to your anxieties, Gloria, not because there's any likelihood, in my opinion, that he'd have been crazy enough to go for a walk on the Heath in weather like this.' They trudged through wild unmown grassland where paths had all disappeared under smooth unbroken snow layers. 'Anyway, he certainly didn't come along here, because nobody came along here . . . unless they had wings.'

'Let's try the other path, where it's trodden. *Somebody* came along there.'

'Could have been days ago. This is pretty old crusty snow . . .'

In the marshy spots the soggy wet ground sagged under their step. Presently they were coming up through managed woodland with Kenwood House glimpsed up on the top of the slope. In half an hour they hadn't caught sight of one other human being. The

ponds were all frozen solid and devoid of visible wildlife.
There was no point going all the way up to Kenwood House and its swept terraces: they were all pristine white stucco and ice. They could count on that whole area being well supervised by staff of the Iveagh Bequest, and so they cut off the loop of Carl's habitual route and picked up his return walk by crossing the ornamental bridge and skirting the lakeshore. In summer, this was one of Carl's favourite stopping places for noting down his thoughts, seated on the wooden bench at the water's edge, watching the dragon flies and the swarms of insects rising from the dense mass of water plants. Today there were only hardy, tall geese strutting over the frozen surface, wings half spread, and this bulky object on the bench, which looked like a children's snow-man. For a moment the absurd thought entered his head that it was Carl sitting there, notebook on his lap, jotting down his thoughts. He was about to make a joking remark about Carl getting to be real eccentric these days when he saw that Gloria had begun to walk faster and, after two or three steps, to run, and then he ran too, with dread in his heart, and both of them were now making harsh urgent blowing noises from the effort of running. As they got nearer they could see that it was a very lifelike snowman, and, although his hair was a white frozen mass, underneath it was possible to make out a human face with eyes and nose and mouth. While still some distance away, Jack told himself it must be one of those old meths drinkers occasion-ally found frozen stiff in doorways in weather like this. Closer up, however, the last hoping against hope had to be abandoned, because the ironic expression on the snowman's face was un-questionably Carl's, and, even when Jack had taken the stiff form into his arms in a desperate attempt to transfer to it some of his body heat, and had sought to move the rigid arms and tried to force warm breath into its lungs, there was no responding sign of life.

34

The Home Office pathologist said Carl had taken around 400 milligrams of Secobarbital, which was a large dose, between twice and three times the dose normally taken as a somnific, but not in itself lethal. Death was due to hypothermia and exposure. In response to the coroner's questions, the pathologist said it was conceivable that, after taking the capsules to calm himself, Mr Schmidlin sat down on the bench to rest and fell asleep. No suicide note had been found by the police. The coroner brought in an open verdict: death due to causes unknown.

There was no cortège: a single funeral car was taking the coffin to the cemetery which was situated in a remote, chaotic, semi-industrialized area of northern London, beyond the North Circular Road, an area of signmakers, glass merchants, driving schools, discount furniture depots, DIY stores, second-hand car dealers.

The rabbi officiating at the service, although he had not known Carl personally, spoke movingly of his life — 'the life of the artist' — on the basis of what Carl's old mother and Jack and Gloria had told him. He said that Carl Schmidlin had come to England as a refugee with his mother, fleeing from Nazi persecution: he had made a life for himself in England and later in the United States, learning to speak and write a language not his own, and had struggled with the despair all artists felt at times. He was a man ill at ease in the world, said the rabbi. And here he quoted Nathaniel Hawthorne: 'the world owes all its forward movement to men ill at ease.' Carl Schmidlin, the rabbi said, may have considered himself a failure, on the basis of his own rigorously demanding and rather unpardoning nature, but to some of those who were close to him he was a teacher and an inspiration and a loyal and loving friend who would be sorely missed.

It was snowing as the rabbi led the handful of mourners through a maze of new graves, with their standard black or grey marble headstones, to the stark spot where the newly dug-up ground was being protected by a muddy tarpaulin sheet. The tarpaulin was rolled back, the rabbi said Kaddish, and Jewish people in the group responded at the appropriate points, and then the plain pine coffin was lowered softly into the wet earth.

After the interment, Carl's eighty year-old mother, supported by a woman friend not much younger, stood under an umbrella that one of the black-coated undertakers held over her head, receiving condolences. When Jack Strawley began to explain who he was she stopped him: 'I know who you are, Mr Strawley. You're Jack. I know. I know. Of course I know you. I know you very well. Though we didn't ever meet. But Carl often talked of you. He was proud of you being his friend. And of course I know what a great film-maker you are. Carl didn't have many close friends. He preferred reading. I think people got him down. Disappointed him. I used to say to him,' and a bright smile illumined the ancient face with its dense cross-hatching of dark lines, 'you should live in the world more, don't be such a critic of everything, people are people, everybody's got to live, but he didn't like the world, Carl, didn't like where it was going. He used to say, "Look at my friend Jack Strawley. An unread genius! That's where the world is going." I don't know really what he meant by that, but he admired you.'

'I'll tell you something, Mrs Schmidlin,' Jack said, 'Carl had a special quality, he could be your friend even if he didn't admire you. And he was a good writer.'

As they were all leaving the cemetery — a small, damp and cold little group of people huddled under umbrellas that were being buffeted by the strong wind — Gloria was saying, 'Oh, I feel it's wrong, it's wrong. Not even a drink or *anything*. I would have liked him to have a better send-off. I wanted to ask people to the house for a drink, but there weren't enough who could come, and I felt. . .'

'We'll have the drink,' Jack proposed.

They went into the nearest pub they could find, a gloomy, shabby old place with dark brown linoleum on the floor and just a couple of old fellows up at the bar drinking pints. Sitting down at a round cast-iron table, Jack raised his glass of whisky and said above the noise of road drills: 'To Carl,' and they were silent, thinking about Carl and his habit of walking away from things that he did not care for.

'He was too proud to let you see he was in a bad way,' Jack said. 'But I should have seen it. Should have done something.'

As they were leaving the pub, he took her hand and said quietly: 'Gloria, I want to come home. I can't live without you and Anna. It's too painful.'

She looked at him with her beautiful dark eyes and said: 'Yes, it's time you came home, Jack.'

When Moira got back from the studio, she realized that she was out of cigarettes and said she was going round to the pub to get some, and he said he'd come with her. The sky was cold dark purple. The Thames had partly frozen over for the first time in years. It was not snowing anymore, but there was a whiplash wind. On the mud flat around the boat the bits of rusty iron and the planks of wood and the dead pigeon and the thrown-out rubbish had all become petrified deep within the milky ice.

The pub was warm and noisy and lively, with an impromptu darts tournament going on in one corner, supporters loudly shouting their side on and decrying their opponents, and in another part of the pub three old dearies were giving an out-of-tune rendering of 'Moon River', washed down with Guinness, and others were trying to make themselves heard above the shouters. He let Moira fight her way to the bar while he went to make a phone call, and then re-joined her. She was asking the bar tender if he had Gauloise, and he said, 'No, dear,' and started to reel off what he did have — Guards, Strands, Consulates, Weights, Benson and Hedges, Black & White — and as he was coming to the end of the list, Jack said: 'I'm going back to Gloria.'

She told the barman: 'Give me twenty Benson & Hedges. And matches.' A particularly loud burst of jubilation and countervailing catcalls from the darts players' corner forced her to wait until she could make herself heard again, before asking: 'Did you just say what I think you said?'

'Yes.'

'Tell me again . . . can't hear a thing in here.'

Her eyes were on his mouth and she was lip-reading him as well as listening intently as he repeated it. She examined his face tightly, nodding her head up and down for a while, letting the news sink in deep, and then she said: 'I want to get out of here.' She was already rushing ahead of him, as if escaping from a room on fire, and in the grip of the glacial air outside her face became screwed up, eyes closing tight, mouth opening wide, wide, and then she let out the scream that she had been holding back inside, let it come out of the back of her throat and the depths of her lungs.

He put his arm around her and said: 'Come on. Come on, Moira.'

'Can't I scream? Now that I've been hit,' she demanded angrily.

'Yes,' he said, 'yes. You've got that right.' She was shivering inside her coat, her lips blue, and though he had his arm around her and was pressing her close, she was not getting any body heat from him. Her throat had gone into spasm, and dry harsh sobs were coming out.

'I'm sorry, I'm sorry,' he said, 'but you did sort of know — suspect — this was going to happen one day.'

'I suspect I'm going to die one day but that won't make me not mind when it happens.'

Her teeth were chattering violently, and he said: 'Let's walk, you're freezing.'

They walked fast, almost running, smoggy river mist in nose and throat, along the embankment where the moored houseboats creaked against their ice binding: under the iron bridge, and along the riverside promenade, not talking.

'When?' she asked him as they got nearer to her boat.

'The taxi said about fifteen, twenty minutes.'

'The taxi! You already called a taxi? You shit! We're not even going to talk?'

'Talking's not going to change anything, Moira.'

They had got inside the boat, and she was looking around confusedly, as if she didn't know where she was. Automatically she went to the record player and switched it on. The LP that dropped from the changer mechanism was Lena Horne. She wasn't listening to it, it was to fill the empty space. She took out a Benson & Hedges and tapped it aggressively against the box. Her eyes were fierce: he thought she might hit him. The port-holes were curtained by condensation. She looked at her watch and then all around, trying to work it out in the time left. 'This isn't going back to how it was . . . before. This is a whole new deal. This is going to be on Gloria's terms. You've accepted her conditions. Means I won't be working with you either. Am I reading the small print correct?'

'You always were good at reading the small print.'

'So I've also been fired from my job — a job I've been doing, on and off, pretty competently, you have got to admit, for . . . what? Fifteen years? Call this a clean break? Yeah, a broken neck's a clean break too! You packed and everything?'

'I packed,' he said. 'Wasn't much. They'll ring . . . when the taxi's here.'

His bags were up on the narrow bunk bed he'd been sleeping in. She looked at her watch again. 'Then I've just got you for another few minutes?' She looked around distraught, damming back tears, biting into her knuckles. Her face was raw and blotchy from cold and misery. 'What'm I going to do now?' she demanded. 'What am I going to do?'

'Get on with your life, like you always said you would. You have such a lot going in your life, Moira.'

'You're a part of my life now. Why? What did I do wrong? I know it hasn't been so great, in one way, but that wasn't my fault, was it? That was the medication, you said. And it was getting better recently. You've been coming out of it.'

'A lot of it's due to you.' He took a last look round the place. 'I got better here. You let me find myself again, in my own time. Nobody picks me out of the gutter as good as you, Moira.'

'Gee thanks!' Her voice had gone hard and bitter and derisive. 'And now it's: I'm better, 'bye 'bye . . . Thanks for the lift, babe. God, men are such selfish pricks! People like you, they use up people and then they throw 'em away like garbage. I put in fifteen years of my life with you, always accepting that you were with Gloria and that nothing was going to change that. But I also thought I had some role in your life, that I wasn't just going to be thrown out like after a one-night stand. I've lived a big chunk of my life with you.'

'You had others in your life, during those years. That was what we agreed.'

'Others!' she said self-mocking. 'Big thrills with Big Movie Names at a loose end. You think I could have a relationship with anyone while I was there for you, all the time?'

'You could have had whatever you wanted,' he said, 'you were always free.'

He knew it wasn't a very good defence he was putting forward because he didn't have a very good defence. Whatever you did, somebody always got hurt. There wasn't any way of living painlessly like in a Noel Coward play.

'Jack, we've had good times, and I've helped you professionally, I'm valuable to you, I work well with you, you need me . . . and you know that. It's so unfair that that has got to stop too, that we can't even work together. Because she's laid down the law.'

'Moira, I don't know if I'm ever going to make another film. And you must see — don't you? — that if I'm around you five days a week, eight, ten, twelve hours a day, going on locations together . . . knowing what Gloria knows, she couldn't be exactly tranquil about that.'

She said nothing, staring at him hard, engraving his face deep in memory. Then she gave a shrug and appeared to get calmer. 'I have to let you go, don't I? Which I do know about. I've got no choice, have I? ' She looked at him with exhausted calm eyes and then told him flatly he could go.

'You're a lovely woman,' he said, 'and you've given me a lot. Hope I gave you something as well.'

'You did. You taught me. A lot! You enriched my life, you shit!'

'Go on writing your scripts and you'll make it, I'm sure you will, you're so very capable and bright.'

'Bright but not very clever.'

'You are. You'll get there. You'll end up running MGM.'

'It's still on my list.'

'That's it. You've got to stake your life. It's the only way.

You're going to be all right,' he told her firmly. 'I know it.'

'Yeah, I'll be just fine.'

'Do that and be great.'

'Yeah, you too.'

He and Gloria decided to give a big party in Carlyle Square for friends and people in the business to show everyone they were together again.

The invitations were for 9.30, and Carver arrived at quarter to nine, carrying two scripts, one bound in blue, one in red. He joined Jack in the bathroom while he was finishing shaving.

Carver was wearing a Prince of Wales grey check suit with a yellow carnation and a mauve Sulka shirt and brown handmade shoes, elasticated at the sides.

'So? What's next?' he asked 'Ready to go to work?'

'Getting around to that.'

'Any thoughts about what you'd like to do?'

'I've been thinking about *Heart of Darkness* again.'

Carver's face became pained. 'I know you like the material,' he said, 'but I'd hoped to hear you say something a bit, well, less . . . heavy. Less *dark*. A picture with a part for Maureen. She's dying to make another picture with you, and she's big right now, *really* big, all the studios would love one from the big win combination: Strawley, Carver and Wynner! Couldn't you come up with a contemporary sex comedy like *Polly & Jane?*'

'Sydney, I have a whole new slant on *Heart of Darkness.*'

'Well, we won't go into it now, this is a welcome home party, let's keep it that way. We'll talk next week. Meanwhile here's a little house *re*-warming present,' he said, putting down the two scripts. 'Read them and tell me what you think. Either'd be a good subject for you, and finance wouldn't be any problem. Jack, wanna just say this, as somebody's known you now . . . been close to you, what is it? Almost twenty years? Let me say this to you: you got smart, you came back to Gloria. Moira's a spunky smart-ass Jewish broad, I love her, but she's not in Gloria's class. Gloria's an aristo. You did right. Carl was a rare human being, intelligent, a brain! A friend! He's dead. That's the past. Now look to the future. Do a picture audiences will want to see. Because, believe me, your brightest glory days lie ahead of you, Jack.'

35

It was a glittering party that the Strawleys gave to celebrate their coming together again and to advertise to the world that everything was going fine, that his problems with alcohol and wild behaviour and depression were in the past, that he was in good shape and perfectly employable once more. The 'Spanish affair' had got into the newspapers in various versions, and — even more damagingly — there had been allusions to his subsequent prolonged stay in the psychiatric wing of the East Anglia health farm. Hence it was essential for him to demonstrate that he was not this crazy hellraising 'genius Jack' figure that the press had been writing up, but a serious, responsible, talented film-maker who could be trusted to bring big-budget pictures in on schedule.

The 'together again' party included those journalists and critics who were basically well-disposed towards him and could be relied on to spread the positive story. I was there myself and heard Jack speak of Gloria as his life support system, as necessary to him as breathing. And I observed that after one glass of champagne for the formal celebration, he was drinking San Pellegrino the rest of the evening.

As part of his public rehabilitation, organized by Carver, and undertaken by a very expensive international PR firm, he gave interviews to the quality press in which he made frank reference to past misdemeanours, saying that that was all over now, and paid glowing tribute to Gloria, to her indispensable role in his life: she had educated him and civilized him, a savage from the streets of New York, had turned him around into an award-winning director. She was beautiful, a wonderful mother and hostess, and a great actress too. He had everything he wanted. His wild days were over.

Anna was now seventeen. At her birth he had adored her helplessly, bowled over by the beauty of this fragile new life to which he had given rise. And then, as with everyone else, passion was followed by loss of interest, boredom, indifference, and a certain degree of irritation as she went through the commonplace troubles of puberty and adolescence. One day he saw that his little girl was not just thin but was wasting away, and realized that she had made a hostage of her frail body and that he could no longer put her out of his mind until later. Faced with the real possibility of her death — that was clearly what she was threatening them with — he put other preoccupations to the side and threw himself fully into the struggle to save her. She was his baby and he was not going to let her die, as he had let Carl die by not caring enough.

Bound together by this emergency, he and Gloria became closer than they had been for many years. He became a father in spirit as well as fact. And then his great struggle was rewarded: Anna started to eat again. He had triumphed once more, had brough her through the valley of death and was euphoric with joy. The dark shadow had passed. Within six months he was making a film about a troubled marriage and a daughter with anorexia, and it turned out to be a fine film, a mature film, full of understanding of emotional pain, full of humour and tenderness and insights into adolescent states of mind. And middle aged states of mind. The critics lavished praise upon him anew, it won a prize at Venice, and he was once more high in prestige. I remember saying to Gloria how happy she must be that he had won through and proved those critics wrong who had been writing him off, and her replying cryptically: 'Winning is always bad for Jack.'

And sadly she was right about that. For if she was as necessary to him as breathing (as he kept saying), he was again taking crazy risks with his oxygen supply. Whenever I ran into him now I sensed that the shackles were chafing once again, that he was embracing the enemies of promise anew, the charlock's shade, the slimy mallow, drinking hard . . . And I saw in Gloria's face the dark, tautly strained expression of someone who loved him deeply but was coming to realize that he could never love another person in that way, except in brief bursts. Whenever I saw them, I could see that their relationship was being put to harsher and harsher tests all the time. In public she rarely let the mask slip, but I had the impression that she could not much longer continue to bear the things he was making her put up with. On one occasion, when I was doing a formal interview with him, for an article I had been asked to write for an American magazine, I asked him why in his films women were often depicted as creatures of chaos, unreliable, unpunctual, untrustworthy, prick-teasers, castrators . . . betrayers: the wicked witch. He'd often been accused of being a mysoginist. His films tended to show the impossibility of men and women ever getting together, ever being able to satisfy each other's needs. And yet, I said, I knew that he had benefited greatly from what Gloria had given him and, for that matter, by what someone like Moira had given him. I said I thought he had been greatly helped by the women in his life. He had replied: 'Problem with women is they're on a monthly moon cycle, like the tides, while men are circadian. And especially if you're someone whose moods swing minute to minute makes it difficult for men and women to get it together. You know the story about Giacometti going to one of those great French brothels before the war? The Sphinx, I think it was . . . a great place . . . and seeing these great girls who were so unbelievably desirable at a certain distance and then when he began to approach one . . . as he got nearer she'd start to disappear,' — he gave a hard little laugh, he was gaily mocking himself — 'see, women when you try to catch hold of them, they vanish . . . maybe that's why his sculptures disappear. Or maybe not. Maybe its got nothing to do with that at all. In answer to your question, Stephen: I recount what I have seen. If others have seen other things, let them recount what they've seen. That's all any of us can do.'

We got onto his ideas about cinema, and he had illuminating

and provocative comments about Welles and Antonioni and Fellini and Bergman. He said that cinema was in the 'the myth business', that humans need myths to keep alive as they need food, that myths were what enabled us to reconcile the dream part and the reality part of life. He said myths were 'stories that lose hardly anything in translation.' Cinema was a medium that drew very largely on those sorts of stories, hence the universal appeal of Hollywood films, which seemed to be equally comprehensible in Minesotta, Patagonia and Timbuctoo . . . 'Because we are always basically telling the same story, which the whole of mankind can respond to, the story of a quest. Of an endeavour.'

He was better value when depressed: that was when you could reach him and make contact with him on a human level. That was when he stopped kidding, and showing off and being invulnerable. His claim was that you needed to be depressed to want to make a film, and *maniaco* to actually do it. That was why so many artists were manic depressives: you needed the two aspects to function.

Shortly after this interview something occurred between Jack Strawley and myself — I have no clear idea what it was — that led to a breach between us, and I was no longer invited to his house. Perhaps he had not liked the article that came out of our interview, perhaps he had not liked how I made him sound. He was unpredictable in his reactions to what you wrote about him. It was impossible to work out all the twists and turns of Jack Strawley's mind.

36

Felix M. Riesner of the firm of Riesner, Greenshein & Sylvester was a small dapper fellow with a small dapper Vandyke beard, a low, soft voice and a reassuring manner. He was famous for saying that there was always a solution. Some solutions were more costly than others, that was all. While Felix Riesner was among the very costliest of these, he would tell you that you couldn't afford to not be able to afford him.

'Compounding deficits,' he was explaining with his benign smile pointing all around, 'can become exponential. Just as compounding interest will build up amazingly over time, so the converse will erode your capital base.'

Their meeting was taking place in the august, if slightly musty and faded, surroundings of the great London club of which Riesner had recently had the honour to have been elected a member. The club's bar was nine-tenths empty. In the one tenth that wasn't, elderly former rulers of nation and empire were asleep in their wing armchairs. Riesner's table was discreetly situated behind a marble Corinthian column.

In reply to Strawley's question about how he had got himself in a position of 'exponential debt growth', Riesner beamingly replied: 'By spending too much. Over the past fifteen years, you've spent every year more than you've earned. Even when you've earned a great deal, you have spent more. It may not have seemed to you all that much more, sometimes only six, seven per cent more, but then there were years when you didn't earn anything between pictures, and your outgoings remained just as high. And taxes . . . and interest on unpaid taxes. And those everlasting loan repayments that you saddled yourself with early on in your career. Oh, it can easily happen.'

'What's my situation then?'

'A lot of your real assets are hypothecated.'

'You better write these things down for me,' Jack Strawley said. Riesner shook his head.

'No, we don't write anything down *here*. In a club such as this

it is not permitted to engage in "professional activity". For now,
I will simply outline to you the broad nature of the situation in
which you find yourself. The full details and my proposals I shall
put to you in a letter.'

'All right. Go ahead.'

'To put it very generally,' he gave his big beaming, all-round
smile, 'on paper, your combined debts are greater than your
combined assets.'

'What about the house, the pictures . . . and the rest?'

'Heavily hypothecated . . . whether there is any surplus equity
would depend on current market prices, which we wouldn't
know until we came to sell.'

'I bought the houses outright.'

'Yes, but subsequently, when you needed money to buy other
things, your producer, Sydney Carver, advanced you the cash.'

'Those were advances against the earnings of our films.'

'In the first place, yes. But in case your film earnings didn't
cover the advances, you issued personal guarantees, collateralized
on your houses and other assets and then, when the advances
were not fully earned, the shortfall was converted into long term
debt.'

'In other words, they own a piece of me?'

'Yes. Sydney Carver owns quite a big chunk of you.'

'In which case, you better send him your bills.'

Mr Riesner chuckled. 'It's not quite as bad as it sounds, Mr
Strawley. In any other field, someone in your position might
have to be considered bankrupt. But in the case of the artist, his
assets reside in his genius . . . that is your capital. You can
command very high fees and percentages of the profits of your
films. So there is no need for us to be *unduly* alarmed. All you
need is a big hit, of the kind you have had in the past, combined
with sound financial management.' He beamed reassuringly.
'We shall have to restructure the companies so that some of the
rolled up debt can be written off. I shall put all my proposals in
my letter.'

'Can you explain to me,' Jack Strawley asked the accountant,
'how it is that Sydney can afford to live as he does and I can't
afford to live on my rather less lavish scale?'

'I have no idea how Mr Carver lives, since I am not his accountant.'

'It's high, it's very high. He has a house in London, a house in the South of France, an apartment in New York, a yacht.'

'His earnings are probably higher than yours.'

'That can't be. On the films we make together, he's paid less than I am, and the profits we share equally.'

'He also makes films with other directors.'

'His biggest successes have been the films he's made with me. For our company.'

'Well, that might be the explanation.'

'What d'you mean?'

'He has complicated cross-collateralization deals.'

'Meaning?'

'It means that if he makes three films for United Artists, and two make a loss, and one makes a profit, the losses on the two that made a loss are taken off the profits of the one that made a profit. You didn't know that?'

'No.'

'You should have known. It's something that in principle should not have been done without your knowledge and agreement.'

'Carver takes care of all that side.'

'That is quite evident.'

No sooner had Carver sat down at his usual table at the crowded river end of the Savoy restaurant than a porter arrived with three telephone messages, each in its own small envelope. The first two were quickly crumpled up and left on the table for the waiters to dispose of, the third occupied him longer and caused him to frown.

Jack Strawley, when he arrived, saw that the table was laid for three and asked if they were being joined by somebody else.

'Yeah, my date,' Carver said.

'Thought you wanted to talk storyline.'

'She won't take up our time,' Carver promised and added: 'Thought we could maybe use her in a small part.'

'We don't have any small parts for coltish South Kensington

gels. Remember, the setting of our story is a semi-tropical Span-ish-speaking Central American republic?'

'She doesn't have to speak. And, if necessary, we can cut her out after. Don't worry about it. How you feeling?'

'I'm feeling fine.'

'God, you're looking great. I mean that.'

Carver had the smoothly polished look of one who has stepped straight out of his sauna and into his jacuzzi and thence into his chauffeur-driven Bentley convertible. His purged cheeks were fragrant with *Chanel Pour Gentilhomme*. He looked at his watch. 'She's ten minutes late,' he said with annoyance. 'She doesn't get here in five minutes she doesn't get to eat, that's all. Am I right? I hate women being late, don't you hate women being late?'

'Yeah.'

They gave their orders, and Carver took out a sheaf of papers and ran his eye down the typed notes.

'I'm going to leave these with you to think about. I just want to raise a couple of questions right now. I've got here: "Opening shot. Marlow on boat, heading up river." I've written here: "Make more sympathetic. How?"' He looked up, and repeated the ques-tion: 'How?'

'I don't know, we'll have to see.'

Carver seemed dissatisfied with the answer but pressed on.

'Page 4. The prologue/flashback. The making of Kurtz. Berlin in ruins. Bodies dangling from lampposts. Young Kurtz in dying city. Negotiates with General Wolff. Okay, this is the deal with the devil. My question is: do we need it? It's going to run ten, fifteen minutes. That's long for a prologue and long for a flash-back. And it has nothing to do really with our story, it's what happened before our story starts. Do we need it?'

'We need it,' Jack said.

'This prologue is going to add a million dollars to our budget.'

'It's what the script lacked before. It gives it a historic dimen-sion. Gives Marlow and Kurtz a history. Shows they both come out of the same mould.'

Carver's date had arrived, a little breathless and very apolo-getic about being late. A wanly pretty English colt of the sort he favoured. Called Sylvia. Carver didn't get up for her, just handed her the message slip. 'Better go make your call. Be quick about it! Jack and I still got one or two things to discuss. You're not back in under five minutes,' he warned her with ostensible jocularity, 'we don't give you dinner.' She laughed and said she would only be a couple of minutes.

'Whaddyah think of this broad?' Carver demanded when she'd left. 'Comes on a date with me, and gets sent a message from her boyfriend, *at my table*. Can you believe that?'

'Got to punish her for that, Sydney. It's an insult. Calls for something. Maybe you should let her go without dessert.'

Carver shook his arrow-shaped head from side to side at the same time lifting his thick eyebrows with an expression of hauling heavy weights up a steep slope.

'These girls these days . . .' he began to complain bitterly.

'Yeah. Go out with eighteen-year old girls, you get eighteen year-old girls,' Jack said. 'It's tough.'

'Okay, let's get back to basics,' Carver said, shaking his head. 'I'm not insisting, Jack. But my advice to you would be . . . *Look,* I just want you to remember that you have given personal guarantees. A 15-minute prologue that adds a million dollars to cost, may cost you personally in the end. If the picture should go into loss . . .'

'It's going to be a fine picture, Sydney.'

'I know that. But will it make money?'

'Don't know about money. I leave that to you. You're the money magician. You must be since you're rich and I'm broke and yet we make the same pictures and get the same points . . . in fact, you're supposed to get less than me. And look at you, and look at me.'

Carver did so: he looked at Jack with deeply knowing eyes, chin nodding, eyebrows rising. 'It's because you don't take my advice. I told you to buy gold, did you buy gold? No. I told you to set yourself up in the Dutch Antilles, did you? You didn't. Result is you pay all your money in taxes. Simple. What d'you suppose she's doing? Whaddyou think of her? You like her? She's eighteen years old! That's the age you like 'em.'

'Too old for me.'

'Don't worry, I wasn't offering her to you.'

'Oh, I thought you were for a minute. Which, I realize, is not at all your style: not like you to give presents. Let me ask you something, Sydney? Are you robbing me?'

Carver shook his head with deep sadness. 'Jack, you don't have any money because you're profligate. You buy houses that you never live in, you give a £3,000 engagement ring to an airline hostess you haven't even got down on the ground. And your pictures run over budget and eat into your profits.'

'Do you eat into my profits, Sydney?'

'You getting sick again?' Carver looked deeply hurt that such an accusation could be made, however lightly, however unmeant. His grapefruit segments had arrived, and he stabbed at them angrily with his fork. 'How can you say something like that to me? If I didn't know you don't mean it, I'd get insulted.'

Sylvia had returned from her phone call. She was an actress from Salisbury rep. and she wanted badly to get into the film business. Carver switched his attention to her.

'So how's the high-flyer?' To Jack he said with a wink: 'Her boyfriend's an airline pilot. Flies to Australia. Leaves her lonely and deprived.'

'I said — I hope you don't mind, Sydney — I said I'd see him for a coffee . . . later. He's only here for a few hours . . .' Seeing the effect of this statement on Carver, her voice had begun to falter guiltily. 'He's leaving tomorrow. Shouldn't I have done that? It's just for a coffee . . . ten minutes. To say hello. And goodbye.'

'To say hello, huh?' He shook his head and turned to Jack in incredulity. 'You wouldn't think she comes from a good family, that her father's an honourable. My dear, it's no skin off my nose who you have coffee or anything else with, since I henceforth cut you out of my life.'

'Don't be nasty to me, Sydney,' the girl pleaded in a soft submissive little voice. 'I won't have coffee with him if you don't want me to. I'll phone him back and say I can't.'

'My dear, I wouldn't want to deprive you. Have coffee with him, have anything you like with him.' He half turned his back on her, addressing himself to Jack. 'I think you're right. I don't think there's any part for this girl in our film. She doesn't have the class. I don't even know if we should give her dinner since she has such bad manners. Are we going to tolerate that? Getting phone calls from her boyfriend at my table! I think we should let her go and have dinner with him. Let 'em go to Lyons.' He chuckled, relishing the thought of them having to eat at Lyons.

'Sydney,' she insisted, 'it was just going to be for a coffee, I wasn't . . .' She shot a quick glance at Jack and decided that she had to make a public act of contrition for what she had done. 'I'm sorry, Sydney, if I've offended you. I didn't mean to.' She lowered her voice to an intimate whisper. 'I'm going to spend the night with you, Sydney. I want to. I really do . . . very much.'

'You think we should give her dinner?' Carver asked doubtfully. 'You think she's sincerely ready to make amends?'

Jack Strawley considered the question carefully and then, leaning towards the girl, said: 'You know what I'd do, Sylvia? When your dinner comes — throw it in his face.'

Carver glared a little at first, then said with the sort of Sydney Carver grin that could cut throats: 'She doesn't mind a little kidding, do you, baby?'

'No, no . . .' she professed, looking up into his eyes adoringly and squeezing his hand.

When he got home, he phoned Moira, even though it was well after midnight.

'Well, isn't this a voice out of the past?' she said with a certain sharpness in her tone. 'Let me guess. You're at a loose end and, leafing through your tattered little black book, you come on this old phone number, somebody you used to know once, and you think: give it a try, what've I got to lose?'

'You misjudge my character,' he told her. 'So what's been happening to you? Am I interrupting something?'

'Only my sleep.'

'I'll call you in the morning.'

'It's okay, I'm awake now, and since I don't get calls out of the past all the time . . .'

'How's the work?'

'Up and down. Slow, if you want to know.'

'How'd you like it to speed a little?'

'What d'you have in mind?'
'I need an associate producer.'
'Isn't Sydney your producer?'
'I need a producer to watch my producer . . . he's robbing me.'
'How much will you pay me?'
'Say . . . $4,000 a week basic.'

There was a brief silence on the line, then she said: 'Call it $50,000 for ten weeks minimum, pay or play. After that each extra week pro rata.'

'Okay, Moira. Whatever you say. Write your own contract. I have to have you with me.'

'It won't open old wounds with Gloria?'

'No, this is strictly a business arrangement. In any case, Gloria and I have come to an understanding.'

PART IV

THE MYRMIDONS

37

Following our unexplained falling out, I had not heard from
Jack Strawley for some months and had assumed I was permanently banished from his life, as so many others had been, when
I received a phone call from Spain one evening, and it was Jack
calling, just as if we had met the night before, and I had not
caused him a great harm. Clearly I was forgiven for whatever it
was that I had done because he was inviting me to come to
Seville. He had a proposition to put to me, he said. He would
rather not tell me about it on the phone. Could I come out for a
couple of days to talk it over? Seville was very lovely, I would
enjoy it. He would soon be starting shooting on his new film, a
modern adaptation of Conrad's *Heart of Darkness*, and I might
be interested in that.

There had been a great deal of advance talk about this production. It was going to be a very big picture with a budget of
something like ten million dollars (which was big money in
those days), starring Nik Ransom, and it was going to be made
entirely in Spain, twenty kilometres south of Seville. The press
was being kept away — all the more reason for me to accept his
invitation. They were building a vast film set, out in the wilds
somewhere, to represent the heart of darkness, and there had
been clashes and mishaps — a Spanish workman had fallen from
high scaffolding and been killed. There was talk of conflict
between Strawley and Carver, and of Strawley behaving 'grandi-
osely', which from my knowledge of him I took to mean that he
was probably sticking to his guns and refusing to compromise
with the money men. I knew about his ferocious determination to
do things his own way, and I knew how arrogant his behaviour
could sometimes seem to be when he was in this phase of his
mood swings. I also knew that this was when he was at his most
creative. It sounded as though he was pissing at the moon again,

and that things were likely to get pretty lively out there in Spain. The prospect of a ringside seat at the spectacle naturally drew me. I was glad, too, that our breach was not definitive and was looking forward to seeing him again. With all our up and downs over the years, and his sometimes weird and terrible behaviour, I had retained my high regard for him as a film-maker, even if that regard now fell short of considering him a 'genius', whatever one wishes to understand by that emotive term (and it is worth bearing in mind that the begetting of evil is not excluded from the dictionary definition of genius).

I had no clue as to what he wanted to talk to me about, but it did not sound to me as if it was going to be an entirely wasted journey. And so two days after his phone call — he was insistent that I must come right away — I took a plane to Seville.

From the airport I went straight to the Hotel Alphonse XIII, where Jack was staying. A room had been reserved for me there. I told them at the desk to announce my arrival to him and was told that Mr Strawley would meet me in the bar in an hour's time. I checked into my room, had a shower and ambled down to the bar at the time we had said. I had to wait another hour before he showed up. He apologized for keeping me hanging around. They were shortly to start shooting — at last! — and there were lots of problems, as I could imagine. I certainly could and was amazed that he should have wanted to see me at such a time — for whatever reason. His one vague allusion to what had occurred between us in London was his remark: 'Yeah, Stephen: you can bathe in the same river twice, only it's colder.'

Seated up at the bar, we looked out onto the patio with its high ferns in huge ceramic pots and the fountain in the centre. Jack asked the head bartender for a brandy. I, suspecting we were in for some hard-drinking and wanting to postpone the worst for as long as possible, claimed an upset stomach and asked for mineral water. We sat chatting easily, as if there were no great pressure on him, and he told me about the marvellous locations they had found. He said they'd started from a fine script by Carl Schmidlin, the last thing Schmidlin had written before his death. And he added matter-of-factly that this film was going to be his own personal 'masterwork'. The story had evolved and become a modern fable, and it was a story that he himself felt strongly involved in. 'You'll see, Stephen, when you come out to the set . . . the whole first part is the journey upriver to find Kurtz, who's out there somewhere in the darkness, this drunken, renegade CIA guy. It's a quest-story, like all the best stories are . . . It's different . . . you'll see, got a modern slant to it. Carl adapated Conrad freely, and I've adapted Carl freely.'

I could see the incipient febrility in his eyes, the first stage of the speeding-up that always happened, to some extent, as he was getting ready to start shooting. The bar was beginning to get full, and he called for his bill. He signed it sight unseen, which was always his way with bills.

Taking me by the arm he conducted me out into the quadrangle. It was still too early for lunch and there were only a couple of people in the restaurant beyond the giant ferns. In any case, he didn't feel up to lunch, he said. Did I mind if we didn't eat just yet? As we walked around the great lobby with its richly decorated mirrors, their opulent frames heavily laden with cherubs and flowers and grapes, I began to get the feeling of being in a Jack Strawley film with too many mirror shots, for which he had a known weakness. I was being steered into an abrupt about-turn. His fast-scanning eyes were restlessly looking for something or somebody. 'Glad you were able to come out, Stephen,' he told me, all friendliness once more after our recent breach. 'It's really great to see you.'

We made our way down the Avenue de la Constitucion, walking fast, as if somebody was after us, or perhaps simply because he couldn't manage to do anything slowly. Across from the cathedral and the Giralda tower, we cut rapidly down a side-street. He seemed to know his way through the maze here. Thick ropework blinds hung down over windows as protection against the great summer heat that was soon going to descend in earnest. We were heading towards the part of town where the bullring is situated, and, in these streets and alleys, there were lots of small dark bars with bullfight photographs on the walls. Jack, a world-class expert on bars, rejected the first three and selected the fourth: although dirty, its floor littered with cigarette ends and discarded lottery tickets, it had an atmosphere of serious drink-ing that appealed to him.

The inside of the bar was the ubiquitous Seville sand-yellow: stripes of light lay across the old cracked *sangre de toros* floor tiles. The bar was stucco, made to imitate marble. Beyond the sharp light at the entrance, the room was deeply shadowed. Jack chose a table in the dimmest part. He called for two brandies, forgetting or choosing to ignore my 'bad stomach', and with his head indicated the house across the alleyway.

'Those fancy enclosed balconies that you see all over town, legend has it they were to stop Don Juan getting access to the daughters.' He gave a wry smile. 'No connection, but I'm writing my autobiography.'

I mumbled something feeble about that being a hazardous undertaking for any man.

'You're so right,' he said at once. 'Plus I'm starting the picture. And there's my peculiar memory, very vivid for some things. Some things I can reproduce in minute detail. I remember places, an atmopshere, something somebody said. Other far more import-ant things have been completely wiped. And my chronology is all haywire, no sense of cause and effect. For me calamity always came out of the corner of the eye: wham! In addition, there's stuff I can't use because of . . . the fact that I still have to . . .' He was starting sentences that he wasn't finishing. 'Question of steering. So . . . need to steer. I'd need someone, a professional in the field, that I could talk it out to, who knows how to handle this kind of material and knows me. Who can get the stuff out of me. *Knows where to dig.*'

'Yes. You need a ghost writer.'

'I have to write it myself. That's what they want. It's got to come from me. Got to have my voice. What I need is a . . . a . . . collaborator. You interested?'

'It's not something I normally do.'

He glared at the ground, dropping his head low, his hands knitting together, his eylids heavy, then fluttering quickly as the brandy went down and shook him back to life.

'Ought to tell you. Gloria and I've split. It's definite this time.' His eyes narrowed, squinting up to the Don Juan-proof balcony.

'I guess it had to happen, and now it has. It's best that you know that. Of course I'm very broke up about it. We'd been drifting apart a long time, and finally the drift went too far, and there was no going back.' He pushed brandy down his throat and flared his nostrils wide as his bloodstream took the jolt. Head nodding, his eyes went round and round trying to find something to focus on and came back again to the enclosed balcony. 'There it is. There it is,' he said. 'Feels like a whole part of my life's shut down. And the worst is I've lost Anna too. She blames me. Has turned completely against me . . . with a rage. You can't imagine! She's gone lesbian. To spite me, I think. To let me know that men are not to be loved, that they're goatish destroyers, blind, untrustworthy, of no use. I can see how she'd get that picture. That whole family scene is going to be very tricky to handle in the book. I don't want outsiders digging into all that, but you, Stephen . . . you could handle it. I'll be speaking it all out, talking it onto tape. You'll have my voice. I'll get you all the material. You'll have free access. My most private thoughts and memories. We'll be so close you'll think you're me.'

'Why would you want to . . . lay yourself open like that?'

He drank brandy, wincing as it went down and travelled through his bloodstream. He was silent for so long I thought he wasn't going to answer. Then he said flatly: 'I've got a lot of expenses. Sydney's been robbing me for years, and there's the back taxes, and . . . and I'd like to get ahead of the game for once, and also . . . to set the record straight for Anna. I want her to understand what it was like to live inside my skin. Maybe she can profit from that, maybe help her come to terms with her delinquent father. No apologies, I'm not going to *apologize* for any of it, I'm just going to say this is how it was.' He paused. 'Don't dismiss it, Stephen. I know it isn't what you normally do, I know you write your own books.'

'Ghost-writing is a specialized skill. There are people who do it very well. Somebody'll want to take it on. You won't have any trouble,'

'I want *you* to do it, Stephen.' He pointed his finger at me aggressively. 'I think you owe it to me. Since you did me a great harm once. And, besides,' he added illogically, 'there's nobody else I'd trust. Because I have to tell it all . . . only way I can do it. Decide afterwards what goes in and what doesn't. There are aspects of my life . . . well, there are things in my life I'm not too proud of . . .' He pulled himself up before going too far in what he was saying. 'I won't hide anything from you, Stephen, and one day, when I'm dead, you can write it your own way.'

I laughed and said: 'You and I are about the same age.'

'Yeah but you haven't lived the way I have.'

He was peering out of the dim interior into the white alley marked by violent shadows at this time of day. He'd become suddenly restless again, restless to find another bar with another ambience. Was restless, too, to have my answer. Yay or nay, he wanted to know now. He kept drinking without visibly getting any drunker; he just seemed to be maintaining the same alcohol level in his blood all the time. Drinking and burning it up. I saw that his eyes were glistening.

'Last time I came here was with Gloria and Carl . . . on a recce. It was for this same film which we're finally doing now. And there was this mishap that happened to me, I got sick, and everything turned out different than expected. Gloria and I . . . were still close then, at the start, despite our problems. What happens is you get used up. Gloria and me, we got used up. Used each other up. Happens with everything. We had wonderful times at the beginning and even later, even a lot later, but it didn't last. Suddenly it's all used up.' He shook his head in bewilderment. 'That time in Seville it was Carl's turn . . . to get used up. I let him go. He could be a pain in the ass with his quibbles and his endless analyzing of everything and his fucking moralizing. He wasn't going to be any movie hack writing to order. I got impatient with him and I listened to Sydney when I shouldn't have. Sometimes I listen to the wrong people. Don't know who my good angels are. I needed him badly but I got rid of him. Let him get rid of himself, if you like. Because I thought I could do without him. I got into some bad trouble with the Spanish police over a little whore in a red dress, and Sydney had to get me out of that, and he's never let me forget it. And I got sick, you see . . . had to go to the health farm. For three months. And all this time, though I didn't know it, Carl was going downhill fast. I was on the mend but he was going down, and I was so totally preoccupied with my own affairs, with getting myself out my hole and up again, that I never realized what was happening to him, and so did nothing. You can see if I'm going to tell my story with any truthfulness I need somebody who knows who I am. I can't just go to some professional ghost-writer, he'd make me sound so shitty. Think about my proposal, Stephen. We'll work out a good fee for your participation.'

I couldn't think about it too long, though, because the American publishers were asking for an outline and one chapter before they would actually commit themselves contractually, and he didn't want to lose the offer.

By the time we left the bar I had accepted. I realized it might not work out. At the best of times he could be very prickly, and here we were, about to get into very dangerous waters; a man's life, who he is. Our relationship had been on the edge just a few months back, it might not survive an experience such as this, but I somehow felt I couldn't refuse to do it.

We began the same day, sitting in the spacious quadrangle of the Alphonse XIII, a small tape recorder between us on the table. 'Is that thing switched on?' he demanded before starting. He wasn't going to waste his breath if it wasn't.

'Yes, its on.'

'Then let's get started.'

And so we began.

38

Jack Strawley had recreated the geographical heart of darkness of Joseph Conrad's story on the west bank of the Guadalquivir, some twenty kilometres south-west of Seville. There, Percy

Drummer, his art director, had discovered a wilderness of rampant vegetation advancing upon, and in parts invading, the derelict country estate of some long dead Spanish nobleman and Francoist general. Artfully re-modelled by Drummer, it became in the film a CIA out-station, ruled over by Kurtz. From this place he runs his rogue operation and the banana/cocaine republic's puppet dictator. When Marlow gets his first glimpse of the place through field glasses it looks as if it has an ornamental stockade all around, then when he adjusts the focus he sees that the 'ornaments' are severed heads on sticks. The buildings are mostly in an advanced state of decay — and so is Kurtz when finally found. The script called for a great wall of vegetation — 'the riotous invasion of soundless life,' in Conrad's words — to have encroached upon the out-station in a stranglehold of whip-like creepers and tendrils, and the decaying estate of the Francoist general fitted the bill perfectly. The orange groves had not been tended for many years; the hot thick clammy air swarmed with insects; the unruly jungle-like vegetation reached right up to the doorsteps; and buzzards circled endlessly overhead.

It was an elaborate and remarkable set that Percy Drummer and his art department had constructed within the shell of the estate. Some parts of it had been restored so that the former grand reception rooms could be used to represent the puppet dictator's presidential palace. Wine cellars had been converted into the torture chambers of the regime's secret police. On open land to the east, Percy Drummer and his Spanish crews had erected the massive facades of unfinished neo-Fascist government buildings, inspired by Mussolini's never-finished new city outside Rome, and all around there were modern luxury villas, some consisting only of frontages and others only of interiors. There was a deer park in the dictator's grounds; a great driveway lined with newly-planted palm trees and shrubs; fountains; a heliport — and, conveniently nearby, as a matter of practicality for the shooting and also serving as a metaphor, there was 'the jungle', where the rebels had their hide-outs in marshy woodland where the branches so thickly intertwined that only meagre quantities of daylight ever penetrated the tree-tops.

Building this set, two-thirds of which would never be seen on the screen, had already cost over a million-and-a-half dollars and the life of a Spanish workman. Start of shooting had been postponed several times. First, because the set was not completely ready, and Strawley wanted the feeling of the whole thing before beginning to film in part of it. The second delay was caused when it was found that the passageway behind the neo-Fascist facades was too narrow for the Technirama cameras and the big arc lamps to pass through, and so they had to demolish parts of the 'Mussolini set' and widen the passageway.

And then Strawley had wanted to create the startling suddenness of nightfall in the tropics. The film was already behind schedule, and Sydney Carver had pleaded with him: 'Jack, shoot it day-for-night, and we'll do it later in the lab.'

But Jack Strawley didn't want laboratory darkness: it did not have the same quality as the real darkness of nightfall, he said. And this was a film about darkness, about true darkness. So you couldn't fake it. It had to be real. In particular, and this made the task especially difficult, he wanted the *suddenness* of night falling. To create this effect, the Spanish dusk had to be prolonged by the use of arrays of powerful arc lamps. Then by extinguishing these lamps in swift succession, night was made to fall at one stroke. But with the time of the real nightfall changing daily, and natural light varying unpredictably, it was a complex business getting all the elements coordinated correctly. They were having to do endless numbers of takes to get it right. Strawley's method of shooting relied greatly on the interplay of accidental factors and his instantaneous reactions to them, and often it was only at the last moment that he would decide where exactly he was going to put the camera, where he wanted the extras, what the focus of the scene was going to be.

Before the start of shooting, he had observed the buzzards with their slow, heavy wing-beats circling around the edges of the dense vegetation, lying in wait for lizards and field mice emerging from the undergrowth. With their brick red or reddish brown backs and broad grey wings, their barred underbellies and short rufous tails, and their way of killing by still-hunting, these birds sparked off a chain of imagery in his mind that he was determined to get onto film. Having seen the birds circle overhead, on the lookout for small prey driven out by the flames of a grass fire, he conceived the idea that by making fires he'd be able to summon them at his command. There were already enough difficulties filming in the artificially prolonged dusk, and to these he now added the buzzards. Fires were lit, and seeing the flames from a distance the buzzards with their zoom eyes came silently plunging down for the kill. Jack wanted reaction shots of Kurtz and the dictator watching the birds hunt. To coordinate birds and actors proved to be a long business, and many hours were spent on getting these shots. At the end of ten days of shooting, the film was eight days behind schedule. Carver was chewing up cigars, screaming that the fucking buzzards and the sudden nightfall had cost half a million dollars, and all they had to show for it was maybe two minutes of usable screen time.

'Don't worry about it, Sydney,' Strawley told him, 'we're getting some great shots.'

'Of buzzards and darkness, yeah.'

'The film's about buzzards and darkness.'

By week three of the shoot the picture was two weeks and two days behind schedule. Carver referred to it as exponential regress. But Jack Strawley was very determined, and nobody could shake him from his resolve. This film was going to be made the way he wanted — it was going to be his 'masterwork' — and there'd be no compromises. One highly complicated shot, in the third week, to be done in a four-minute continuous take, called for break-away walls to be hoisted out of the camera crane's path. Assistant directors with headphones were synchronizing the action in different locales with the overall camera plot. The shot had already used up twenty takes, all of them spoilt. Toward the end of the day's shooting there was nothing in the can, and everybody was on overtime. Carver was tearing his hair out. And then, in the last ten minutes, Strawley got the whole scene on the twenty-first take.

'Okay, welcome back from the brink,' Carver said. 'Congratulations. It's a great shot that we almost didn't get. You going to give yourself a heart attack, you're going to give us all heart attacks. Make it a little less great and a little faster . . . *please,*

please. Because if this film goes down the toilet, we're all going down with it. You have any idea what a shot like that cost us?'

'You'll just have to steal a little less, Sydney.'

Carver tried to laugh, but the laugh stuck on his lips. 'Jack, I have New York screaming down the line three times a day, threatening to cancel the production . . . if we don't speed up. We're eyeball-to-eyeball with catastrophe here.'

'Hasn't happened so far.'

'Only got to happen once, baby.'

'I'm going to speed up,' Strawley said glinting, and Carver didn't know if this was a promise or a threat, but seeing what he took to be a faint sign of reasonableness he reminded Jack about Sylvia.

'You won't forget Sylvia, Jack. You going to find her something? Doesn't have to be big. Something where she'll be noticed.'

'She has no talent, Sydney. She doesn't even have tits.'

'I find her attractive. I'm . . . fond of her. Do something for her, Jack. I'm asking for a favour, haven't I done enough for you? Do I have to remind you?'

'Yeah, remind me, Sydney. It's slipped my mind.'

'I think you remember pretty well. Just ask yourself where you'd be today without me.'

'A lot richer.'

'You're paranoid.'

'Even paranoids get rolled.'

'I don't know why I take this shit from you.'

'Because you're still flying high on my coat-tails, Sydney. That's why. And you daren't let go.'

When Carver had gone, Strawley said to Moira, 'Keep him away from me, because I'm liable to kill him.'

'How can I keep the producer away? He signs the cheques. And hands out the liquid in the right places to keep this whole operation afloat.'

'Watch him for me, Moira. He has an evil aura, that man.'

She was trying hard to get Jack to eat, because most of the time he'd order meals at the hotel that he ended up not touching. Instead of eating he drank whisky and swallowed little brown pills which kept him going. He was getting great stuff on the screen, some of the footage looked truly amazing, but he was burning up nervous energy at a tremendous rate to do it, and she could not tell how much he had left in reserve. When he couldn't sleep, she came to his room and took notes that he gave her for the next day's shoot. Elaborately inventive notes that took little heed of practical or financial considerations, and none at all of other people's limits or frailties.

'If I keep going, so can they,' he said.

'You have a crazy kind of energy, Jack,' she warned. 'You keep going by driving everybody else crazy, but some don't have that outlet, and the strain is showing. There's somebody in tears every single day. It's becoming a very hysterical set. If you don't go easy on them, people are going to crack up. Nik's on the verge now . . . and you know Nik, he's liable to say fuck you all and take off . . . or have a heart attack.'

He shook his head up and down ruminatively. 'I can handle Nik. Nik's going to win an Oscar with his performance, I can do it for him, and he knows that, so I'm not worried about Nik even when he storms around. It's Carver from whom I get the bad vibes, he's eviltown.'

'Don't get obsessive about him, Jack.'

'He bugs me with his Gucci bags stuffed with the liquid. Fucking paying everybody off, mostly himself . . . out of my pocket!'

'Listen. They all do it. You just have to look out for yourself better.'

'Will you do that for me, Moira?'

'I always did, when you let me.'

'Do it.'

Jack Strawley kept changing his mind: he thought a scene should be played a certain way, then he saw it in rushes and decided it was all wrong, it was shit, and had to be redone in a different way, the opposite way from the way it had been done yesterday, then he decided that that didn't work either and reverted to the first way, which yesterday he'd said was shit.These continual changes of mind were costly not only in terms of production costs but also in terms of the actors' loss of faith in the director's directions, since they were liable to be reversed from one day to the next. And although he was causing the confusion and the tension, he blamed the actors and the technicians. He kept saying: 'I've never worked with such a bad crew, with such unprofessional actors.'

Moira warned him: 'You're going too far, Jack. They're not going to take much more. People are going to quit. Ease up.'

Whereupon he turned on her. 'Goddammit, Moira, don't tell me what I should do. I'll decide when I have to ease up, not when you tell me.'

'You told me to look out for your interests. That's what I'm doing.'

'You look out for my interests the way I tell you to.'

In the car, going back together to Seville, he apologized to her for his unreasoned outburst. 'You're doing good, Moira. Don't take any notice of me. I'm all messed up. Don't know where the fuck I'm going, what I'm doing. Don't know whom I can trust . . . apart from you, Moira. Because the others are all waiting for me to fall on my face. Including Nik. He's gotten to be . . . poisonous.' She knew the symptoms and said in the same practical, efficient voice as when she was asking about what time he wanted actors to be called next day: 'Want a girl?'

'Yeah,' he said. 'But I don't want a prostitute. Get me somebody young and fresh and real.'

'Did you like the Danish?' she asked him.

'Which one was that?'

'The one who was making eyes at you the other day, the journalist you wouldn't let on the set.'

'She was making eyes at me?'

'Yeah — she fancies you. She told me.'

'Don't believe it. She wants a story. Nobody fancies an old wreck like me.'

'You're not a wreck. You're just are driving yourself too hard, you're tired out . . .'

'Yeah, the Danish was all right, I vaguely remember.'

'Want to have dinner with her?'

'Oh, God no. Say I'm busy working until ten. Say I'll have dinner with her some other time. You have dinner with her,

Moira, and bring her up after. I want you there, Moira. I don't want to be left alone with her. I don't know what to say to these girls any more.'

'Poor guy, doesn't know what to say!'

Afterwards, when he'd had his little excitement, which was all in the coming towards, never in the realization — these girls had a way of disappearing as soon as you got close to them — he told Moira:

'What's beautiful about it is that you bring me these girls. You bring them to me . . . as an offering. That's what is so great. You were never jealous in that way. You always understood what that was about. Gloria never did. I should have married you. You are great, Moira. And smart. And know the ropes . . . all the different ropes. What I don't understand is why, pushy and bright as you are, you didn't get farther during all these years, why you're still other people's assistant. You deserve better.'

She gave a sour, self-mocking laugh. 'I'm taken for granted, that's why . . . I'm "good-ole-Moira'll-fix-it". I usually do too. Be it a hot ticket, or a production snarl-up, or a rotten marriage, or a little erectile problem, or whatever else besets the lives of the great. I fix it so good I'm not needed any more. Remember?'

'What happened to that project you had with Tony? Your Anais Nin script.'

'He went cold on it. Went cold on me same time.'

'He's crazy. Doesn't know what he lost.'

'Like someone else?'

'You're a great girl, Moira. You really are. You're the best.'

'I know, I know. Except . . . I'm no girl. I'm forty. Yeah, the years pass, don't they? I missed a lot of those famous boats that are supposed to come in for you if you wait. Not so many coming now.'

'One'll come for you one day, I'm sure of it.'

For the scene of Kurtz's final collapse, Jack Strawley had worked out an elaborate *mise-en-scène* that called for the rogue CIA man to be leaving the presidential palace after having witnessed something that has brought about in him a deep, if belated, sense of moral revulsion. Walking through the dusty hot streets, he is coughing and choking, drinking from a hip flask and sweating. And when he gets to his apartment building, the elevator isn't working. There's no electricity, the country's falling apart, and he has to walk up six flights of stairs. The camera was required to follow his progress, from outside the building, as he climbs to the top of the grey-white concrete pile. He's going up and up, becoming drunker and drunker. At the top he collapses into a messy pile-up of flesh, a beached whale of a man.

The camera was set up on a narrow crane platform which had to hold the lighting cameraman, his operator, and the director, all in one tight space. On the ground two burly Spanish grips were working the hydraulic fulcrum lever to raise the platform in sync with the actor going up the stairs. Nik's drunken progress from floor to floor was carefully timed with stopwatches, and, while the cameras rolled, an assistant director inside the building signalled to an assistant director outside the building exactly where Nik was on the stairs, and the second assistant director passed on the info to the grips raising the platform. If the timing was off even slightly, Jack called 'Cut' and signalled for another take. Nik was having to go up the stairs again and again and he was getting pretty exhausted. Jack didn't want it done by the stand-in. He wanted Nik's face: he wanted to see it crumble . . . the disintigration of Kurtz. Nik was raging at this treatment, calling Jack a fucking sadist, shouting that the whole production had got out of control and he'd had enough and was quitting. At this point Jack came down from the crane and himself climbed the stairs and got down on his knees next to Nik. He put his arm around the actor in a hug of iron.

'Nik, I know you're exhausted, but this is going to be such a great scene for you, it'll be one of the highpoints of the film. This scene will be remembered. We've got to get it right. This is where he starts to break, and sees "the horror, the horror". That's what breaks him. He's poisonous and mad. Maybe he's been poisonous and mad all along, but this is the point where he knows it, and that's the horror. That's what this scene is about.'

'You want me to play him mad in this scene?'

Jack Strawley thought about it for half a minute, in silence, nodding his head up and down slowly. 'Yes,' he said finally. 'Try that.'

'Before, you said to play him "terribly sane".'

'He's terribly sane too. That's right, that's right. They're not that far apart, Nik. You understand what I'm saying? Things fall apart. They just fall apart. That's how it is, that's the process. Things fall apart. '

Jack Strawley's face was a sodden, grey sponge. He had a tumbler of whisky in his hand from which he sipped meditatively, every so often, keeping the alcohol level in his bloodstream constant. He didn't let himself get any drunker than this, nor any soberer.

Nik, jagged-edged, without a drink all day — when he was acting he laid off it — said: 'Jack! make up your mind: IS HE MAD OR IS HE TERRIBLY SANE?'

Jack Strawley gave a sphinxy smile. 'What d'you think, Nik? Play it the way you feel. Mad or sane . . . whichever.'

The buzzards were getting on everybody's nerves now with their unsummoned presence. 'You're not on call, not on call,' Jack Strawley shouted at them as they clustered on the telephone wires and the trees, waiting to pounce. Finally, their constant presence annoyed Jack Strawley so much that, having finished with them, he ordered them shot. Two Spanish crew members arrived with carbines and blasted them bloodily out of the sky.

In the middle of all the turbulences besetting the shooting, Strawley amazingly found time to give his attention to a question of his billing. He'd decided that he wasn't going to share his major billing with Evil Carver and instructed Moira to phone New York and tell them that. What he wanted was solo billing above the title, in the same size as the title, so that it would read:

JACK STRAWLEY'S
HEART OF DARKNESS

All other names, above or below the title, including 'A NorthStar

Production', had to be smaller than his name. Carver could have a producer's card in a separate frame in the main credits, before the final credit card which was to read: 'Written, produced and directed by Jack Strawley.' There'd be a separate card saying: 'based on the novel by Joseph Conrad and an original screenplay by Carl Schmidlin'.

He wanted a new clause in his contract, specifying that on all hoardings and marquees and advertisements, anywhere that the film's title appeared, his name would appear the same size, and that it would not be linked, as previously, with Carver's in the logo: 'A Strawley/Carver Production.' That formula was dead. Carver was dead. 'This'll be the last time I let him ride on my coat-tails,' he told Moira.

Though far from happy, she accepted her instructions and phoned New York to relay Jack Strawley's demands. She was told that there were already enough other problems on this production: the size and form of credits were not to the forefront of their minds, right now, and, in any case, changes to contracts already agreed and signed could only be made by mutual agreement, and furthermore NorthStar could not impose on exhibitors a legal obligation to always couple Strawley's name with the title of the film. There might be marquees and other spaces where there was room only for the title. That was their official reply. Unofficially they said to Moira: 'What kind of megalo shit is this?'

She wrapped up their reply with diplomacy, alluding to legal formulas and guild rules, but he saw through all that and was furious.

'Syd-the-Knife doesn't just rob me of profit participation, I'm also robbed of my rightful credit.'

'Wait, Jack,' she advised him. 'If the film's as great as we think — as we know — it will be, we'll get everything we want. Wait till you're in a better negotiating position. It's not the moment now.'

'What d'you mean not the moment? The rushes are great.'

'I know, I know. But the costs, Jack. The costs.'

The storyboards with which Strawley was annotating the script were becoming increasingly menacing in aspect as the film moved towards Kurtz's discovering that the likeable young Marlow has been sent to 'remove' him.

Under the image of Marlow, Jack had written 'the myrmidon'.

39

In the thick of all that strife and mounting paranoia — he'd say with much acrimonious mirth that it was a case of 'the survival of the most paranoid' — we were putting in an average of a couple of hours a night at the tape recorder. He was having trouble sleeping, and these sessions served to fill the sleepless hours with what seemed like purposeful work at the same time as ridding him of what he called 'the heavy stuff' in his mind. He was searching for an underlying 'form' in his life, the hidden pattern of events that had taken him to the present point, and my being there, tape recorder running, gave him a sense of structure. Something that his life singularly lacked.

He'd phone through to my room in the middle of the night, mumbling, 'Hey, I wake you up, Stephen? Sorry. Look, I'm not sleeping. And you can sleep tomorrow, so how about us doing some work on the book?' I usually said okay, because I could sense the underlying urgency behind the casual request, and it seemed to me I could not refuse.

As soon as the tape recorder was switched on and he could see the spools turning, Jack would start talking. I'd try to keep him to some sort of storyline, feeding him dates or other kinds of prompts, but he wouldn't stay with any preordained structure.

'Putting it in the right order's your job, Stephen, you're the one's got to find the structure,' he snapped back peremptorily.

Having rid himself of that bothersome responsibility, he was chasing along whatever trails of memories the day's events had evoked in him. I wanted to call the book 'Bad Continuity' and let his thoughts and memories pour out in disorderly fashion, but he said no, he believed in storyline, the book had to have continuity, and I'd have to put that in. That was what he was paying me for, although he hadn't paid me a penny so far: to give his life a structure! If it was just going to be chaotic outpourings, he didn't need me for that. And so he dug around in his past, looking for his 'invisible mistakes', and his mistimings, and reminiscing sardonically about all those trains he'd got on that you couldn't get off once you were on them. I tried to steer him as best I could, but with all the tensions of the production, and the psychological and emotional strains that he was under, and his drinking, and his fury in regard to past and to present events, it was impossible to keep him en route.

Some nights there were calls from Fred Spinola, the president of NorthStar. These became more frequent and highly charged as the overages kept mounting. 'Fred,' I heard him shout down a crackling line, 'you want it good or you want it cheap? It's hot here, we are working with talented, temperamental people and they're not remote-control toys you can wind up from your air-conditioned nightmare, and nor am I. We are getting great material on screen. And it's going to go faster now. We've solved a lot of the major problems. Listen, I don't even have the time to think about stuff like that with all the other stuff I have to think about . . . we had to have those air-conditioning units. We had to have the ice-making units. They were essential. You try working in this heat. The stages are furnaces, how d'you expect people to stay sane? You want us murdering each other down here? That's gonna happen soon. I know I will carry the can. I know that, I know that. Fred, if you're at all unhappy, just say so and I'll call Warners, they'll take the picture off your hands any time. I did it with you because you wanted it so bad, and you promised hands off. If you want to change your mind, I'll talk to Warners. Fred, that's entirely up to you, if you want to incur the extra expense . . . let 'em all come, you come too, make it a junket.'

When he'd hung up, he turned to me with a frenzied smile, a hold-on-tight smile. 'He's going to send out his "guys" — his myrmidons! To check us out. Like we're putting money in our own pockets. That's what it always comes down to, the money. The deals. The points, the cuts . . . the percentage. Who's going to make what out of this. God!' He shook his head with great sadness that the world should turn out to be so venal. 'You always end up paying, like I've been paying Sydney all my goddamn life, and still he's not paid off. You play the future. You sign away this little piece and that little piece. A percentage of this, a percentage of that, it's only 2%, it's only 5%, it's only 10%. When you've added it all up, you're in up to the neck and you don't own yourself anymore.' He fixed me with his mock-smiling eyes so that you couldn't know how seriously he wanted you to take any of this and then demanded fiercely: 'Tell me, will you, how can we be sure, how can we be sure, Stephen, any of us, that we are not imposters? That we are who we tell ourselves we are?'

There was often a discrepancy between the painted smile on his face and what he was saying, the two just didn't fit together. There were self-contained compartments of his mind that I was not let into, and then suddenly one of the sealed hatches burst open and it all poured out.

'God, he's an evil man. Been robbing me for years. I'm talking about the Carver. Cross-collateralizes his other ventures with mine, so I'm paying for his losses out o' my profits. Filters it all through these companies in the Dutch Antilles. Which put up the completion guarantees. It's to do with end money, and I don't know what.' He waved his hands about in flurries to designate ever-growing mountains of indescribable financial manoeuvring. 'I still haven't learned things the Carver was born knowing, like what "off the top" means or what is 3½% of 70%. The fact is it's the distributors who make the money out of films, not the producers, so Sydney manages to wear two hats, he does distribution deals for our films, and the distributor never loses money, and Sydney manages via the Dutch Antilles to be distributor and producer at the same time. You've got to talk to Riesner about all that stuff. I'm not a financier, which is evident from my finances. Riesner, my accountant whom I can't afford and can't afford not be able to afford, he'll tell you how it's done. You know, I don't want to sound *too* obsessional about this, but the only kinds of women he can do it with — the Carver — are those in his power that he can humiliate. Little publicity girls or typists that can't type whose uncle . . . and oh yeah . . . almost forgot they've got to be called Chloe or Daphne or Sybil or Deirdre, for Christ sake. Or Sylvia, can you imagine? Who is Sylvia, what is she? Got to be coltish otherwise he can't get it up. The Carver can't get it up with somebody called Ruth or Jane or Jean.'

By now he was talking very fast, without stops, running one sentence into the next, cutting off phrases, a cacafuego of foaming words. There was an odd kind of inappropriateness in some of the things he said and did at this time. His words were the wild and venomous utterances of somebody who felt himself in a corner. 'I know you're not supposed to mock the misshapen but Sydney's dwarf cock is so eminently mockable . . . see, the length's all in his arms, in his grabbing greedy arms. God shrunk the rest. . . .' He emitted a richly exaggerated chuckle, really over the top now. He couldn't stop, having got started, and was finding himself enormously funny. 'See he can do it better with his nose gets in anywhere with his nose no squeamishness where that overlarge organ of thrust is concerned he'll push it in any crack the dirtier the better and get there and get there where the shit-gold is he's a lousy producer . . . doesn't know nothin' about movies has terrible taste Christ you should see his women he likes them "coltish" well, you've seen Sylvia.' Another wild chuckle, followed by sad regret and a huge effort to slow down his speeding mind. Braking, braking hard. 'Don't know why I kept him around all these years. Hell, I'm not the best person to explain why I do anything. You heard of the death of the author theory that the Frenchboys invented? Well, treat me as dead.' He was doing some exercise to slow his breathing. Sombrely taking charge of himself. 'I'm an unreliable witness of my own life. So don't take any notice . . . just treat me as a dead author.'

Did I realize that he was stretched too tight and about to snap? There were times during the filming of *Heart of Darkness* when I thought he was talking pretty crazily and acting pretty crazy too, but I had been around a lot of people in the movie business who were big drinkers and manics and I had seen them take off on great big binges of words and alcohol and sex and God knows what else. I'd seen them raise hell and next day I'd seen them sobered up, down-to-earth, honoured citizens. The bigger they were, the better they were able to get away with it. It's only when the outside world doesn't go along with the crazes that it's called madness, and, when you are successful enough, the outside world doesn't consider you mad. And I have to admit that neither did I consider Jack mad at this point. I could see that his mind was poised at an edge but I didn't feel he had gone over it . . . yet. Movie history abounds with stories about the excessive behaviour of great directors: there was the case of Stroheim getting those extras burnt during the making of *Foolish Wives*, and there are plenty of other examples. A great director's behaviour could always be justified on the basis that it's better for others to have the nervous breakdowns because, after all, he's the one who has got to bring in the film. 'Yeah, Jack was a little crazy out there in Seville,' people said afterwards, but at the time, while he was functioning — that was the sole criterion — and getting magical images on film, nobody, myself included, thought any of it was what you would call *really* mad.

40

At first sight, the myrmidons didn't look too bad. Their suits were lightweight with narrow lapels, narrow shoulders and loose-waisted jackets. The big kid with the big glasses was in beige gabardine, the wiry one in plain linen. Their shirts were decorously white, unostentatious, with button-down collars, and, despite the stifling heat, they both wore ties, narrow and of plain colours. Their shoes were loafers. They didn't carry their badge of office, the brief case. They were non-smokers and young and relaxed, and determinedly unencumbered. One of them was called Dave, Dave Grunwald, and he had a large, round, freckled, eager young kid's face with auburn tousled hair and huge wire frame glasses and a big friendly grin. He was about thirty something but looked twenty something. The other one, Tim Tomkins, was taller and had a wiry build and an amusedly knowing expression, a slightly turned down mouth and a calm way of hooking his thumbs into his trouser belt like the good guy in a Western waiting for the bad guy to draw first. They were deferential and played down any power they might have vis-à-vis such an important artist of the cinema as Jack Strawley, making only laughing roundabout allusions to the reason for their presence in Seville. 'One of our rare chances to get outta the air-conditioned nightmare,' they said grinning.

While all of them were having a drink in the silk-walled Alphonse XIII bar, Jack Strawley found a hand in his pocket. Caught in the act, the pickpocket gave an elegant little shrug and delicately withdrew the hand with a muttered, 'Excuse me,' as if it were a case of inadvertently brushing against someone in a crowded place. It had been done with such sleek furtiveness that it almost resembled a sexual approach.

'Fella there,' Jack Strawley said, indicating him casually to the others, 'you'd think he was an aesthetic surgeon or something, wouldn't you? Well, no. Actually he's a pickpocket. Put his hand in my pocket just now. Just goes to show you can never know whose hand you'll find in your pocket, huh? Just watch him. See how good he is? Almost as good as Sydney.' It was said with a broad kidding grin, and everybody chuckled, except Carver. Lately, he wasn't so amused by jokes against himself.

The young execs seemed altogether too amiable and polite to get around to what they had come here for, and to help them out Jack Strawley said: 'I know you fellas are worried about costs. And to prove to you how economical we are here, I'm going to take you to a real cheap place to eat. It happens also to be the best. It's a great tapas bar, a little crowded, that's all.'

The place he took them to was indeed crowded, as he had

warned, but Carver with swift strike action got them the one table that was just becoming free. There were people at the bar who'd been waiting half an hour or more for the table, but the Carver didn't believe in waiting and sat down, unashamedly, before the current occupants had all got up to leave, thus hurrying the laggards on their way while at the same time preempting other claimants. '*Occupado, occupado*,' he smilingly snarled at belated hoverers, flapping his arms to disperse them.

Soon the appropriated table was heaped with a colourful array of small delicious dishes: Jamon de Guijuelo, Tortillitas Sevillanas, Filete de Pez Espada. Jack told them to bring all the specialities, and they were regaled with amazing cured hams, Spanish omelettes, meats in pepper sauce and combinations of smoked fishes and bacon-wrapped giant shrimps.

In the course of their light conversation, the freckled one, Dave Grunwald, admitted shyly to having a Ph.D in Classics: he had done his thesis on the Aristotelian principles of drama as manifested in American TV crime series. The second exec, Tim, had majored in pre-Rennaissance Italian art before going on to do a year as a foreign student at the Ecole Normale Supérieure in Paris. And he spoke good Spanish as well!

'Didn't know Fred recruited his myrmidons from the intelligentsia nowadays,' said Jack Strawley.

'Oh, I know what people say about Fred,' Tim Tomkins admitted knowingly. 'But don't you believe it. Fred is smart. Fred is dead smart. It's easy to knock him, what's not easy is to fault his record. He knows what the paying public wants to see — and what they don't want to see — and in the end it's they who are our lords and masters.'

'Great food here,' Dave Grunwald said, 'but kinda noisy for talking . . . huh?' He looked around uneasily: their American voices were a powerful magnet to shoe-shine boys and street-vendors and beggars. They were constantly having to be waved away. He moved his chair closer to Jack Strawley's and said with intimate sincerity: 'What I think Tim is trying to say is that ultimately everything has to be performance-related.'

'That what he's trying to say?'

The elderly shoe-shine boy who had been waved away just a

minute ago from one side of the table was back on the other side now, trying to get in there. Sydney Carver said: 'Yeah, okay,' and, indicating the others, added expansively: 'All of them.' Jack said he didn't want his shoes shone, they were okay without any shine.

'Have them shone,' Carver insisted. 'It's on me.'

'See how he spends money,' Jack Strawley told the young execs. 'Now you know why we're two million over.'

The shoe-shiner sat on the floor, brushes and rags and jars of polish spread around him. After dipping his gnarled stained fingers into the black cream, he spread it deeply into every crease and crack of Sydney Carver's lordly British shoes, hand-made in Jermyn Street from the finest, softest of leathers. Looking downward and observing with what conscientiousness the wizened old man applied the polish, massaging it profoundly into the leather, Carver took from the edge of his plate a scrap of Guijuelo cured ham, consisting largely of fat, that he had felt disinclined to eat himself, and held it with two fingers above the face of the sweating man, tickling his dark, lined and cracked face with it until he responded by opening his mouth and snapping the fatty morsel into his jaws. Now he tackled the shoes with renewed vigour, polishing the leather with a variety of cloths and finally with the sleeve of his ragged old jacket, until the shoes had become black mirrors.

Dave Grunwald was in the course of explaining their position:

'Basically, Jack, remember we're on your side, don't go thinking we're a bunch of morons in the front office who don't appreciate quality — we *fought* for this picture, Jack. Tim and I fought for it. I'm telling you that not to sing our own praises but to convey to you how much we *care* about this project. We said to Fred, we have got to make this picture, it's a duty to ourselves, to the company, otherwise why are we in this business, might as well be manufacturing . . . uh, shoe polish . . . and Fred said, all praise to him, fellas, he said, I wouldn't want to keep you from your duty . . . make the picture, fellas!'

The shoe-shine boy, having finished with Carver's shoes, had crawled along the floor pushing his tubes and tins and rags and brushes ahead of him, until he was at Dave Grunwald's feet. In mid-sentence, becoming aware of the frenzied dark straining face below him, of nimble blackened fingers fervently working at his feet, Dave Grunwald absent-mindedly followed Sydney Carver's example and found some scraps on his plate to drop into the shoe-shiner's mouth.

'. . . here's what I want to say,' he was saying, building up to it, 'the thing is, we have a duty to our profession as film-makers but we also have a duty to our stockholders, and, in the climate of today, that doesn't give us a lot of leg-room. If you can't show sustained *growth,* they hit you over the head via the share price . . . and that is something you cannot ignore because you can be flushed down the toilet before you know it. Jack, you have made wonderful profitable films in the past, and this one can be too, but we're two million bucks down the drain and four weeks behind schedule . . . and that is a pretty serious situation to be in.'

Sydney Carver, calm and restrained, said: 'Dave, it's a situation that we are very fully aware of and can remedy. I've worked with Jack on twelve films. I know his work pattern. He starts off slow and then he speeds up. That's his style. This is his speeding-up phase now. You just watch him. You'll be amazed how he can speed up. We had a lot of start-up problems at the start. But we can catch up. Believe me.'

Tim Tomkins, whose shoes were currently being shone, frowned briefly downward and then, clearing his brow, said: 'I'd sure like to believe that. You saying you can bring the film in on schedule and within budget?'

Carver considered the question gravely, honestly. 'No, Tim,' he said at last, 'in all honesty I cannot say that. I'm not saying that we can do miracles. I'm not in the miracle business, I'm in the movie business. What I'm saying is the haemorrhage can be stopped, will be stopped, and some of the lost time made up. Jack will back that up, I'm sure. Jack . . .'

Tim Tompkins, hand stuck easily in his gun-belt, but conveying a bland promise on his face that on no account would he draw first, turned to Jack Strawley for the promised back up.

'Yeah, I'll back that up.'

They were waiting for something more detailed, more persuasive, but he didn't seem to have anything more to offer just then. Grunwald and Tompkins exchanged looks.

'Think,' said Dave Grunwald, 'we'd better show you what we have in mind.' He slid a neat hand inside his breast pocket and with some delicacy extracted a couple of sheets of NorthStar notepaper embossed with the logo of a star of many rays. 'Here's our action plan. In summary,' he said, handing the sheets to Jack Strawley 'it takes into account costs so far incurred that we cannot now realistically expect to recoup. This is a plan relating to future costs. It specifies that production costs have to be kept to the approved budget unless there is specific authorization from Tim or myself or another designated NorthStar executive.'

The plan, he explained, while rigorous, was realistic and need not affect quality. He asked Jack to study it and to say by tomorrow whether or not he felt able to comply with its provisions. Quickly running his eye down the tables of figures making up the 'final revised budget', Jack Strawley seemed untroubled, was nodding steadily, casually.

'I can see Fred's myrmidons are reasonable guys,' he said, 'and being reasonable myself . . . we'll do it.'

'Don't agree until you've had a chance to study it,' Dave Grunwald warned. 'We want you to know exactly what you're agreeing to, so please study the figures carefully. We'll come out to the lot tomorrow and, provided you're able to accept the terms, we can go home.'

'Sounds okay,' Jack Strawley said, handing the 'plan' to Moira to look over while the rest of them continued talking pleasantly — about Spain and Franco and what was going to happen after his death, and they talked of bullfighting and the mysterious beauty of the confrontation between man and bull, and of current shake-outs in the movie business, and then Moira looked up from the 'plan' and she had worked out some figures with paper and pencil.

'It's very, very tight,' she said. 'A lot of it is difficult to do but just about do-able. If things all fall right. Some items, however, are simply not do-able, and we should say that straight away so as not to arouse false expectations.'

'What's not do-able?' tousle-haired Dave asked mildly.

'It's going to be hellish difficult, for example, to reduce daily travel time. I know that travel is taking three hours out of an eight-hour day, but the Spanish crews have got family and girl-friends in Seville that they want to go back to . . . and, anyway, unless we all stay in hotels too, and there aren't enough of those close by, what are the crews going to be doing while we're making our way out? If crew members quit that will cost us a lot more in hold-ups than we can hope to save.'

'What else is a problem?' Tim asked, thumb in belt, quietly looking at Dave.

'I'd rather not say off the top of my head. I'd rather do some detailed calculations and give you exact figures of what is and what isn't.'

'You do that, Moira. Have it for us by tomorrow. When we come out to the filming,' Dave said.

'I'll try.'

'We can do it,' Jack Strawley said. 'Moira'll do the figures, but I can tell you now, we can do it.'

'Well, I'm glad,' Dave Grunwald said. 'But Moira's right. Work it out carefully. Because you're going to be asked to sign a binding legal undertaking, Jack. To the effect that not one single item of additional expenditure will be incurred without a specific signature of approval from either Tim or myself.'

'Yeah, that's okay,' Jack Strawley said easily.

'And that any expenditure incurred without such approval from us will be paid for by you, Jack, out of your own pocket.'

'That's fine, that's fine,' Jack said. 'I have no problem with that.'

'And remember, Jack, this is on top of your existing guaran-tees, not in place of them.'

'Fine, fine.'

The evening ended very cordially, Fred's myrmidons saying that the stuff they had seen was great, if rather long. They were sure it was going to be a fine and profitable film, provided costs were strictly controlled henceforth.

41

Next morning, Grunwald and Tomkins were driven from Seville to the lot in a studio car, Tomkins timing the length of the
journey on his Rolex chronometer, and he and Grunwald had to
admit that not much could be shaved off travelling time.

At the entrance to the movie set city, they were stopped and
barred from going further by one of the Spanish policemen on
duty. He said he had orders from Signor Strawley to let nobody
onto the set whose name wasn't on the call sheet. Tim Tomkins
made use of his good Spanish to explain exactly who they were,
giving their full titles in the NorthStar hierarchy, explaining
patiently that Mr Strawley's instructions did not apply to them.
But the Spanish policeman said they applied to everyone, and no
exceptions could be made. That was what Signor Strawley had
said. No exceptions. The execs asked that Carver be called, and
he arrived within a few minutes and told the Spanish policeman
that he was taking these gentlemen onto the set, but the policeman was adamant, he had his instructions from Mr Strawley, and
not only could the two American gentlemen not go on, Carver
couldn't either. By now two other Spanish policemen had come
to the gate to back up their colleague. 'I'm the producer of this
film, I'm the one who pays your salaries,' Carver told them,
making a strenuous effort to smile. Yes, they knew who he was,
they said, but they'd been told by Mr Strawley not to let *anyone*
on. The set was closed. Even crew members were not allowed
on, if they were not directly involved in the scene. Carver demanded that Moira come out to see him, and she arrived within
ten minutes. She said, worriedly, that it was true, the set had been
closed: Jack was filming a difficult scene. It involved Sylvia. She
hoped they would all understand. 'It's a nude scene,' she added
apologetically.

Carver didn't know whether to be angry or pleased about this.

'What kind of a nude scene?' he demanded. 'I know nothing
about any nude scene. I haven't been told.' He turned to the
young execs with a kidding air of being affronted. 'I'm the

producer and even I don't know about it. Sylvia didn't even tell me.'

'She didn't know until this morning.'

'Be that as it may,' Dave Grunwald said, his big freckled face showing signs of crumpling into peevishness. 'Jack knew we were coming today. Why'd he have to do this scene today? He knows we have to settle these vitally important matters. Why couldn't he have filmed this scene another time? Why didn't he tell us last night about this scene? Why let us come out if he can't see us?'

'I don't think he knew last night that he was going to do this scene today,' Moira said uncomfortably.

'It wasn't scheduled?' Tim Tomkins asked.

'It was a scene that Jack realized he needed. I think he may have forgotten about you coming out,' Moira explained.

'That's very disappointing,' Dave Grunwald said. 'I thought last night that we were moving towards an agreement, but this is,' he shook his head with an air of having been badly wronged, 'a setback.'

'I realize that,' Moira said, 'and I apologize on Jack's behalf. He gets very caught up in what he's doing and forgets . . . about other things.'

'That's evident from the way costs have gone completely out of control,' Dave Grunwald commented. He exchanged looks with his colleague, Tim Tomkins, and then said with an air of patient reasonableness: 'Here's what I propose, Moira. Why don't you go in and talk to Jack. Since you think he may have forgotten, I suggest you remind him of what was arranged last night, point out to him we're here waiting, and that it's essential for us to see him so we can come to terms, in order for the production to continue.' He paused to let the threat sink in. Measuring each word, he went on: 'Let him finish this take. Let the girl put some clothes on. And as soon as she has, we'll come on the set, or he can come out, whichever he prefers. While the next shot is being set up, we should be able to clinch this whole thing . . . provided he's ready to accept the terms we discussed last night.'

Moira went away and came back fifteen minutes later, looking pale and upset.

'I'm sorry,' she said, 'I don't know what to say, I'm embarrassed. He won't let you on the set. And he won't come out. Sometimes he can be very . . . fixed. He says no way can he break the mood of this crucial scene that he's doing in order to talk to you about finances. It would completely destroy his concentration. You'll have to excuse him. He'll see you this evening at the hotel. He apologizes, hopes you'll understand.'

The execs looked at each other with an air of bewilderment. Finally Dave said: 'There's no nude scene in the script I have.'

'It's a new scene.' She looked very uneasy, averting her eyes from the two executives and from Carver.

'It was agreed last night that there weren't going to be any new scenes without the prior approval of Tim or myself. That was the basis of our understanding last night,' Dave Grunwald pointed out.

'Jack decided it was needed,' Moira said. 'It's a scene that directly leads up to Kurtz's big breakdown scene which we filmed a few days ago. Jack decided the new scene is necessary to show Kurtz beginning to crack.'

The scene was going to be done in a single shot to create a claustrophobic feeling, and, for the same reason, the art director, Percy Drummer, had substantially lowered the ceiling of the late Francoist general's wine cellar, which meant everybody was going about stooped. The ceiling was a crumbling, leaky concave. The impression was of being inside some filthy dripping underground culvert, lit by a single electric light bulb at the end of an extension lead. The lamp was to be hand-held by one of the policemen and shone into the face of the girl being questioned, and sometimes it would shine directly into the camera.

Earlier, Jack had had Sylvia brought onto the set.

'Sydney was telling me the other day what a good swimmer you are.'

'Yes, I am rather good,' she admitted.

'Good at the underwater stuff?'

'Oh yes, rather. You mean snorkelling and . . .'

'What about without a snorkel?'

'Underwater swimming?'

'You know about holding your breath . . . and all that?'

'Oh, I do, yes. Of course.'

'How long can you hold your breath under water? Fifteen seconds, twenty seconds? Twenty-five?'

'Oh, I can do that all right. That's no problem for me.'

'You have any problem about appearing nude?'

'Nude?' She gave a strained little laugh.

'Yeah. If you do have some problem about that, tell me right now, so we don't waste time.'

'It's a nude swimming scene, is it?'

'Well, no . . . they're not exactly doing nude swimming.'

'What kind of a scene is it?'

'It's a torture scene. Okay?'

He seemed preoccupied and not ready to tell her much more about the scene before she'd agreed to do it, and she gave a laughing frown and said quickly, so that he wouldn't get the idea she was unwilling or difficult: 'Well, if it's a good scene . . . and as long as it's artistically *called for*, I don't really mind what I do.' She gave a slightly hysterical little laugh.

'Yeah, that's what I gather from Sydney.'

'I'm game,' she said chirpily. 'I'd be very happy to . . . Thank you for giving me the chance. I appreciate . . .'

He cut off her formal expression of thanks. 'Go and talk to Moira. She'll fill you in about it.'

Nik Ransom, as Kurtz, was squashed in a stooped position in a corner of the cellar where the walls glistened with damp penetration. The shot was to begin on Kurtz, sweating profusely, watching something going on off-camera. He hears low voices, a girl's choked cries, cut-off screams, gasps. He hears scuffling. Violent movements. Water sounds. Frenzied splashing. A desperate gasping for air. The camera trails along the dirt floor and up over the claw legs of an old iron bath tub, very rusty on the outside, very chipped and grimy and discoloured with rusty water marks inside. In the crumbling plaster around the tub there are the imprints of clawing, bleeding fingers. A thick, hairy arm with rolled-up sleeve and coarse fingers is pressing down on a girl's face half-submerged in scummy water, hair floating in bodily effluvia. The face is going under in a fit of choking, the heavy hand pumping down. The head surfacing. Questions being shouted at the head. To which the head does not reply. As a result of which the head is pushed under again and again and held down for longer periods each time — ten seconds, fifteen, twenty . . . 'Cut!' Strawley called. He told Sylvia: 'You're not shivering, dear. It's an ice cold bath. I want you shivering so your teeth rattle. Once more from the top. Action.'

The operator with the camera harnessed to his body moved shakily over Nik's face in the same tight trajectory as before, but when he came to the bath-tub, Jack Strawley wasn't satisified.

'Cut! Cut! I can't see her shivering. Bathwater's too warm. It's supposed to be glacial! It's not a warm bath, dear. It's so cold your lips are blue, dear. Your tiny hand is frozen, baby. I want you to rattle your teeth . . . I want to see goose-pimples. Jimmy, run the cold on full. And let's have some ice in there.' The cold tap was opened full, containers from the ice-making unit were emptied into the bath-tub, and, in a minute, Sylvia was shivering convulsively, and her teeth were rattling, and her lips were blue. Strawley called: 'That's much better. Action!' He gave a signal, and the secret policeman once more leaned towards the girl, took a bunch of her wet hair in his massive fist and pushed her head under the water. Strawley counted silently and then gave the signal for the actor to let go of her head. 'That was better,' Strawley said. 'But it's got to be rougher, Pedro.' The Spanish actor playing the torturer was beginning to get the feel of the scene now, entering into it fully. This time when he held the girl's head under, the count was longer, and, on being released, Sylvia's gasping for air was harsh and laboured and realistic, and her teeth rattled to Jack Strawley's entire satisfaction. But still it wasn't quite right. He wanted it done again. He instructed: 'One more time, Sylvia. Hope this isn't too much for you. You managing?'

'Freezing to death,' she said, shivering violently but gamely. 'I'm okay. Just about.'

'Good girl,' he said. 'Big breath now. Make this a good one, Pedro, so we can wrap it up.' On the call of 'Action', Pedro pushed the head under again, and the scummy bathwater was

churning with the girl's violent struggle as she fought against the
big hand holding her down. There were clusters of air bubbles in
the scum. For one instant the screaming head rose up as from the
dead and before it could utter its scream was pushed under again.
And held down . . . and down. It was getting to be long. Pedro
was waiting for the signal to let go, but for some reason the
director was not giving it, and the water was being churned up
more and more violently, and finally the actor felt that he couldn't
hold the heaving head down any longer and let go, and Sylvia
came up spluttering and choking and retching.

'Don't ever do that again, don't ever cut a scene before I've
said "Cut",' Jack Strawley told the actor.

'Jack, she was in trouble,' Moira told him quietly. 'You can't
blame Pedro, you lost count. If he hadn't let go . . .'

'She's a good underwater swimmer.That's what she told me.
She said she was okay.'

'You lost count, Jack. You kept her under too long.'

'I think it worked well that time,' he said, pleased.

'Jack, she almost drowned!'

'Now don't exaggerate, Moira. She played it well. Good girl!'
he called to the shivering frightened girl, now wrapped in towels,
shaking, unsure of what had happened. 'Very good, Sylvia. We'll
print the last one,' he said, turning to Moira once more, 'that was
definitely the best one.'

The NorthStar executives had cancelled their return flight and
were meeting with Moira and Carver in the latter's suite.

'I wanna know what happened today,' eager Dave said, fixing
his eye sternly on Moira.

Carver was in a state of grim silent rage.

'There was a control failure,' Moira said quietly.

'Whaddyuh mean, Moira?'

'We — Jack — temporarily lost control of the situation.'

'Temporarily? This production seems to have been out of
control virtually from day one,' Tim Tompkins said, hands dangling loose now.

Moira was still not looking at anyone, speaking into the middle distance quietly. 'Jack's a perfectionist, and this film means a

lot to him. It's a project he's had for years. I think maybe he has driven himself and others too hard. I think he realizes that now and will ease up. Today he got so absorbed in the scene that he lost track of how long Sylvia's head had been underwater. The actor should have let go sooner, but they're all scared of Jack, and Pedro was waiting for the signal . . . which didn't come. It was a *grave* mistake on Jack's part. Jack's deeply sorry, of course, and he'd like to make it up to Sylvia. Incidentally — I know this doesn't excuse it in any way, but I saw the rushes, and the scene is amazing. Amazing and truly horrifying. It is *so* real. It says everything about that situation, about those people, and about the state that Kurtz has reached.'

'And the state that Jack has reached,' Carver added with sombre satisfaction that his air of sorrow couldn't entirely mask. A long silence developed in the room with nobody looking at anyone else. The freckled boyishness of Dave Grunwald's face behind the big glasses seemed to be undergoing rapid ageing.

'Look,' he said. 'Today a girl's life was put in danger for reasons that, at best, could be termed insane perfectionism, at worst . . . murderous acting out of some . . . some . . . personal grudge or grievance, or whatever. Secondly, the understanding reached last night that there would be no departures from the agreed script and schedule without Tim's, or my, approval was flagrantly breached, less than a day after it had been agreed upon. He just went ahead and did what he wanted, while we were kept off the set . . . I mean that's as flagrant as you can get.' His tone was one of pain, of a man who had been sorely disappointed — and misled. He was shaking his head in incredulity and mild outrage. 'This production is two million dollars over-budget. His overages have eaten up half the entire budget of a film we were due to start this week, and that film must now be put in turnaround, and the costs already incurred on it may have to be permanently written off . . . Tim and I took the decision to finance *Heart of Darkness* because of our admiration for Jack's work, against the grave misgivings of Fred, who was all along against the project and, as company president, could have vetoed it, and only gave his approval,' he shook his head several times by way of indicating his hurt at having been so let down, 'as a gesture of faith in Tim's and my judgement. If that judgement is now proven to have been faulty, Tim and I will carry the can. Our jobs are on the line. Not to mention Fred's. And if we go down the toilet with this one, the whole company may go down with us. That's how potentially disastrous it is. And Jack, who just doesn't grasp any of this at all, blithely goes on.'

He paused to stare at Carver, to see if any of what he was saying was going to be rebutted by the producer, but Carver didn't seem to be in a rebutting mood. He was nodding his head noncommitally, trying to determine what was going to happen before it happened. Unopposed, Dave Grunwald continued: 'Tim and I talked to Fred on the phone earlier, and it's become clear to us all that we simply cannot go on like this and so we have reluctantly come to the decision.'

Moira cut in before he could say what the decision was. Those sorts of decisions, she knew, must be nipped in the bud before they became implanted in the mind as irrevocable. 'Dave, listen, I know we have got big problems here but let's not lose our heads. A lot of what Jack has shot is great. Don't you agree it's great? I think it's his best film, and Nik's going to win an Oscar . . . We've got another four weeks to go.'

'With Jack that can easily become six or eight,' Tim said gravely, 'and each week costs us another half million.'

'With the safeguards written into your proposals, to which Jack agrees, you'll be fully protected.' She looked at Carver for support, but he wasn't providing any for the moment. 'Sydney,' she challenged him, 'you support what I'm saying, don't you?'

Carver was stroking his cheeks, looking thoughtful and listening with concentration. She considered it a dangerous sign when Carver listened like this. It meant he hadn't quite made up his mind whom to sell down the river. He could come down on your side or on their side, dependent on how the play went and the advantages moved.

Tim Tomkins, getting thinner as he lounged against a wall, said: 'We've got to remember that in the first twelve days of shooting, Jack fell ten days behind schedule. You know what he told Fred on the phone? He said: "Fred, it takes as long as it takes." On the basis of his own words, four weeks to completion means the same as the length of a piece of string. It's pouring money down the drain. Up till today we thought there was still a chance to make him see sense. But now, after what happened, well . . . I frankly think he's out of his mind.'

Carver had worked out now which way the wind was blowing and that it was definitely blowing against Jack Strawley. Standing up, his nose seemed to be jutting out more than ever: he had come to resemble an arrowhead about to be let fly. His manner was seeking to belie this, was seeking to give the impression of someone who, having listened to all the arguments, is reluctantly forced to a hard but inevitable conclusion.

'As I see it, we have three options.' He splayed his fingers and counted them off. 'One: to continue as is. We'd have to convince Dave and Tim and Fred, and I doubt we can do that after what's happened and what they've been saying. To be perfectly honest, with all the good will I have got for Jack, I don't think I could convince myself either.' He looked towards the young execs, and they said nothing by way of confirming his assessment so far. 'Option two is that NorthStar shuts down the film, everybody goes home, there's a loss of between $9,000,000 and $11,000,000 chalked up to the company, and *everybody's* down the toilet. Which brings us to option three.' He stopped lengthily in his tracks, his nose conducting in the air.

'Which is?' Moira prompted him angrily. She looked at the young execs, but they weren't looking back. Grunwald was examining the carpet. 'Which is?' she said again insistently. Nobody was meeting her eye. 'Spill it out, Sydney.'

'Which is,' Carver said with ominous rotundity of phrasing, 'that since we cannot persuade Jack to meet our concerns, we may have to go around Jack.'

'*Go around Jack,*' she echoed scornfully. 'You mean fire him.' Moira threw it out with angry incredulity. 'You know that'd destroy Jack *and* the film.'

'I have come to the sad conclusion,' Carver said sadly, dressing his words in the mellifluous tones of one big enough to rise above personal considerations and loyalties and see the larger picture, 'that Jack has already destroyed himself — mentally, and physically, and professionally — with his drinking and his drugs, and we either go along sentimentally backing a sick man and a *loser*, or we have the courage to act decisively . . . and cut our losses.'

The arrowhead had been let fly and was now planted deeply in Jack Strawley's back. Moira's eyes were making the circuit of their tense faces, going round and round, trying to find a weak point where she could break the tight ring of resolution that she saw. But it looked to her, from their quiet, set positions, that everything was already decided between them, and this meeting was a charade: the death committee had already sat, the sentence was decided, and it was now just a question of carrying it out.

She said, snappily businesslike: 'If we're talking about cutting losses, let's not be vague, we have to know what we're cutting and what we're gaining, right?'

'Right,' Dave Grunwald agreed with her. 'Both Tim and I would agree with that formulation.'

Tim Tomkins nodded, standing watchfully by, hand on belt. He was sweating despite the air-conditioning, and he took off his lightweight jacket and loosened the narrow tie. With deliberate calm, he proceeded to the mixing of dry martinis in a chromium shaker.

'Go ahead, Moira,' he told her while doing this, 'we're ready to listen to what you got to say.'

'Yeah, you better be,' she said standing up with an air of squaring up to tall Tim Tomkins and his dry martinis.

He interrupted his stirring and turned towards her with an understanding smile. 'We know you're close to Jack, that you two go back a long way. And we respect that. So does Sydney, but Sydney's being realistic . . .'

'Yeah, that's one word for it,' she said.

'Dave and I are fully cognizant of how valuable you are to this production. We want you on board, Moira, because anyone brought in to replace Jack would have to count heavily on your help. I hope we can count on you for that. We would, of course, show our appreciation in tangible ways.' He smiled at her with all the warmth that such a thin man could muster. Moira didn't smile back. Her face showed nothing.

'Get Fred on the line,' she told them, 'because anything that's decided will have to be done fast and have his full approval.'

'Moira, we are empowered to take the necessary steps,' Dave Grunwald said.

'Yeah, those you've danced before. I may show you some new ones you don't know yet. Get Fred on the line.'

The two young execs exchanged looks. The decisiveness in Moira's voice seemed to make an impression on them, and Tim nodded to Dave Grunwald and said: 'Dave, maybe that's not such a bad idea. Why don't you call Fred and see if he's free to come to the phone.'

Dave Grunwald went to the phone, and Moira said: 'If he isn't free, get him to make himself free.'

While the call was being put through, and the two NorthStar execs were huddled together, impressing on Fred Spinola's secretary the urgent reason for which they were seeking to interrupt the conference he was in, Carver had gone up to Moira, an air of paternalistic concern on his face.

'Moira,' he said, 'I don't want to play the heavy here . . . but you've got to realize these fellas mean business and they're smart. I wouldn't try to fool with them. There's a lot at stake here, and there comes a point when no matter how beautiful your eyes, *they* don't fool around.'

'I'm not fooling around, Sydney.'

Tim Tomkins was signalling to them with an air of achievement that they had Fred Spinola on the line. Dave Grunwald was in the course of filling him in. Having done that, he now turned to Moira.

'Okay, Moira, say what you want to say, and I will relay it word for word to Fred.'

'Tell Fred this . . .' she said, standing up very straight in the heavy air, arms folded, doing absolutely nothing with her eyes, which were as cold as cold print. 'Look at it step by step. Okay, he fires Jack. Then what happens? Not many directors of any standing are willing to finish off another director's picture, especially if he goes protesting wrongful dismissal and demanding guild arbitration. You're liable to be held up for two, three weeks minimum.' She paused, glaring at Dave. 'You telling Fred all this?'

'I'm telling him.'

'Is he listening?'

'He's listening, Moira. Go on.'

'Second, once you've found another director and got him out here,' she went on slowly, giving Dave Grunwald enought time to relay what she was saying, 'once you've found this director and he's familiarized himself with the hundred and something hours of film that we've shot — even if he watches ten hours of film a day it's going to take him two weeks just to get through what we've shot, and there are other details of the production with which he has got to acquaint himself . . . motivation lines, plot lines, thematic interweaving . . . Say three weeks? We're talking about a hold-up of three weeks minimum, possibly as much as six or seven. All the time with the clock ticking, and costs mounting at a rate of half a million a week. You telling Fred all this? He's going to end up with *additional* costs, which are pure losses, nothing to show for them, of close on two, three million.'

Dave Grunwald was softly summarizing Moira's argument on the phone, while Tim Tomkins and Carver and Moira remained locked in their separate silences, not looking at each other, awaiting the response. There followed Fred Spinola's answer, which only Dave Grunwald was hearing.

'What does Fred say?' Moira demanded when the response seemed to be going on too long to suggest simple acceptance of her argument.

Dave provided his own summarized answer: 'Fred says a lot of things, but the bottom line is: solutions to disasters are never without pain.'

'So what's he in favour of doing, precisely?' Moira asked. 'Let him spell it out.'

'He wants to invoke the over-budget clause and the health clause in Jack's contract, terminate his services and fly out Jim Robinson to finish the picture.'

'Jim Robinson is a third-rate hack,' Moira said. 'He'll finish the picture all right, he'll ruin it.'

'As you have just pointed out yourself,' Tim Tomkins said, 'we're not going to get a major director to take over in twenty-four hours.'

'I have another solution,' Moira said quietly.

'Go ahead,' Dave Grunwald told her.

She took a breath and then spoke rapidly, not looking at any of them in the room, but addressing herself directly to Fred Spinola in New York via Dave Grunwald. Her face was as impassive as if she were reading off a shopping list.

'My proposal is this. With the assistance of Sydney and Wladislas, I take over the production, and meanwhile you look for a name director to replace Jack. I'll make sure that the picture is shot the way I know Jack wants it shot. This way there's no hold-up, the concept remains Jack's, and there's no danger of some third-rater fucking it up.'

Tim Tomkins, without waiting for Fred Spinola's answer, said: 'That's quite an interesting proposal.' He looked across at Dave on the phone who was answering some objection that Fred Spinola had raised. He had lowered his voice so that what he was saying into the mouthpiece couldn't be heard by the others, but it was evident that he was arguing against Fred Spinola's point of view. After five minutes he looked up and his boyish grin had come back. In the faces of the young execs a clear shift had been perceived by Carver, who now scrambled on board the new bandwagon.

'With Moira and me working in close harmony, we can get this picture under control, cost-wise, while maintaining the artistic quality,' he avowed. 'It's our best bet. Our only bet.'

The crackling objections coming over the telephone line had abated. A convergence of views appeared to be occurring. Tim Tomkins added his formal vote. 'Yeah, I agree. Seems like our best bet.'

Dave Grunwald, with the full return of his lost boyishness, directed towards Moira a big smile of relief: 'Well, you've convinced us in this room, and it seems you've convinced Fred.'

'Good,' she said. 'Because now comes the hard part.'

'Oh, you thought that part was easy?' They were all looking at each other, and Dave Grunwald's grin had become shaky again.

'Carrying this through will fall largely on my shoulders,' she told them, 'and I'm gonna have to be a prick, for which I want to be properly recompensed.'

'We will certainly want to show our appreciation, I think we'll be talking about a substantial bonus . . .' Dave Grunwald began, but Moira cut him off.

'I don't want a bonus,' she told them. 'I want my present contract torn up and replaced by a new one. Instead of associate producer, I get to be co-producer with Sydney. Instead of four thousand a week with a minimum of ten weeks, I want nine thousand, backdated to the beginning, with a minimum of twenty-four weeks, up to final cut. Same percentage of the gross as Sydney's getting. And this picture to be the first of a three-picture deal.'

Dave Grunwald was conveying her terms to Fred Spinola, after which there was a long silence while Dave Grunwald waited, tapping his fingers, and Tim Tomkins waited lounging stiffly against the wall, his long legs tightly interwoven, watching Dave Grunwald's face, and Sydney Carver waited, looking down and watching everyone, and Moira waited looking at nothing, staring blankly ahead. There came a crackle from the telephone, suggesting a decision from New York.

Dave Grunwald listened carefully, repeated one or two things to get them straight, and then turned to Moira:

'Fred's offering eight thousand a week for minimum twenty weeks, backdated. You get co-producer credit. He'll give you 2% of the gross. And make it the first picture of a two-picture deal. And on the second picture you get sole producer credit if it's your own project.'

Moira said without her blank look wavering from the wall, or any emotion in her voice, 'Tell Fred he's got a deal.'

42

The telegram from New York read:

Mr Jack Strawley,
Hotel Alphonse XIII, Seville
Dear Jack: Ever escalating problems and costs on 'Heart of Darkness' having now reached totally unacceptable levels I am forced with regret to take the painful step of relieving you of any further responsibility in connection with this production with immediate effect. I want you to know how heartily sorry I am to have to do this but your intransigence in the face of our repeated efforts to reach accommodation with you leaves me no alternative. The full contractual ramifications of my decision will have to be gone into between our respective lawyers but it is necessary that I indicate at this stage the legal basis on which we are terminating your contract namely that your are in breach of clause 7(c)iii relating to 'egregious and unapproved budget excesses' over and above limits defined in clause (b)ii above as well as giving cause for the activation of clause 27 (d) (the ill health clause which we are invoking as per sub-section ix.(d.) ('mental ill health'). Kindly turn over to Sydney Carver or Moira Goldberg all materials including all scripts notes storyboards etc relating to the production as well as all moneys and monetary instruments furnished by this company and please note that company responsibility for your personal expenses including hotel expenses ceases as of 12 noon today. Very truly yours, Fred W. Spinola, President and Chief Executive Officer Northstar Pictures.

Jack Strawley's reaction to this telegram was to toss it in the trash bin to which he normally consigned unwanted advice from the NorthStar front office. The car that normally came to pick him up from the hotel and take him to the set arrived at the usual time, and as usual he telephoned through to Moira's room to ask if she wanted to drive out with him. They normally did this and discussed the day's shooting during the journey. This time he was told that she had already left and so he went to the car alone and was driven out unaccompanied. At the turnpike, where entry to the lot was controlled by a Spanish policeman, he was told that his car could not proceed further, and the barrier was not raised. Jack got out and started to walk round the wooden bar and, when the cop came running to stop him, he pushed the cop out of the way.

'I'm firing you,' he told him. 'Pick up your money and get outta here.'

By now there were a number of production people standing around watching what was going on, although without anyone looking him directly in the face. He didn't look at them either but walked ahead to the set which was swarming with extras and stand-ins and stunt men. The scene due to be shot was of the rebels' attack on the out-station, their overrunning it, and their killing of Kurtz and the puppet dictator. The scene was to begin with the final phase of the fighting, with mortar shells being fired out of the surrounding vegetation, and corpses and the wounded scattered around the courtyard. The explosions were going to be produced by means of sticks of buried dynamite, which would be touched off in sequence by an explosives expert, a heavy-bellied Spaniard in Spanish army fatigues. Stuffed dummies with breakaway arms and heads and legs had been set up at the spots where the dynamite was due to go off, and cameras were arranged to record the bodies being hurled into the air and blown to pieces. A doctor and two ambulances with first-aid teams were standing by.

The first assistant director called through a loudhailer, first in English and then in rudimentary Spanish:

'Presidential guards, this scene here's where you panic. *P-A-A-N-I-C!* Ah wannah see it on yuh faces. Casualties and corpses, do not — repeat do NOT — at any time take off wounds, blood or bandages. Okay, everyone, we're gohnna do a trial run of the smoke and flames.'

The second assistant director was working with the stuntmen who would fall dead. Five cameras were going to be used to

capture the scene, two on dollies, two hand-held with the opera-
tors moving amid the extras and one on a large scissor crane. The
assistant to the second assistant director was working with the
corpses and the wounded, arranging their positions on the ground.
Moira was watching tensely over these preparations.

Jack Strawley called her over to him. 'Moira,' he said, 'there's
not enough blood on the injured and the corpses. I want a lot of
blood. This is a bloody battle. These are savage people, they cut
off heads . . . and put 'em on poles.' He looked through his
viewfinder at the walking wounded, framing them from different
angles, shaking his head:

'They're too casual, they're supposed to be stoned out of their
fucking minds with fear and tequila and hash . . . because they're
all going to have their heads cut off and they know it. Hand out
the booze, Moira. If they can't act soused, we got to get 'em
soused.'

'I made a note,' she said gravely.

He was sipping whisky out of a cup, wavering on his feet: he
had the impression of being on a rolling boat on a high sea. 'I
want to see the head,' he said suddenly,'want to see what sort of
job they made of Kurtz's head. Got to look like it was recently
alive.'

'They've done a good job with the head . . . it really looks like
Nik,' Moira said.

Without any change of tone, he told her while gazing through
the viewfinder at different sections of the scene: 'You know my
big mistake, Moira? Not realizing how much I really need you.
And not just as an assistant. Is it too late?'

She said quietly: 'That time's passed, Jack.'

'Yeah,' he said, eyes blazing. 'I guess it has. I guess I missed that
one. Yeah. Gee, but this is going to be a great scene. This is the
slaughter of the Galitheans. You know they couldn't say the word
"shibboleth", they couldn't pronounce the sibilant "sh" and they
said "sibboleth" and that identified them to the Israelites, that
weeded them out and they slaughtered 'em.' He had an excited look
on his face. A smile had set on his lips like jelly. 'This has got to be
a very bloody battle scene, Moira. This is Kurtz's final
downfall . . . paying for all the hubris, all the crimes.'

'Jack . . . you got the telegram?'

'The telegram?' he asked vaguely.

'The telegram from Fred Spinola.'

'I got some damn telegram from Fred, yeah . . . know the way David took Jerusalem? He sent in Joab up through the water-tunnel, so they penetrated behind the defenders into the heart of the city. They come up out of the darkness. That's what I want, I want to show the rebels coming out through the wood-work . . . everywhere. Suddenly it's crawling with 'em.' The view-finder slipped out of his hand, and he stood for about a minute watching it fall to the ground, where it slowly shattered.

'Jack, you read the telegram?'

He looked around and saw Nik walking by himself, acting like crazy into thin air, getting himself into the part, the situation. Preparing himself. 'Nik's going to be great,' he told Moira. 'This is going to be his best performance ever. An Oscar-winner. We almost ready to go?' he asked her. She nodded, and he looked all around to establish where everybody was, because it was going to be a big complex scene with a lot of elements coming together, and with all those explosives going off and stunt-men taking dives there was a real danger of somebody being injured.

'Looks good to me. Okay, let's rehearse it,' he told Moira. 'No explosives, just smoke.' He called to Nik. 'Nik, we're going to run through it.' On the walkie-talkie he shouted: 'Smoke! Smoke! Sam, get the guards falling back, they're firing wildly into the crawling vegetation all around . . . firing crazily . . . Okay, let's go for it. This is a camera rehearsal, everybody. I want the cameras moving with the action . . . Okay, go for it. Smoke!'

The smoke canisters should have gone off in half a dozen selected spots, and the grips should have started to draw the dolly back on the laid tracks, and the actors should have started walking towards camera, but nothing happened, nobody budged, the entire set and crew had become immobilized as if stuck to the ground. 'Let's go,' Jack Strawley said again, and out of the corner of his eye — the place from where disaster always struck — he saw, by the side of the trailers and trucks, the little huddle of sobrely suited men: Carver and Grunwald and Tomkins, the myrmidons, dressed for the occasion, carrying their briefcases now. 'Who let them on?' he demanded. 'I gave firm instructions they weren't to be let on the set. No myrmidons on my set. Get them off my fucking set, Moira!' He turned to the second assistant director, Sam Walker. 'Okay. Let's go, Sam,' he said again and called 'Action!' once more. Nobody budged: the cameras, whether hand-held or on tracks, remained immobile. Crew and extras and stuntmen and technicians were looking away. 'What's going on here?' he demanded. Nobody answered. Only Moira was meeting his eye.

'What's the problem, Moira?' he asked, turning to her since nobody else was paying any attention to him. 'We got a strike here or what?'

'You said you'd received the telegram,' she said quietly. 'From Fred Spinola. You did get the telegram?'

'Yeah,' he said.

'That's it,' she said softly.

'So Boreham Wood hath come to Dunsinane,' he intoned sonorously. 'Is the production closing down?'

'No, Jack.'

He looked puzzled and beckoned to the suited men to come over, and they approached docilely, Dave grinning boyishly, Tim with hands dangling loose, Sydney Carver to the fore.

'Sydney, what is this? Fred decide to throw his weight around?' He fixed his eye on the two execs from New York. 'I got the message,' he told them. 'We're going to have to speed up, right? And keep costs down. Got it! We're losing time now, and time, like you fellas keep saying, is money. So let's go, shall we?' He slapped his thigh hard. His body had the jumpiness of a nervy horse. When they didn't respond, he added: 'Let's work it out after we finished shooting today . . . so's not to lose production time.' He examined their grey, serious faces closely. Dave was nodding his head up and down, a kind of behavioural tic that Strawley took for agreement. 'If that's okay, Dave?' Dave continued to nod automatically but his expression was negative as he looked towards Moira.

She said gently, firmly: 'Jack, they fired you and they won't go back on that.'

'It's a negotiation ploy,' he patiently explained to her. 'They're not going to close the picture down, having spent all this money.'

'They're not closing it down,' she said.

'So who's going to run the show? Hacker Syd?'

'I'm going to,' Moira said in a low shaky voice.

He gave a hoarse, shocked laugh. 'You Moira? You're going to direct this picture?'

She stood her ground, looking him directly in the face. 'No. I'm not capable of that, I know.' Her speech was staccato from lack of breath. 'But I can keep it going.' She took a deep trembling breath. 'Following your . . . your storyboards. And notes. Things you've told me.' She added tensely, almost inaudibly. 'And taught me.' Her voice got stronger. 'It's what was decided, Jack. There wasn't any other way, where we'd gotten to.'

He scratched his head. His eyes had gone dull and lifeless. 'You're a smart cookie, Moira. I always said you were. Smart . . . very smart. It's perfectly true: you're the only person could do it, you're the only one that knows the whole footage, how it all fits together. You're the only person I told. They had to have you. Without you they couldn't do it. You're holding this whole thing together for them. Well, all I can say is I hope you got more'n thirty pieces of silver, baby, because you don't want to make yourself *too* cheap, do you?'

'I'll tell you exactly what I got, Jack,' she said white-faced but with a strong, controlled voiced. 'They doubled my salary, and they made me co-producer with Sydney. It was what I demanded and it's what they gave me.'

'Always knew you were smart, Moira. But I guess I didn't realize how smart. Underestimated you. Your capacity for betrayal.'

'Jack, you blew it. They were going to fire you whatever.'

His eyes had the flashy crazy light in them. 'You sold me down the river, Moira. You sold me to the myrmidons.'

Carver interceded. 'Jack, it was done in your best interests. Spend a little time at the health farm, Jack. The good Dr Saltie. You're worn out and you need a rest and, if you do this right, nobody'll even know you didn't finish the picture. It'll be yours. We're going to see to that. Moira and I.'

'Yeah. Guess I have a lot to thank you for, Sydney,' Jack said. 'It's got your imprint, your filthy fingers all over it. You figure this way you can steal *all* my points. Figure you can fly all on your own now, Sydney? Don't need my coat-tail to hang on to anymore. Well start flying, baby . . .'

Mouth frothing, he leapt at Carver, grabbed hold of him by the neck. The two NorthStar execs tried to tear him off, but he was too strong for them in his maddened state, and Carver was getting his protrusive nose set back into his face, and his neck squeezed into a narrow funnel. Seeing that the young execs hadn't the weight to deal with him, Moira ordered two Spanish grips to come and grab hold of Jack, pin back his arms and march him off to one of the ambulances. They were burly fellows, but he was enormously strong in his wild rage, and they needed the help of the ambulance men to overpower him. Moira asked the young Spanish doctor on duty if they had Haldol in the ambulances. They didn't but they had morphine, and the attendants and the grips held Jack down while the doctor got the needle in.

On the dusty road back to Seville, before the morphine had fully taken effect, Jack tried to open the rear doors of the ambulance and to leap out. It was travelling at 120 kilometers an hour at the time, and the ambulance attendants had to wrestle him down to the floor. They couldn't subdue him completely and had to call to the driver to stop and come and help them. It took the three of them to get him flat on his stomach with his hands pinned behind him so they could be tied up, and they bound his legs as well, to make sure he wouldn't try to leap out again.

43

This time Jack Strawley was put in a part of the psychiatric wing of the health farm where they took away his belt and his tie and his shoelaces and his pyjama cord, so that he had to knot his pyjama pants to keep them up. And he had to ask one of the nurses to light his cigarettes, not being permitted to have matches, and where he slept the dormitory windows opened just six inches. They injected him with Thorazine three times a day, and when he attacked one of the male nurses (who was refusing to let him leave), they raised the Thorazine to four times a day.

When Dr Saltie arrived she found him strapped down on a gurney at the wrists and ankles, another strap across his chest, claiming that the Devil was sitting on top of him and piercing his heart with his pointed nose. She held his hand, and he hung onto her so determinedly that a male nurse had to come and force his hand open. The doctor stroked his forehead, and her eyes were sad and gentle and shining, and he thought of her eyes as a lighthouse shining in the heart of darkness, and then they were giving him an injection and electrodes were fastened to each side of his head, and as the shock waves passed through his brain he thought that he was the man in the Memling painting being flayed alive by medieval surgeons with knives. They were peeling off his prickly skin as if skinning a rabbit. He knew that someone who was in his body, this imposter pretending to be him, was screaming and that they were trying to burn him out. The electric shocks passing through him had the force of kicks in the head from an enraged horse. The shocks stunned him and made his eyes roll out of his skull and his teeth clamp down on the rubber bib jammed tight in his mouth, so that he wouldn't bite his tongue off. All of these experiences and sensations and sights, Dr Saltie told him afterwards, were creations of his imagination, since he had been given a short-acting anaesthetic prior to electroconvulsive treatment. But what Dr Saltie did not know was that the eye of the savage could see even under anaesthesia.

Between electroconvulsive treatments, he was pumped full of a drug that wrapped his body in blankets of thick coarse felt through which he felt nothing. Having first rendered him skinless, they were obliged to zombify him for his own good. He was raw-fleshed, devoid of any covering except the felt which was like an artifical reptile skin covering him all over, body and hands and mouth and nose and eyes.

With the second, third and fourth courses of electric shock he discovered what it was like to be a 990-pound fighting bull having his head lowered by Fred Spinola's myrmidons of death jabbing their lances into him. He could see the mess he made on the floor, all that blood running down his hide, and the grey-green matter of his brains splattered everywhere. He was straining against the leather restraints with the veins bulging through his skin.

He was allowed no visitors and observed constantly through spyholes in his cell.

When he had had several of these death sentences by electrocution carried out on him (and been reborn little by little), Dr Saltie with the sympathetic eyes came in to 'have a chat'. He asked her if the electric shock treatments were over, and she said yes, for now, and she hoped permanently and she said how very reluctant she had been to have recourse to them, but they had been made necessary by the severity of his condition.

'I was mad again?'

'Yes,' she said so very gently that it was almost all right to have been mad. She asked him what had happened, and he said that his partner Carver had been robbing him for years, as a result of which he had no money, and certain personal guarantees that he had foolishly signed were going to be enforced because he'd gone egregiously over-budget, and his house and his paintings and Gloria's jewellery and his vintage Jaguar XK150 and everything else that he loved and prized would be taken away from him. Dr Saltie put him on lithium and said she'd see him again in two or three days' time.

In the first couple of weeks of his conversations with Dr Saltie he kept up his splenetic commentaries on the ways and means of the Carver, the high-flyer on other people's coat-tails, the knife-nose not of woman born, the Rat Man. Then he told her:

'I feel so low, I don't think I can go on living feeling as low as I do. I preferred being mad . . . it was better than this.'

She stroked his forehead and said softly: 'I want to quote to you something Jacques Lacan said once. "Man's being," he said, "cannot be understood without reference to madness, nor would he be man without carrying madness within to the limits of his freedom." But, Jack, you have to come back from there. And you are doing that now.'

'How's it,' he asked her, his eyes full of uncontrollable weeping, 'that you know my mind so well?'

'Because I've been there myself.'

'You?'

'Like you, I sometimes didn't take the lithium, because I hated what it does to me, the way it makes me dull. But I have to take it, and so do you.'

After seven weeks, he was sufficiently balanced out to be moved to the other wing, where they specialized in body massage and water cures and aerobic exercises, and since his financial affairs were in a terrible mess he was allowed a visit from his unaffordable accountant, who said that NorthStar had attached all his asssets under the various contracts he had signed, but not to worry, they would only be able to actually take over these assets if *Heart of Darkness* failed to earn back what it had cost, and then only to the extent that he had gone over-budget without their authorization. Meanwhile, of course, he had the use of all his properties, and they could not stop him 'living normally' and using money in his accounts, although he was not allowed to transfer funds out of the jurisdiction of British courts.

44

After coming out of the East Anglia health farm in cold, wet late November, a winter sheen lying over the flat English-smelling countryside that matched his wintry state of mind, Jack Strawley simply disappeared. At any rate, he was lying low, not making his presence back in London known. When one phoned the Carlyle Square house one was told by a woman who did not speak English at all well that Mr Strawley was not there, at present, and was asked if one wished to leave a message. I left a message that Stephen Dall had phoned and that I wished him well, and for him to call me when he could. I left two or three such messages, but my calls were never returned. Having been in Seville with him at the time of his breakdown, I of course knew what had happened to him and understood that he was not yet sufficiently recovered to face the world.

More than ever, it looked as though he was going to need the money that the publishers had offered him for his autobiography, and so I continued to work with the tapes we had made so far and to fill in the gaps in his narrative by means of interviews with people in his life. Since his removal from *Heart of Darkness* was obviously going to be a key incident in his story, I talked to all the key players in that event and obtained their versions of what had happened and why. Moira, in particular, felt the need to set the record straight and, within certain legal constraints imposed on her, talked freely to me. While she vigorously defended the action she had taken to 'save the film and save Jack's professional life', it was not difficult to see that she felt badly about what she had done and was shattered to have incurred his animosity. At the same time, she was keenly aware that the disaster that had befallen Jack had furnished her with the once-in-a-lifetime opportunity to make her way in the film business after many years of getting nowhere, and there was a gritty determination in her not to miss out on that chance.

What Jack Strawley was engaged upon when he did not return the phone calls I and others made to him, was trying to put his calamitous financial affairs in some sort of order. Riesner, his expensive clever accountant, had advised him that while NorthStar was struggling with 100 hours of unshowable film 'threats that we will remove your name, denounce them at press-conferences and expose their mistreatment of the artist somewhat lack oomph.' He advised that they would have more clout when NorthStar had a two-hour film they were about to release and were committed to a major world-wide marketing campaign. 'That's when we make our demands. Say we want your personal guarantees annulled on the grounds that you were egregiously hindered and obstructed in the shooting of the film.'

His financial adviser and his psychiatrist were in agreement about his need to play it cool, lie low, gather strength for later, and since he was still shaky and melancholic, and the lithium was making him feel as if he was wrapped from head to toe in heavy bandages, he went along with what they said and sat in his Chelsea garden reading nothing that could possibly be turned into a film while he endlessly played the *Stabat Mater* of Rossini on the record player.

As part of the policy advocated by Riesner, he made no attempt to impose his point of view as far as the edit and the other post-production decisions were concerned. 'We want to have a case for a counter-suit saying they ruined your film.' He stuck to this plan for a while but eventually couldn't help himself and wrote a guarded note to Moira saying: 'Putting aside all personal feelings, if I am needed for the good of the film, call me and I will do whatever I reasonably can at this stage.' She wrote back a typewritten letter, saying she had much appreciated his offer and would bear it in mind. It sounded as if the reply had been drafted by NorthStar's legal department. He kept cool and reasonable in the face of the rejection of his reasonable offer and carried on reading Pessoa, according to whom nothing mattered, therefore why get excited about a picture, especially since excitement was what had got him into trouble in the first place. Dr Saltie was trying to instil into him, at their irregular therapy sessions, a method of dampening down upsurges of unreasonable excitement. She seemed to be right about their bad effect on him. Yet he missed the upsurges keenly, missed the 'madnesses' that made him feel real and alive. She insisted that calm, mature creativity was possible and was the highest kind: this was something her training and her knowledge and also her personal experience told her. But it meant having to sacrifice some of the highs.

'If it's so clear-cut, why didn't you do it?'

'Because I was crazy like you, Jack. You've got to decide, if you want to burn out before you're fifty' — his eyes said *if it makes a fine blaze* — 'or blaze a little less and stay alive.' He said he'd have to think about that. Staying alive wasn't necessarily all it was puffed up to be.

'The worst thing that could happen to you,' she warned him solemnly, 'is that *Heart of Darkness* is a huge success, because that will just make you cling to your manias, prove to you that you were right all the time.'

He pulled a face. 'If it's not a success, I won't have a place to live and nor will Gloria and Anna, and we won't get to eat, and I won't be able to pay your fees, so on balance we may all have to grit our teeth and live with the bitch-goddess Success.'

Four cutters were employed on the film, working under the supervision of a redoubtable Hollywood lady called Deb Boothroyd, a woman who had cut all the old greats — directors like John Ford, William Wellmann, William Wyler, Raoul Walsh — and knew about storyline and relevance. No matter how exquisite a scene, her attitude was: where's it get us? And if it didn't move the story forward, out it came.

By the end of the third month of editing, *Heart of Darkness* had been reduced, on this principle, from over a hundred hours of footage to a slaughtered but still unmanageable rough cut running four and a half hours, which NorthStar screamed was longer than *Gone With the Wind*. Jack Strawley's 'compromise' suggestion that the film should play for ten hours, in three instalments on three successive nights, was dismissed with derision. Miss Boothroyd was urged to get out her scissors again and reduce the four-and-a-half hours' playing time to two hours. Even she found this hard to do: the Berlin prologue alone, depicting the education of agent Kurtz in the final phase of World War II, ran for fifteen minutes, and the epilogue another ten minutes. In a film of two hours, this did not leave enough time, even rigorously adhering to storyline and cutting out every irrelevance, for the complex narrative to unfold. It left too much unexplained, too many loose ends: made the plot look disconnected and haphazard — at times, surrealistic. Nonetheless, this was the version NorthStar decided to submit to the test of sneak previews.

The long silence which followed suggested either that he was so much out of the picture now that nobody felt obligated to keep him informed of what was going on, or else that a secretary had forgotten to put something in the post, or a P.A. had forgotten to make a courtesy telephone call: there were no courtesies coming his way these days.

His crazy behaviour in Spain and his deep, lingering anger distanced him from all the leading players in the set-up; there was nobody to ask lightly, 'Hey, what's going on?' If Riesner rang up to enquire, he was going to be given a legalistic reply, but since it was the only line of communication left open, he instructed Riesner to ring.

The accountant came back, determinedly putting the best face on a worst-case situation. 'They *say* the previews have been disastrous, and they're re-cutting the picture. My interpretation is that they want us to think that the film is unshowable. It's a bluff.'

'Ask to see preview cards.'

'We need a lawyer's letter for that. A major lawyer in a major law firm . . . to scare them regarding costs.'

They got a suitably expensive lawyer, and in response to his formal request the comments of audiences at a series of sneak previews held in Pittsburgh, Dallas, Denver, Oklahoma, Atlanta, and New Orleans were sent to Jack.

In answer to the question, 'Did you like the picture?' there was a 65% negative response, 20% in between and 15% positive. He ran his eye down the answers.

'Yes. It's a great film. I'd put it in the same class as Welles's *Touch of Evil.* Regrettably it hasn't much chance in a place like Dallas.'

'I didn't like it. I couldn't understand what the characters were doing or why. They seem to be a bunch of weirdos and jerks.'

'The best part was when Kurtz gets his head cut off. That should have happened sooner, then we wouldn't have had to sit through this bilge.'

'The atmosphere is great and the photography and acting are superb, but it has got too many plots and the photography's too dark.'

'I liked the buzzards. The rest stinks.'

'I've never seen such an artifical studio jungle! Grows right up to the back porch. Where's this place supposed to be?'

'The naked girl they drowned in the bathtub runs away with the picture.'

'Nik Ransom overacts as usual. I can't believe that an officer of the CIA would act this way.'

'I was upset watching it, but afterwards I couldn't stop thinking about it. I don't know what it's supposed to mean, but it's an experience to see it. It doesn't leave your mind.'

There were hundreds of comments in this sort of vein. At best, the audience was affected against its will, at worst — which was the most part — they hated it.

Another re-cut was ordered. Strawley wanted to take charge of it, saying: 'I'm the only one who can put it together, they must realize that now.' But Riesner advised him not to do it. 'If you put it together, and the film goes down the drain, we haven't got a leg to stand on, and they'll implement the guarantees. *But* . . . if they put it together, after having illegally dismissed you, we can make a case that NorthStar ruined the film through their incompetence and ill-will toward you. And therefore they are in default and cannot implement the guarantees.'

It was a convincing legal argument, and Strawley had gone along with it at first but, rereading the preview cards, he rebelled.

'I'm not going to stand by and see them destroy my work,' he said. 'I have longer-term considerations than losing my house and my paintings. In any case, they're never going to implement that. Think what that'd do to their image in the business.'

The problem was getting back into a position where he could have any effect on the thinking of these people. Fred's myrmidons were not going to listen to him: he was the profligate overspender, the mad artist, the uncontrollable genius-boy who knew better than everyone else, the man who had almost drowned Sydney Carver's date.

He couldn't go to Moira. He didn't trust Moira now. Gloria had been right: the most upwardly mobile ass in the business. She obviously had a vested interest in keeping him out, making it on her own. Here was her big chance, and she was seizing it. He knew about that driving force, how it could roll over anybody:

he'd rolled over Carl that way, so he knew. In any case, his pride wouldn't let him go to Moira. Damn it, she was his assistant, he'd taught her everything. He wasn't going to go running to her saying 'help me'. And he couldn't go to Sydney, after having tried to strangle him. He tried a phone call to Fred Spinola and was amazed by the acrimony in the man.

The chief executive of the suited ones shouted down the line: 'Jack, I always thought you were a shit, now I can tell you to your face that's what you are. You're a man who wants to make arty films for the critics and for the glory of his own ego, *at other people's expense, at this company's expense, at my expense!*' It was obvious he was not going to get anywhere with Spinola. His only other chance was Nik. He wrote him a letter.

Dear old Nik,

I've been staying out of people's hair ever since my disgraceful behaviour in Seville, for which I have no excuse except stress and overload and too much booze, but now that I'm in tip-top shape again, calm and stone cold sober, I can't bear to see the assholes ruining our work, yours and mine, and with that your shot at an Academy Award, which I firmly believe you have a strong chance of winning for your performance *provided* that it's not cut to shreds by the dwarfs in suits. You are the only one with the clout to stop the bastards. The film has got to run minimum three hours. It will be a hell of a job to get it down to that length. I would like it to be four hours, but I'm ready to be bargained down to three, provided they leave alone the essentials of your performance, and that includes stuff which is so *good* that even if it is not strictly speaking plot, we have *got* to keep. What they don't understand is that the film *has got to* move slowly at the beginning, it has got to take time to develop, it's scene painting YES . . . but that's got to be or the violence in which everything explodes is just fuckingshitbang movie violence. We have to see Kurtz's solipsistic world. The perfection of his delusional system. We have to see that system *working, succeeding in the beginning.* In order that it isn't just macabre melodrama we have to take the time to show all that. Kurtz *is* keeping the Commies at bay, standing out against the dominoes tumbling. All that takes time and criss-cross plot lines. Cutting out everything that isn't strictly mainline story, they've cut the heart out of the film. Nik, if for you this is a question of an Oscar, for me it is a question of professional survival because, however well you've done for them in the past, if you lose that sort of money they don't forgive you ever, not to mention that my house and Gloria's jewels are mortgaged to this picture and therefore everything is at stake for us. You and I have a common interest here and should act in concert. If you still have belief in me, as you once had, then you will know that only I can save this picture. This is not arrogance — although I admit I have been known to behave arrogantly in the past — it's just plain fucking horse sense. Because it *is* my picture, I know all its rhythms and what cutting this or that out does to the underlying emotional structure of the whole and to your performance. Nik, you are not helpless. You can refuse to do the retakes I know Moira is asking you to do, you can refuse to cooperate in doing publicity for the launch, you can threaten adverse statements to the press, you can be your wonderfully difficult self . . . and this time for a good cause. Do this for me, Nik. And for yourself . . .

I wait to hear from you — hopefully & soonest.

All the best, Jack.

Two weeks went by without any answer from Nik, and then Jack Strawley got a letter from Nik's agent. It read:

Dear Mr Strawley,

Nik has asked me to reply to your letter because he says he is not good at 'Dear Jack' letters. Therefore that awkward task falls to me as his agent and friend. It's a tough one, because I sympathize (and Nik sympathizes) with everything you say, but I have had to advise him that in the real world he has to accept the powers-that-be in this business, and they are plenty mad about this film and the way they were held-up for millions of dollars of needless costs, and they are convinced that this film, if it is to have any chance at all, has to be got down to around two hours ten. Which is fifty minutes less than your minimum length, and having seen the film two or three times now, I must say I personally agree that at three hours it is a hell of a lot too long.

On a personal level, Nik is really sorry he can't be of more help to you, but we both think you know this business well enough to understand how the cookie crumbles when it does.

Nik sends you love and best wishes,
    Sincerely yours,
      Arnie P. Schwarzkopf

45

Heart of *Darkness* finally came out in September 1976. I attended the press show with considerable misgivings. From my time with Jack Strawley in Seville, I knew more about the making of the film than my fellow critics, and I also knew more about what it had cost him personally, and what was now at stake for him, and not just financially. I knew that a vital part of his self-esteem — perhaps of his appetite for life — was tied up with the fate of this film.

I tried in my review to be as objective as possible without being gratuitously unkind to a film-maker for whom I continued to have a high regard. I summarize the essentials of what I wrote:

'Jack Strawley's new film *Heart of Darkness* comes out of the honourable American cinema tradition of looking at the failings of American society in a spirit of savage self-criticism. Its antihero is one of the best and the brightest who loses his way in a steamy Central American dictatorship: Joseph Conrad's Kurtz updated as a CIA station chief gone rogue in the tropics.

'Nobody in Strawley's *Heart of Darkness* deserves our compassion — certainly not the drunken Kurtz, brilliantly if sometimes self-indulgently played by Nik Ransom at his most operatic. Kurtz having escaped the control of his masters in Virginia, another agent, young idealistic Marlow, is sent out to secure the loose cannon. And in the course of doing so learns how contaminating evil can be. The extraordinary thing is that while none of the characters deserves our compassion, we have it forced out of us by the powerful emotional blackmail to which director Strawley subjects us. So murkily mysterious is the film (possibly due to the heavy cuts), it becomes at times quite surrealistic, which may be what life in a mythical central American dictatorship is like.

'This is Jack Strawley's most grandiose and most way-out film, full of bizarre touches, rococo characters and brilliant imagery and technique — the much-discussed torture and drowning of the girl in the bathtub is done with dazzling brio.

'If other directors have been known to fall between two stools, Strawley with his appetite for excess falls between many. This film is a sort of updated classic, it is a sort of political thriller, a sort of South American novel of magic realism and a sort of success and also — alas — a sort of failure.'

If I was ambivalent in my views, my colleagues were much less so. For the most part they condemned the film roundly. One called it the biggest and most expensive disaster of all time. The words 'boring', 'confused' and 'pretentious' appeared in many reviews, and one or two drew an ironical parallel between Kurtz going rogue in a mythical Central American dictatorship and the, by then much publicized story of Strawley getting out of control in Francoist Spain. One or two critics saw qualities in the film, but on the whole opinion had turned against him; he was being punished for his Palme d'Or, for his Oscar, for his hubris, for being called 'genius Jack'. Now he was being called a fake genius, someone who had come to believe his own publicity to such an extent that he permitted himself to ride roughshod over everyone else in his quest for glory, as evidence of which his sadistic treatment of poor Sylvia, nearly drowned in a bathtub in his perverse pursuit of realism.

. Those who had always seen through him, now congratulated themselves on their perspicacity. Those who had once acclaimed him looked wistfully back on the inexplicable enthusiasms of youth.

The reviews might have been lived down if the public had liked the film. In its opening week at the Ritz, in Leicester Square, it took £2,390 when films that were finding public favour were taking between £15,000 and £20,000. The Ritz take didn't cover the cinema's running costs. Second and third weeks were no better, and after that it was withdrawn. Takings in France were higher and also in Italy and Spain, but not sufficient to encourage NorthStar to embark upon a major promotions campaign in America. The film was experimentally released in selected areas where it was thought it might do well: New York, Washington, Chicago. But it did badly in all these places, the reviews also were bad, and wider release plans were cancelled, since there was no point in playing places where not even opening costs would be recouped.

It was a time when other films were meeting a similar fate. Films were either a triumph or a disaster with nothing much in between, and every major company had some that were not worth releasing. On the company's books, an unreleased film was a property that went into the balance sheet as capital invest-ment, valued at cost, whereas once released, an unsuccessful film went straight into the red column of the ledger and became a drag on the stock price. What was more, the cost of a major film release — promotions, advertising, and prints — added millions to the amount that had to be recouped before the film was in profit, and the conventional industry wisdom said there was no point throwing good money after bad.

Given this harsh climate and the polarization of success and failure as never before, Strawley's arrogantly extravagant flop inspired punning commentaries about its being *the last Straw-ley* . . . Hundreds of thousands of dollars spent on filming buz-zards, dozens of hours of excess film, vast sums incurred to obtain the effect of sudden darkness, a self-indulgent performance from Nik Ransom that consisted, it was claimed, of so much silent brooding that you could save half an hour of running time by just cutting out his silences — these were all sticks with which to beat a man who clearly had gotten too big for his boots and was ripe for a comedown. And the sticks were used savagely. Jack Strawley became the whipping boy for all the crazy excesses of the movie business.

In the boardrooms of the conglomerates that now owned most of the major film companies, Strawley was held to be a prime example of what was wrong with the business. His flagrant disregard of the rules had to be punished. And so his guarantees were going to be enforced, not simply to defray some of the crazy costs he had incurred but to discourage others from thinking they could infringe contractual undertakings with impunity.

To drive home this lesson, the executives responsible for letting *Heart of Darkness* get out of hand also had to be punished. The first to fall was Fred Spinola, president of NorthStar; shortly after him came Dave Grunwald and Tim Tomkins, the executives who had argued for Strawley's film and then failed to keep him under control. And to make the lesson absolutely clear, what remained of NorthStar was restructured and reborn as Sunrise, with a new logo in which the bright night star was replaced by a blazing sun. The new order of the day was going to be sunshine and not night-time brilliance.

After this debacle, nothing much was heard of Jack Strawley, except for occasional snippets in *Variety.* He was said to be planning a film of Graham Greene's *A Burnt-Out Case,* of Patrick White's *Voss,* of Malcom Lowry's *Under the Volcano.* He was working with a script-writer on a project entitled *Joanna Faust,* an updated version of the Faust legend, set in the film business, with Faust as a fading sex symbol and Mephisto as a plastic surgeon who will restore her glamour. In connection with these and other projects he was constantly jetting around the world, and the occasional letters I received from him were written under the letterheads of the Hassler in Rome, the Crillon in Paris and the Plaza in New York.

If he was broke, as he sometimes airily claimed in these

communications — never neglecting to mention that this was the thief Carver's doing — it was being broke on a very grandiose movie-business scale. I supposed that even if these projects were not materializing for the present, he must be getting development money from somewhere. I did not imagine he was spending his own money.

And then 'genius Jack' was once more in the news. It was one of those stories the media couldn't resist. A famous film director selling his house and valuables at auction to pay off his creditors. 'GENIUS JACK' UNDER THE HAMMER was one of the headlines. And THE FALL OF THE HOUSE OF STRAW(LEY) was another. The special viewing that Christie's laid on at the Carlyle Square house turned into a media event. It was a unique opportunity for the press to peer into the secret nooks and crannies of a major film director's life, and the papers sent their star photographers and their bitchiest columnists or most sobbing sisters to tell the tale of how the mighty are fallen. Strawley was allowing it because he wanted to realize the maximum from the auction sale. He was selling everything. Since he was losing his big London house, he'd have nowhere to store the valuables and the junk accumulated extravagantly, and often thoughtlessly, over the years. And besides, he had had one of his drastic mood swings as a result of which he'd decided he did not want to be encumbered with possessions. He was going to travel light from now on. The journalists ironized and speculated about the signs of grandiosity and extravagance in the director's lifestyle — and about the leather-bound scripts, some of which were inscribed with intimate messages from female stars who had appeared in his films. All was up for sale. He had no use for it anymore. Gloria had returned to the United States, and his own plans were to be mobile. And maybe he was also enacting a sort of public penance in ridding himself of all the rich and useless accoutrements of his life.

After the auction he moved to Paris and took a tiny apartment in the Rue de Bucci. 'It's just big enough for a telephone and a *baise-en-ville*. What more do I need?' he wrote to me on a postcard. He'd chosen Paris because that was where he was most admired and where one of his films could usually be found playing in a small cinema somewhere. Some French critics who had seen a four-and-a-half hour version of *Heart of Darkness* had pronounced it a masterpiece, so the attitude towards him was definitely friendlier there than in London or New York.

Living in Paris was pleasant enough. He hung out at the Closerie des Lilas, at La Coupole, at Lipp and Fouquets. He was the great American director who was not a prophet in his own land but was in France, where they appreciated the worth of such a man. Bernard Pivot asked him to come on *Apostrophe*. *Libération* interviewed him at length, and so did *Le Monde*. Postgraduate students wrote theses about *Le Cinéma de Strawley*, one even attributing to him its 're-invention'. Important French stars and producers expressed interest in working with him and many came to his table at the Closerie or at Lipp to discuss projects. But the fact that he spoke so little French and that his style was so strongly 'Anglo-Saxon' presented difficulties that in the end could not be overcome.

For quite a time the postcards kept coming from Paris, providing me with unembellished snippets of news that no longer found their way into the columns of the press. He was planning a film with Belmondo, with Depardieu, with Delon. No: he was going to direct a play, instead; no, an opera: *The Damnation of Faust*. And so on. He was going to Mexico at the invitation of the Mexican government to set up a Mexican film industry. He was preparing a co-production with China.

None of these projects came to anything. Then, in 1982, I received a longer card than usual, from New York this time, in which he'd written:

'I hope you've still got those tapes. I'm going to need them. I'm going to make an autobiographical film, part fact, part fiction, which is what my life has been. It's going to be fun to do, I'm going to throw everything in. Out-takes from my old films. Chat shows. Filmed interviews with people in my life . . . Nobody's ever done this before about himself. A sort of fictionalized documentary about my own life. The camera turned inwards. Zoom in on the 'I'. So hang onto the tapes with your life! Will be in touch soon.'

Then I heard no more of him for the next four years. In fact, not until I received the phone call from Alice in New York, in February 1986, telling me: 'Jack wants to see you.'

46

It was a definitive move. For the first time since selling his London house and putting his remaining personal belongings in storage, he was shipping out everything he owned and starting on a new phase of his life: going back to New York, his roots.

He stayed first of all in the Drake Hotel because it was big and anonymous, and there was a special deal with the airline whereby he got the room at a reduced rate. He was having to be careful about money now. He was trying to sell his Magritte, the masked apples, through the dealer in Paris, Laforge, who had handled the sales of his other paintings. It was the last of the paintings — the other important ones had all been sold by this time — for which he could expect to obtain a substantial sum of money: between $100,000 to $150,000 was the figure he'd been quoted by art experts. He was going to have to live on that while setting himself up in America.

He had been back to New York many times in the last thirty-five years but under very different circumstances. Those visits had taken place when his career was flourishing and he was considered a 'top name'. In those years he'd always had a suite at the Plaza or at the Carlyle, and lived almost entirely in the very small world of restaurants, clubs, bars and nightclubs that other 'top people' frequented.

Now he was in a quite different New York. He'd come back to stay and to remake his life. A real life, it was going to be this time, he promised himself. To his different eyes there was a feeling of melancholy about the glittering buildings. The energy hum in the air was the same as in his youth, what was different was that he no longer felt elated by it, it all seemed an unnecessary hassle. He was keeping himself tightly in check, stamping out the first signs of any speeding up, taking his tablets regularly.

His first task was to find an apartment from which he could operate, and he spent a depressing week running all over town looking for a place and not finding much in the price range he had set himself. He was learning about mundane things that had never concerned him before: that a deposit against breakages, as well as first and last month rentals, had to be paid over at the start of a tenancy, which meant he had to come up with three months' rent straight away. That was going to eat up a sizeable chunk of his available capital. His finances were going to be very tight until the Magritte was sold. And re-establishing himself in New York required funds. Looking at the less expensive places, he found himself drawn back towards the neighbourhoods where he had lived and hung out in his youth. It was all much changed from thirty-five years ago when he and Carl had frequented the bars and cafés around Tompkins Square. What had been part of the Lower East Side then, with the El running down the middle, was now the scruffy-fashionable East Village. Chinatown had spread upwards along Mott Street, swallowing up the lower reaches of Little Italy, and the small-time gangsters and pimps of West Broadway had been pushed out by the chic art galleries and realtors' offices and Bohemian richies. The areas where it was fashionable to live and hang-out had extended down beyond the Village into SoHo, and westward to what was now called Tribeca, which was the area where he had began his career, all those years ago, at the Tramline Theatre. Times Square was, if anything, sleazier and more vibrant and alive with all the dangers than it had been in his youth, but he was in no mood to sample the dangers, not wanting to follow anything through, not wanting involvements, however peripheral. Remembering how he had walked in these same streets with a wild clamouring in his bloodstream, he had to laugh at the way time had changed all that, turned him into a lithium junkie. All wrapped up in felt. He remembered, at Sardi's, people clapping him as he came in, and how important that had seemed to be. Getting up speed was everything then, and now he was taking medication to keep himself slowed down.

Somebody had suggested to him he should look at hotel apartments that could be taken on a monthly basis. The midtown ones were all miniscule, but the third or fourth place he went to, the Alexander Hotel, on the Upper East Side, between Madison and Park, had appealed to him straight away with its atmosphere of sedate, old-fashioned comfort and graciousness. It was a part of lost New York that he had refound. The available apartments he was shown all had a rather standard hotel feeling to them, but the manager mentioned that in a week's time the lady occupying a nice sixteenth-floor apartment was moving out. She'd been living there for several years, the place would have to be redecorated and furnished, and so wouldn't be available straight away, but why not take a look at it? He found it very much to his liking. It was one storey below the penthouse and bright and spacious, with a large living room, two bedrooms, two bathrooms, and a long balcony that afforded views across Manhattan. Since it was late May, and the summer hotel season in New York was a desert, the manager frankly confided — he was a portly, florid old world character called Norbert Beauregard — that he was eager to have 'someone of standing' in the place, who was going to be staying a while, and since Jack Strawley was willing to sign a year's lease, and was a distinguished artist of the cinema, Norbert Beauregard was ready to make him a preferential rate of $1,500 a month — no more than what was being asked for some real dumps downtown — and this rental included heating and electricity and daily maid service. There was a small but fully equipped kitchen, room service if required and a restaurant on the ground floor. He could have a direct phone line installed, and also use the operator-controlled hotel lines. There were all the usual hotel services. The most important of which was that messages could be left for him when he was out. There was no deposit to be paid, no last month's rent to lay out, and he could settle his account with his American Express card, which meant in effect that he'd be paying his rent in arrears, not in advance. The redecoration and furnishing of the apartment would be carried out to his taste: he could pick out his furniture from the hotel's furniture depository in the basement, where he could also store his papers — some sixty or more boxes. Amid the standard hotel stuff, he found one or two nice old American pieces and a selection of turn-of-the century New York prints that Beauregard was willing to have framed for him. The standard hotel sofas and armchairs were going to get new loose covers, which he could choose.

All in all, it seemed to him a piece of good fortune to have found this place and have got it on such reasonable terms, and he decided that his life was now about to take a new and favourable turn, after the years of the doldrums.

Once installed, he began to put about the news that he was back in the United States and looking for projects. He put out feelers among independent producers and distributors and with the agencies. To make his presence known, he lunched regularly at '21', at Lutèce, the Caravelle and the Côte Basque, and when he came back from these long and amply lubricated lunches there were usually a few message slips for him at the reception desk, with numbers to ring back, and these phone calls occupied his afternoons.

The early evenings were the hardest for him. Then he sat on his balcony in the fading light, which gave a bronze-like lustre to the Citibank tower directly in his sightline, and drank neat whisky until dark, at which time he ventured out to witness the racing start of another New York night. The sudden glitter was the quick fix in the bloodstream. He observed the burning bodies hectically converging. In no time you were at the flaming centre with the burnt-out stars of Brooklyn and the Bronx and Staten Island out there on the periphery. He was remembering how alluring the centre had always seemed to him, how he had striven towards it, staking his life on getting there.

As he walked by himself one evening, pausing now and again to frame with his fingers images that kept leaping out at him from the past, he found himself heading downtown, towards what he still vaguely thought of, even after all the years he'd spent abroad, as 'home territory'. He was not watching too closely where he was going, letting himself drift wherever the homing spirit wanted to take him. And suddenly he was in a long narrow street of deeply scarred house fronts, black iron doors covered in graffiti, overflowing trash bins. He saw a dim orange light coming from a below-stairs porthole, and, as he went towards it, the sidewalk was vibrating with music. It seemed to be a bar and he couldn't refuse its vague promise and so went in. The long narrow space had something familiar about it straight away: the tunnel-like layout, the bare blackened brickwork, the cellar-like smell, the way the illumination from overhead lamps petered out as fast as it fell, creating a series of small light pools with dark spaces in between. Oh yes, oh yes. There was something reassuring about the fact that this place still existed: the old Hole in the Ground bar, his one-time haunt. Sitting down in a booth near the entrance, he drank his whisky and watched the lively concourse. It seemed to be a place favoured by young, attractive girls. They looked as though they might be showgirls or actresses or models. They seemed to be at home in the place, called out greetings to the barman, Alexis, from whom they picked up message slips before heading for the wall phone. One of these girls had come in carrying a cello. Another wore black leotards with a parka top. There was a girl with long crimped brown hair who laughed a lot and seemed to be breathing too frequently and too hard. She kept asking Alexis if he'd seen Giorgio, where the fuck was Giorgio? And after she'd taken off abruptly, handsome Giorgio showed up and was told by Alexis that Angel had been asking for him. Giorgio was powerfully built, dark and ruggedly unshaven, and wore Ray-Bans despite the almost non-existent lighting. He shrugged, said Angel was a crazy bitch. He had a smell of Sensimilla about him and a permanent unpleasant grin, like some kind of prothesis attached to his tight jaw. Jack Strawley found himself wondering if Giorgio also did black eyes, and broken noses and arms and complete disposals where somebody had it coming. Or was that another person's department in this age of specialization? Anyway, it was useful to know where to go if he should find his nervous system in need of some quick chemical readjustment.

There was a woman sitting up at the bar whose sudden shotgun bursts of laughter had a ring that stirred in deep memory. She had on a shiny figure-fitting evening gown with a heart-shaped

neckline that plunged some way down into her substantial, pow-
dered bosom. Her lips were scarlet cupid bows. She was talking
animatedly with Alexis and laughing in these sudden deep sharp
bursts from the back of her throat. Oh, there couldn't be another
woman with a laugh like that. After all these years, it was
recognizable straight away, even if not much else about her was.
She was smoking through a long cigarette-holder and swaying
about on her high stool. He called to her softly, questioningly, in
case he had made a mistake:

'Lila! Lila?'

Hearing her name, she swivelled on her stool and, peering
through a mist, attempting to focus and finally succeeding, uttered a yelp that could be heard the length of the bar, all the way
to the backrooms. 'Jack Strawley!' With reckless precipitation
she slid off her stool, and he had to grab hold of her arm to stop
her from falling over. Feeling his hand on her, she gave him the
smile that promised all. The old smile. She did a few unsteady
steps of a mock-slithering walk, eliciting ironical applause from
men at the bar. 'How long's it been?' she asked him. 'Twenty
years?'

'More like thirty, or more.'

'I kept track of you and all your fabulous successes,' she told
him. 'You going to be shooting in this neighbourhood?'

'I hope so. What's been happening to you, Lila?'

'I got thirty years older, that's what's been happening to me.
I'm not a great big success story like you are, Jack.' She had her
hands full with her drink, her cigarette-holder and her mock-
snakeskin clutch bag. He steered her into a seat in the booth and
signalled to the bar waiter to bring refills.

'You were so good in *Killers Kill,*' he told her, 'you got such
good reviews. I really thought you had a career ahead of you.'

'Me too. Shows how wrong we both were.' She laughed like a
mocking machine gun: ratatatatat. 'Oh, it got me a contract at
Fox. But that didn't amount to much in the end. You must know
about those contracts.'

'A shame. You had a quality.'

'Yeah, a slithery quality.' The machine gun again. A short
sharp burst. 'It was a showy part . . . typecasting.'

'But God! You looked sensational. Why didn't you get in touch with me? I'd have tried to do something for you.'

'Now he tells me! Don't you remember the walk by the river? Get out of my life! Let me soar! Wouldn't let me come to your first night. I was going to be in the way. And did you soar! Won the Oscar. Prizes at film festivals. I've seen you on Cavett and Johnny Carson . . . and Dinah. I'd say to people . . . I know him. He and I used to be an item. Since you mention it, as a matter of fact I did ring you a few times . . . *since you ask*. Oh, that was way, way back. Could never get through to you, I left messages but . . . I must have chose bad times, when you were busy.'

'You should have kept trying.'

'Oh, you know. You get discouraged.' The animation of her face slowed. 'You still with Gloria?'

'No, no. We split up a while back.'

'Yeah, I remember now . . . I remember I read about that. You have . . . a daughter? Right? Just the one?'

'Just the one.'

'I've seen pictures of her in magazines. Lovely girl.'

'Yes, she is. And you, Lila? You . . . married?'

'Uh-uh.' She shook her head.

'Never?'

'No, I never married.'

'Never wanted to?'

'I guess I got involved with all the wrong men.' Another quick burst of the unmistakable laughter.

Over in shadowland there was a continuous febrile bustle of moving figures, some of them disappearing together into the deeper dark further back, while others remained lingering and looking, hands low.

'In back there,' Jack Strawley said, 'that's where Eddie Max used to deal drugs, basically marijuana when I was a kid. And girls, of course. That was the racket then. This is where I first set eyes on Slither Slither. I must have taken you here when we were doing the film, to show you.'

'I think you must have done.'

He could smell New York river slime and shaling black brickwork exuding dankness, and rust gradually eating into metal. He could smell the passage of time here.

'I haven't been here in thirty-five years, I wander in and run into you, Lila! Isn't that amazing? How d'you know this place?'

'I know it. We must have come here. Like you said, you must have showed it to me.'

'It was a real seedy place in those days, and I can see it hasn't changed much, except for the girls who come here, better class than Slither Slither . . . fringe showbusiness? Or what?'

She gave her quick-fire laugh. 'Why? You in the market for a little action? That why you came here? Wouldn't have thought a man like you needs to come to this sort of place to find some action.'

At the bar a girl with long straight dark hair, wearing a very short tight skirt and knee-high suede boots, was checking out her messages with Alexis. 'Rachelle,' Lila called to her. 'Want to see you before you go.' The girl held up the fingers of one hand to show she had five minutes. Lila turned back to Jack Strawley, and her voice had gone hard. 'Got to go now. What you come here for, Jack? To gloat? See how the ones who didn't make it live?' She fidgeted with the heavy Mexican jewellery at her neck. She seemed angry and weighed down all of a sudden: the alcohol level in her blood stream had got a little too low for her liking, and she signalled the bar for a refill.

'I just wondered in by chance,' he said. 'And you?'

'I own the place.' Her voice rattled without quite getting to be a laugh. 'And as you noticed, it *is* seedy.'

'But a good investment, I should think.'

'Seedy but profitable.' This time it was one of her full rip-roaring laughs. He remembered when he'd first seen her standing at the phone at Stella's, in her crumpled linen skirt, which had given him ideas, and she had emitted that laugh — and it was an enticing mating call then, whereas now it was really offputting. 'See,' she went on, 'I had a career change when the acting didn't work out.' He nodded. 'You don't really wanna know. Any more'n you did then! About the seven-year Fox contract which wasn't worth a fuck? With those six-monthly options on their side? So that if you didn't do what's expected . . . and I don't have to tell *you* about *that.*' She felt around in the air, seeking some support there, and then steadied herself against the back of the booth and closed her eyes. She opened them again sharply, and they glowered now with heavy sarcasm. 'In the press I was referred to as an up-and-coming Fox starlet, which in those days was still supposed to mean a budding star. Oh, *boy* was I up and coming! Making hundred and fifty a week. Getting a small role every now and then but mostly doing the other thing that they expected of their up-and-coming female contract artists. One day I met this guy in a nightclub. You spent a lot of time in nightclubs if you were an up-and-coming starlet in those days. So I met this guy, and he said to me, a girl with your looks, somebody who's on the silver screen, however flittingly, you could make a hundred to a hundred and fifty a time, not a week . . . in other words, I could be making seven, eight hundred dollars a week instead of a lousy hundred and fifty. Now I have a super de luxe apartment in Sutton Place with maids and a butler and a mirror room, and I can make a thousand to fifteen hundred a week with my girls. I have the best girls. My clients are all top drawer men, people who can afford the best. It's not what I dreamed of, Jack, when I studied acting at Stella Adler's but . . . I have money in the bank and I'm not dependent on anyone.' Her mocking laugh.

'You seem to have made the best of it,' he told her. 'Like we all had to.'

She gave a snort of disgust. 'Yeah. Except that I O.D. every so often, and the medics have to pump me out. And waking up alive, when you've put your money on the other alternative, is the daddy of all hangovers. Know the worst thing about being a madame? You have all these gorgeous girls around you, and all these high-flying men . . . and it's a ball seven nights a week, you know the worst? The worst is the loneliness. The fucking loneliness is the killer.'

47

Slowly he was getting a taste again for the New York scene, the lunching life and the night-time life and the phone calls in between. There were one or two independent pictures in the offing, but not much colour of money to be seen, and the only actual cash offer that had come his way was from a cheapie producer who wanted him to make an exploitation documentary about the low life of New York after dark, and the money from him was a trickle. It was going to be done on a budget of $50,000 of which $15,000 was his fee. None of which he'd got yet. All he'd got was 'research money', a few hundred bucks at a time, which he used conscientiously to explore the low life. In his mind he'd isolated a few settings for the film and got one or two characters lined up. He wanted Lila in the film. He wanted to use her story as the centrepiece, if she'd agree, so he had to work on her and, to this end, was hanging out a lot at her place. He wanted to call the film *The Hole in the Ground* and to shoot part of it in the long narrow tunnel bar. He had discovered that the place was frequented by young free-spirited girls with a drug habit, and that Lila used it to recruit 'occasionals', a type especially appreciated by her jaded clientele. The right sort of girl could earn a good sum just for one night's work. And so there were always girls drifting in to see Lila, toying with the idea of a remunerative one-nighter. And handsomely unshaven Giorgio was there in his white shoes and Ray-Bans to make them feel good with whatever they needed to make them feel good, and, if they were pretty enough, they could have credit, since Giorgio knew where they could get the money if they needed to.

There was one with very short, razor-chopped pale blond hair and a white glaze in her eyes, beyond which you could not see. Jack was interested in her sad toughness of spirit. She was thin and taut as a wire sculpture. She sat at the bar, the white glaze over her eyes, listening to Lila's spiel, not showing much interest in what was being outlined to her but not turning it down either. She was passively nodding her head up and down while her ankle rotated as if she was wanting to jump out of her skin. On the look-out for characters for the film, he was interested by this nervy/sassy urchin in her scuffed down-at-heels shoes and torn jeans, drinking straight vodka on the rocks and hiding herself behind the white glaze.

He thought he must have been staring at her too hard, because after Lila had left, the girl got off her stool and ambled over to him.

'You're Jack Strawley, aren't you?' she said. 'Mind if I sit down with you a minute?' She didn't wait for him to consent but pulled up a chair. 'Lila told me who you were, said she was an old friend of yours.'

He said: 'Yes, that's right,' noting the extreme pallor of the girl's face, the faint film of perspiration going all the way down her neck.

'I recognized you when she pointed you out,' she said. 'See, I know all your films. I was doing a Ph.D. on the Erotic Motif in the Cinema of Jack Strawley . . . so I feel I know you pretty well.'

'Am I talking to a philosophy doctor?'

'Not exactly. I didn't finish.'

'That's a pity. You might've told me what my erotic motive is.'

'Motif, not motive.'

'Lila give you some new material on me?'

'She . . . uh . . . hinted she could. I didn't let on about my dark academic past. Wasn't what she was interested in, vis-à-vis me. I'd seen her in *Killers Kill*, of course . . . Slither Slither, she was great . . . but I wouldn't have recognized her if she hadn't told me. That was a wonderful film. I also liked *The Interloper* a lot, and *Polly & Jane* . . . and *Heart of Darkness,* oh and a few others that you did. I know it wasn't a success, *Darkness.* But I think it's one of your best.'

'Why didn't you finish the thesis?'

'Because . . . oh, because of lots of things. Because I'm not really cut out to be a bluestocking. Because I found writing hard, and there were problems . . . family problems, money problems. Health problems.'

'I know that can happen,' he said sympathetically.

'You don't,' she corrected him bluntly. 'You don't have a fucking idea.' She stopped and collected herself. 'I was in the film course at NYU.'

'But you didn't finish that either?'

'I found the teaching too technical. I don't think making films is about camera technique and sound effects, that's what they were teaching mostly, very little about content.'

'What d'you do now?'

'Right, *right* now I'm trying to find a way of getting Giorgio off my back.' She shot a glance towards the white-shoed dealer. He had shifted his operating base to the jukebox and selected a Judy Collins number. 'D'you like Judy Collins?' the girl with the chopped off hair asked Jack Strawley. 'I think she's great. Leonard Cohen? You like him? He's one of my cultural heroes. You're another, matter of fact.'

'That's a heavy responsibility,' he said.

'There's a bunch of us interested in movies,' she went on. 'In making a movie . . . you know? Just a small movie. But with content. We get together. We don't have any money, we just have a Mitchell and a Moviola and we cadge some film stock here and there and shoot each other. Now you're going to think this very suspect,' she added quickly, without breathing in between. 'but you couldn't advance me four hundred dollars, could you? So I can pay off Giorgio. He's getting to be quite a pain. I know it looks as though I just came over and said all this stuff in order to touch you for some dough, but that isn't how it is. Okay, okay, I can see the idea doesn't grab you too much, so forget it. Just an idea.'

She was hyperventilating and, every so often, took a really big gulp of air as if she was about to run out of it. And she was swaying about in her chair. One foot was in continuous movement as if treading water at high speed. He watched her expression change about five times in the space of a second.

'What's it you're all out of?' he asked her.

'If you really wanna know, I do half an ounce of coke a day,' she said, 'and today has been a *nuit blanche*. I'm out of the money and that asshole Giorgio won't renew the prescription till I've paid what I owe. But don't worry. I can get the money.

Wouldn't want you to think . . .' She got up to go. 'I'm very bucked to have met you, anyway and I'm sorry if you think what I said before was a line. Because it's all true.'

He suggested: 'Let me get you another of what you're drinking.'

'Look. . .' She seemed uncomfortable about what she was going to say. 'I'd like to stay and have a drink with you but I really do have a problem that I have to resolve . . . *now*. So I don't really have the time right now, unless . . . you said to me that if I stayed and had a drink, and maybe we have dinner or whatever, that you could help me out.' Her eyes were reckless bright. 'I need the four hundred tonight.'

'You don't need that much for a fix.'

'It's not so much the fix. I'm not that hooked on it. It's an instalment that's way overdue.' She shot a glance in Giorgio's direction: he was leaning over the jukebox, selecting the next number. 'You won't help me then?'

'What'll happen if you don't have the money?' he asked her.

'I'll have the money,' she said, throwing back her head. 'I got to have it.' He looked at her hard. 'If you can't help me, it's no problem.' She gave a violent shrug, was starting to get up, and he put a hand on her arm to detain her. The white glaze in her eyes was impenetrable as a wall.

He told her: 'Some trains once you get on them you can't get off so easy.'

'You giving me fucking fatherly advice or something?'

'Or something. Don't do it.'

She threw her head to one side, glaring at him angrily. 'If you're referring to what I think you're referring to. Seems to me Lila's not done so bad. She's got an apartment in Sutton Place, maids, a butler. She eats at "21". And gets to test the girls herself.'

He made a casual gesture as if agreeing. 'Yeah, I know. She tell you about the times she overdoses, and they have to pump her out?'

'Trrra-rara-rum!' she sounded off. 'Here it comes. The Lesson. That's the older generation all over,' she mocked. '*They* do what they like, and having studied your films I do know what you like . . . and then they come on heavy on the moral issue. You better die out, you old guys. Die and leave our generation to make our own lives.' Angrily she got up and went to the bar to get her own refill and came back with the ice cubes clinking defiantly in her glass, eyes glinting.

'Okay,' he told her, 'you made your point. You can buy your own drink and your own dope. Because you've got this valuable capital resource you can always cash in .'

'So?' she threw back at him. 'I'm going to tell you something. Guys think when they pay for a girl, they're in control but they're wrong. It's the guy who's got the hard-on — or more likely can't get one — who has to get the help, and that means it's the girl who controls.'

He gave a light shrug. 'That what appeals to you about it? Being in control.' He spoke softly, almost tenderly. 'My problem about giving you $400 is that it won't solve your situation. You'll pay off what you owe and you'll get more shit on credit and then you'll fall behind in the payments, and it'll be a choice again between getting that pretty face of yours all broke up, or Lila.'

'Can you tell me, Mr Gladstone: what's wrong with prostitution?' she said mockingly.

'You don't know?'

'No. Tell me.'

'It makes you a prostitute. That's what's wrong with it. You can make yourself a film-maker, if that's what you want, or you can make yourself a prostitute. Your choice.'

She had become very pale and trembly. Her eyes had gone liquid, dissolving the white glaze, and he could see fright and desperation and panic. She bit her lip trying to hold herself together. Her jaw was shaking. 'How can I make myself a film-maker? Who's gonna give me that chance?'

'Nobody gives you the chance. You have to make your own.'

'That what you did?'

'Yes. I won't say it's not costly. You have to stake your life . . . and other people's.'

'Suppose you don't have that much ambition?'

'You don't make it. And listen, I don't want to sound like your father again, but . . . you don't have to make it. You don't have to be like me. Your life's worth more.'

She had quietened, lost some of the brittleness. 'Why you giving me all this good advice, which I won't take, and you know I won't take.'

'Way of talking to myself.'

'You do a lot of that?'

'Quite a bit, lately.'

'I'd have thought, guy in your position, don't need to talk to himself. There are plenty who'd be glad to listen.'

'You have to talk to yourself too.'

'Yeah, okay. I see that.'

Over at the jukebox Giorgio had selected Quincy Jones' 'Body Heat', complete with expressive moans and groans, and was grinning across at the girl with the chopped-off hair. 'Wanna come pay off your debt, baby?' he mouthed at her.

'I'll pay cash,' she called back to him, stretching out her smile to its sickly end.

'You savin' it up for somebody?' he called back.

She nodded, smiling hard. 'Yeah, shithead! My beloved.'

Jack Strawley was staring into the bottom of his whisky glass.

'Here's what we're going to do,' he told her after some moment's reflection. 'I'm going to give Giorgio the four hundred, and you're going to give me an I.O.U. It's not a present and it's not a loan. It's an advance. You'll pay me back out of your first pay-check as a film-maker. Whenever that is. Okay?'

She nodded, biting her lip and hyperventilating. He tore a corner off the bar menu and passed it across to her with a pen. 'Write the I.O.U.,' he told her. 'Do it properly. Name. Address. Date. Signature.'

When she had written it out and signed it, she said: 'Thank you, sir. Guess doesn't mean all that much to you . . . expect you're pretty rich. But I want you to know . . . I appreciate it. Fact is, I think you just saved my life.'

He got up, stuffed the scrap of paper in his pocket and started towards where Giorgio was lounging against the bar, rhythmically rolling his body in pantomime accompaniment to the moans and groans.

Jack Strawley called back to her: 'Have a good life. And I suggest you get yourself some new cultural heroes.'

48

A sudden stifling heat had descended on New York with noon highs in Manhattan of 99 degrees, and the radio broadcasters were repeating all day long that it was one of those days when you could fry eggs on the sidewalk, and the night was going to be pretty hot and muggy too, so why not try one of Sygurnie's cool refreshing daiquiries in the air-conditioned ambience. Air pollution levels were such the newspapers were advising people not to breathe unless they absolutely had to.

At the height of the heat-wave the producer of the documentary about New York after dark, disappeared. His phone was permanently off the hook, his office closed up. Jack Strawley made inquiries through the F.B.I. and the Missing Persons Bureau, but neither organization had any information concerning the missing film producer. Nothing new there. These shady film producers were famous for their disappearing acts. According to Giorgio, who was better informed in these matters than the F.B.I. or the Missing Persons Bureau, the producer had defaulted on the one kind of debt you must never default on and was either at the bottom of the East River, or, if lucky, merely in intensive care. Whichever, he was not going to be in any position to produce anything in the foreseeable future. Or to pay the first $5,000 instalment that Jack Strawley was due on his contract.

He had been using his American Express card to pay his rent at the hotel and was now getting phone calls and telegrams about the sum outstanding: Amex was threatening to cancel the card if payment of almost $4,000 due was not received immediately. He had counted on the money from the documentary to pay the account and now found himself having to stall for time. He phoned the accounts office and said there had been a technical hitch concerning the sale of some of his securities in Europe: the settlement date was not for another week, and the mechanics of the transfer, although supposedly instantaneous, sometimes took anything up to ten days, as they must know. He was trying to be both offhand and tough with them. He reminded them casually that he'd had the card for thirty years and had charged hundreds of thousands of dollars. Oh sure, the girl said, but now there was $3,985.35 outstanding, and she didn't make the rules.

'Who's the head of American Express nowadays?' he asked roughly. 'Lemme talk to him.' But it seemed she didn't know who the head was and, in any case, doubted if Jack Strawley would be able talk to him.

'You know who I am?' he asked her gruffly, and she had to admit she didn't. 'Listen, stupid. Go find somebody who does,' he told her. The girl went away from the phone and he could hear her talking to someone, and after a few minutes another woman, whose voice sounded older and more accommodating, came to the phone.

'I'm sorry about this, Mr Strawley. How long d'you say it'll take for your securities to clear?'

'Couple of weeks.'

'Should be all right, sir. I'll make a note on your account. You shouldn't have any trouble.'

So he had got two weeks. He'd have to reactivate the sale of the Magritte. Three years ago the Paris art dealer Laforge had got him $249,000 for a small Klee, 12 1/2 x 18 3/8 in., pen and ink, gouache and pastel on paper, from a private American collector, and that had allowed Jack Strawley to keep going for another couple of years. When the proceeds from the Klee had almost run out, he'd sold a small, indifferent Foujita, done in 1951 when the painter's talent was on the wane, for the not bad price of 450,000 francs . The small Magritte left with Laforge was one of a dozen versions of the same subject, two masked apples beneath a cloudy blue sky. One of the other versions had been sold for 2,700,000 francs. His was less good and smaller. Laforge had estimated being able to get him between 800,000 francs and 1,300,000 francs, less commission and charges. He could reckon to make around $100,000 clear. It was the last of his valuable canvases, and he wanted to get the best possible price and had told Laforge to hold out until he got it. But now, clearly, he was going to have to take whatever he could get.

Ringing up to find out what was happening, Jack Strawley sought to keep the tone of the phone call as casual as possible — it didn't pay to show need. After chatting for a few minutes, he asked Laforge:

'Any bites at the apple?'

Laforge said he had no firm offer at present that was '*intéressant*'.

'I think that's because you like to see it hanging on your wall, Pierre. What'd be a tempting price for somebody? For a quick sale?'

'The market's not good at present. Shall pick up in a year or so. As well, there's the problem that a quick sale is not feasible in the present time.'

'Oh, why's that?' He maintained his light tone with grim determination.

'I haff receive letters. From a firm of lawyers. Oh, they're how do you call . . . who run after the ambulance?'

'Ambulance-chasers?'

'Yes, yes. That is what they are, I am sure.'

'What they chasing, Pierre?'

'The apples. The money we get for the Magritte. They say you owe them money. I think they are gangsters. They buy uncollectable debt and then collect it. Using their own collecting methods.'

'If they don't have any sound legal claim. . .'

'Even so, even so! They can hold up the sale, while the courts haff to decide if they haff sound legal claim. And our French courts, you know how long they can be.'

'What do we do about that, Pierre?'

'Do nothing. Iss my opinion. To wait. In one year these people can be out of the business, in jail . . . floating face-down in the river. Let us hope. And then you sell for big fat price . . . the market should haff improve by then.'

'Suppose I can't wait a year, suppose I would like to have the money right now.'

'That shall be a problem. But I take it you don't *absolutely* need the money now.'

'Depends how you would define absolutely, Pierre.' Jack Strawley laughed. You had to keep your tone light when you were desperate. When people knew they had you by the throat they had a tendency to throttle you. And the estimable Pierre Laforge of Paris was not necessarily any different from the rest of the shitty human race. So Jack Strawley kept his voice light.

'Pierre, listen. I'm sort of bored by the whole thing. I don't even have the picture hanging on my wall, you have it hanging on your wall. What d'you say, suppose *you* take it off my hands? I'll give you a good price. And *you* hang onto it and sell it in a year's time and make a big fat profit. Huh?'

The phone seemed to have gone dead it was so silent, but he didn't demand, 'Are you there?' so as not to sound anxious. He judged that it was probably a strategic silence to get the price down.

'Is attractive proposition,' Laforge said returning from the dead. 'I shall be glad off it. Only at present time everything is very slow. France is having its usual *crise*, and I haf lay out a great deal recently, and there not many buyers in the market . . . but perhaps in a few months' time, when things improve.'

The way these people got you by the balls. 'Well, I may just come and pick it up and sell it myself, Pierre. Or hang it on my wall.'

'As you like. Of course. Of course. Completely as you like.'

He had stopped taking the lithium tablets now. The lithium kept him on an even keel, stopped him getting manic, but it also made him dull, wrapped him up in felt, blunted his edge, and permitted him to let things drag on, and if he let them drag on much more they'd drag him under. He had to get something off the ground fast, now that his last source of liquid funds, the American Express Co., was about to dry up on him. He decided that his mistake had been getting tied up in cheapie projects like the New

York documentary. That was the lithium keeping him under. Right, he decided. Forget about these piss-ant little hole-in-the-corner films with shady producers like the one now probably residing at the bottom of the East River, according to Giorgio. Go for the Big One. The one he'd been saving up for the right moment. Well, there was never a fucking right moment. For anything. Do it now.

He started putting in calls to Maureen Wynner and, after three days of continual phoning and leaving messages, finally got hold of her.

'I have a wonderful subject for us,' he told her, 'that can be as big as *Polly & Jane*. It's a trenchant sex comedy. By a very good French writer. The script is being translated now. The central character is this woman who's just been made American Ambassador in Paris. It's a fabulous part for you, Maureen. She is someone who has been involved with the world's richest, cleverest, most powerful and, above all, *sexiest* men. Including — and here's our story — the American President (hence her appointment) *and* the new French President. It's political-sexual high comedy. And a love story of the great.'

Maureen was making appreciative sounds. 'Sounds good, Jack. Love to read the script.'

'I can have either Delon or Belmondo to play the French President, and I can get Nik for the American President. I want to move on this, Maureen, because it's a great chance and the option on the material runs out.' He said he didn't want to send her a script, wait until she'd read it, then wait until she'd given it to somebody else to read . . . then wait until forever. He wanted to cut through all that, he said. 'So, let me tell you the rest.' She said okay, and he spent an hour on the telephone to L.A. telling her the entire film, in detail, acting all the main parts scene by scene, delivering love speeches, punch lines, gags, and she was laughing all the way. He vividly described the clothes she was wearing in each scene, including underwear: he told her in graphic terms, with camera angles, how the sex was going to be filmed, and she was cooing. He *knew* that he was through to her from the tease in her voice. If she turned on, you were through. If she didn't, she said: 'Talk to my agent.'

If he could direct the picture with the amount of whizzbang that he'd put into selling it to Maureen, they'd have an enormous hit. He told her he needed a quick decision, and she agreed to come to New York to talk over a deal. It was going to happen, he knew it in his bones, felt the certainty creep up his spine; the certainty that happened when everything was suddenly speeding up for you.

He said to her: 'Let me take you to the Five Hundred for lunch. I haven't been there in ages. Last time I went it was with you. Remember?'

She laughed gorgeously. 'Yes, I do remember, Jack. I do . . . Better book a table for three,' she added in a more practical tone of voice. 'And I'll get Judy to come along as well.'

It seemed to be a good sign that she wanted to bring her agent.

'Great,' he said. 'Tell her to come at half past. I want us to have half an hour by ourselves first.'

Arriving at the entrance of the Five Hundred, you had only to look at Emil's face to know how you were faring. Day by day, like a chronicle of the times, Emil's face, as he seated people, reflected their box office takings, their updated track record, the critical acclaim or pannings they had just received, the fame or oblivion that awaited them. Going by Emil's face, Jack Strawley understood that he was currently nowhere in the maitre d's ratings. It didn't dampen his spirits today; he had got nicely hyped up on dry martinis and refused to be snubbed when Hugo Trelawny determinedly avoided noticing him. Damned little squirt. 'Hugo!' Jack Strawley called to him. 'Still living beyond your over-ample means?'

'One does what one can. What are you doing here?'

'I firmly believe I'm going to have lunch.'

'Well, isn't that a coincidence? So am I. With Gore, as a matter of fact, I do rather like Gore. He's so good at loathing people.'

'Almost as good as you, Hugo.'

'I don't want to boast, but not quite.' Hugo was wearing a white suit and drinking what seemed to be eggnog. 'How's business?' he asked looking around to see if anyone worth recognizing had come in. But nobody had in the last minute or so.

'You saw that Dustin is here,' he said informationally. 'And Ricky von Opel.'

'Who *is* Ricky von Opel?' Jack Strawley asked, peering through the indoor jungle trained over white trellises and up pearwood walls.

Hugo Trelawney laughed cursorily at such affectations of ignorance. 'So what are you up to, Jack?' he demanded without the slightest degree of interest in the answer.

'Pictures,' Jack Strawley told him. 'Moving pictures. Trains coming into stations. That kind of thing.'

'I meant — lately.'

'Lately I've been having lunch.'

'Well, as long as it keeps you off the street.'

Jack took his place in the atrium, under the plant-filtered daylight, and the octahedral thick-glass lanterns. The place was filling up. The refrigerated air kept bare female shoulders crisp as frozen lettuces. Presently, he sensed a faint stir in the air and saw that Maureen Wynner had made her entrance wearing a green patterned silk top diagonally buttoned across the bodice, white kid shoes with peep toes and high heels, and a teenage-style mid-thigh-length skirt. Beaming Emil conducted her to Jack's table, and he felt his ratings with the maitre d' shoot up.

'Long long time, eh?' Maureen said as they kissed tenderly on the lips. 'Shhh! Don't say how long. Somebody might hear.'

Sitting down, her skirt very noticeably didn't reach anywhere near her knees.

He said: 'Looks like you've obtained an exemption from the passage of time. You look sensational, Maureen.'

Her boldly flashing eyes flirted with him when they weren't flirting with the rest of the room.

'You look pretty good too,' she said. 'Don't happen to be free at the moment?' she asked, 'because *I* am again, yeah *again*, what a bore, all that rite of spring stuff at our age. Shhh! Getting too old for the dating game now. All those phone calls! All that getting to know you. Think of the phone bills we could save. Because we do know each other, don't we?'

'Yeah, we do.'

The passage of time, while it may have necessitated a face lift or two, and a constant regime of dieting, hadn't diminished her capacity for sending out inflammatory messages.

He carefully didn't get round to the project until the intimacy between them had been securely reestablished. Then he told her easily:

'It's a good role for you, because she's got to be your sort of age to have known all those amazing men and, at the same time, she has got to be able to run rings around the younger competition. Aged — what? Let's say forty, forty-five . . . but she outperforms the kids in the romantic sex stakes. It *is* you, Maureen. I *see* you play it, darling, I don't see anybody else. This is going to be a performance like Carole Lombard's in *Nothing Sacred,* like Garbo's in *Ninotchka,* dammit like Wynner's in *Polly & Jane.* I know that audiences will be in love with you because I am already. Or rather, *again.*' He was aware of laying it on like his former producer, and it made him feel a little sick.

'Well, oh gee!' she said with a mock fluttering of eyelashes, 'how you do manage to turn a girl's head, Jack. You're still as good at that as ever. I love the idea of working with you again. Sounds like it could be a wonderful *adventure.* All round.' Her voice was as thrilling as it had been the very first time he'd met her. 'And I'm going to prove myself to you. I know you used to think I can't act, and that was so hurtful to me. I know you — and others — used to call me Maureen Talentless, Except on Her Back.' She gave him a gorgeous teasing smile from way back.

'That was because those of us who didn't know you in that respect were so wildly envious of those who did.'

'Male chauvinist pigs! All of you!' She tagged on a forgiving smile. 'I showed you, didn't I? And I'm going to show you that I have a lot more talent of *every* sort — than you ever gave me credit for.'

She had arranged for her agent Judy Rhinehart not to show up before 1:30, so as to give her and Jack half an hour alone to get re-acquainted, and, at exactly 1:30, the agent arrived. She had the pasty looks of someone who spends most of her life on the telephone or in dark restaurants. There were rather a lot of lines around the mouth from having smiled too much in her youth, a habit of which she had seemingly cured herself now that she was a powerful agent. At lunch, her smiles were few and far between. She asked all the questions he expected her to ask, and he gave his prepared answers. What companies had he been dealing with? What was the size of the budget? Who else would be in the film? Was Nik going to make a fuss about accepting secondary billing to Maureen? What about Delon? He really wasn't a name in America. What about Sean Connery or Michael Caine instead? Jack Strawley pointed out that the French President should be played by a French actor, and she conceded the point without any deep-down conviction. He said that he'd been talking to Ray Stark, to Dino de Laurentiis, the Orion people, John Calley. Salary and billing were discussed, and he didn't flinch when Judy said that Maureen would be paid $5.5 million and take 5% of the gross and would get top billing whoever else was in the picture, even if it was Paul Newman. He said that five and a half million was not going to be a problem, and on the billing question he was sure they could come up with a solution since Paul Newman was busy anyway.

The Rhinehart woman had the kind of passion for details that pasty-faced women who didn't have other kinds of passion tended to have. She kept asking things like: 'Oh, so when did you see Ray last . . . he's in London, isn't he?'

'I know, I know,' Strawley said. 'He's got a couple of things going there, in any case I'm not really sure I want to do it with Ray . . . maybe Dino, maybe Orion. Maybe, I don't know, Alan Ladd.'

'Carver?'

'No, I would doubt it. We no longer work together.'

'Ever? That's a pity, you and he were a good team. At Orion are you dealing with Arthur?'

'Arthur and I go back a long way,' he reminisced. 'I like Arthur a lot and he leaves you alone, but there are times when knowing somebody too well can be a handicap. Of course Arthur, as you know . . .' He filibustered his way around the traps.

At the end, he considered that it had gone pretty well. He had drunk almost the whole bottle of Pomerol that he'd ordered, since Maureen was watching her figure and only willing to have a sip, and Judy drank only Perrier water, and then he'd had two

large brandies with the coffee . . . and the clicks in his head were building up like an electric storm.

When they'd finished coffee, Judy said she would discuss the whole thing with Maureen this afternoon, and let him know their answer quickly, hopefully later in the day or some time tomorrow: where was he going to be? Did he have the impression that Stark or Orion were willing to commit to *pay or play* right out? Because Maureen had two other firm offers and was going to have to give definite answers very very soon. He said he was sure that either Stark or Orion would find that acceptable. He decided: time to wind this up, before the prying Rhinehart bitch started demanding sworn transcripts of phone conversations. He called for the bill, scribbled 'add 20% service' across the bottom, and slapped down his American Express card. The waiter came back after some minutes to whisper in his ear that they were having a problem passing his American Express card through their machine, did he have another card — Diner's or . . .? He said no, he'd only brought American Express: he told the waiter to bring a cheque form and he'd make them out a cheque. The waiter went away and returned after several more minutes to say that they were not accepting cheques except by special arrangement. Strawley, smiling, quietly suggested their card machine must be stuck and to ring up American Express and clear it on the phone. Maureen and Judy were deep in tête-à-tête and seemed to be taking no notice of what was going on. The waiter went away and came back with Emil who stood beaming and nodding and smiling on the far side of Strawley's chair, beneath the giant ferns. Discreetly, out of earshot of the ladies, in a delicately pitched low voice, he said that the American Express Co. had been telephoned and had indicated that they were unable to accept the charge.

'They can get things pretty mixed up, sometimes,' Jack explained, 'especially when they have to cope with changes of address. That seems to be beyond them. Why don't I just sign the bill?'

Emil said smiling strongly: 'I don't believe you any longer have an account with us, sir.'

'I used to have.'

'Must have been some few years ago, sir. You don't now.'

'That's a technicality I think we can.' He became impatient. Snapped his fingers. 'Okay, give it to me. . .'

'I'm afraid,' Emil began, lowering his voice to the lowest possible pitch without making himself inaudible, 'that I'm not permitted . . .' he was starting to explain.

'That's too bad! What d'you want me to do in that case?' He was raising his voice deliberately, so he'd be heard. His voice was mocking. 'Want . . . me to stay and wash dishes, Emil, with Maureen wiping?'

There were appreciative chuckles from people at adjacent tables enjoying the joke of Maureen Wynner drying dishes, and Emil gave a little chuckle too, then said in a terse undertone:

'Let us just step over there, sir, where we can . . . discuss this. Shall we, sir?'

Jack Strawley got up and accompanied Emil to the walnut bureau in the entrance where the big leather book of reservations was kept. Emil turned the pages slowly, as if engaged in searching through his seating plan. Under his breath he asked:

'Please tell me, sir, how you propose to settle the bill?'

'You tell me, Emil.'

'How about cash, sir?'

'I don't have that much cash on me.'

'Well, that *is* a problem then, sir.'

'What d'you suggest we do, Emil?'

Emil looked perplexed. 'What would *you* suggest, sir.'

'What I suggest, Emil, is that I sign the fucking bill,' and he proceeded to scrawl his signature across it, 'like I always have done here, for years and years, or . . . if that doesn't suit you . . .'

'Yes, sir?'

'That I stuff it down your throat, Emil.' He had said it loud enough for one or two people to hear, including Hugo Trelawney who seemed tickled by the situation.

'Need a loan, Jack? I'm not offering, mind you, but you could try Ricky. Ah, but you don't know Ricky, do you?'

Jack returned to his table, with Emil stuck to him like a fat Siamese twin.

'Let's go,' he told Maureen and Judy.

Maureen stood up, and Emil, bowing, pulled out her chair for her, and, bowing again and smiling, whispered something in her ear.

She said crisply: 'I'll take care of it, Emil,' and the three left, bowed out by Emil and the waiters.

Outside the restaurant, as the taxis were drawing up, he and Maureen embraced warmly, and Judy said: 'I'll phone you later, Jack.'

49

Back in his apartment at the hotel, he considered tactics. Should he stay all afternoon by the phone waiting for them to call him, or should he be out when they called and so oblige them to call back? Or should he wait an hour or two and then call Judy? He thought that the lunch had gone well, apart from the incident with the bill. Best to wait for them to phone him. Showed more confidence. He waited for two hours, sitting by the silent phone, and then decided to hell with it, only *unconfident* people played those games. He put a call through to Judy Rhinehart at her office.

'Was really nice seeing you again, Judy.'

'I enjoyed it.'

No chat. Get to it. 'So what d'you say? You talk it over with Maureen? Do we have a deal?'

'I was just about to phone you,' Judy Rhinehart said, her voice chirpy. 'Jack, we're going to pass this time.'

'I got the impression,' he said, keeping his voice low and level, 'that Maureen was keen to do it.'

'She was. She was thrilled at the idea of working with you again and she thinks it's a wonderful story, and you will do it beautifully. Only she does have these two other firm offers . . .

and, being practical about it, we both feel they are somewhat nearer to going forward.'

'Which one's she going to do?'

'That's not 100% decided yet.'

'She at the Sherry?'

'Should be.'

'Okay. I'll talk to her. Speak to you later, Judy.'

He couldn't believe that the decision was irreversible. It was a snag that had arisen, but the movie business was all about snags arising and being overcome. Maureen needed more coaxing. Big women stars expected to be chased. So, okay.

'Maureen,' he told her on the phone, 'I really am disappointed by your decision. I want you for this picture, you're so right for it. We can have a very big success with it, and . . . it would be meaningful for me, and I think for you, with the history you and I have. You know, for me there always has got to be the personal element for a picture to really work. And this film will have that, if we do it together. It's something that'll be so moving and glamorous and sexy for audiences.' She wasn't saying anything: but it was a warm silence, and he had the feeling he was making an impression on her. 'Do it, Maureen. Do it for me . . . just close your eyes and lie back and trust me. Hey, you're so great with your eyes closed.'

'And on my back?' There was a faintly taunting note in with the teasing.

'Please. I need you for this picture . . . and for myself too.'

She gave the teasing warm little laugh that he knew: sometimes you had to insist with her, had to bully and coax, crank up the emotional ante . . . he got the feeling she was coming round. She wasn't saying anything, playing the coquette. But in the end she was going to say yes. He knew that.

'Jack,' she said at last, 'I have to admit it's awfully tempting . . . for all sorts of reasons. Personal reasons and . . . because you *are* a good director, probably the best I ever worked with, I know that.'

'I can do something exceptional with this story, with you in the part. We'll make a terrific film together . . . and, who knows . . . you're free, I'm free, let's give it a chance.'

Her silence was even longer this time, and he thought maybe I shouldn't be pleading with her, maybe that's the wrong approach, Carver would have made her feel insecure, made some remark about her age, mention that Orion had wanted Liz Taylor.

'Maureen, what d'you say?'

'Nice as you make that all sound, Jack, let's be realistic, you and I: I know how good you are but I also know that the films you make have been known to run into trouble . . . , and I don't want to battle anymore. I'm too old for that now. And I made a rule to never let personal sentiment enter into business decisions.'

Her voice and words sounded pretty unbudging now.

'I thought at lunch we were all set. At the beginning, anyway. Until Judy arrived.'

She gave a laugh that, despite what she had just said, seemed to contain all sorts of promises. Leading you on was what she did best, whether it was on the screen or in life. 'I do have to decide this with my head, Jack, tempted though I may be at other levels.' Even turning him down, her voice was full of enticements. Sending out erotic dares. You would think she meant yes when she was saying no. The stop-go nature of her signals was always the problem with the unwinnable Wynner.

'You're a great tease, Maureen. You always were. You can't get out of the habit, can you?'

'Jack, it's a business decision. It's got to be. And on that basis, after careful consideration, we are regretfully declining.'

It sounded very final and businesslike now: that 'we' bit, she and all her advisers and managers and guiding lights. You were up against a whole fucking board meeting. He felt the bitter anger rising in his throat, making his voice shake. 'What you're saying is I haven't made a major film for over ten years. I drink too much and sometimes go a bit crazy, and, in addition, fucking American Express doesn't accept my charge card, so you end up paying for lunch . . . hence I must be on the skids . . . hence the business decision has got to be no.' He hadn't played this correctly, not according to the Carver rule book which said to always argue from strength, never from weakness. To keep the upper hand and not show yourself to be desperate, however desperate you were. Because people always took advantage of your desperation.

There was an even longer silence this time, and when she spoke, finally, every last note of enticement had gone out of her voice: it was sheer as a cliff face where you can obtain no hold.

'I have to be practical, Jack. It would have been nice, but you know better than anyone how hard I had to fight to get where I've got. I have to do what's best for me.'

When he'd hung up he drank what was left in the whisky bottle and then flung the empty bottle at the bathroom mirror, shattering the raging face into a thousand shards, some of which flew back at him cutting his brow and cheeks. Going into the sitting room, he set about smashing up the place, starting with the pictures, the lithographs of New York at the turn of the century: hansom cabs, and men in silk top hats, and women wearing high-stand collars and lace blouses and large brimmed hats trimmed with ostrich feathers. He smashed up the world of the past. He was yelling his rage at the top of his voice as he picked up chairs and threw them against the wall.

Presently, through all the noise he was making, he became aware of an insistent knocking on the door, which he chose to ignore while he was continuing with the systematic demolition of the apartment. No result having been obtained by knocking, a pass key was eventually turned in the lock, and there stood Norbert Beauregard, flanked by two sturdy black bellhops, all three with aghast looks on their faces as they took in the devastation.

'Looks like I've done some damage, Norbert,' Jack Strawley said, calming down and sobering up instantly. 'Got annoyed with myself, and — uh — you know how it is getting annoyed with yourself . . . caused some damage. Just put it on my bill, Norbert. I'll take care of it.'

Norbert Beauregard looked around, shaking his head with an air of bewilderment. 'Mr Strawley,' he said after a while, 'I think we better talk about this in my office.'

They rode down in the elevator in silence, Jack Strawley feeling like a prisoner between the two large black bellhops, Norbert Beauregard staring fixedly at his highly polished shoes.

When they were in his poky little ground-floor office, the door of which was left open, with the bellhops standing guard outside, Beauregard took a manilla folder from a pile on his roll-top desk and frowningly leafed through pages, his face getting redder and redder as he did so. 'Mr Strawley,' he asked eventually, clicking his tongue against his dentures, 'how d'you intend paying these bills, may I ask?'

'In the usual way.'

'American Express has informed us that they will not accept any further charges in your name, Mr Strawley.'

'Seems to have been some sort of mix-up there. Let me give you a cheque till I get that all sorted out.'

'Those you gave at the bar have come back marked "refer to sender",' he pointed out.

'I don't know why that should be. I'm going to look into it straight away. I'll do it right now.'

'It distresses me to point this out, sir, but you are two months in arrears with the rental for the apartment,' Norbert Beauregard said, blushing deeply.

'Funds I'm transferring from Europe are going to be through in the next few days. A matter of a few days, that's all.'

Norbert Beauregard was making little tchk-tchk sounds with his tongue and teeth as he considered the matter. Finally he said: 'Mr Strawley, I do think that it might be best if you were to find somewhere else to stay, while you sort out the transfer of funds.'

'That's out of the question right now,' Jack Strawley patiently explained. 'I have important deals that are at the point of being signed and people have this address and this telephone number. They know I'm *here.*'

'We shall make sure that all messages and mail are forwarded to your new address.'

'This is a crucial moment for me, I can't leave at present.'

'Unfortunately, I do not see any other alternative.'

'I'll cover all your costs, every cent, Norbert,' Jack Strawley said expansively. 'I'll pay for all the damage I did. I'll give you a signed undertaking to that effect. And the rent of the apartment will be paid, just as soon as. . .' Seeing the blankness of Norbert Beauregard's expression, he cut in on himself: 'Let me make a couple of phone calls. I'm going to work something out for you right now.'

Norbert Beauregard's lips became pursed as a rosebud. 'Oh dear, oh dear,' he sighed, 'oh dear! I like things to go smoothly, Mr Strawley. I don't like all this bother and trouble! Well! It would have to be . . . cash, or a certified banker's draft . . . the amount outstanding . . . plus next month's rent, plus the unpaid bar bills and the cost of redecorating, refurbishing the apartment. We are looking at a sum of . . . around $10,000, I should think.'

'I'll arrange that,' Jack Strawley said. 'Right away.'

He went out into the lobby and from a phone kiosk rang Sydney Carver's office. The chairman of WorldVista was in conference, he was told. Giving his name, Jack Strawley said: 'See if you can break in on him, I have to talk to him . . . say it's very urgent.'

He heard clicks and hums and cut-off words, and then the terse, busy voice.

'I'm in conference,' Carver told him. 'I'll get back to you soon as I can.'

'Listen to me a minute, Sydney.'

'I'm listening.'

'Expect you're surprised I'm calling you.' The silence with which this was received was evidently strategic. 'I'm surprised myself that I'm calling you.'

'Can you make it brief?'

'Briefly, very briefly, I need $10,000.'

From the other end came a mumbled sound, the meaning of which, as was often the case with Sydney Carver's utterances, was difficult to decipher.

'You heard?'

'I heard.' The reply was a noncommittal rasp, followed by another of those strategic silences that you were meant to fall into head first.

'I wouldn't think that such a petty sum presents much of a problem to you, Sydney,' Jack Strawley said, and he heard his voice bounce back at him. The long silence expanded, forcing out further explanation. 'I know we haven't talked in a long time . . . I'm asking you this . . . because, frankly, I sort of feel entitled to ask. Your present position is not unrelated to the association we used to have and the films that I made when we were in partnership.' His voice sounded strange to himself, hollow and artificial and oddly resonant.

'You're in the big shit, in other words?'

'You phrase it with your usual delicacy, Sydney.'

'Talk to my secretary, Jack. She'll fit you in soon as I have a spare half hour.' His voice had the sound of winding up the conversation fast.

'Hold on, hold on there. Sydney, this is something that can't wait.'

'I'll try and fit you in during the next couple of days.'

It sounded as if he was doing half a dozen other things at the same time as conducting this telephone conversation.

'It's more urgent than that. I don't have a couple of days. There's been some mix-up with American Express. You know how they can be. Result is the hotel's demanding I pay them right away, otherwise . . . I have to leave. If you made a phone call to the manager, guaranteeing the amount, they'd accept that, I'm sure. You wouldn't even have to lay it out. I just need a little time to get something organized. I have that Magritte, the two masked apples. It's with Laforge in Paris. It's worth a hundred and fifty thousand. You can take a charge on it. For the ten thousand. If your guarantee was ever called. Which it won't be. It's a question of gaining some extra time until certain of my projects come through.' The echoing sound of his voice gave him the impression that he was on the air, broadcasting his troubles to the world.

'Jack, why don't you stop kidding yourself? Your projects are not going to come through. You're all washed up as a filmmaker.'

'Sydney, we are talking privately, I take it?' he asked with sudden suspicion.

With a note of satisfaction: 'I told you I was in conference.'

So now the entire movie industry knew his exact situation. That he was all washed up. That he didn't have the money to pay his hotel bill and was being thrown into the street and had had to go on his bended knees to Sydney Carver to bail him out, and that Sydney had shat on him. Which was what Sydney did to people he could afford to do it to. And he evidently could afford to do it to Jack Strawley, which was even worse than the act itself. It was letting it be generally known that he was someone who could be shat upon without risk. All the industry would know it now. Every studio he approached, every producer, every potential guarantor would know.

He said softly: 'Listen, Sydney, let me just add this for the benefit of all our listeners: the reason I called you to ask this little favour is because I felt I had that right, since you've stolen millions from me . . . for years. Like you steal from everybody.'

He heard the click of the conference speaker being switched off and then the sound of the phone being slammed down hard.

Okay, no point panicking. Who can you call? What are your fallback numbers? The people you can go to in the last resort. Which this is, now. Not a hypothetical last resort, a real one. He got out his tattered little black book and started leafing through the pages. He began to dial Gloria's number, and then stopped. I can't ask Gloria: I lost her her home . . . I've never paid her a penny of alimony, I can't ask her. She doesn't have $10,000 lying around in loose change, but she'd borrow it against her apartment or her pension fund, she'd get the money for him, but he couldn't do that to her. So who else? Anna? I can't go to my own daughter for money. The daughter who hates me. Besides, Anna never has a penny. Lives from hand to mouth in her queer world, and I don't even know where to get hold of her, her girlfriends change so fast. Forget pride, forget anger, forget shame: who? Moira? He hated to ask Moira, had not talked to Moira since their breach in Seville over ten years ago. Moira was a big-shot lady now, *Fortune* magazine listed her regularly as among the ten highest paid women executives in the United States, her salary as head of World Wide Arts Associates was said to be over a million a year. He rang World Wide and asked to be put through to Moira Goldberg. Ms Goldberg, they said, was in Rome. Did they know where? At the Hassler. She would be back after the weekend, they said. He thought of ringing the Hassler but she was unlikely to be sitting in her room by the phone, and in any case he didn't have enough coins to call Rome from a phone booth. Enough coins! He didn't have enough money. He had a few dollars in his pocket, and that was it. To ask Beauregard for phone money when he was trying to persuade the manager of his ability to magic up $10,000 would be counterproductive, he decided. So, forget about Moira. Who else? He tried ringing Nik. No answer. Nik was never home: at the best of times it took three or four days to locate him. Bruce Tucker? He crossed out Tucker's name: he'd died, a couple of years back. His friend Otto. But Otto was sick, didn't remember who people were these days. How could you ask a man who couldn't remember who you were to lend you $10,000? Jim Jones in Paris? But Jim Jones was no longer in Paris, Jim Jones was dead. Of congestive heart failure. The drink. Not a good way to go, Irwin had said. Irwin? Irwin was dead too. Last year was the year everybody died . . . Irwin and Joe Losey, and Truffaut, and Carl Foreman. Try Lila, he told himself. He had her card somewhere. Here it was. Sutton Place. The crème de la crème, slave scenes for the connoisseurs. She must have a few bucks.

The girl who answered wasn't Lila. Lila was very occupied right now, but could she do anything for him, anything at all. She said she was very very close to Lila, that her name was Candy . . . Candy by name, candy by nature, she added, and entirely in Lila's confidence.

'I'm an old friend of Lila's,' he explained. 'Would it be possible for you to go to her and ask her something?'

Candy gave a faint sigh and said it might be if it were not too complicated.

'Can you say it's Jack Strawley, that I've run into some temporary financial difficulties and could she possibly lend me a few thou?'

'I'll ask her,' Candy said. She came back after five minutes. Lila, she said, sent her love and said she was sorry she couldn't lend him the money, that it was one of her golden rules never to lend money to a friend because you lost the money and you lost the friend.

He flicked through some more pages, tried some more numbers, but everybody it seemed had left town suddenly. Wasn't really surprising. How many people with $10,000 to lend remained in the city on a steaming hot Friday night in August? In the end he had to go back to Norbert Beauregard and say no luck, everybody was away for the weekend. But he was sure that by the middle of next week. . .

Norbert Beauregard become quite flustered, quite upset and even redder than usual. 'I regret but you absolutely can't stay in the apartment, I cannot take that risk . . . it's out of the question, besides which I have now arranged for the decorators and carpenters to come in.'

'Let me stay in another room . . . any . . .'

'I can't, Mr Strawley. I'm sorry. It's impossible. I'm an employee of the company that owns this hotel, and there are company rules I have to abide by. I already have a lot to explain . . . all the . . . the damage . . . hundreds of dollars worth of damage. If I let you stay after that I would be considered remiss. I can't . . . it's more than my job is worth. You understand, of course, that we have to hold onto your luggage until your bill is fully settled.' His voice took on a tone that might almost have been considered kindly. 'The only suggestion I can make is . . . try another hotel, Mr Strawley. Where you are not known.'

50

He went out into the hot street and started to head downtown. The heat rose from the ground in heavy spirals and wrapped around him moistly as he walked. His lightweight jacket was sticking to his back, glued on through the sodden shirt. He passed his fingers through his damp hair and touched his face, and his hand came away sticky with sweat and blood. He was keeping close to the sides of buildings for the small amount of shade they afforded. The temperature at noon, he'd heard on the radio, was 102 in the shade. Didn't feel like much less now. There were no fresh air currents, no breathing space: the atmosphere had congealed into a sticky paste. He inhaled dust and grit and stagnant gasoline fumes. Central Park offered a brief respite from heat and concrete, but he could not stay there. Had to find somewhere to stay. A hotel where he was not known, where it was not known that Jack Strawley, the film director, was all washed up, a finished man. Only he was known everywhere, and therefore everyone knew.

He walked into the lobby of the Plaza and asked for a room.

They looked at him, his sodden jacket, his cut face, his strange luminous unpresent eyes. 'Your bags outside, sir?' No, he said, he did not have any bags. How long was he planning to stay? Two or three nights. Perhaps four. Perhaps a week. Or a month, or longer. How did he intend to settle his bill? With money, he said. Behind the desk they smiled: in what form, credit card . . . cheque? No, he said, cash. He would pay in liquid. Unfortunately, they said, looking at their reservations plan, they had no single rooms available. Nor any doubles. Seemed there was no room at this inn. He would take a suite, he said. They did not have a suite either. That was impossible, he said: in August, New York hotels were all empty. The Plaza, however, was full, they said. He went to use their marble washroom facilities to make himself a touch more presentable, but as soon as he was in the streets again the heat of sky and earth tightened around him like a vice, squeezing out his body waters.

Checking through his pockets he found that he had eight dollars and 65 cents. He went into a liquor store and bought a half bottle of the cheapest whisky they had. He drank as he walked, letting the whisky tear through his chest with the promise of a magic click. It was all that was keeping him standing up straight: the ballast of spirits in his underbelly. Since the Plaza didn't want to give him a room, he'd have to try some place where they were less snooty about people without bags or credit cards. He took a downtown bus, got off at Grand Street. Should be able to find something in Lower Broadway. Making his way along Walker Street he had only a vague notion of where he was headed in this uncharacteristic, eerie New York quiet, was pursuing the swampy smell of decay and disintigration, of open trashcans and damp mould. Dank, stored heat coming at him out of blackened old brickwork. Where was everybody? The entire population was fleeing from the heat, the unbreathable air. Purposeless forms slouched in the barred and padlocked doorways of wholesale textile companies, psyches simmered in the dimness of entrances: when it was hot and heavy like this, murder figures shot up, people at the end of their tether exploded . . . had to kill somebody to get if off their chest. He could understand that. Could quite understand that. He was running out of air, traversing a city that was moving towards meltdown. He dissolved the dust in his throat with regular swigs of whisky, pressing on towards the Hudson with its promise of air from the Atlantic. He read a scrawled sign at the entrance to an alleyway: 'No Pissing or Shitting. People Live Here.' Beyond the sign, he stopped at a crumbly dark brown nineteenth-century façade with weather-gnawed cast iron columns and an unillumined neon sign, saying: 'Hotel': 'Singles $30, doubles $35.' It was placed between a steam equipment company and a guitar repair store, its window cluttered with broken-stringed instruments. There were a couple of steps going down to the hotel entrance. The fat night clerk was seated in the dark behind the desk watching TV, where a comedy soap was disbursing regular bursts of hysterical canned laughter. A thick peat-bog smell came from below. He told the desk he wanted a single, and the unsmiling night clerk said without taking his eye off the set:

'That's gonna be thirty, mister, including taxes.'

'I'll settle up tomorrow, okay?'

'You pay for the room now,' the night clerk said, not taking his eye off the flickering screen, not smiling, while the canned audience killed itself laughing.

'I have to go to the bank. I don't have the money on me. You take a card?'

'No plastic.'

'I'll leave you my watch as a deposit. It's a Rolex. It's worth more'n a thousand dollars.'

'They sell 'em for ten bucks brand new in Chinatown.'

'This is a real one.'

'Yeah? How do I know?'

He tore his eye off the television screen and fixed them on Jack Strawley, looked him up and down:

'Listen, bud,' he told him. 'Do me a favour, go away. Get outta here, will ya? I know your sort. You're the sort that pisses in the sink.'

He carried on towards the river. A well-dressed woman walked alongside him, animatedly talking to herself. He had begun to notice lately how many people in New York talked to themselves, angrily as a rule. There were a lot of people angry with themselves. New York was full of these crazies, these weirdos. Nowadays, with all the new drugs to keep them quiet, they let the crazies out of the asylums to wander the streets. The woman striding alongside him was engaged in a furious dialogue with herself. 'So what's it feel like, dear, to be a dried-up, greedy old crow?' Came the quick-fire retort: 'I'll think about it and let you know.' Repartee with the other self. A noodle shop. Red-lacquered Cantonese duck. Chinese signs over stores. He was going east, not west. His orientation was all fucked-up. Thought he was going one way when he was going another. The light was fading. Blood-red brick, shaling brickwork, where the fuck was he? Street stands and stores all selling fake Rolexes. He carried on in the same direction since he had nowhere else to go. He stopped at a store selling kitchen equipment: massive shiny steel cauldrons for hotel and restaurant kitchens. He could see his dark face in the glass. Addressing it gravely, he said: 'A few hours ago you were having lunch at the Five Hundred with the movie star Maureen Wynner and tentatively inviting her into your bed, and now you have no bed to sleep in and nowhere to go. Is that possible?' He tried to think of some quick-fire answer to this riddle, but all his repartees had dried up. People who passed him and saw him standing there, talking to himself, a whisky bottle sticking out of his pocket, seeming not to know which way to turn, thought little of it. It was a sight that was not uncommon around here. With the dust settled thickly in his throat, and the remedial whisky all gone, he went into a bar.

'What'll it be, Mister?'

'Oh, lemme have' — his eye was going over the range of liquor bottles with an air of undecidedness while he secretly counted the coins remaining in his pocket and found them to be insufficient — 'bring me a glass of iced water and uh . . .'

While Jack Strawley was making up his mind, the barman poured out a glass of water and set it in front of him, and Jack Strawley picked it up with a shaking hand and drank the water in a long gulp.

He said: 'Gimme another, I'm thirsty.'

The barman refilled his glass with water. 'So what'll it be then?'

Jack Strawley drank the water. 'Thanks.'

'You decided? What'll it be?'

'That's all.'

'That's all! You don't want nothin'? Jeezus! Go on, get out o' here. Bums! Bums!' He went away to serve someone else and, when he came back and found Jack Strawley still there, began to lose his temper. 'Thought I told you to get outta here, buster.' His face broke into a big sarcastic smirk. 'Unless you'd like another glass o' water.'

'I would.'

'You buy a drink or you get outta here,' the barman told him.

He began a systematic search of his pockets. What was this? A folded scrap of paper. He unfolded it. Torn off corner of a bar menu. With writing on it that was not his own. Somebody's address. Who'd given him this address? A signature, some kind of an I.O.U. Signed Alice . . . he couldn't make out the second name. Alice? An I.O.U. for $400. Who the hell was Alice? Then he remembered the girl with the chopped-off hair in Lila's bar. Whose drug bill he had paid off. When was that? Two months ago, three? Or was it a year? He couldn't remember.

It was a lifetime ago.

He had no idea where he was. He was lost, that much was evident, but whether this was the dark forest, or Hell's Kitchen, or Little Italy, he couldn't say. The layout of New York had escaped him like a word gone out of the mind. It seemed that he had been walking for hours and hours. Possibly in circles, for he did not seem to have got anywhere. He lurched against a grey brick wall used as a urinal. Post No Bills written in large crude letters next to a sign for the Oriental Hotel, all comforts, running water. Perhaps here. Vaporous emanations of scotch whisky interposed themselves between himself and the knowable world. He was holding onto the steep wall with his fingernails and slipping down it. The street was suddenly full of Chinamen, and he was sitting in a puddle of piss. Where was it that Carl lived? Somewhere near here. He recognized the area. Get over to Carl's place. Carl wouldn't let him die. He found a phone booth and dialled Lila's number. This time she answered herself, sounding vague and spaced out and giggly. Could he come and crash at her place? No question of an alienating loan, just somewhere to put down his head.

'Oh, baby, everybody's crashing here tonight. We can all crash together. Come on over . . . though may not be your scene, going by memory.'

He had no idea of how to get to Sutton Place and whether he would be admitted in the state he was in. Candyish Candy might not be so understanding about that. He decided that, all in all, a doorway was preferable for closing his eyes. Then he would see in the morning where he was.

51

She'd found him semi-comatose outside her door. First didn't recognize him: who is this bum? What's he doing outside my door? He had this typical drinker's cut-out and couldn't remember when he'd disconnected. He was hallucinating and paranoid, half out of his mind, but somehow his automatic pilot had led him to her. Alice with the razor-chopped hair. The would-be film-maker. The onetime philosophy student. She took him in. Couldn't leave him lying there. He needed to have some food in him and he needed someone to take care of him. If she didn't want a body outside her door.

When the whisky had worn off, there was the next problem: that he had nowhere to live and no money, and she had practically none, certainly couldn't pay back the $400 she owed him. But she could make a bit of money waitressing, and didn't they say two could live as cheap as one? And he had this painting that he owned, this Magritte painting of two masked apples that was worth quite a lot but he couldn't sell because of some ambulance-chasing crooks trying to rip him off. Once he'd gained a breathing space, he was able to persuade the dealer in Paris to give him advances against the painting, in return for a higher percentage on an eventual sale. That way he obtained a couple of grand and then another couple, enough for them to live on for a while and enable him to make some phone calls and go out and meet people. To try to sell himself.

Projects came up that sounded possible. He was the perfect person to direct such and such a film. They were bound to see that. He'd had a big success with something very similar in '66. So, okay, that was twenty years ago, he could do it again. He was going to be on top again, a name to conjure with. A magician, he told Alice, was an actor who had the power to make an audience believe in his magic. And with a few whiskies inside him, he was a good actor-magician and would come back from lunches at '21' or Lutèce or the Côte Basque flying high on pure hope. And then come crashing down when people didn't ring up next day or the day after.

She got jobs waitressing, which bought them food but didn't pay the phone bills for hour-long phone calls to Major Stars in Hollywood whom he was trying to pursuade to lend their names to one or other of his projects. She was ready to do anything to keep them going, was willing to go to Lila and sell herself to some richie for a good price, to get them through a tough patch, but he wouldn't let her do that. He was going to earn the money. Once, he pulled off directing a porn film. And not just directing, but performing in it too! Suddenly the washed up film genius was rejuvenated into King Priapus, throwing himself into it with a fury and a frenzy. A creaking old sex machine but *functioning,* functioning amazingly for a man in his condition. She thought he must have got himself hyped up on coke or speed or Spanish fly or rhinocerus horn, or some even more potent drug like self-belief. It made them a few thousand, gave them a breathing space. And after that he got one or two jobs teaching film up and down the country at different universities. For the students it was inspirational being taught by this famous film-maker who'd won the Palme d'Or and the Oscar and enough other prizes you would have needed a Kane-size mantlepiece to hold them all. He'd get each class to embark on the actual making of a film, and the students threw themselves into that 100%, but sooner or later there was some scandal, his drinking, or his use of drugs, or the fact that he'd get students to extemporize sex scenes and encourage them to carry on to the point where they became pornography. And so university authorities tended not to renew his contract. Not that he was in the habit of behaving incorrectly towards students, it was they who chased after him. With his ravaged face and his white hair and his beat-up body, he nonetheless exercized a strong spell on the females in his classes, and to him a girl offering herself was some sort of a benediction that he could not refuse. He'd say to Alice: 'Oh gee, I'm so sorry, honey, you know I can never resist another of those flaming bodies', and then he said to her, 'I want to be cremated when I go, I don't want the cold earth and worms, I want the flame . . . and I don't want to be kept in any Grecian urn, I want to be scattered in a river that's big and fat and dirty.'

He kept making fitful efforts to get off the booze and the drugs and the flaming bodies and the hope. The hope was the worst drug of all, but it was pretty clear that he was falling apart fast, and she thought, loving him very much, even though he was impossible to live with, that the only thing that could save him was if he could make another film. He was all the time trying to get something set up: burning up the long-distance phone lines, spending practically everything he made from teaching on these phone calls to talk up projects that really had no chance with him . . . trying to persuade Brando to do *The Deafness of Ludwig van Beethoven*, about a deaf and dying Beethoven . . . and his crazy possessive love for his nephew, or Maureen Wynner to change her mind about 'their' film, this sparkling Parisian high comedy about the mistress of presidents, and there were other good subjects that he was selling hard, that other people ended up making but could not be made by him, since he was that most despised of all creatures in the film business, a has-been. When his projects collapsed he'd mutter violently that it was all fucking carrying water up the hill and fucking killing him, but he kept on, water barrels yoked to his shoulders, slipping and sliding and falling, and dragging himself up one more time, exhausted as he was, one more time up the hill. And gasping, would say to her with a grin of high mania on his crafty, prematurely old face: 'Alice, my dear, it don't get any better than this, that's what you got to remember. The rest is even worse.' And laugh and laugh. He'd ask: 'Who the hell can you complain to? And especially I can't damn well complain, since it's been granted me, in the final phase of my life, to be given one last love.' And he told her: 'Everything that ever happened to me I turned into narrative, like they did 20,000 years ago, covering the walls of their caves with scenes of hunting because a man has this need to portray what his life has been, whether on a cave wall or a screen, that being the only way a man has of seeing himself as a human being and of summing up his life.'

This summing-up was what he had to do, she could see that: he had to make the story of his own life, the life of the film-maker.

Even if they could make this film cheaply, they couldn't make it for nothing, and he'd calculated that they needed $100,000 to $150,000 to do it. Which was a stupendous sum of money for him to raise, now, though when he was making *Heart of Darkness* he'd spent practically that amount filming buzzards at dusk.

They were working on ways of raising this sum of money. The Paris dealer Laforge had re-calculated and decided that if Jack really badly needed a quick sale for the Magritte he'd give him $50,000, which was about a third of what the picture was worth, and out of that he'd deduct, with interest, the small sums he'd been advancing in dribs and drabs, altogether amounting by then, rounded up, to $9,000. Still, a cheque for $41,000 wasn't to be sneezed at. And they did all sorts of cost-cutting budgets and worked out that with another $100,000 they could make the film and have a small margin. But where were they going to get a sum like that?

Their only chance, as far as Alice could see, was Moira, and one day she rang up World Wide Artists Associates and asked to speak to Moira Goldberg. One secretary passed her to another secretary and they were all saying, 'Who?' and 'What did you say your name was, Miss?' and, 'What is this in connection with, please?' and she told them, 'It's in connection with Jack Strawley', and they said 'Who?' and she said, 'Jack Strawley, the film director,' and they said that WWAA only considered projects that came through established agents, are you an agent? and she said, 'Listen: just tell Mizz Goldberg, and then if she doesn't wanna speak to me, fine.' Finally she got put through to her, and Moira was very brisk and not very friendly. 'Yes? What is this concerning?' Alice said, 'It's concerning Jack . . . Jack Strawley,' at which point Moira said not very pleasantly, 'Who are you?' and she said, 'I'm Alice, I'm with Jack.' She added quickly, 'He doesn't know I'm phoning you, he'd kill me.' Moira's voice became less brisk then, and she asked, 'How is Jack?' and Alice said, 'Oh, comme-ci, comme ça.' Moira said to give her a phone number where she could call her later in the day, and she did call back, late in the afternoon, by which time her voice had become a bit more human.

'It's quieter now, tell me about Jack.'

Alice told her about Jack, not mincing words, and after half a dozen sentences Moira asked, 'Is there anything I can do?'

'That's a pretty silly question, of course there is.'

'Come and see me tomorrow at the office. Quarter of one.'

At twenty to one Alice was there. Moira was on the thirty-third floor, she had got the whole floor, with every window offering a Disneyland ride around the Manhattan skyline. There were these great big bronzes everywhere, and the open floor was subdivided into sections by sculptures of circles and triangles, so that you were irising in and irising out all the fucking time.

Alice was kept waiting half an hour before being shown in to the big boss, who was wearing something off-white by Sonja Riekel — this rather petite, dark, handsome-but-harried Jewish business woman of fifty something with a hoarse strident voice — from shouting at people too much, and smoking too much — and it was difficult for Alice to imagine her as this hot number with the most upwardly mobile ass . . . except that she'd gotten there, hadn't she?

No sooner had Alice gone in than the hotshot lady had to take another call, which meant Alice got to see her in action.

'Look, I'll go to two and a half mil, but that's my limit, I've got to draw the line somewhere and that's where I'm drawing it. And I don't want to hear any more about her personal hairdressers and bodyguards . . . or dramaturges, they went out with Marilyn. If she wants them, she fucking pays for them. Just tell her I'm cheap. Ask her, does she want it symbolic or does she want it real? She can't have both. I'm ready to close on this today, but I'm also ready to turn the page, if I have to. Would be great to have her, but if I can't I'll tell myself like my Mama used to say, "Moira dear, it's only a movie." '

When she'd hung up she said straight off, 'I'm going to call you Alice, and you're going to call me Moira,' and Alice could see she was being assessed with those sharp clever eyes that could assess very complicated things in about twenty seconds flat. Right off she'd got Alice summed up, and it was positive.

'So how is Jack's health?'

Alice told her about the drinking and the drugs and his heart condition and his chest troubles.

'And you're looking after him. Yes, he could always find women to pick him up out of the gutter. Why in your case?'

'Why did you?' Alice asked.

'Well, for one thing he was on his way up then.'

'You were very interested in people on their way up, I've heard, Moira,' Alice allowed herself to say.

Moira smiled at that, and said: 'I guess you could call that fair comment, but I also loved him, you see, and I thought he was brilliant — a genius.'

'I still think he is,' Alice said. 'He's just got himself in a hole and needs a hand up.'

Moia said they wouldn't go to lunch because she never had lunch, she was too busy for lunches *and* she was dieting. She ordered in a tub of cottage cheese on lettuce leaves and a bottle of Perrier, saying Alice could have whatever she wanted, at which Alice said okay, caviar and champagne, since she wasn't dieting, and she got caviar and champagne. While she forked down her cottage cheese, Moira asked about how Alice had met Jack and about their life together, and Alice told her how he'd paid off Giorgio for her to the tune of $400, without any angle, refusing her offer of carnal recompense. Moira asked her what she wanted to do with her life, and she said: 'Be a film-maker,' expecting Moira to say yes, doesn't everyone, but she didn't. What she said was: 'Well, you've got a great teacher, Alice. I learnt most of what I know about film-making from him.' Then she asked her if Jack was in any shape to make another film, and Alice said if he had another film to make he would be in a lot better shape. That it was what he needed most. She told Moira about *Scenes in the Life of the Film-maker,* about how he wanted to mix documentary footage and scenes from his films and TV interviews and chat shows with re-enactments of scenes from his life. Moira asked how much would they need to make this film, and Alice said it could be done for $150,000 if they used a non-union crew and that they could lay their hands on around forty thou, only needed another hundred and ten. Moira said okay, she'd finance the production to the tune of a hundred and fifty. That gave them a small margin. But they had to be sure to keep to this budget because that was the limit she could go to for this type of film. She said that given Jack's reputation for uncontrollability and for going over budget, and for eccentric behaviour, she didn't think, frankly, that anybody else was going to back them, and she could do so only within these limits because she was accountable to her board and to stockholders. Luckily she had enough successes behind her to be permitted some high-risk ventures . . . which this was. But the risk had to be limited strictly. Given Jack's record, she was going to be criticized within the company, but she was going to do it because, whether the film made any money or not, it was one that he ought to make, and she said that there had to be room in a great industry for that kind of film-making by a man who had served it well.

Which was how it had got going. They moved into the loft, assembled a non-union crew, partly from students, but with one or two top pros, like Cybotski to do the photography, and Larry Bix as their editor. They knew it was going to be a stupendous editing job with all those hundreds of hours of material, and, although Jack intended controlling every frame, he needed help. They got a good professional for sound and Hal to place the lights and adjust them and move stuff and a student as camera assistant to operate the camera, load and unload the film, and work the hand-held when they double-shot a scene. Alice did everything else, including being the script girl, script editor and cook. They got in some established actors, who worked for a nominal fee because it was Jack. And new young actors who did it for the exposure in a film with and by Jack Strawley.

There were unforeseen expenses and hold-ups. Jack got sick and had to go into hospital. Not surprisingly they ran out of money before the film was even a third done. He said he only needed another $50,000, he was going to cut down, do it on a really tight budget now, he was sure he could finish it for that, and Moira came up with the extra, but she said it was really the last she could give them because WWAA was now the target of a hostile take-over bid, she could be ousted by the shareholders and any evidence of overspending or spending on dubious projects would provide her enemies with ammunition, that was really the limit now. They said they could definitely finish it for that and then didn't because Jack got sick again, and Moira gave them some more money, and then some more, but finally Moira had to say no. And then they were again in big, big trouble with bills unpaid, bailiffs at the door, and simply didn't have enough money to live on let alone shoot a film . . . which was when Jack said he was going to see Giorgio, Giorgio knew people interested in investing in the picture business.

Alice said, 'You know the sort of people Giorgio knows.'

And Jack said yes, he did, but what had he got to lose now?

52

I had been away from the Varick Street loft for three days, during the great standstill of the freeze, and now with Manhattan messily thawing out and getting back to normal, the brief period of frozen time was over. As I started the long climb up the stone steps, there was the buzz of normal activity on every floor, except for the top floor, where all was very quiet. At the top, I knocked lightly on the door and it was opened almost at once by one of the crew members, Hal, the one who had been doing all the heavy moving when I was there last. Apart from him the place was empty. The cameras were hooded, the arc lamps turned off, the Moviola screens dark and lifeless.

'Where is everybody?'

'You not been told?'

'Told?'

'Mr Strawley had to go back to the ho'pital. Was havin' difficulty with his breathin'. Workin' in this cold and all and with the beatin' he took . . . and like havin' a weak chest'n all.'

'Is he going to be all right?'

'Oh sure. Got to finish the film. Expect Alice'll be back soon, she'll tell yah.'

When I'd been here before, Jack Strawley's powerful presence had prevented me from taking everything in. Now I had the time to look around. Everywhere there were boxes — tea chests, packing cases, shipping containers, metal trunks, cartons of different sizes — covered with the labels of shipping lines, of English, Spanish, French and Italian storage companies and the stickers of hotels. Other labels, or sometimes just words scrawled in marker ink, gave some indication of what was in these boxes: film scripts; press cuttings; diaries and journals; notebooks and storyboards; photographs; letters; contracts; miscellaneous . . . From their grimy, battered condition it looked as if these boxes must have been following him around from country to country as he pulled up stakes in one place to move somewhere else. What might one find in them? Undoubtedly there would be source material about the cinema of the fifties, sixties and seventies, the span of his prominence, which would provide the cinema historian with valuable information about the life of the film-maker in those periods. I might find clues in these boxes to why his success had been bought at such a high price, to why he had wanted it so much, what it was that had driven him constantly to 'stake his life'. Perhaps I would also find clues to why it had all crumbled for him. And to why he should have been brutally beaten up by anonymous assailants — one would probably find far too many clues, I told myself, since life invariably afforded far too many clues to everything. I was once more with Jack Strawley in the position of not knowing what to think: where to come down in my overall assessment. Like others, I had gone through the different phases of believing him to be some kind of genius, and then some kind of hubristic imposter, and then a total fabrication that the press, the critics and the publicity machine had created, man of straw blown up into false-genius . . . which, in due course, called for a fall-guy, a sacrificial victim of our hype and our desire for stories that need legend-figures to sustain them. Which one of these he was I could not say. Life affords too many damn clues.

When Alice returned from the hospital she looked wiped out. Seeing the shoe box I had brought with me she asked, before saying anything else: 'Those the tapes?' I nodded, and she seemed cheered by this. 'Oh great, because he's been asking about them. He wanted to know if you'd brought them. So many people promise to do things and then don't. These tapes are important to him.'

'How was he when you left?'

'He's on a drip, and they're pumping oxygen into his lungs and antibiotics in his veins.'

'Could he talk?'

'Yeah, he could talk. I'm not sure he was supposed to, and he's a bit delirious, if you really want to know, but he did talk. As a matter of fact, he talked about you. Oh, he's a survivor, has to be to have survived this far. It's been touch and go a lot of the time. He said you did him a great injury once, wouldn't say what it was. He said if he shouldn't pull through he wants me to finish the film and to get you to help me . . . he says that you owe him that, and that with the tapes and all the material in the boxes, and you being a historian of cinema, you can give it some . . . structure. Which his life singularly lacked.'

Apart from the moistness of her eyes, she was tightly controlled; her face wind-beaten red at the cheekbones, her slight form shivering inside an old US army greatcoat. She pulled the khaki balaclava off her head and shook her chopped off hair. I said: 'Oh, he'll pull through, I'm sure.'

'Yeah, we've been there before. With him, you always expect the worst to happen, there are no quiet moments, you're living all the time on the edge of your seat, and biting your fingernails.'

'Why d'you do it, if I may ask you that?'

She took a long breath, her eyes filled with heavy knowledge, and her voice took on a harsh edge. 'You mean why is this young not-too-bad-looking chick hitched up to a sick, drunken, penniless old wreck? Tell you the truth, Stephen, I don't know. I suppose because I love him, although I also think every day about leaving him.'

'But don't.'

'I couldn't. I just couldn't. I tell myself, if I leave him he'll die. But I also know he's going to die if I stay. So what's my alternative?'

The loft was very gloomy with no movie lights and none of the high adrenaline flow that comes with cameras turning. All that turbulent movement was stopped now and life was still. I saw that she was weeping.

'I'll get a hold of myself in a minute,' she promised. 'I'm quite strong really. Living with Jack you have to be. Oh boy, do you! Yeah. We had a few emergencies like this, and he pulled through. So . . . so . . . I guess . . . What makes me think he won't this time? I'm getting as pessimistic as him and I mustn't, he needs me to be the optimist in the family, he says. He says I'm his life force, what keeps him alive.' She laughed, made a determined effort to shake herself out of the gloom, brandishing her fist like an athlete urging himself on.

'Jack always managed to find somebody to pick him up out of the gutter.'

'Why me? Why has it got to be me! Let somebody else, for a change. Of course, I don't mean that . . . oh, I don't know why I'm saying all this to you, someone I don't even know. Although I know a lot about you. Jack's talked about you. He said you're good at drawing people out. That you drew him out on those tapes. It's true you listen pretty good.'

In the next hour, while she talked and I listened, the crew members started drifting back, asking after Jack, wanting to know how he was, and if they were going to be needed, if there was any chance of the filming being resumed or if they should assume it was over. Alice told all of them that she didn't know, that there was no way of knowing, but maybe in a day or so things would become clearer.

The arrival of the doctor stopped the speculation. He was looking worried, and Alice immediately feared the worst.

'No, he's not any worse than he was,' the doctor said quickly. 'Except that he's gone crazy. He's discharged himself. Got them to take off the straps, and then he pulled out the breathing tubes and told them he was going home.'

'They let him do that?'

'You know Jack. It's hard to stop him when he gets something in his head. He says he's going to finish the film. That's the only thing that counts for him now.'

'He'll kill himself.'

The doctor avoided looking at her. 'He can't harm himself now,' he said flatly.

'What you saying, Doc?'

'Let him do what he wants, what he has to.'

Presently there was the sound of voices coming from outside, and we could make out Jack's, a bit thinner in timbre than his normal shout, but still full of unopposable authority as he yelled instructions at the ambulance men.

'Dumb-heads! Don't tilt me so much, you're going to make me throw up all that pheasant and port wine I had for dinner. You! Higher, higher. Don't shake me up, can't you see where it's marked "old bones, fragile, handle with care"? With care, idiot! Don't bump me. Easy, easy now. Put me down nice and easy now.'

They brought him in, two men carrying him on the stretcher, two others walking alongside transporting the oxygen cylinder and the drip feed. He was as near to being a skull as a living being can be: that great mane of white hair flowing, his intense overlit blue eyes distantly focused, and his skin shining like transparent paper. They lowered him gingerly onto the bed, with him giving instructions all the time. 'Not like that, imbeciles: *there* . . . over a bit. A bit more. Put me down nice and easy, nice and easy: don't jolt the old skeleton . . . put me down right, *chaps* . . . don't expect to be doing much walkie-walkies.' He spent a couple of minutes taking some good long breaths of oxygen and then set the mask aside and reached for the whisky, and as he swigged from the bottle his etiolated features became imbued with a faint, moistly phosphorescent whisky glow, and he announced without raising himself:

'Fellas! This being a non-union production, I'm going to call for a night shoot without any warning or extra pay.' He took another swig of the whisky, followed by a gulp from the oxygen tank. 'Sorry about that, guys. Circumstances. It's on account of our shooting time's limited. Everybody, please. Get set up, will yah? Scene 389. Try not to be too . . . long 'bout it.'

He gave his rough, sandpaper chuckle. His flaming, blue eyes were not of this world, his face acid-etched out of metal. It was a formidable ruin of a man, and, seeing him in this terrible state, but with those blue-flame eyes shining out of the skullhead, I remembered the extraordinary beauty of the man thirty odd years ago, at our first meeting. Only thirty years from that to this! He seemed to know what I was thinking. Between gulps of oxygen and whisky, he managed to get out: 'I know . . . don't I know? . . . you get eaten up . . . it's the process . . . time . . . eats you up . . . it eats you.' He shook that Ancient Mariner head. 'Be all right in a minute. Just need to get some . . . breath.' He was shaking his head and, then having amassed a sufficient quantity of breath out of the tank, said with a sly grin:

'So, we got the critic on board! Ready for your scene, Stephen? It's easy. You just have to be your usual quibbling-equivocating hag-like self. "Though highly gifted, some would say, *whereas others would not,* Strawley failed finally because of the lack of any deep structure in his work. A sadly dissipated talent . . . and a tragically dissipated life." Do I read you right, critic?'

'This may not be dramatic enough for you,' I said, 'but what I want to say, if it's supposed to be me talking and not a parody, is that I think you made some fine films.'

'Don't know how much that counts for at the pearly gates, critic.'

'Who knows what counts?'

'Yeah, that's the problem. Nobody knows. Now I'm going to have a rest while they set up,' he abruptly said, cutting off all further discussion and closing his eyes. We all became hushed, with the grips and technicians moving around in fast, smooth, silent coordination.

While he was resting, Alice, in preparation for the next shot, was switching on the row of Moviolas to provide the images of a life flashing before the eyes. The script called for the dying film-maker to see on the editing machines reconstituted and documentary scenes of his past life. One screen showed a small boy on his bike going past an old-style granite post office building, a Pennsylvania Dutch town hall built of red brick; an A & P supermarket; a dingy, red Unitarian church with tall steeple; coming to a stop in front of a cinema called the Blue Hall, where he looks up at a big poster of Alan Ladd in *Appointment with Danger*. At the same time, screen two was showing a portly, red-faced man in a retirement home, peering through the fog of old age, speaking tetchily to camera: 'How was I supposed to know you were going to turn into this "genius Jack" fella? You were just an ordinary scruffy boy, with bad habits, unteachable, wouldn't learn because you thought you knew everything.' He gave an old man's hee-heeing laugh that made his chest heave and triggered a coughing fit.

Although Jack was resting with eyes closed, the lids were slightly raised at the bottom and in this way he was keeping an eye on everything. On another screen, now, there was Jack on the Johnny Carson show, riding high, sure, arrogant, *manic*. On yet another screen he was in Seville, at the feria, embracing the triumphant bullfighter Antonio Francisco, and in the next flash, you saw a heavier, slower Francisco being jeered by the crowd, having plastic bottles and a cushion hurled at him. Eyes opening a little more, squinting at the flashing images of his life, Jack Strawley's hands moved in a series of fluid, expressive gestures, and the crew seemed to understand exactly what he was after. The student Alberto, operating the hand-held Arriflex, was starting to go around the bed in a circular motion, filming Jack, and in doing so taking his pace and his shooting angles from the director's delicately moving fingers, which were conducting him in a stately dirge around himself, and indicating to Alberto to include in his slow orbit the other camera, the big one, which was doing a panning shot that swung from the row of Moviolas to the man on the bed. A series of quick, urgent pointing movements, like those of a conductor cueing a soloist, indicated that a change in the script had occurred, that the director now wanted the principal camera to stay on the mother's face on the Moviola, and to move in close, while the hand-held Arriflex was to go on filming the son as he watches. The mother had embarked on a rambling story that had been intended only as visual background, but now the director had changed his mind and wanted the camera to go close and heed the words.

' . . . once I came to see you in that children's place, and you didn't recognize me . . . and I . . . was so . . . so very . . . wounded.'

'Cut,' he called in a firm hard voice from the bed. The mother had had her little close-up scene. And now it was over. On to the next one. His eyes opened wide. He called for someone to help him sit upright and, propped up by cushions, from time to time taking gulps of oxygen washed down with whisky, he gave his commands.

'Okay, fellas. I want you to just keep going on me. Whatever I do or say, okay? If I say "Cut", that's in the story, and you don't cut, you don't cut until I say, "Cut for real." Just keep turning till you run out of film. We're gonna do the destruction speech. The old dying director talking about how much he destroyed in his life. If I dry . . . just carry on while they give me the speech. This is real life, and in real life people dry . . . so it's okay. Alberto, I want you filming the crew filming me, okay? Where are we? The critic asks me a question or makes a comment. What d'you say, critic?'

'That you made some fine films.'

'Yeah, and I say . . . I say about not knowing what counts and then I go on . . . I go on to say . . . that I destroyed a lot of things in my life . . . Okay? Ready? *Action.*'

As the cameras started turning again, he had fallen back exhausted, out of breath, unable to go on, needing to gulp oxygen, but even while doing this he signalled to the crew to keep turning. 'Don't worry,' he reassured them, when he could get out some words, 'this'll play like a dream. Deathbed scenes are a cinch.'

His breathing had again become gasping and desperate and he seemed to not have the strength to place the oxygen mask over his face. The doctor had to do it for him. The cameras, in accordance with his instructions, were continuing to turn, although it was very evident that the crew felt bad about it, and they were talking about stopping. Meanwhile, the second cameraman, Alberto with the hand-held Arriflex, was filming the crew, as Jack had directed, recording their distaste for what they were being asked to do, and Jack Strawley was making signs to him and to the man with the sound boom to come in close, so as to capture all the elements of the scene. It was becoming very painful for everyone, and finally Cybotski called, 'Cut.' At which point Jack — as if he had been giving a performance all along — seemed to revive, and with enormous effort — each word was like rolling out rocks — said: 'Don't . . . cut my . . . film, Cybby. That's the director's . . . prerogative . . . nobody else's . . . you don't cut until I say "cut for real." Okay? I just need a minute. Keep them rolling. I still got to say 'bout the eye . . . the eye of the savage, that bit. Doesn't come here in the script but let's do it here anyway.'

Looking at each other unhappily, the crew members followed his instructions and resumed filming, even though he didn't have the strength to say the speech in the script. He was too far gone for that now. Yet was continuing to see everything with the eye of the savage. That eye which could see faster than a normal eye, and saw extraordinary pictures never to be forgotten but also couldn't help destroying what it saw, so intensely did it see, and what he must have seen then was that the 'cut for real' couldn't be put off any more, with his director's eye for the shape of a scene he must have seen that then. Knowing that he did not have long left, he seemed to want to make some final voice-over comment. I leant close to hear his last words, my ears pricked for some resonant mystery like 'Rosebud', but all I could catch was a mumble that sounded like, 'Fucking hell!' After which he slumped into deep coma and his respiration began to sound as if he were breathing in sand instead of air. I looked unhappily at Alice who had her fist jammed deep in her mouth trying to keep control of herself. His face was ashen and the angry rattling went on and on. And then, suddenly, all the sounds stopped and there was a deep silence which was infinitely worse than the noisy struggle that had preceded it. The cameras were still turning, one on Jack, the other on the film crew filming him, since he had not said the words 'cut for real'. Finally, when there was still no movement or sign of life from the bed, Cybotski quietly said, 'Cut,' and this time there was no peremptory directorial voice to overrule him.

Jack had instructed that he wanted to be 'cremated without fuss' and his ashes thrown out into the street. Ashes didn't need a resting place, he'd said. He wanted to be part of the New York street scene, an irritant in the air: 'like I always was, let 'em breathe me in and cough me up . . . and spit me out.' But even if it was what he wanted, it was too painful for Alice to execute such a ribald will and, while she accepted that there should be no formal ceremony, since he detested all ceremonial, she wanted to have some sort of a gathering for the purpose of leave-taking and that his ashes be thrown into a river's flowing water: 'a big fat dirty river', as he had once specified. That seemed somewhat less awful than the ice-white asphalt of Varick Street. The leave-taking was to be held in the loft. He had specified that himself, in his role as director — so there would be some 'appropriate' shots with which to end the film.

Alice and I had phoned around to a few people to break the news of his death, and we said to them to tell others who'd known him that there was going to be a little farewell gathering prior to the cremation, and that anyone who wanted to come could come, no invitations needed.

The leave-taking was scheduled for twelve noon, with his plain pine coffin reposing on the floor of the loft, one more box among all the other boxes and trunks and packing cases. Except that this box was open, and you could see the face with its knowing expression, which seemed to me at once angry and weirdly triumphant, as if with the satisfaction of 'having got a good one in the can'. The film lights were on and the cameras turning as the mourners arrived to pay their last respects. The members of the film crew were there to work, but they detached themselves one by one, stepping in front of the cameras and approaching the coffin to murmur their own goodbyes. Then they resumed their posts and filmed the others. Among the first to arrive were young people who had been his students at the film courses he had conducted during the last couple of years of his life. One girl, perhaps one of the flaming bodies he had not been able to resist, broke down and sobbed in front of the coffin. Others showed their emotion in a more contained way. They were handed drinks while they stood around in an informal semi-circle waiting. Norbert Beauregard, the manager of the Alexander Hotel, arrived wearing a black tie and black arm-band, looking flushed and solemn. Others arrived with whom Jack had had some brief contact in the final years, doctors, nurses, one or two independent producers and agents who had entered into discussions with him about projects that in the end had failed to materialize. Nik Ransom showed up. A glowering presence, he stood in the full glare of camera lights and gave a low bow before the coffin, in the manner of a star actor humbly taking a curtain call. The press photographers who had come to cover what up till then had been a fairly flat event for them, now began to wake up, and they were positively galvanized when Maureen Wynner arrived, dressed all in black, skirt below the knee for once in her life, and stood silent in her thoughts before pressing a kiss to her fingers and her fingers to the coffin, an action that evoked a frenzy of popping flashbulbs. Moira arrived, stern, wearing dark glasses, and she embraced Alice tearfully, and the two women wept together, supporting each other. Then Gloria arrived with Anna, and Anna said hysterically: 'I don't believe Dad's dead, he's just kidding around. He's doing this for a film.' Gloria was tender towards Alice, whom she had never met. She embraced her warmly, and said: 'I am so sorry, Alice. For all of us who've lost him. I can only hope that he gave you some of his crazy strength.' Towards Moira she was unrelentingly hostile, saying not a word to her. The last mourner to arrive was Sydney Carver: an unsure man, who for once made no attempt to push himself forward, but remained silent and sombre, at the back of the room.

Although Jack had said he wanted no ceremony, Alice thought that a few words ought to be said by someone, and that burden and privelege fell on me, because as a critic and historian of cinema I 'would know what to say about him'.

I had accepted with deep misgivings, conscious of having been unable to place Jack Strawley correctly in the many pieces I had written about him and his films during his lifetime: how was I to say something now that summed him up in a few words?

I began by stating the facts plainly:

'Jack Strawley, at one time acclaimed as a genius of cinema, by myself as well as others, died forgotten and unhonoured. For the last decade of his life he had been unable to get any meaningful work in an industry for which he made many millions. It's said in the business that you're only as good as your last film, and since Jack's last film was a flop, that was what he was considered to be by a lot of people he had earlier helped to make rich and famous and powerful.'

I was saying these things with the deliberate intention of discomfiting those in the room, like Sydney Carver and Nik Ransom and Maureen Wynner, whose careers he had greatly advanced and who had failed to come to his help when he needed help. I went on:

'Like many people of large talent, he had large failings as well, and to the end he considered that he had lived his life badly and was sceptical of the idea that he had partially redeemed himself by having made some fine films. Although I believe that Jack Strawley will be reevaluated and will be found to have a place in the history of cinema, I know there can't be any certainty of this. But I shan't be worried for him on that score. He took big risks all his life, and I expect he's ready to take his chances with posterity.

'Balzac wrote in one of his novels, putting the words into the mouth of a critic, so it may be appropriate for me to borrow them, that genius is a terrible malady, a monster that devours feeling, dries up the heart, and that you have to be a colossus to keep your balance. Well, Jack Strawley was not a colossus.' His balance was shaky . . .'

'William James said, speaking of the hero, that to him, too, objects are sinister and dreadful, unwelcome, incompatible with wished-for things. But that he is someone who endeavours and *"can stand this world"*. I don't know what will be the final verdict on Jack Strawley, but whatever it is, it has to be said that he endeavoured and was able to stand this world, right up to the end.'

After the farewells, we all went in different cars and taxis to the crematorium, and, when that part of it was over, it seemed fitting that I should accompany Alice to fulfil Jack's last expressed wish.

We told the cab driver to take us across the Brooklyn Bridge. Turning past the massive abutments and coming up onto the main span, we were sitting tightly still, unable to speak, our feelings uncertainly contained. I couldn't help thinking about how Jack would have filmed the scene we were about to enact. I had a vision that he might have made the characters dissolve into hysterical laughter and spill the ashes, scattering them under the wheels of the heavy traffic and I was fearful that somehow we might be directed from beyond the grave to act out this mockery.

It was now near dusk with Lower Manhattan becoming a loosely knitted pattern of lights, the Brooklyn Bridge twanging beneath the solid streams of traffic. We told the cabby to stop wherever he could pull up, and although he said it wasn't permitted to stop on the bridge and looked at us strangely in the mirror as if he thought we might be intending to jump off, he did stop with the inducement of a ten-dollar bill, telling us to 'hurry it up'. Alice got out first, carrying the quite small, square, black box containing Jack's ashes, and I followed. Car lights were flashing at us, horns hooting in a clamour of protest at the way we were slowing down the traffic. She looked at me, both of us wondering if this last act required some formal words to be spoken, but it was too noisy here, and there didn't seem to be much left to be said, so I told her: 'Just do it, Alice. Do it.'

While she was undoing the top of the box, I was looking down through the cross-hatching of struts and wires and staunchions to the big fat dirty river below, where Jack felt he belonged. Amid the overhead iron girders, the spotlights and floodlights were coming on, and there were the headlamps of the passing cars flashing at us angrily, and I said again: 'Do it,' and touched her elbow, whereupon she lifted the box high, said simply, ''Bye Jack,' and made an arc-like throwing movement, and in the still air Jack's ashes fell straight down like stones.

Hubert Selby Jr

THE WILLOW TREE

Bobby is young and black. He shares a cramped apartment in the south Bronx with his mother, his younger siblings and the cease-lessly scratching rats that infest the walls behind his bed. Barely a teenager, he is old beyond his years. The best thing in Bobby's life is Maria, his Hispanic friend. They are in love, and they have big plans for the summer ahead.

Their lives are irrevocably shattered when a vicious Hispanic street gang attack the couple as they walk to school. With Bobby savagely beaten and Maria lying in hospital, terrified and en-gulfed by the pain of her badly burned face, *The Willow Tree* takes the reader on a volcanically powerful trip through the lives of America's dispossessed inner-city dwellers.

Into this black and smouldering hinterland, however, Selby introduces a small but vital note of love and compassion. When Bobby's bruised and bloodied body is discovered by Moishe, an aged concentration camp survivor, an unlikely friendship begins. As Moishe slowly, painfully, reveals his own tragic history, Bobby struggles angrily with his desperate need for revenge.

As Bobby and Moishe's relationship develops, Selby's searing prose accelerates and sends the reader spinning through their inner turmoil. From the raw ferocity of Bobby's anguish to the silent grief of Moishe's memories, Selby builds relentlessly to an emotional crescendo. Yet Selby's writing is informed by an underlying belief in human virtue. He stares unflinchingly at harsh social realities, yet insists on nurturing the faintest glim-mer of hope. This honesty and clarity of vision makes reading *The Willow Tree* an exhilarating and cathartic experience.

An outstandingly gifted voice in modern American literature, Selby has created in *The Willow Tree* a luminescent statement on the nature of human grace and the need for forgiveness.

THE DEMON

Harry White is a man haunted by a satyr's lust and an obsessive need for sin and retribution. Heartless, cold and dissociated, yet recognizable and almost likeable, he excels at his job in an expanding corporation, but is distracted by lunchtime sexual encounters. Controlling his excessive sexuality, he opts for marriage. As a consequence, financial gain, promotion, a big house in the country, even a vice-presidency, all become his for the asking. But the more Harry succeeds, the more desperate he becomes. Although enormously wealthy, he is driven to rob the secretaries' desks for money. However, what begins as petty crime slowly develops into a nightmare of apocalytpic violence as Harry mires himself still further in his relentless sense of guilt and shame.

THE ROOM

In his second novel, *The Room*, Selby narrows his focus and concentrates on the nightmare world of one man in one room.

Isolated behind the bars of a prison cell, a prisoner awaits trial for some unspecified charge. He soon surrenders himself to self-pity and hatred, indulging himself in morbid sadistic fantasies.

Images of increasing violence and vengeful cruelty obsess him, building so rapidly that the reader is magnetically drawn into this private hell. With his celebrated compassion and insight, so effectively displayed in his seminal first book *Last Exit to Brooklyn*, Selby makes the victim of this seething inner turmoil somehow sympathetic. By creating such a vivid picture of the imprisoned man's hopelessness, Selby forces us to confront the blame that must be borne by a society that can allow such despair to go unnoticed and unalleviated.

'Selby's best book.'   —*The Times Literary Supplement*

'Well-made, sensitively written and a truthful declaration of human desperation. Selby is a natural, self-engrossed writer, a pessimist with a touch of the poet. *The Room* is a serious and harrowing study of a man who does not fit in.'—*The Irish Times*

'One must be grateful to Selby for his fatal vision and strong, original talent.'   —*Newsweek*

Hortense Calisher

'It seems impossible for Calisher to write poorly: she is a master of language.'   —*Contemporary Novelists*

IN THE SLAMMER WITH CAROL SMITH

Pills, homelessness, disaffected youth and the shifting, almost impossible claims of radical idealism are pitted against each other in this powerful and affecting journey through the troubled mind of a girl who finds herself lost in nineties America. The harsh rhythms of the street are used to movingly explore the politics of race and gender and the psychology of terrorism and drug addiction.

'Beautifully written and stirring'   —*Los Angeles Times*

'As consummate as Calisher has become after decades of writing, she is still as fresh on the page as new grass in spring.'
                    —*Booklist, starred review*

'Simply astonishing'   —*San Francisco Chronicle*

'Calisher continues to surprise with the breadth of her knowledge of how we live now and with her supple, ever fresh writing.'
—Publishers Weekly, starred review

As well as being the author of over sixteen works of fiction and the most anthologized short story writer in America today, Hortense Calisher has also previously served as President of American P.E.N. and is a past President of the American Academy of Arts and Letters.

Roy Heath

'There is no longer any doubt that Heath is one of the world's best writers.' *—Kirkus Reviews*

THE MINISTRY OF HOPE

Kwaku, Roy Heath's marvellous literary creation, is back; a small-time chiseller and ineffective healer in a village in Guyana but now down in the dumps: his wife has gone blind, his twin sons brutalize him, he is toppled from his perch as a healer and becomes once again the laughing stock of all and sundry. But fate intervenes, and Kwaku's fortunes are gradually resurrected — but only after barely escaping from a murderous mob does he finally succeed in establishing himself as a respected, wealthy citizen.

'A triumph . . . a wonderfully comic novel. . . . A dramatic display of character in action that has seldom been matched by any contemporary novelist.' *—Kirkus Reviews*

'Heath's observation of the complexities of one man — his generosity and meanness, duty and forgetfulness, tenderness and cruelty — is wise and masterly.' *—The Daily Telegraph*

'Kwaku comes from a long line of literary buffoons who manage to triumph over the "intelligent" people around them. The language Mr Heath employs to describe this process is luxurious and densely baroque in places, sweetly comic in others.'
—The New York Times Book Review

KWAKU
or The Man Who Could Not Keep His Mouth Shut

This is the tale of Kwaku, who was reduced to a state of idiocy by intelligent men but made a spontaneous recovery. Part con-man, part Everyman, part Holy Fool, this picaresque saga follows Kwaku as he pursues his childhood dreams of wealth, happiness and position with a fanaticism that is only defeated by his own magnificent failings. Brilliantly conceived, deftly constructed and, above all, hugely enjoyable.

'A soldier Schweik in Civvy Street.'

—Times Literary Supplement

'A paradise of cartwheeling words and images.'

—New Statesman

'To be good, God knows, is enough to ask; to be astonishing into the bargain is a bonus.'   *—The Guardian*

'Simply one of the most astonishingly good novelists of our time.'   *—Edward Blishen*

'A beautiful writer.'   *—Salman Rushdie*

Roy Heath was born in British Guiana and came to England, at the age of 24, to become a lawyer and teacher. He is the winner of the Guardian Fiction Prize and was shortlisted for the Booker and Whitbread Prizes.

Carlo Gébler

W9 AND OTHER LIVES

'The mass of men lead lives of quiet desperation,' Henry David Thoreau noted in *Walden*, and *W9 and Other Lives* is Gébler's provocative response to that assertion. Where Thoreau's retreat on Walden Pond in Concord, Massachusetts, had a specific geographical location with a universal significance, *W9* refers not only to a West London postcode but also represents those vast enigmatic stretches of human day-to-day experiences which exist without maps. The characters depicted in this volume lead lives which are quintessentially modern: lonely, rootless and uncertain. These are not, however, stories of complaint, or lament, or melancholy. On the contrary, they illuminate and celebrate the courage and joy that are to be found flourishing in the most unlikely corners of human existence.

An essential primer for the way we live today, *W9 and Other Lives* spans the entire globe as each story gently shifts the reader's attention from one location to the next. A good number of them are also situated in the author's native Ireland, where possessing a keen sense of place has a special significance all of its own. From Cuba to Connemara, from the Mediterranean to London's Maida Vale, Gébler captures scenes that are delicately observed yet down to earth, his prose gently unfolding to reveal how events can darken or illuminate ordinary lives in extraordinary ways. The choice of narrative tone in each story reflects a kindness towards people and a general sympathy for its principal characters which are extremely rare in modern letters. Quiet these voices may be, but despairing they most certainly are not. Strangely haunting and resonant in their effect, Carlo Gébler has fashioned in *W9 and Other Lives* stories that will linger long after one has finished reading them.

Novelist and broadcaster, Carlo Gébler was born in Dublin in 1954, grew up in London and is now a resident of Enniskillen, County Fermanagh, in Northern Ireland. His novel, *How To Murder A Man* was one of the final ten books short-listed for the 1998 Booker Prize.

'Gébler's pellucid prose style is the perfect instrument with which to probe a reader's heart.'   —*Will Self*

'A writer of extraordinary talent and originality.'
                                              —*Kate Saunders, Cosmopolitan*

'Carlo Gébler's special subject is proving to be the pain and unease that trickles into the space between the events of everyday life.'   —*John Melmoth, Times Literary Supplement*